Wrecked

Priscilla West

DISCARD

This is a work of fiction. All characters appearing in this work are fictitious. Any resemblance to real persons, living or dead, is purely coincidental.

Contents

Chapter One

THE NOTE

There would be no happy ending for us. He was too damaged. I was too broken. Things between us shouldn't have gone this far in the first place. Then this never would've happened. If only I'd been stronger. If I only I hadn't said those words, if only we were different people—not the lost, scared and broken people that we were . . . then we wouldn't be in this wreck.

***

I was okay. Just okay. Not good, not bad—just okay. After what happened to Mom, I answered a lot of questions with that line.

"Lorrie, how are you coping?" they would ask.

"I'm okay."

Or: "I'm so sorry Lorrie, this shouldn't have happened to a woman like your mother. How are you dealing with things?"

"I'm okay."

Before the trial, during the trial and after the trial, I gave that same answer. What the hell did they expect me to say?

Sitting on the edge of a low stone bridge spanning a narrow part of Lake Teewee, I looked out across the dark waters, idly gazing at the old, towering trees along the distant shore as if they somehow knew the answers I was seeking.

I dangled my legs over the side, my snow boots almost touching the high water. The bridge spanned over a narrow part of the half-frozen lake that eventually turned into a stream winding through and around the west side of campus. Some of the students liked to call the lake "Lake Peepee." I thought it was a stupid name at first but then someone explained that there were frequent rumors of frat boys pissing in the lake. Whether it was true or not, the water in the lake was still covered in a disgusting layer of green algae.

I had finished unpacking and setting up my dorm room last night, and decided to take a walk this morning to refamiliarize myself with the campus layout. It would be nearly a week before classes officially started so there weren't too many students roaming the campus yet which made the place rather quiet.

I exhaled deeply and my breath fogged in front of me.

After taking three semesters off, I was back on campus again at Arrowhart College, ready to start the Spring semester in the middle of the coldest winter ever experienced in Studsen, Illinois. The crappy weather made the timing of my move from my aunt's house in Indiana back to Illinois unfortunate, but I didn't want to delay coming back to school.

Aunt Caroline had suggested I take another semester off, but that was the last thing I wanted. I wanted to feel normal again. I needed to go beyond the denial, the anger, and the depression. The therapist had told me I was one step away from reaching the last stage of grief, which was "acceptance", then I could move on with my life. She'd said this last step was the hardest for most people. For some it takes months, others years, and the rest . . . well, they never make it. I didn't know which category I'd fit into; all I knew was being away from school didn't help me cope. If anything, it just gave me more time to dwell on the past.

A high-pitched squeal to my left made me jump. Frantically reaching for a grippable stone on the bridge, I managed to find one and regain my balance, saving myself from falling into the water. I turned toward the noise and caught a glimpse of a black cat disappearing into the thick brush with a mouse in its mouth. It was probably a stray trying to collect enough food to last the remaining winter.

I wrung my hand like a disgruntled old woman warning kids to get off her lawn. "Hey buddy! You almost made me fall into the lake." The cat had almost lived up to its reputation for being unlucky.

The cat poked its head out of a bush for a moment, looked at me curiously with its green eyes, lost interest then vanished again.

"That's right. Get out of here kitty," I said, a bit disappointed that he left. No one else was around and I could've used the company.

The cat was like most of the friends I'd made freshman year at Arrowhart; we had a momentary connection but then we quickly went our separate ways and lost contact. I'd only kept in touch with Daniela Stauffer, who was now going to be one of my suitemates this semester. Maybe I'd make new friends this semester. Thinking about that, I frowned when I imagined students' reactions to me telling them that I was a twenty-year-old sophomore. I could almost hear the questions. *Did she get academic probation? Could she not afford to pay for school?*

I had good reasons for being a first semester sophomore when I should've been a second semester junior, but I'd prefer they didn't know.

Unfortunately, most probably *did* know—through the media covering the trial and through campus rumors. Word tended to spread fast on a college campus with only a few thousand students.

I sighed heavily then inhaled through my mouth. The crisp winter air entering my lungs felt refreshing. The thick puffer jacket I wore kept my chest warm, but the cold stone beneath me sucked the heat from my bottom through my jeans, leaving my ass slightly numb.

My ass matched my feelings. I was numb when I should've been excited. Wasn't it supposed to feel good returning to college? To go to fun parties and meet hot guys? To be moving on with my life again? Wasn't that what Mom and Dad would have wanted?

Reaching into the inner pocket of my jacket, I pulled out a folded piece of notebook paper. I unfolded it and stared at the black letters shakily written in cursive by Dad. My chest grew tight and my fingers trembled but there were no tears in my eyes as I read the letter again, for the thousandth time.

Dear Lorrie,

Whatever happens after this, I want you to know that I love you and that this had nothing to do with you. Even after the divorce, I still loved your mother. I guess you always knew that. I can only blame myself for what happened to her. Maybe if I hadn't worked so much, had paid more attention to her, we would've never gotten divorced, and she would've never met that monster.

I'm so sorry Lorrie. I'm sorry to you, and I'm sorry to your mother. She was so beautiful. She was the best thing in my world, and even after the divorce, I was happy to just be a part of your lives.

I know that you need me now, more than ever, but I can't. I just can't Lorrie. I'm too weak. It hurts so much that she's no longer here. You're the strong one Lorrie, you've always been strong. Ever since you were born, you were always so strong. You have to keep going, don't make the same mistakes I made.

I'm sorry Lorrie. Goodbye.

Love,
Dad

I should cry now, I thought. That's what normal people did right? In the movies, whenever someone read their father's suicide note they cried afterwards. I'd cried the first hundred times I read it but now I couldn't cry. I couldn't feel anything. Not even when I wanted to. It was like there was a switch in my brain that was connected but nothing was transmitting. No sadness, no pain, no joy. Just numbness. Was that what dad meant when he said I was strong? That I could numb away the pain and move on?

I dipped the toe of my boot into the water and nudged a thick ice piece floating by.

Dad took his own life a few months ago, after the trial was over. It was a hell of a thing to do to your loved ones. It was a hell of a thing to do to his sister, Caroline. And to me, after I spent most of my time living with him after the divorce. Didn't he know how much we cared about him? Didn't he know how broken we'd be when he committed suicide?

I folded up the note and put it back into my pocket. When I patted my jacket for my phone to check the time, I remembered I'd left it back in my room. I should probably head back.

A soft gurgling drew my attention to the water beneath the bridge and I looked down. I almost didn't see it at first, but then

I spotted it. There was a large goldfish making slow circles under the water.

"Hey fishy. What are you doing? Aren't you freezing in there?"

The fish glugged a few bubbles to the surface and I took it as a yes. It was slow but looked alive in the bitter coldness of the water. I envied that feeling of being alive. My ass was numb and I was numb on the inside. I wanted to feel something. Anything. Just to know that I was still here.

I tucked my legs beneath me and leaned over the side of the bridge, dipping my fingers into the water. A frigid chill spiked up my arm invigorating me.

I could still feel something.

I leaned further over the side of the bridge so that I could reach deeper into the water. My wiggling fingers must've looked like dinner because the fish approached and started nibbling at me. The icy bite of the water made me alert and awake, clearing the numb fuzz that I thought had settled permanently on my mind. I pushed up the sleeve of my jacket with my other hand, before leaning further, to plunge my arm deeper. The edge of my sleeve was getting wet but I didn't care. The cold had a cleansing quality, even as the tips of my fingers were starting to lose their feeling.

I thought about leaning further, but it was already the furthest I could go without losing my balance. If I fell in the freezing water, I might die—there was certainly no one around to help me. I might have been numb but I wasn't stupid.

Something felt odd around my shoe.

I twisted my head and saw a black, furry creature tearing viciously at my shoelaces.

"Hey!" I yelled.

The cat screeched and jumped three feet in the air, scaring the shit out of me. I wanted to pull my hand out of the water, but it was too late. I flailed for a split second, trying to grab onto the stone I'd used earlier to save myself, but this time I missed.

I tipped forward, losing all balance

Then I was under

Chapter Two

SWIMMING

I panicked when my head went beneath the surface and I opened my mouth to scream. In an instant, my lungs inhaled a mixture of water and algae, making me choke and sputter. The cold soaked through my heavy winter clothes immediately, piercing me to my core. I struggled to surface but my jacket was suddenly ten times heavier. I felt myself sinking.

A dreadful thought tore through my mind.

This is it. It's all over.

I was going to drown. I was going to die. Aunt Caroline was going to think I ended up taking the same path as Dad. Killing myself. She had lost her sister-in-law, then her brother, and now her niece.

But I didn't choose this! I didn't want this. It was an accident caused by a stupid cat.

And then a silly thought flashed.

I can't die like this, in a lake full of piss-eating algae. The embarrassment would be too much.

Fighting against the weight of my clothes, I furiously kicked my legs, forcing myself upward. My head bumped into a hard ceiling—a large piece of ice had floated above me. I reached out with half-frozen fingers, desperately trying to find where the ice ended. Or a hole. Anything.

I felt nothing. Everything was solid. I flailed my arms in a frenzy, frightened because I couldn't hold my breath much longer. Suddenly, my hand burst through to the surface and I felt the cold air against my fingertips. Frantically thrashing my legs, I torpedoed my body toward the hole. Finally, I broke through to the crisp air.

I never thought I could feel so much relief in my life. I panted for air, sucking it in like it was my last breath. I had made it. I had survived. I had a near-death experience and was going to appreciate life so much more after this moment. I silently thanked the powers-that-be for a second chance.

I wiped the water from my eyes and my relief turned into despair.

The bridge was nowhere in sight.

As I violently roiled the water around me, I tried looking for the shore but I couldn't find it. *Where the hell was it?* My teeth chattered violently and my limbs were turning into frozen icebergs, numbness overtaking my muscles. Suddenly, a sharp sting knifed through my stomach, and I clutched my abs in pain. *Perfect time for a cramp!* Unable to move, for a brief instant I was left with the thought of sending a letter to Kellogg's telling them the Frosted Flakes I ate this morning turned out to be the death of me. Then my legs gave out. I stopped treading water. I stopped floating and started sinking.

I was going to die.

"What the fuck?!" someone shouted.

"Help!" I screamed instinctively with the last of my breath. "HEL—" My head submerged beneath the freezing surface.

Water blurred my vision, making me lose my orientation. Distantly, I heard a splash then I felt something grasp my shoulders. I struggled against it thinking it was going to push me further into the depths.

Someone was shouting at the surface but the voice was faint beneath the water. "Stop fighting me dammit! Or we'll both die out here!"

Strong arms wrapped beneath my armpits raised me above the water.

I tried to tilt my head to see who the voice was coming from, but a wet mass of my own hair covered my face. Powerful arms and legs stroked the water around us propelling us toward the side of the lake.

Before long, we collapsed onto the bank.

"What the hell were you thinking?" cried a deep male voice, breathless.

On hands and knees, I tried to respond but ended up coughing water onto the gravel. My clothes were completely drenched and my muscles were coiling into tight balls. It was actually colder now that we were out of the lake.

God this was so embarrassing. I could see it on the campus paper now: *Sophomore goes for a swim in Lake Peepee in the middle of winter.*

My savior took several deep breaths before dragging himself to sit on a large rock beside me.

When I had finished coughing, I brushed the hair out of my face and looked up at him. He had short, dark hair matted with water and a sharp, sculpted nose set between two dark grey eyes. His brows were furrowed in concern. His strong jaw was covered in a rough layer of stubble that framed his full, shapely lips. He was so gorgeous, my breath hitched in my throat. Had I died and gone to heaven?

Steam rose from his body as if his outrageous hotness physically manifested and clashed with the frigid air. His gray sweatshirt was soaked, and it clung tightly to his chest, enough to see the outline of the wide shoulders and thick muscles underneath. I rubbed my eyes, figuring the contaminated water I swallowed was making me hallucinate. No way this was real. I looked again and realized it wasn't an illusion.

Wow.

A hint of a tattoo peeked out the side of his sweatshirt collar along his neck. I squinted but couldn't make out what it was because it extended further down beneath his drenched clothing. It made me wonder what other tattoos he could be hiding. Finishing my assessment of his dazzling figure, my conclusion consisted of two words: Padded and tatted.

My face was becoming warm despite the cold, and my heart started beating faster. As an attempt to calm myself, I wracked my brain to pick a better-looking savior from any of the thousands of students I'd seen before on campus. But I couldn't pick anyone. Who could rival him?

"What was that?" he shouted again but softer this time. His voice was rough and husky—though laced with concern.

As if almost drowning in Lake Peepee wasn't embarrassing

enough already, I had to be fished out by the hottest guy I'd seen in ages—maybe ever. If he hadn't jumped in to save me, I might've been a goner.

My teeth chattered. "I-I-It's the cat's fault."

He stared into the distance then furrowed his brows. "What are you talking about? What cat? There's nothing there."

I followed his gaze and spotted the bridge. The stupid black cat was still there watching us but it was motionless, blending in with the dark foliage behind it. It had an impassive expression as if it was smugly saying, "What a bunch of idiots."

"It's right there." I pointed desperately with a wet finger. "Can't you see it?"

He squinted. "I don't see anything. There's nothing there."

God. This guy might have a stunning face and a great body but his eyesight is terrible.

Groaning in frustration, I shook my finger at the cat. "Look again. It's right next to that bush." As soon as I finished my sentence, the cat hopped into the bush and disappeared along with any evidence proving that I wasn't a crazy person who saw imaginary cats. *That little bastard.*

"You're crazy. You know that?" he yelled. "Crazy." Those accusatory gray eyes pierced deep into mine, sending an unwelcome flutter through my belly.

"I'm not crazy," I cried. "I know what I saw. I swear it was right there. And don't call me crazy."

He shook his head. "You almost got us both killed, flailing around like some kind of idiot. That was probably the least helpful thing you could've done. Did you *want* us to die?"

A wave of embarrassment and annoyance washed over me as I threw my hands up. "I was drowning, dude. What did you expect?"

Tattoos and Muscles sucked in a deep breath, his chest rising. The intensity in his eyes seemed to dissipate. "Do you know how dangerous it is to be out here alone? Do you know how cold the water is?" he asked, as if I was a two-year-old.

Yeah, we were both in it, remember? God, this guy's an idiot. All brawn, no brain.

It took too much effort to be a smartass though and my sides hurt too much. "Yes I know how cold the water is," I said, controlling the urge to be snarky toward the man who just saved my life. "I didn't mean to go in. I fell."

"No one's around at this time, students haven't arrived yet, the ground is slippery. You've gotta be some kind of special to be fooling around here by yourself. Ya know if I hadn't been jogging past at that moment . . ." Mid-sentence, he narrowed his eyes at me, a startling look of realization crossing his face. "Wait. Was that . . . was that . . . Were you trying to commit suicide? Are you depressed or something?"

"No! I just—" I thought about mentioning the cat again, but decided that was a lost cause. "I just lost my balance, that's all . . ."

He studied me a bit longer, as if considering if I was lying to him or not. I didn't have the energy to pretend I was okay, so he would just have to take my word for it. "What were you doing on the bridge?"

Oh, you know. Just hanging out, playing with the fish, reading my dad's suicide note. The usual.

"I was enjoying the view." As I got to my feet, my wet clothes dripped onto the icy gravel. Tattoos and Muscles—T&M—eyed me up and down carefully. He was watching me like I was going to jump back into the lake at any second. "I'm not going to jump in again. Chill out."

He straightened from the rock he was sitting on and approached me. I took a step back afraid he took offense to the unintentional pun I made about "chilling out". He violently rubbed his hands together then grabbed a handful of my jacket.

"What are you doing?"

I tried to take another step back but he held firm. He was right in front of me and I looked up him, heart pounding. My eyes flickered to his lips. I was suddenly aware of the acute fluttering effect he had on my nerves when in such close proximity.

He twisted the front of my jacket, wringing out a splash of water.

"We need to get ourselves somewhere warm, before we freeze to death," he said, his tone softening. He continued to wring out my jacket, first the front, then the back and sleeves. Then he went to work on himself, squeezing the icy lake water from his sweatshirt and sweatpants.

I nodded in agreement then took a few steps towards the direction of campus. I couldn't wait to get back to my room—to forget this day ever happened.

"Hey, where are you going?" he snapped.

A gust of wind blew across my face as I answered. "D-D-Dorm."

"Fuck the dorms, you'll be frozen stiff by the time you get there. My place is just past that trail." He pointed to a jogging trail leading into the forest. "Let's go there and get you warmed up first. Get us both warmed up."

As much as I hated to admit it, he was right. If I wanted to go back to my room, I'd have to walk halfway across campus. My clothes would probably become ice armor by the time I got there.

I thought a moment about how I knew nothing about this guy and was going over to his place. Ordinarily I'd be cautious, but these were unusual circumstances. This was a matter of life and death— literally. Besides, T&M didn't seem dangerous; he'd just saved my life. If anything he probably thought I was the unstable one.

Deciding to follow his suggestion, I tried to walk over to him but faltered when the cramp returned.

He sighed, his breath steaming up the air. He came over to me and stopped. The next thing I knew, he was turned around and kneeling in front of me. For some reason, the sight of him in that position made my pulse skip a beat.

"What are you doing?" I asked.

"It's called a piggyback ride. C'mon, we don't have all day."

"I can walk just fine," I shot back, annoyed by his condescending tone.

"No you can't. Don't be a brat, hop on before we both freeze to death."

I opened my mouth to protest but closed it when another gust of wind hit my face like an icy baseball bat. Knowing he was right, I begrudgingly mounted him, feeling my chest press against the hardness of his back as I wrapped my arms and legs around his torso. His body exuded enormous heat—probably because he had been running not long ago—and it permeated the layers of wet cotton separating us. The sensation was warm and comforting making my pulse beat a steady staccato in my ears.

I didn't have the will to protest, especially considering how comfortable the ride was, so we kept each other warm as we walked through the trail.

Five minutes later, my cramp had gone away and we arrived at a brick apartment complex. He'd been right: his place was much closer than the dorms. It was one of those off-campus student apartments. They weren't officially owned by the college, but a lot of the upperclassmen stayed in them, and they were usually much nicer than the on-campus dorms.

After walking up the steps to the second floor with me on his back, he set me down in front of apartment "2E". We went inside and he closed the door behind us. My shivering stopped almost immediately. I was so grateful the apartment was much warmer than outside. I released a deep breath, relieved I was no longer in danger of freezing to death.

"You're wet," he said. "Wait here."

He disappeared into another room while I awkwardly stood near his door, water dripping on the carpet. Not knowing what else to do, I surveyed the surroundings, noticing the tidy kitchen and an old brown couch positioned in front of a small TV. It was surprisingly neat for a guy's place. I was expecting empty beer cans, posters of half-naked swimsuit models, and maybe a bong or two—the typical college guy setup.

He returned with a few pieces of neatly folded clothing and a towel. I expected him to be in a new change of clothes but he was still in his drenched sweats.

T&M offered me the clothes. "Sorry, but this is all I have. I don't exactly keep women's clothes around." He pointed past the couch. "Bathroom's around the corner."

"What about you?" I asked, eyeing his hair and clothes dripping on the carpet.

"I'll be fine for a bit longer, go on . . ."

"Are you sure? You can go first. It's your place after all."

The edges of his lips curved upward. It was the first time I'd seen him smile and the look of him with wet hair and a boyish grin sent tingles down my back. "I appreciate the concern but I'll be fine. Go on, warm up. I'm gonna change out of these clothes while you're in there."

"Okay." I gratefully took the items he gave me and went into the bathroom, closing the door behind me. The inside matched the neat efficiency of the rest of the apartment and smelled faintly of disinfectant. Setting the clothes on the counter, I looked at myself in the mirror.

Wow, I look like a mess.

There were bits of algae and ice caught in my hair. I was suddenly feeling self-conscious about my appearance, when I normally wouldn't be. The inappropriateness of the concern given the circumstances kind of pissed me off. I'd almost died and here I was fretting about how I must've looked to T&M. What's gotten into me?

Shaking my head to clear my thoughts, I turned on the shower, and steam slowly filled the room. I removed my boots and socks then peeled off my wet clothes that had been clinging to me like a heavy blanket. I placed the items on top of the toilet but when I tried to step into the shower, I accidentally knocked a wet sock into the nearby trash bin. Grumbling in annoyance, I reached into the trash and fished the polka-dotted sock out along with a wad of tissues clinging to it. When I took a closer look, I noticed a used condom crumpled up among the tissues.

Ew.

Scrunching my face, I gingerly pinched off the undesirables and dropped them back into their home in the waste bin. I spotted at least two more condoms poking out from the pile of tissues. Apparently this guy either had a lot of sex or he didn't take out his trash often. The unusual neatness of his apartment suggested it wasn't the latter.

Figures, a hot guy like him would be getting a lot of action.

I stepped into the shower and let the heat of the water wash away the pinpricks beneath my skin. T&M—or Tim as I decided to refer to him for simplicity—clearly lived a spartan lifestyle. One bottle of shampoo and one bottle of body wash stood next to each other in the shower cubby. They almost looked lonely. I considered using the loofah that hung over the showerhead, but when I imagined him lathering up the creases of his abs and his junk in the front with it, I decided against it.

Just warm up and dry off Lorrie, no distractions. Just as if it's a quick rinse before sex . . .

I sighed. What a great return to campus. It was just supposed to be uneventful semester; one that was going to help me return to a normal life. One without people dying. But before it even began, I almost died myself. Now I was showering in some strange guy's apartment who probably thought I was depressed and suicidal.

Unfortunately, he wasn't too far from the truth. Being depressed was a shitty place to be and telling others about it only fed the condition, making it worse. It was like rolling an impossibly large stone up a hill and if you asked for help, the extra hands got in the way more than they helped, pushing the stone in all sorts of directions until you realize that you'd have been better off pushing it alone. But you know you can't do it by yourself. The only solution then was to not roll it at all. Just walk away, pretend it wasn't there, that there was no point to moving it to the top of the hill in the first place. And that left you feeling numb—which wasn't great but at least it wasn't bad. Feeling numb was at least better than feeling depressed.

I turned the water off, stepped out of the shower, and dried myself with the towel he'd given me. I took a closer look at the clothes: there was a large black US Air Force t-shirt and a pair of jeans. I put them on and laughed when I examined myself in the mirror—the clothes were huge, making me look comically small in them. I had to hold the jeans up with my hand otherwise they'd fall down. At least the bagginess of the shirt would help hide the fact that I was no longer wearing a bra.

After ensuring I looked presentable—at least as presentable as possible in baggy clothes and without makeup—I gathered my wet clothes in my arms and opened the bathroom door, preparing to thank Tim for his hospitality. When I stepped into the living room, my jaw dropped at the sight of him naked.

"Oh, I'm sorry!" I quickly turned away but not before the sight of him was seared into my memory. Images of carved muscles and exotic tattoos danced across my mind.

"Wow, that was quick. I thought you'd be in there longer." I heard him laugh and the subsequent thud of his drenched sweats being thrown into a corner hamper. "You can turn around. I'm not naked, ya know. Unless you consider being shirtless as naked."

I turned around and noticed he had a white towel around his waist. His torso was still fully bare though. Tattoos ran along the side of his chest and extended down his arm. They were mostly a mix of tribal designs but one tattoo stood out for me. A picture of a large hammer was boldly etched on his upper arm. An unwelcome desire flittered in my stomach as I imagined running my fingertips over the inked lines.

I wasn't opposed to seeing him shirtless at all. Not. At. All.

I forced myself to make eye contact with him, but was surprised to find him not doing the same. His eyes were wide, and they were roaming down and up my freshly showered body.

When his eyes finally met mine, his lips curved wickedly. "You clean up well."

My cheeks flushed. "Thanks," I replied, slightly uncomfortable. "I feel a lot better without all that lake gunk on me. I really appreciate the clothes, although they might be a little big for me." I gestured to the jeans that were threatening to fall down my hips.

He looked me over again, dark eyes subtly lingering at certain parts: thighs, chest, lips. "No, you look good—real good." His hand gestured to the couch. "Have a seat. I'll get you some warm tea and a belt. I can get you back to your place after I wash up."

He grabbed my wet clothes from me and set them down on the kitchen counter while I took a seat on his couch. I thought it'd be a relief to sit down and relax but I found myself tense and restless, wondering who this guy was and what I'd gotten myself into by agreeing to come to his place.

He went into the kitchen and brought me a cup of tea. It smelled fragrant and spicy and the hot mug felt good in my hands, calming my nerves temporarily. I sipped slowly, enjoying the fluid warming up my chest as he went into his bedroom to search for a belt. Moments later, he returned.

"Thank you so much," I said as he handed me the belt and sat down on the edge of the coffee table inches away from me.

He, in his shirtless glory, carefully watched me bring the cup of tea to my lips. I brought the edge to my mouth but didn't drink, too distracted by the desire to touch my lips against the soft skin of those hard pecs right in front of me. I flicked my gaze to his to avoid staring at his chest. The concerned way he studied me with those dark irises matching the color of his damp hair was making me squirm in my seat. Not to mention the peripheral view of that towel around his waist was approaching scandalous. He didn't cross his legs like I would if I were wearing a skirt and I fought the urge to snag a glance down at that distinctly male area. But it was hard to resist. Was this what it was like to be on the other end of someone trying to cop a peek up your skirt?

"How's the tea?"

His voice interrupted my thoughts and I hurriedly swallowed a big gulp that burned my throat going down. "Very good, thanks," I choked. "I feel bad you had to go to so much trouble to make it though. Sorry for being such a burden."

". . . Polite too." He grinned. "Don't worry about it. It was no trouble at all." His demeanor was almost the opposite of what it had been at the lake—it was relaxed and warm now. But then again so was mine. The feeling of almost dying must be wearing off for both of us.

"Are you going to have some yourself?" I asked, uncomfortable with how he was just sitting there. Right there. Half naked in front of me with a 'V' shaped muscle around his pelvis tempting my eyes to look down to where the slanted lines met. Wasn't he going to take his shower?

"Probably in a bit."

Seeing him in no hurry to leave, I wracked my brain for a conversation topic. "So . . ." I looked down at the shirt I was wearing and pinched the lettering to try to end the silence. "Are you in the Air Force?"

He paused for a second longer than I was expecting. "No, I'm just a student. Senior, actually. You go to school here too?"

I nodded. "Yeah, sophomore."

"Cool. So why did you come to campus so early?"

"I thought it'd be good to have some time by myself to prepare for the semester. You know, mentally prepare and all that."

He nodded. "Alone time, yeah. Helps to work things out on your own sometimes. People can be stressful, especially at this school where people like to gossip. I swear it's like every student's minor here."

I wondered if his comment was specifically directed toward me and my circumstances. Did he know who I was and my reputation? "Yeah, I'm not too interested in rumors. They're often wrong anyway." I shifted my legs and happened to briefly brush against his. I felt my nipples tighten from the unintentional intimate contact.

His eyes narrowed and he glanced at the offending leg. He looked at me for a while, apparently deep in thought. When his eyes glanced down at my chest, I saw an intense flicker in those dark irises—or was it a spark? "Haven't met anyone here who doesn't like gossip," he said smoothly. "You do know you're at Arrowhart right? Gossip is big here. It's only normal that you'd be interested."

"Yeah, I know," I replied. *And boy did I know.* "But maybe I'm not normal."

The smile he gave had an edge to it that made me uncomfortable and aroused at the same time. "I'd say so as well. Seeing imaginary cats and falling into frozen lakes isn't exactly normal," he teased, before his voice lowered intimately. "But then again, normal's boring."

A heated ache moved through me. Was it my imagination or was he flirting with me? It didn't seem like he realized who I was. I noticed again how unusually neat the place was. Did he have a girlfriend that cleaned for him? Or his mom? "So do you live here by yourself?" My voice came out huskier than I intended and I cleared my throat, hoping he didn't notice.

He smiled. "Yeah, I get plenty of alone time here."

I found that difficult to believe given his devilish good-looks. It would be easier for me to believe if he'd said he had a ticket system for girls lining up outside his apartment door. Maybe even a BYOC policy—Bring Your Own Condom. That could explain the contents of his bathroom trash.

I forced another gulp down my throat, uncomfortable with how being so near him made me restless. "What do you like to do in your alone time?"

"In my alone time?" He cocked a brow and looked at me with curiosity.

I glanced at his sculpted chest because I couldn't help myself. "Yeah, like when no one's around, just in private." I was thinking about how I liked to mope and draw in my alone time and was hoping to find common ground between us. He probably didn't sit on icy bridges in his alone time but maybe he did something relatable so I could convince him I wasn't just some depressed girl trying to kill herself.

A glint in his eye, his grin widened. "What do I like to do in my alone time?" he repeated, suggestively. "Oh, just the usual stuff guys do when they're by themselves. You know, normal stuff."

Oh no. Was *I* flirting with him? I'd unintentionally said something that could've been interpreted as a reference to his masturbation routine. *God, how awkward.* This was not my lucky day. I glanced at his towel and noticed a towering bulge that hadn't been there before. My face flushed. Shit, did I do that?

I tightened my legs together in my seat and giggled nervously. "Cool. Um . . . you can go take your shower now, you know. I don't want to be the reason you catch a cold."

His brows narrowed. "You gonna be okay here?"

I took a sip of my tea and forced a slight smile. "I'm not going to off myself if that's what you're asking. Really, I'm okay."

"I'm asking about your comfort." His expression became serious and a quick glance at his crotch revealed the bulge had disappeared as mysteriously as it came. "We both just had a near-death experience. It's normal to be shaken up. Hell, even I'm still a bit affected. It might help if we kept each other company, that's all."

His words sent a shiver down my spine, as if he had caressed me with his hands. He was too concerned about me, too caring. I pictured everything that could happen. The whirlwind romance, the heartbreak that would come afterwards. Guys as hot and flirty as him were always dangerous, and in my current state, getting my heart broken would shatter me. What I needed was a normal and boring return to campus, and Tattoos and Muscles was clearly going to be none of those things.

I put on a more convincing smile. "I'm more than comfortable. Thanks for saving me. Thanks for everything."

His expression relaxed and he nodded. "You're welcome."

"Go take your shower, we'll have plenty of time to chat afterwards," I lied. "Can I watch TV?"

"Sure, the remote is on the coffee table." He nodded slowly to himself, before seeming to make up his mind. Finally he got up and headed to the bathroom.

He got up and it took an extraordinary amount of effort on my part not to check out his butt as he strolled to the bathroom. I was sure it was divine anyway. After being so close to him, I felt like I needed another shower—a cold one.

Shaking my head from a stupor, I realized I definitely needed to get out of here.

After hearing him close the door, I turned on the TV, straining my ears to listen to what he was doing in the bathroom. The TV was on ESPN. I flipped a few channels until I reached one of those juicy daytime talk shows, waiting to hear him turn on the shower. As soon I heard the showerhead running, I stood up and placed the mug on his coffee table.

Then I went over to the kitchen counter and gathered my wet clothes. I tried to be silent, but when I slipped my feet into my wet boots, they squelched loudly on the carpet. Fortunately, the woman on TV screaming at her boyfriend about how he cheated on her with her own mother was loud enough to drown out the noise.

I was about to rush out the door when I realized that I'd be stealing his clothes. Frantically thinking of some quick way to repay him, I spotted his kitchen trash can and decided to take his trash out as a way of thanking him. It wasn't a fair payback—he'd saved my life after all—but at least it was better than nothing. To appease my guilty conscience, I ended up taking his recyclables as well.

"I couldn't help myself. Your mom's a MILF," the TV blared.

It was the last thing I heard before I opened the front door and stepped outside.

I planned on looking for the dumpster around his apartment

but when I reached the bottom of the stairs, I heard his door open. Panicking that he'd catch me, I slung the garbage bags over my shoulder and sprinted in the direction of my dorm. Running across campus in an oversized shirt and jeans, wet, dirty clothes in hand, and two black trash bags jangling over my shoulder, I probably looked like a deranged homeless person. A homeless person who saw imaginary cats.

After a fifteen minute dash that had my heart pumping, I arrived back at my dorm. Large, golden letters across the entrance read "Floyd Hall". I threw the garbage bags into the dumpster and took the four flights of stairs up to my floor. I opened the door to my suite and promptly went into my room.

Reaching into the pocket of my still dripping jacket, I pulled out Dad's letter. The ink was starting to run a little and the room was turning blurry.

Stupid. Stupid. Stupid. I should have been more careful. I gently placed the letter on the window ledge next to the radiator. Hopefully it would dry off and still be mostly intact.

I rummaged in my closet for a while before changing into my pajamas. Tears started falling down my face as I curled up in my bed. Why was I crying now when I couldn't before? I grabbed my pillow and held it against me. I thought I couldn't feel anything anymore, but I was wrong. I knew it was stupid, but I had felt a lot of strong conflicting emotions from just being around Tattoos and Muscles—or Tim or whatever his actual name was.

Worst thing though, it was probably the most normal thing I had felt in a long time.

Chapter Three

SLOBBERING DOG

Plagued by dreams and daydreams of Tim and his naked torso, I was still recovering from the entire episode several days later as I was sitting in class. It was an 8:30 AM session of Psychology 102. I hated morning classes, especially classes in a lecture hall with a hundred-plus students. We were in the very back row. The only reason I had signed up for the course was to be in the same class as my suitemate Daniela.

We had met freshman year before everything happened. She was the only person who had consistently stayed in touch with me after I took time off. Now that I was back, she was my main connection to the school and my best friend.

She also had more than a passing interest in psychology, unlike me. I thought it would be a good class to take to get some social science credits, but the only thing I was taking this semester that I was passionate about was my drawing class. This class was an exercise in staying awake.

Totally sleep-deprived after staying up too late again watching *Grey's Anatomy*, I started doodling. It was something I did a lot. My therapist back in Indiana—Dr. Alice Schwartz—had recommended that I find a creative outlet to express myself, and for once that was advice I had no problem taking. I loved to draw. Zoned out, I dragged my pen across the top of my page, waving it up and down to make a little river.

It was still hard to believe the whole episode with the lake had happened. The look on the guy's face after he saved me was burned into my memory. He had asked me if I had tried to kill myself. Even though he didn't know my family history, the question stung. After everything I'd been through, I still would never take the cowardly way out. There were people who cared about me.

Thinking about putting myself in that much danger turned my stomach into a pit. I looked to my left and watched Daniela soaking in the lecture. What if I hadn't been saved out there? She'd be devastated. Thank god T&M had come and saved me.

He was causing his own problems, though. I'd spent most of my time since that fateful morning thinking about his strong hands and reserved personality. When I first saw him, I thought he was just your average incredibly hot college student, but the more I thought about him, the more curious I became. Who was this guy who had tattoos and muscles like a gang member but kept his apartment as clean as a soldier's?

It would still be best if I didn't run into him again, though. I'd come back to school just trying to get through the semester with as even a keel as possible. The last thing I needed was a bad boy who thought he had something up on me trying to get into my pants. Especially if I started letting him. My emotional state was fragile enough as it was.

Returning my attention to the important work of doodling on my page of what should have been notes, I began to sketch a big warhammer modeled after a tattoo I had seen on Tim's arm just before he went into the shower. It reminded me of the hammer Thor used in *The Avengers*. Even if I didn't want to see Tim again, it was a cool tattoo. Not something I would get myself, but cool nonetheless.

"I'll just pick a name from this list," I heard the professor say from the front of the class. I perked up. "Ms. Burnham, please."

I looked around, horrified. What was the question he'd asked? I had been totally zoned out. Squinting, I saw that the Powerpoint slide had something to do with a guy named Ivan Pavlov.

"The question is: what is Pavlov most famous for, Ms. Burnham." He was balding with gray hair at the sides and silver wire-framed glasses, and he sounded foreign. German, maybe. What he didn't sound was amused.

I looked to my left at Daniela. Her eyes flicked down to my notes, apparently saw I hadn't been even kind of paying attention, then turned to the front of the class. "The Dog Slobber Principle," she called.

Several people in the class laughed. The professor tried to keep a straight face for a moment, but he smiled too. "I was looking for 'conditioned reflex,' but dog salivation was an important part of the experiment Pavlov used to discover it. Thank you, Ms. Burnham."

I smiled at Daniela. That was the second time I'd been saved in the space of a few days. I really needed to start paying closer attention in class. It was my first semester back, and getting off to a bad start wouldn't help me in my goal of making it through the whole semester.

The rest of class went by without incident. I did my best to actually take some notes, leaving my sketch of Thor's hammer unfinished, but I would need to copy Daniela's for all the stuff I missed. Having a class with my best friend was already beginning to pay off.

After class had ended and everyone was packing up, Daniela poked me in the ribs. "Hey, are you okay?" she asked. "You look like you have something on your mind."

I shook my head. "I'm fine. Just have to get back into the swing of school is all." I finished packing up and slung my bag over my shoulder. "Thanks for saving me on that question. How did you know the answer?"

She laughed. "For one, I was paying attention. Two, Pavlov comes up in a lot of books about psychology. He's kind of one of the founders, I guess."

"So that was a pretty easy question?"

"If you were paying attention, I guess. It doesn't really matter. I doubt Professor Muller is going to remember what Ms. Burnham looks like."

"That's true. It's a big class."

"Yeah. Want to hit up Starbucks and get some coffee? I need to kill an hour before geology."

I didn't have anything until the afternoon, but I didn't feel like going back to the dorm to sit and do nothing, so I agreed. We walked the ten minutes to the Starbucks in the student union. Daniela got a mocha and I got a venti black coffee. Caffeine was the only way I was really going to operate in the morning for the foreseeable future.

The Starbucks was crowded, but we found a small table with two chairs by a window and took our seat. Daniela took a sip from her steaming drink and eyed me carefully.

"So what was that badass hammer you were drawing when Muller called on you?" she asked.

My face grew hot. I hadn't told her—or anyone else—about the incident with the lake. It was too embarrassing, and I was afraid that people would think I had fallen in on purpose no matter what I told them. A lot of people, Daniela included, knew about my family tragedies. My mom's murder had been major news. After such a sensational story, my dad's suicide made a juicy follow-up. The coverage of the whole thing made me sick, as did thinking about people's opinions on it.

I could just imagine their thought process: maybe I had inherited the temperament to go through with killing myself. If my dad could do it, why couldn't I? I clenched my jaw. If anything, the way my dad had passed made me certain I would never do the same. I knew how it affected the people left behind.

"Whoa, hey, I was just asking. There's no need to get mad," Daniela said.

I blinked and snapped back into reality. "Sorry, what? I'm not mad."

"You have a nasty scowl on your face for a girl who's not mad."

I smiled. "Sorry, it wasn't you. The hammer's something I saw on a tattoo recently, that's all."

Her eyebrows shot up. "Are you thinking about getting a tattoo?"

"No, I just thought it looked cool."

"Where did you see it?"

"On this guy a few days ago."

She squinted. "Where? What did he look like?"

My chest tightened. Did she somehow know the guy who had rescued me from the lake. "Why? Have you seen it before too?"

"It sounds familiar. Where did you see him?"

"He was out jogging," I said. That was true, at least.

"It's January. He was out jogging and you saw his tattoo? Was it on his leg? His face?"

Shit. I was a terrible liar. "No, I was sitting inside and he came in. Here, actually. He rolled his sleeves up and that's when I saw it."

She stared at me for a second and said nothing. Did she realize I was lying? My guess was she probably did. Daniela was very perceptive; it was part of the reason she liked psychology so much. She'd taken several other more advanced psychology classes that only required Psych 101 and was just now circling back to take Psych 102.

She shrugged. "Fair enough. Was he hot?"

"I guess. I don't know, I feel like me and guys is still kind of weird. Like I'm just trying to get myself right, you know? I don't need to complicate that by trying to keep someone else happy too."

"That makes sense." She hummed in contemplation. "Yeah, I'm pretty sure this hammer guy is ringing a bell but I can't quite put my finger on it."

Hoping to change the subject, I asked, "Speaking of getting myself right, can I copy your notes for class? I have like nothing from the first half."

She laughed. "I saw. Yeah, that's no problem."

"Who is this Pavlov guy, anyway? You said he was important."

"He is. Basically, he did studies on how everyone has reflexes to certain things. The first was a study on how people reacted to overwhelming stress or pain. Everyone shuts down eventually. They go in shock, become numb and stop doing things. The difference between people is when they shut down and how long it takes them to get out of it."

"Sounds depressing." And disturbingly familiar.

"Yeah, kind of. Basically, more sensitive people shut down sooner and have a harder time getting out of it. Anyway, he did that, but he also did this thing with dogs where he would give them food at the same time as he rang a bell. He measured how much they slobbered every time. Eventually, he would ring the bell without any food present, and the dogs would slobber the same amount."

"And that's called conditioning?"

She nodded. "Exactly. See, this class will be no big deal for you!"

I scrunched my nose. "I still want to copy your notes."

"Of course. By the way, what time is it?"

I looked at my phone. "Ten-forty."

"Ah, I need to get to class. Listen, I know you don't want to get too involved with any guys, but that doesn't mean you can't have fun, right? If I can find us dates, do you want to come out Friday?"

"I don't know, Daniela, I might just stay in."

"Come on, it's first week of classes. There will be free drinks and a little flirting. Worst case, we ditch them and go back to the dorm to watch bad TV with a little buzz on. At least we won't feel lame for not going out."

It *had* been a long time since I'd been out for a fun night. Living with my aunt and uncle hadn't really allowed that. Going out with Daniela would probably be a good time, and she was right: worst case, we could come back home. If I stayed in on the first Friday night of the semester, I would probably feel lame because everyone else was out drinking.

"Okay, if you can find us dates that aren't total creeps, I'll go."

She smiled. "Good! I'll let you know. Anyway, I've got to run. I'll see you later."

After she left, I stared into space for a few minutes. Maybe going out would be fun, maybe not, but it would definitely help get me back into the swing of normal college life. I still didn't feel like going back to the dorm. It was too quiet. Instead, I took out my notebook and continued working on my hammer sketch, filling in more details than even the tattoo had.

It was beginning to look pretty good.

Chapter Four

BEARDED SQUIRREL

Classes on Thursday and Friday were a breeze. Since it was the first week of school, there wasn't much homework or studying to do. Still, I found myself glad that Friday arrived. It had been a difficult experience returning to school. I found myself questioning people's stares—and there were plenty of them. Did they know who I was? Did they see the trial on TV? It made me uncomfortable to think that they were silently judging me, pitying me, or thinking I must have a lot of issues after what I'd gone through. I just wanted to feel normal again, and having people stare at me didn't help.

"That's such a cute outfit," Daniela said as I stepped out of my room into the suite. She was seated on the couch waiting for me to finish getting ready for the double-date she had set up for us. She had met a pair of guys—Cody and Justin—in her Sociology 101 class earlier in the week. So Daniela set up a double-date at a bar off campus called the Bearded Squirrel.

We were both underage by a few months but Daniela got us fake IDs. "And here I thought you were reluctant about going. You look ready to break some hearts!"

I smoothed out the front of my blue dress, adjusting the fabric at my hips to ensure the bottom wasn't riding high in a way that could be misinterpreted by my date. "Hey, if I'm going to go on a date, I'm going to do it right. Otherwise there'd be no point, right?"

"I like that attitude! We're gonna have so much fun tonight!"

I still wasn't sure about doing this whole date thing. I wasn't really looking for any kind of romantic relationship at the moment given the craziness going on in my life but it was a step toward normal. Regular people dated. They went out to parties, laughed, got drunk, and took embarrassing pictures that they would post on Facebook the next day. They didn't sit in their rooms on Friday nights sketching and moping.

Daniela hadn't even given me many details about Justin, my date. She'd gone on about how mouth-wateringly scrumptious Cody was and how she would stare at his crotch all lecture long. "If he's half as well-developed down there as the muscles in his arms, he'd be one serious catch," she had said.

"So this Justin guy—" I said, making last-minute adjustments to my hair in the full-length mirror we had in the suite. "What's he like?"

"Oh! He's also a catch. Frankly, I would've been fine going out with either of them. I've heard other girls say that he has celebrity looks. Like a musician, you know?"

"What kind of musician? Like a rockstar?"

She tilted her head toward the ceiling and put her finger on her chin. "Don't think so. Maybe more alternative? Not sure."

Hmm . . . someone artsy. If he was down-to-earth and not an egotistical rockstar type, maybe we could hit it off. Who knows? I decided to be optimistic about Justin.

"Well as long as he doesn't have high expectations, I could see us getting along. I'm not exactly the perky, blonde sorority-type, if that's what he's looking for. You did tell him a bit about me right?"

"Oh yeah. Of course. I said Lorrie Burnham is my best friend. She's wonderful, has a wicked sense of humor, and is overall a great girl."

I frowned. "So basically you told him as much about me as you've told me about him."

The edges of her lips curved into a smile. "Sure, whatever. It's more fun if it's a surprise anyway right?"

"I guess."

I knew where she was coming from. Daniela had good intentions. Except in my experience, surprises could be a bad thing. A very bad thing.

The plan was to meet Cody and Justin at the bar so we called for a cab to pick us up outside our dorm. The driver was a young guy with brown hair and lovely green eyes who turned out to be not much older than us. He explained that he was a senior English major and took a part-time job driving cabs on weekends to help pay for his tuition. He was friendly and I found myself thinking that if my date turned out to be half as pleasant as him, I would consider the night well-spent.

The cab slowed to a stop outside the front entrance to the bar. There was a large pink neon sign out front of a bearded cartoon squirrel that had a beer mug in hand. Toward the side was the parking lot which was mostly full with cars and trucks. A few vehicles even spilled out onto the open grass area nearby. This place was apparently very popular. I hadn't been to many bars but from what I could tell by the number of people flooding inside and the cars parked all around, this one was unusually large. From the outside, the wooden square building didn't seem that big, so it either extended further back than I could see from the front or it would be ridiculously packed when we got inside.

"Ladies, here you are," the driver said. "I hope you have a wonderful night. Name's Ryan by the way. Here's my card. Call me if you need a ride back to campus." He winked one green eye. "My shift goes until five AM."

"Thank you so much!" Daniela said, handing him a twenty and taking his card. "We'll definitely give you a call when we're ready to head back."

I offered my thanks and gave him a tip. After giving us a salute, he drove off.

Daniela turned to me. "Night's off to a great start already huh? Aren't you glad you came out?"

I had to admit it felt good to be out instead of being cooped up in my room like I usually was. "Ryan was actually kind of cute," I found myself saying to her.

"If you thought he was cute, you're gonna love Justin!"

I smiled. We followed a gaggle of girls up the wooden steps to the entrance to the bar. A big burly guy with a black skullcap and a scruffy beard with braids in it stood by the door with his arms crossed across his barrel chest. Uh oh. Security.

"Ladies, welcome." His voice was low and gruff.

Daniela reached into her purse for her wallet and flashed her fake ID. Her hand was still and she beamed a confident smile, having practiced the routine more than a few times. I was about to do the same when the guy waved his hand dismissively. "No worries, you're good. Just don't get too rowdy or I'll have to kick your asses out. Got it?"

We both gulped and nodded.

He smiled, uncrossed his arms, and gestured inside. "Enjoy your night." He flashed us a pearly white grin that seemed too kind for someone that looked like he manhandled "rowdy" college kids on a nightly basis.

Once we got inside, I turned to Daniela. "Did that just happen? They don't even check IDs here? Won't they get shut down?"

Daniela shrugged. "Who cares, right? That's not our problem. As long as we're in, we're good to go."

We scanned the bar, craning our necks over the crowd of people to try to spot our dates. I didn't know who I was looking for, but that didn't stop me from looking. The bar was brimming with people but not wall-to-wall crowded as I imagined it would be. I didn't recognize the loud rock music playing probably because I was more a Taylor Swift fan than a Nine Inch Nails one. It was probably a fifty-fifty mix between college students and recent grads but there was definitely nobody older than forty.

Daniela's cell phone chimed and she checked the new text message she received. "They got a table near the back. It's supposed to be next to a giant moose head mounted on the wall."

We maneuvered our way through the crowd toward the back and spotted the moose head. It looked like an ordinary mounted moose head except it had black X's over its eyes and it had a long tongue sticking out. The decoration fit the over-the-top grizzled animal theme they had going on.

"Cody!" Daniela shouted over the noise.

Two guys seated across from one another turned to us, smiled, and waved. The one named Cody had brown eyes with flecks of amber in his irises and donned a white baseball cap turned backward. He wore a pink polo with the collar popped and sleeves that showcased his muscular arms. There was only one label flashing to my mind: frat guy.

"Daniela!" Cody shouted. "You guys made it! Come sit with us." He patted the seat beside him.

Daniela sat next to Cody and I took my seat next to Justin.

"Cody, Justin," Daniela said gesturing to each person in turn, "this is my suitemate and best friend Lorrie. Lorrie, this is Cody and Justin."

"It's great to finally meet you," Cody said, smiling.

"We've heard such good things about you from Daniela. You're much hotter than I expected," Justin said, as he put his arm around my shoulder and rubbed gently.

"Thanks..." I said, unsure how to react to his sudden contact. I'd barely gotten to know him and he was already acting like we were dating. It made me uncomfortable. "You look good yourself."

Justin had mid-length, brown hair in a layered purposely messy look that was popular with teenagers these days. He had a boyish grin and large dark brown eyes that matched the polo he was wearing. The collar was also popped but his arms were scrawny unlike Cody's. Daniela had said that he looked like a musician. Now I knew what she had meant. Looking at Justin made one word come to mind: Bieber.

"Yeah, I remember seeing you on TV during that whole trial thing going on. Man, that's crazy. I can't imagine having my mom being killed by my stepdad. That must really suck."

I looked at Daniela and she looked back at me with wide, concerned eyes. I coughed. "Um . . . yeah. It does suck," I said, suddenly making a one-eighty on my decision that I was glad to come out on this double-date. I took his hand off my shoulder and set it in his lap.

"What's the matter?" Justin asked.

"It's a bit warm in here. Your hand is making my shoulder sweat," I said sarcastically.

Justin grinned. He apparently didn't take the cue. "There's a lot of heat between us I know. But it's only going to get hotter, I assure you."

"Well." Daniela clapped her hands together. "Let's order some drinks shall we?

I was considering calling Ryan and having him take me back to the dorms, but I didn't want to leave after just arriving. I hoped to god that Justin only made bad first impressions and that the rest of the night would be better.

We ordered drinks. Daniela got a margarita, Cody got a mug of Miller Lite, Justin got a Coors Light, and I had a mojito.

"This is a cool place," Cody said taking a sip of amber liquid from his mug. "I've been here once before but it was never this packed. I think they opened like a year or so ago."

"Yeah," Daniela said. "I heard this place is pretty hype. A lot more exciting than the bars around campus."

"No doubt. This place is ill," said Justin. "Check out this moose head." He pointed to the large pink tongue hanging out. "Doesn't he look like he's thirsty?" Justin poured a little bit of his beer on the tongue and it sat there while he and Cody laughed. Daniela and I laughed as well but we weren't laughing with them. We were laughing *at* them.

"So are you guys seniors?" I asked, hoping to divert their attention so that they wouldn't get our asses kicked out of the bar for messing up the decor. I'm all for having fun, but Cody and Justin were just being dumb.

"I'm a senior econ major," Cody said. "Justin's a junior. Anthropology major." He snickered at Justin.

Justin snickered back and brushed his bangs away from his eyes before turning toward me. "I study people. That makes me specially attuned to people's needs and desires. You might say I'm a sensitive guy." He grinned mischievously. "You want to hear my insights on you?"

I really didn't want to hear anything more from Justin's mouth after what he'd already said about me but decided against being rude. It would make things more awkward than they already were and it would ruin Daniela's date with Cody as well. Considering Daniela invited me out, it would be a pretty bitchy move for me to do that to her. "Uh . . . okay," I said then took a big gulp of my drink to prepare myself for his response.

"You're a smart girl, but lack direction in life." He took my hand in his. "You're kind of down a lot, especially after what you've been through. You need a strong man to care for you, to take care of you."

He wiggled his brows then pointed his thumb to his chest.

Wow, just when I thought he couldn't get any worse. This guy was a real catch all right . . . a real catch right out of Lake Peepee. I wasn't sure if that was the most insulted I ever felt in my life, but it was definitely up there. I clutched my drink in my hand and lifted it off the table. A vision of throwing the contents into Justin's grinning face flashed through my mind. Just as I was about to make that vision a reality, someone nearby slapped a nearby lounge seat in exclamation.

I turned to see a group of guys and girls standing near us talking excitedly.

"No way. It's starting? Now?" one guy said.

"Yeah, let's go. I don't want to miss it. I don't want to miss seeing *him*," a girl replied.

They filed out the back door. Soon, another group hurried after them, followed by another group. People were streaming out the back door like squirrels rushing after a pile of acorns. Some stayed, but nearly half the bar cleared out.

"What do you think they're all excited about?" Cody asked.

Sensing this was the perfect getaway excuse, I said, "I'm going to go check it out. I'll join back up with you guys in a bit."

I glanced at Daniela and she flashed me an apologetic expression for Justin's behavior. "Okay, I'll keep these guys entertained while we finish our drinks," Daniela said. "Let us know what you see."

I snatched up my jacket then grabbed my clutch that had been strategically placed between Justin and me to act as a barrier. I stood and hurried out the back door, eager to escape from my "date".

I didn't know what I expected to see, but this certainly wasn't it. There was a large tent set up outside that looked like it came straight from a carnival. People were huddled around an elevated octagon stage surrounded by metal fencing. The whole area was lit by bright spotlights. What was all of this?

Attracted by curiosity as well as the energy of the crowd, I found myself wiggling through a sea of bodies to get a closer look at the stage. Inside the octagon was a mat that had a large logo of a squirrel wearing fighter gloves that said "The Bearded Brawl". After noticing faint blood stains on the mat, it became clear to me that this was some kind of fighting arena.

A suave man in a white suit entered the cage with a microphone. "Ladies and gentleman," he announced with dramatic flare. "We just had an exciting opening match but we've got something even more exciting in store for you. The match you've all been waiting for. Our main event."

The crowd cheered and whistled. Some rattled their beer mugs against the fence.

Two men stepped up onto the stage and entered the cage. One was wearing a red hoodie with matching trunks and the other was wearing a dark blue version of the same outfit. They both had their hoods over their heads so I couldn't see their faces, but their sweaters were partially open and I could snag a peek at their torsos. And what a peek it was. From the teasingly little I could see, it was clear each had ripped abs and sculpted pecs like they were carved by a sculptor. The one in blue particularly caught my attention. He was bouncing on his toes and shaking his arms to stay loose and to keep himself warmed up for the fight. Each bounce sent ripples through his hard muscles, which in turn made my own heart bounce. A surge of desire through my body made me realize how affected I was just by the sight of him. I was unwittingly reminded of Tattoos and Muscles, except I couldn't tell if this guy had any tattoos underneath his hoodie. Tim had a gorgeous bod but I don't think he could compete with blue trunks.

"On my left, standing at six feet, two inches and weighing in at two hundred pounds of pure, raw muscle. Don't let his friendly face fool you, he'll squeeze the life out of you if he gets you in his hold. We've got Abram 'Mr. Hyde' Wallace!"

The crowd cheered for the man in red trunks. Abram hopped around, shadow-boxing the air, displaying his quick fists and dexterous footwork. I squinted, trying to get a view of his face but I couldn't see much beneath the hood. I could see his smile though; it was wide and showcased neat rows of white teeth, which made it seem like he was just happy to be here.

"And on my right, standing also at a height of six feet, two inches and weighing two hundred and five pounds with fists of steel, it's your defending champion, Hunter 'The Hammer' Jensen!"

The crowd erupted once again but louder than they did for Abram. I heard a girl cry out, "I love you Hunter!"

Hunter didn't make as much of a show as Abram. He simply continued shaking out his limbs and bouncing on his toes. Although his head was down seemingly in deep focus, he seemed to be soaking in the cheers, absorbing the crowd's energy to channel later in the fight.

"It's exciting isn't it?" a male voice said next to me.

I turned to see a tall guy around my age with a smooth head standing beside me. He had hard, chiseled features that complemented the defined muscles stretching against his t-shirt and jeans. I wasn't really a fan of bald guys, but this dude was quite attractive. A quick scan of his build and I wondered why he wasn't in the cage himself. He had a smile on his face that looked friendly.

"Yeah, I've never seen this before," I responded. "What kind of fighting is this?"

He chuckled. "So you're not a devoted fan of Hunter, apparently. It's mixed martial arts. Punching, kicking, wrestling—pretty much anything goes except for biting, crotch shots, and eye gouging."

I narrowed my eyes. "That sounds brutal."

"It's exciting to watch for sure. And it's not too bad for the fighters when it comes to safety. Probably no more dangerous than playing professional football or doing boxing. I'd even say it's safer than boxing."

Curious, I asked, "How can it be safer when you can do much more than punching?"

He shrugged. "Some fighters win through holds and submissions. Usually the guy in the submission just taps out before he gets really hurt." He pointed to red trunks. "Abram's strength is in his submissions; he has a wrestling background. As for striking—" He pointed to blue trunks. "Hunter's strength is his stand-up game. He throws a mean punch, which is why he earned the name 'The Hammer'. But the refs tend to stop matches before fighters get seriously hurt. There's no ten count that allows a fighter to get back up and continue fighting again after a mild concussion. Once someone goes down after a good punch, the ref pretty much always ends the fight."

"Wow, you know a lot about this."

He grinned. "Name's Gary." He extended his large hand.

I took it and he shook firmly. "Lorrie."

His grin widened. "Well Lorrie, all I got to say is you're in for a treat if this is your first time watching this."

"Is this like a sanctioned event or something? Why are they having a mixed martial arts fight at this bar?"

"It's sponsored by the Bearded Squirrel. As far as being sanctioned . . ." He shrugged. "Let's just say it's semi-legal. Legal enough—and good enough for business—that they're willing to take the risk."

The announcer stepped out of the cage and a man in a light blue button-down and black pants entered. Judging by his formal attire, he was the referee. He stepped into the center, rolled up his sleeves and pointed to his left.

"Red corner, are you ready?" he shouted.

Abram peeled back his hood and removed his sweatshirt, throwing it over the cage to his coach. He tilted his chin up, beat his fist against his chest, and nodded. He had neatly combed brown hair parted on the side and a soft face with a wide nose. He reminded me of Mr. Rogers from the kid's show *Mr. Roger's Neighborhood*—except this version of Mr. Rogers was on steroids and too big to fit in sweaters.

"Blue corner are you ready?"

Hunter removed his hood then slid the sweater off his massive arms and threw it over the cage. That's when I saw his face; and the tats around the side of his chest and neck.

My heart stopped.

He *was* Tattoos and Muscles.

I heard women screaming Hunter's name and one or two of them shouting for him to marry them. He didn't seem to notice, rather his focus was solely on the opponent before him. The hammer I'd painstakingly drawn in my sketchbook was etched on the side of his arm. There was no mistaking it. I'd finally found out his name.

Hunter Jensen.

I watched anxiously as both men stepped forward and approached one another.

The referee addressed each fighter. "I want a clean fight, you know the rules. No crotch shots, eye gouging, or anything dirty. If you do, I'll have you disqualified. Are we clear?"

Each fighter nodded.

Abram and Hunter tapped gloves then each took a step back. The referee slashed his arm between them like a knife cutting palpable tension. A silence fell on the crowd.

I looked at Gary who had wide eyes and a grin on his face. He seemed pumped to see the action start.

"Fight!" the referee yelled, pulling his arm away and stepping back.

Abram immediately rushed for Hunter, brown eyes blazing red. His friendly expression now maniacal, he lived up to his name "Mr. Hyde". Hunter ducked and hopped to the side, avoiding what would've been a knockout blow.

Abram threw lightning quick jabs left and right but Hunter dodged each of his strikes. A wild jab caught Hunter across the cheek but Hunter quickly shook the blow off as if it was a light tap.

Hunter circled around the ring and Abram followed. They cautiously circled each other until Abram's back was toward me and Hunter was facing my direction.

Abram went for a punch again but dropped at the last moment to tackle Hunter's legs. The punch had been a feint. Hunter quickly hopped backward and thrust his body weight forward as Abram slammed into his legs. Hunter managed to keep his balance, preventing the immediate takedown but they were still struggling. I could clearly see Hunter's face. I could see his mouth guard behind his grimacing lips. He was straining with every ounce of energy to lift Abram off the ground so that Abram wouldn't have leverage to pull Hunter's legs out from under him.

"Uh oh," Gary said. "Hunter has a shitty ground game. If he gets taken down, it's over."

I watched in horror as Abram was about to overpower Hunter and take him down. Once on the ground, he'd probably only be able to defend himself until the round ended. I was barely aware of my hands cupping the sides of my face in disbelief. My savior was going to lose.

I watched him with fierce intensity. My breathing slowed as my heart rate jumped. Hunter must've sensed the tension because he tilted his head, diverting his attention from Abram. His dark eyes locked onto mine. He stared at me. My breath caught. A millisecond passed. Or a second. Or an hour. I didn't know. It had to have been my imagination.

There's no way he spotted me.

Suddenly we broke eye contact. Hunter returned his attention to Abram. Hunter growled, summoning strength from who knows where and picked up Abram and threw him to the side like a two hundred pound rag doll. The move was good enough to buy Hunter enough time to regain his footing.

Abram got to his feet and lunged with a wide hook. Hunter ducked and shot skyward with powerful legs, landing an uppercut under Abram's chin. A mouth guard flew across the ring and clattered against the fence. Abram crumpled to the ground in a daze. Hunter was about to jump on top of Abram to land the finishing blow but the referee stepped in between.

"Stop! Stop! It's over!" the referee shouted, waving one arm over his head. Hunter backed off.

A bell chimed three times.

Hunter was declared the winner. The crowd cheered. One girl fainted with her hand over heart and her friend had to fan her with a "Go Hunter!" sign they made with blue glitter.

Hunter paraded around the ring with his fists in the air. When he walked over to my side of the cage, I ducked behind Gary's wide back to hide from him. The last thing I wanted was for Hunter to acknowledge my presence. It would be completely awkward considering I'd ran off from his place without explanation. He probably still thought I was suicidal. I also still technically had his shirt and jeans. Maybe he'd demand to come over to my place to take his clothes back. Or demand that I'd bring them to his place. Either way, I didn't want to get involved with him. I had enough shit in my life to deal with already.

After seeing Hunter win, I decided to leave before we ran into each other. I could've been mistaken—it very well could've been my imagination—but I was almost certain he had recognized me right before he delivered the knockout blow.

"It was nice to meet you Gary," I said. "Thanks for explaining to me how this all works."

"Leaving already?" he replied. "A little too violent for your tastes perhaps?"

"Eh . . . I just have to get back to my friends in the bar. They're probably wondering what I've been doing out here for so long."

He grinned. "It was nice meeting you Lorrie. Enjoy the rest of your night."

I smiled at him then turned to the crowd and began wiggling my way through the sea of excited bodies. Although everyone was packed in tightly beneath the tent, most were gracious enough to make room for me passing through. I had to push a few people aside though. The endeavor was like an obstacle course and I already felt the first signs of sweat prickling my skin despite the cold weather. I finally caught a faint glimpse of the familiar beer-guzzling squirrel sign atop the bar before more energetic bodies piled in and obscured my view. It took a lot longer than I expected to weave through the crowd probably because more people had trickled in when I was watching the match. I was nearly out, when I ran into someone tall wearing a gray, zippered sweater.

"Excuse me," I said, trying to push my way past him. He wouldn't move though, not by will and not by force.

Who was this douchebag? I moved to step around him.

A firm hand grasped my arm. "Not so fast."

The familiar voice halted my footsteps. I looked up and saw beneath the gray hood, those dark eyes I'd seen before both in real life and in my daydreams.

Hunter.

Chapter Five

NEVERLAND

"I thought I saw you." His presence was powerful and his voice, although no louder than normal, somehow seemed to drown out the raucous around us.

His sudden appearance was alarming. "H-How did you get out here so fast?"

"I saw you run off so I threw on a new sweatshirt and came out here before you could run away again. Gotta be quick to catch a thief." He winked. "Don't think I've forgotten you still have the clothes I lent you."

Damn it.

He continued, "So you came to cheer for me huh?"

"I don't know what you're talking about," I shot back, suddenly unnerved by being so close to him. Not to mention his hand firmly around my shoulder and the warmth from his palm seeping through the thick fabric of my coat. It should've been comforting but I found myself becoming edgy and restless.

"You were right in the front. You seemed really concerned about me during Abram's takedown attempt. I was touched."

We were surrounded by Hunter's adoring female fans but he was hooded and in inconspicuous attire so nobody noticed who he was. Except me. Was that his intention?

"What makes you think I was concerned about you? Maybe I was concerned about 'Mr. Hyde.'"

He grinned. "I doubt that."

"You're a little full of yourself, Hunter."

His grin widened. "You know my name now, that's not fair. Now you have to tell me yours."

Realizing I had the upperhand on him, I couldn't help a small smile from breaking through. "Sorry, that'll have to remain a secret. Now if you'll excuse me, I need to get back to—"

"My boy!" said a male voice.

"Gary!" Hunter responded. Sensing an opportunity in Gary's distraction, I tried to make my escape but Hunter's hand remained firm around my shoulder. I moved but he hugged me closer to him, my face mooshing into the soft cotton covering his chest. I caught a whiff of his just-been-fighting scent and my brain fried for a moment.

Gary appeared by my side, shook Hunter's hand, and they bumped shoulders.

"Congrats on the win. Didn't look like you even broke a sweat out there. Looks like all that practice defending takedowns paid off."

"Couldn't have done it without you man," Hunter said.

Gary noticed my presence and eyed Hunter's arm around my shoulder. "Lorrie! Didn't expect to see you here. I thought you were going back inside."

"*Lorrie* huh?" Hunter looked down at me with a grin that made my heart skip a beat.

Shit. He knew my name now.

"It's such a pretty name. Here I was referring to you in my mind as Dorothy. Looks like I was somewhat close."

Double shit. He had a nickname for me as well. Except 'Tim' was nowhere close to 'Hunter'.

"So how do you guys know each other?" Gary asked.

My stomach dropped. Not only did Hunter know my name now, he was going to spill about how he saved me from committing suicide last week. It would draw more attention to me and wreck my attempts at a normal semester.

Hunter looked at me carefully then turned to Gary. "I was out jogging last weekend. I slipped on the ice and fell flat on my ass. She rushed over to see if I was okay and we got to chatting."

I was shocked that Hunter had just lied to Gary. Why was he covering for me? And at his own expense?

Gary laughed. "I've been telling you man. You gotta work on your footwork." He laughed again and slapped Hunter on the shoulder.

"C'mon let's go inside, I'll buy you a drink. Although you should really be the one buying with all that prize money you just won."

We made our way through the crowd. Hunter kept his arm around me, holding me close so I wouldn't get lost—or run away. When we made it into the clearing, a pair of blonde girls with large breasts and slim waists approached. Hunter turned away to hide his face.

"Gary? Gary Wilkins? Oh my god we're like your biggest fans!"

Gary grinned and opened his arms. "Why hello ladies. It's always great to meet my adoring fans." He turned to us. "Sorry guys, I'm going to have to catch up with you later. I have some important business to attend to. You understand." He winked at us.

Hunter and I walked off toward the bar and I looked over my shoulder to catch a glimpse of Gary laughing with his arms around both girls. The two girls had their hands all over his shaved head, relishing the smoothness beneath their fingertips. I had a feeling those girls were going to get a very special "autograph" by the end of the night.

Hunter suddenly stopped. "How are you feeling?"

I froze, thinking he was referring to the day he saved me from becoming an ice cube at the bottom of Lake Peepee. "How am I feeling about what?"

"About getting a drink. I'm not really that thirsty right now. I'd rather walk and talk. You interested?"

"I'm flattered but I really have to get back to my friends . . ." The thought of returning to Justin almost made me gag. It would be uncomfortable but at least it was an uncomfortableness I could handle. I had no idea how to handle being around Hunter Jensen, especially now that I knew he was a badass cage fighter.

His expression turned tender but serious. "I'm not going to bite ya know."

I'd just seen him uppercut a guy's mouth guard out so I didn't know how to react to this side of him. "I never said you would. What makes you think I have that impression of you?"

"Because you're trying to avoid me."

I laughed. "No, I'm not."

"Yes, you are Lorrie." Hearing my name uttered from his lips sent a jolt through my system, heightening my already strong awareness of him. "You ran from my apartment. And now you're trying to give me the slip. What's the deal? Do I smell bad?"

I had to suppress a grin at his line about smelling bad. If anything, he smelled *good*. Strong, musky, manly. Which was strange. I couldn't put my finger on it but I did know that a guy wasn't supposed to smell as good as he did after working up a sweat. My mind swirling, I decided to go with a standard brush-off line. "It's not you. It's me. I can't explain it, it's complicated."

He narrowed his dark eyes. "If it's not me, then why do you act this way only around me? I noticed you didn't have the same reaction around Gary."

I wracked my brain for an answer. "Gary's friendlier."

Hunter smiled. "Hey, I saved your life, lent you my clothes, made you tea, and let you shower at my place. And you're saying Gary is friendlier? Psh, and here I thought you were polite."

"I am. I'm politely stating facts."

"Alright, since you don't think I'm such a friendly guy, I'm gonna have to charge you for my hospitality."

"See? Proved my point." I folded my arms across my chest but I was eager to settle my debt to him so I wouldn't have to deal with him anymore. "So what do you want in return?"

"You're going to have to join me on my cooldown walk. I usually go alone, but this time I want company. Unfortunately that means you're going to have to ditch your friends."

I frowned. "That's not very nice."

"I'm Mr. Not-So-Nice remember?" A smile played at the corner of his full lips. The combination of boyish charm and rugged brawler was becoming too difficult to resist.

"Alright, fine. We'll walk, but just to make us even. Then I don't owe you anything, okay?"

"Sounds good." His smile turned into a wide grin. "Go tell your friends you're ditching them."

I took a step then halted and turned back to him. "You're willing to wait?"

His grin remained firmly in place. "Not nice isn't the same as mean. Give me a little credit here."

"Aren't you concerned I'm just going to go inside and end up ditching you?" The question rode a thin line between teasing and serious. I didn't know which way he'd interpret it maybe because I didn't know which way I meant it, myself.

"We have a deal remember? You seem like someone who respects that. I trust you."

"Maybe you're a little too trusting."

I went back inside the bar, leaving Hunter out back. I seriously thought about ditching him. What was I doing agreeing to go on a walk with him anyway? I wanted a normal life again. I wanted peace. I wanted to feel like a regular person again. I had to keep telling myself that going on one walk with Hunter wasn't going to ruin any of those things. I had to convince myself that the feelings I felt while being around him weren't real, that it was a fluke the numbness I constantly felt somehow magically disappeared for a moment when I was near him or thought about him. It was hormones. A "biological quirk" as my therapist liked to refer to disorders. Just a result of being without a boyfriend for over a year. If I allowed myself to fall for Hunter, I could really get hurt. Guys like him had women literally fainting to be with him. Hadn't I been hurt enough already?

I spotted Daniela, Cody, and Justin across the bar still at the same moosehead booth where I'd left them. For a moment, I considered making up a good excuse to tell them in person but decided that I didn't owe Justin anything. I pulled out my phone and texted Daniela.

There's a mixed martial arts thing going on out back. Gonna hang out with one of the fighters instead of Justin :P.

A moment later she replied. *Can't blame ya :). You gonna be okay by yourself?*

Yeah, don't worry about me. I'll catch a ride back. Tell Justin and Cody I got sick and had to leave.

Leaving out the back door, I saw Hunter leaning against the side of the bar, alone. His warm breath made billows of fog in the cold air. I'd half-expected him to be surrounded by women when I returned, but the only thing around him was his gray hoodie. People were still gathered beneath the large tent, chatting excitedly about Hunter's fight. I couldn't help but wonder what some of those fan girls would do if they got the chance to be in my position.

"Congratulations, I just lost my friends," I said. It was Hunter's fault that I'd ditched my group so I figured I might as well give him a hard time.

He smiled. "If that was all it took to lose your friends, then they weren't good ones to begin with. Besides, you just made a new one."

I cocked a brow at him. "You?"

"See anyone else around?"

I looked around for Gary but didn't see him anywhere in sight. "I guess I don't see Gary here. . . Speaking of which, why did you lie to him about the lake incident?"

He shrugged. "I didn't want you to look bad. Friends look out for one another."

I took a deep breath of the crisp air and cleared my throat. "Just because we're walking together, doesn't make us friends. This is just a deal. Let's just get this over with okay?"

"After you, *Lorrie*." He grinned wickedly.

We walked away from the clamor of the bar along a dirt path leading into the dark forest surrounding the bar. For a popular venue, it was kind of in the middle of nowhere. I was concerned about going into the darkness of the forest but strangely felt safe around Hunter. However, neither of us said anything. The silence was awkward.

Once we entered the forest, I broke the silence. "So . . . you go on cooldown walks after you fight?"

"Yeah, it's a good time to reflect and clear your head, ya know. That's why I usually go alone."

"You don't go with any of your female fans?" I asked, nonchalantly. "Why walk with me then?"

"Most of the time I like just hanging out by myself or with Gary—I don't get along with most people . . . You're different though. I don't know what it is exactly but I feel like we can relate, you seem cool." He looked at me and grinned.

"Thanks, I guess. Always nice to be thought of as 'cool.'" I didn't know what he meant but it sounded like a compliment and my face flustered anyway. "So, I've been wondering, why did you think my name was Dorothy?"

He stopped to pick up a large branch on the ground. "'Cause you remind me of Dorothy from the Wizard of Oz except you almost got swept away by an icy lake instead of a tornado. Then you ran off from my place because you were in a hurry to go home."

I stooped to pick up my own branch but it was smaller than Hunter's because my hands were smaller. "What can I say? There's no place like 'Floyd Hall!'"

He chuckled as he idly tapped the leaves and bushes with his branch as we walked. "I suppose that makes me the cowardly lion?"

I smiled despite myself. "From what I saw tonight, you definitely found your courage."

He chuckled again.

"So what's it like being a fighter?" I asked.

"Not bad. I like the competition."

"Aren't you scared of getting hurt?"

He paused. "Nobody likes to get hurt. That's where training and preparation come in. You keep your head on straight, and the worst you come out with are some cuts and bruises most of the time."

"I think 'Mr. Hyde' would have to disagree with you—you forgot concussions."

"Sometimes it happens. It's not like I intended to give him a concussion. Besides, Mr. Hyde's a big boy. He would've done the same to me if he had the chance."

"Not nice, but not mean right?"

"However you want to put it." He smirked. Suddenly, he swatted at my face. I was frightened for a moment but quickly realized he had saved me from a nose-diving mosquito. Damn thing must've been resistant to the cold. "So Lorrie, how about you? I know you're not a good swimmer; I know you don't like my apartment; now I know your name. What else can you tell me? Or do I have to figure it out?"

"By the way, I am a decent swimmer," I corrected him. "It's just different when you're trying to swim in heavy clothes and freezing cold water. But other than that, there's not much to know. Nothing of importance anyway. I'm just your average college girl."

"Normal right?" he teased.

"Exactly."

"Any major?"

"Ugh, I wish. I'm 'undecided'."

"'Undecided' is legit. It's certainly honest. I think most people are in that major whether they want to admit it or not."

"I guess . . . How about you?"

"Physics."

I raised my brows. "Physics? Wow, that's quite a brainy major. Physicist by day, brawler by night?"

He chuckled. "The matches help pay for the tuition. But physics isn't all that bad. Most of it is just memorizing a lot of formulas. Once you realize that, it's a lot less intimidating."

"Do you have a particular interest in being a physicist?"

"Eh, not really. I was just kinda interested in planes and stuff when I was growing up and thought learning physics would be cool. I'm kinda less interested in it now."

Hunter's expression seemed to turn unusually despondent and I decided not to pursue the topic. "I see."

We came to a clearing and found ourselves in front of what looked like an abandoned amusement park. There was a beat up sign over the entranceway that said "Neverland".

"Are we walking in there?" I asked.

"Sure, why not?"

"It looks sketchy. What if it's dangerous?"

He smiled. "You're walking with me. If anybody tries something on us, they'll be sorry. Trust me. I saved you once already, remember?"

"Okay," I said tentatively. I was intrigued by the idea of exploring an abandoned amusement park. What would a place for fun and laughs be like when it died?

We carried our sticks with us as we hopped over a broken turnstile and entered the park. There were yellow and red flags, tents, game booths, a ferris wheel, a merry-go-round, and a bunch of other fascinating things. Everything was covered in dirt and rust. Small crevices were filled with iced water. I'd have thought some of this stuff would've been salvaged but it was as if one day people decided to abandon everything.

"This is pretty crazy. They just left all this stuff here," I said admiring the surroundings. "Do you walk around here often?"

He prodded a broken styrofoam cup on the ground. "I like to walk around this place whenever I've got a match here. Kind of always had a thing for amusement parks since I was a kid. There was a fire at this place a few decades back. You can see some burn marks on the carousel over there." He pointed with his stick.

I looked at the carousel and saw half the horses blackened by ash. The other half were shades of gray and white. It seemed like all of them were supposed to be white.

"That's terrible. What happened?"

He shrugged. "Nobody knows how it started. But it happened at night when almost no one was around. I think it took one or two people's lives. Not enough to be a huge tragedy but I'm sure it affected the family members of those that died—if they had any. I think the owners got a bunch of insurance money and started another park somewhere else. It must've been a big a deal when it happened but people kind of forgot about this place over time."

The story sounded horrible and hit a little too close to my own personal tragedy. I wanted to change the topic. "Did you go to a lot of places like this when you were young?" I asked.

"That's the thing. I didn't go to any amusement parks when I was a kid. I wanted to but my parents never took me. All the other kids in grade school would talk about how awesome Disneyland was. Or Six Flags, or Sea World."

"What kind of parents don't take their kid to an amusement park?" I said jokingly. "That's like the stuff childhoods are made of."

"Deadbeat ones." He paused, his mouth a thin line. "They were druggies. Real assholes. Cared more about their drugs than taking care of me. That's why I got away from California and came here."

"Oh. I'm sorry to hear that." I suddenly felt bad for asking him about his parents.

We were both silent for a moment. I contemplated what Hunter had told me about his parents. Was fighting a way for him to cope with his troubled past like I used drawing to cope with mine? I didn't know, but it sounded like he and I might not have been as different as I initially thought.

Hunter ended up throwing his branch into a pile of debris near one of the game booths. It fit right in with the other junk.

"How about your parents?" he asked.

I was surprised he didn't know about me after learning my name. I would've thought he heard about me from rumors around campus. Or seen my picture in the paper. It was certainly big news across Illinois.

I could feel the numbness settling in once again. "They're not together."

"Divorced?"

Without skipping a beat, I answered. "And dead."

"Oh. I'm sorry."

"Yeah."

I could feel the past creeping up on me again like it always did. Images would flash. Scenarios would be relived. The stone would appear again, bigger than the last time, intimidating me like it always did. It would dare me to roll it up the hill. I'd consider it for a while, maybe even try to push it a few times, but every time, I'd end up quitting.

"Hey, check out that booth!" Hunter pointed in the distance, breaking me from the spell. He tugged my hand and we rushed over. "Look there's an old milk bottle still standing up. Did you ever play these kinds of games before?"

I thought about the time I went to the carnival with Mom and Dad. I must've been eight at the time. Dad handed the operator a few bucks and I was given a ball to throw at a stack of milk bottles. It was silly for an eight-year-old to think she had the strength to knock those bottles down. But for some reason I thought I could do it. I thought I could win. I wound my arm back and threw the ball with as much strength as I could muster. It ended up hitting the poor operator right in the nose—a fountain of blood sprayed my overalls. That was the last time I played.

"Yeah," I said wryly.

"Let's play." He touched my hand holding the small branch, sending a tingling through my arm.

"You can play. I'll watch."

He smiled. "Nah. I threw my stick away. This one's yours."

"Um . . . I don't really feel like playing."

He laughed. "C'mon, let's knock the hell outta that bottle. You could win a prize."

A small smile tugged at the corners of my lips. "And what kind of prize would that be?"

"Anything you like. How about that beat-up looking doll over there." He pointed to the corner of the booth. There was a dirty-blonde doll—emphasis on 'dirty'—with a pink dress and a dimpled smile on its face as well as various dark stains.

"Eww. That's gross." I made a disgusted face but laughed as well.

"Okay, no doll then." He looked around. "How about some cotton candy from that machine over there?"

I looked at the decrepit cotton candy machine stand with cobwebs inside the glass and a bird nest sitting on top of it. I chuckled. "Why don't I just scoop up a bunch of dirt and dump it in my mouth?"

He grinned. "Alright, alright. How about the reward for knocking down the bottle is the satisfaction in itself for having done it."

"Wow, that sounds lame. I'd even take a gold sticker over that."

He laughed. "Just throw the stick already, Lorrie. We both know the bottle ain't gonna knock itself over."

Feeling in a better mood, but still kind of annoyed that Hunter was making me play this game, I wound up my arm and chucked the damn stick as hard as I could. I missed and hit the back flap of the tent, tearing a hole in it.

"Wow, you didn't win but man that was quite a throw."

I held my arm up and squeezed my spongy bicep through the jacket sleeve. "I hope you bought tickets to the gun show."

Hunter smiled at me with his dark eyes then lifted both his arms up and flexed. Thick bulges peaked through the gray cotton. "I didn't need to bring tickets. I'm a vendor."

We both laughed before the tent housing the game booth suddenly started collapsing. I jumped into Hunter's arms and he pulled me back until we were both out of the way.

"Holy shit!" I cried.

"I take it back," he said, flabbergasted. "You won. Definitely won.

Feeling satisfied?"

Still tight against his body, I thought about it for a moment. "You know what, that was satisfying. Really satisfying actually."

"Good. It sure looked like it."

We both looked into each other's eyes. I felt like Hunter was the first person at this school besides Daniela to treat me like a real person—not a victim, object of pity, or some freak in a circus show. I hadn't really felt much of anything recently but ever since I met Hunter, I've felt so many emotions. Annoyance, desire, embarrassment, anxiousness, fun—anything but numb.

A heavy silence passed between us. Being this close to him, I could feel his heart beating. Or was that my own? He was so good-looking it was painful. But I couldn't tear my eyes away from his dark irises. He tilted his head down slowly. My breath hitched. His eyes became heavy-lidded. I tilted my chin up to meet him, closing my eyes along with him. Just before our lips made contact, I snapped to my senses, panicked, and pushed him away.

"Is there something wrong? What's going on, Lorrie?"

Flustered, I blurted my unfiltered thoughts. "I'm not going to sleep with you. I know what guys like you are like."

His eyes widened. "Whoa, whoa. What? Did I miss something? Where did you get the idea that we were going to sleep together?"

"You were going to kiss me."

"Yeah so? Did you think we were going to then roll around naked on the ground, crushing styrofoam cups and getting dirty as hell?"

"No, but I'm sure you were thinking about a place. Maybe you weren't thinking we'd do it now, but you were definitely thinking about it sometime."

He sighed. "One, it looked like you were just as into kissing as I was. Two, kissing is a far cry from sex."

"I was just caught off guard, that's all. I wasn't *into* it like you're suggesting."

"What's going on? I don't get you, Lorrie. Why are you freaking out over a kiss? You can't get pregnant from a kiss ya know."

"Hurr, hurr. Gee, thanks for the bio lesson." I sucked in a deep breath. "Are we done with this walk yet? Can we go back?" I turned and took a step in the direction of the way we came.

"Wait," he said. I pivoted to face him again and saw he was looking at the ground.

"Wait for what?"

He seemed to be deep in thought for a moment then he met my gaze. "You wanna go on a date?"

It was my turn to be surprised. "Whoa, whoa. Where did that come from?"

"You think I'm a player and that all I want is to have sex with you. But it isn't like that."

"What's it like then?"

"I don't know. I can't spell it out for you."

"You can't or won't?"

"Dude, Lorrie. I'm not exactly a walking pile of answers. I may be a senior but if you think I've figured out everything about girls or life, you'll be pretty damn disappointed. I don't even really know what you're thinking, why you're acting this way. Hell, I don't even know what *I'm* doing half the time. But I do know I like being around you. I want to see you more. So I'm asking if you want to go on a date sometime."

"I'm sorry Hunter. You're a really sweet guy but . . . I'm going to have to say no. It's not a good time for me, I'm really not into dating anyone right now. It's nothing personal. Really, it isn't."

He studied me for a moment. I could tell he was debating whether to ask me why I wasn't into dating at the moment and I was already preparing a deflection, but his response surprised me. "If dating doesn't work for you, then how about being friends?"

"Um . . . What's your definition of 'friend'?"

"People who enjoy one another's company, who generally enjoy hanging out, talking about random stuff, grabbing food, watching movies, pulling each other out of frozen lakes, you know. *Friends*. Why? What's your definition?"

I scratched my chin, looking for objections but not finding any. "Hmm . . . I'd say that's a decent definition. I'd agree with that."

"Good." He nodded eagerly.

"—But, 'friends' is not the same thing as 'friends with benefits'. I just want to make sure we're clear on that."

He gave a sly smile. "We enjoy one another's company. Is that not a benefit?"

"You know what I mean, goofball." I punched his shoulder lightly but it felt more like his shoulder was punching my fist.

He smiled. "Okay, let's be 'friends' friends then." He held out his hand as if expecting a handshake.

I looked at it, wondering the implications of completing the handshake. What would it be like to be friends with Hunter? There were perks to be had but caution overrode eagerness. "I'm not sure, Hunter. You've already made it clear you'd like to date me. What if that's going to be a problem?"

"And you've made it clear you're attracted to me. So it evens out," he said smoothly.

My eyeballs nearly popped out of their sockets. "Huh? How is it clear I'm attracted to you?"

"The way you look at me, the way you try to blow me off . . . us almost kissing."

"Yes, I try to avoid you," I said, correcting his particular phrasing of 'trying to blow him off'. "But doesn't that normally mean I'm *not* attracted to you?"

"Doesn't apply to you. You're not normal, remember?" He grinned.

I sighed, concealing a smile tugging at the edges of my lips. I didn't want him to know that I was enjoying his company. "Hunter, I don't want to be friends with a guy knowing he's just being friendly to try to get into my pants. That's not real friendship. That's playing a game."

"Then good luck finding any male friends." He laughed but I didn't find his joke particularly funny. "No, but seriously. I meant it when I said 'let's be *friends* friends.' I don't really have any female friends so I hope you realize that I didn't make that suggestion flippantly."

"You have stalkers and girls fainting to be with you," I replied, pointing out the inconsistency between his words and reality. "Maybe I'm just the first girl to turn you down. Everyone else probably drops their panties at the snap of your fingers. I'm surprised if you even have to ask at all."

He shook his head slightly, calmly registering his disapproval.

"You're not the first girl to say 'no' to me. And you're right, I don't usually ask girls to date me. But so what? I'm not doing this to get into your pants—not if you don't want it. I'm asking for friendship."

Maybe I was just giving him a hard time. It was clear that Hunter was pretty different from most of the other guys on campus. And he seemed genuine when he said he just wanted to be friends. But I couldn't let him off the hook too easily, I wanted to make him sweat so I decided to play my trump card. "You got a boner when I was in your apartment."

He cocked one brow, his composure disrupted. "What?"

"When you were just wearing a towel. I saw the bulge . . ." I teased, smiling at him.

His head tilted in concern and he paused for a moment to think. I eyed him carefully, curious how he was going to respond. Would he man up and defend himself? Or deny it?

"Okay, okay," he finally said then sighed. "I did get a boner, I'm not ashamed to admit it."

Reacting to his admission, I folded my arms across my chest and raised an eyebrow. "Don't you see how that's a problem for us being friends? I mean I'm flattered, but friends don't make friends get boners."

"I'm glad you're flattered," he said, amusement in his voice. "But it just happens sometimes, like sneezing or coughing. And even if I did, it doesn't mean I'd act on it."

I tightened my arms across my chest. "So you weren't attracted to me?" I puffed.

"You were asking me about 'what I did in my alone time'. I thought you were flirting with me and given how good you looked in my clothes, biology kicked in. But the bigger question is: why were you looking at my crotch?"

My cheeks heated from embarrassment. I didn't expect him to throw that curveball at me. "I wasn't looking! I just glanced out of the corner of my eye. Besides, you were practically shoving it in my face the way you were sitting in front of me with your legs spread eagle. You could've poked my eye out."

"Psh, I was just sitting normally." He waved his hand dismissively. "It wasn't in any way as ridiculous as you implied. Plus you just said you glanced it outta the corner of your eye like it was barely noticeable and then you said I could've poked your eye out. Those two statements together make no sense."

"Makes perfect sense to me."

His brows narrowed. "Is this really about your own self-control? After running across campus in just a pair of jeans and a t-shirt, I thought you were a strong girl. Are you saying you can't handle yourself when you're around me? Are you *that* attracted to me? Maybe we should go on that date after all." A mischievous grin spread across his full, shapely lips.

I shifted on my feet, knowing there was a kernel of truth in his ridiculous statements. "I *am* a strong girl," I retorted. "I'm also smart enough to know this is a bad idea."

"You don't know that. Neither of us knows that. Hell, if anything, I should be the one saying this is a bad idea. You stole my clothes. You even stole my trash. You're one weird girl, Lorrie. But I can't help myself. I like your company."

"Hey, I was taking out your trash to repay you!"

He laughed. "Wow, what kind of person does that to repay someone? Here I was thinking you wanted to sift through my trash or something like some kind of stalker."

"I was in a hurry," I said, flustered. "It's not like I had time to write a nice thank-you card."

"Let's face it," he said taking a smooth step toward me and placing his hands warmly on my shoulders. Liking the thrill I got from his close proximity and his hands on me, I didn't possess the will to resist. "We both don't know each other well but I know you're different from other people here. It takes a weirdo to know a weirdo. We need a proper chance to hang out instead of just meeting up by chance all the time."

I looked into those gorgeous dark irises, still only half-believing I was with him in this odd place, alone together. "How are you a weirdo? You seem pretty well-adjusted to me."

"Do I? I suppose that's a pretty big compliment. Thank you."

"Whatever."

"C'mon, Lorrie. You're running out of excuses." He extended his hand to me as he had before.

He was right, I was running out of excuses. Was I really going to become friends with Hunter Jensen? What did I know about the guy? He was a fighter, had tats, was a senior, was incredibly gorgeous. And on top of that, he had saved my life. Come to think of it, what did he know about me? I'd tried avoiding him; I'd given him a lot of sass; I'd even stolen his clothes. What did I have to offer as a friend? He'd said he liked my company. But why? I thought about asking him why he wanted to be friends with me, but decided it was a dumb question to ask. What if I asked that to every person that wanted to be friends with me? "Hey, umm . . . so what are the reasons you want to be friends with me? Please present a list of bullet points on a 5x8 notecard." It was a stupid question and for some reason had only occurred to me because of Hunter.

He made me uncomfortable and comfortable, restless and calm, annoyed and entertained—all at the same time. I was wary about his bad boy allure and how he could fuck me up worse than I already was. But as long as we were just friends, there wasn't any harm right? It's not like I was going to lose my head and fall for him. Dad said I was strong and I'd even told Hunter as much. Maintaining a friendship between us would only help prove that. Besides, didn't I want to make new friends this semester?

I took a deep breath, looked him confidently in the eye, and shook his hand. "Alright, let's be friends."

He beamed.

"—But promise you won't get boners around me. It's awkward."

He scoffed. "Are you cock-blocking me against yourself? You can't say that. What if I asked you to not get hard tits when you're around me?"

My eyes widened. "W-What? Where did that come from?"

"You think I didn't notice? You weren't wearing a bra after you showered at my place and I could see your nipples poking through your shirt after you touched my leg. And you were talking about getting *your* eye poked out . . . I could say the same thing."

"Oh my god!" I shouted, completely embarrassed that he'd noticed that. That damn baggy t-shirt was supposed to hide my chest. "It was the temperature, not because I was aroused!" I lied. "It's not like I can really control it."

"Well, I can't really control whether I get an erection or not." He crossed his arms in mock distress. "Besides it's my body, I can do whatever I want with it. And there's no way you'd know anyway."

I knew he was right even before he finished. "Fine, fine, fine. You have a fair point, but at least you know where I stand."

"Great, now that we have that settled, as a first sign of our friendship, Ms. Lorrie, I suggest we exchange digits."

I pulled out my phone, brought up the Contacts screen, and handed the phone to him. "Okay, here type yours in."

He quickly tapped in his name and number then handed my phone back to me. I looked at his handiwork. It said *Gunther Handsome.* I laughed.

"What's so funny?" he said.

"Nothing, Gunther Handsome." I showed him my phone.

He grimaced. "Stupid auto-correct. My thumbs are too big to type on your tiny phone properly. Lemme fix it."

He reached for my phone but I snatched it away. "I think I'm going to keep it this way. It's much more amusing." And adorable.

"Alright," he grumbled, apparently displeased with the name Gunther. "Gimme a call so I can get your number."

I called and his pocket vibrated. He pulled his phone out and began pecking at the screen.

"Lorrie, what's your last name?"

I hesitated. "I don't usually give out my last name to people I don't know very well," I lied, deciding that it was better Hunter didn't know exactly who I was—my past included. I'm sure it wouldn't be hard for him to look it up or catch word of it, but I got the sense he wasn't the prying type. I could at least delay the inevitable.

His brows furrowed. "But we're friends now aren't we?"

"Friends, but not *good* friends. I gotta trust you before I give you more personal information."

He looked at me funny.

"I know it's weird," I said. "But that's just how I roll. Can you dig it?"

"So to most people you're like Madonna? Only a single name?"

"That's right."

"Alright, I'll make up a last name for you then," he said, a glint in his eye. He tilted his head up and tapped his finger against his chin. "I'm thinking Lorrie Hide."

I stuck out my bottom lip. "Are you saying I'm the wife of 'Mr. Hyde'? That I'm two-faced like him?"

He laughed then shook his head. "Hide as in H-I-D-E. 'Cause you like to hide yourself from me, whether that's trying to give me the slip or avoiding telling me things about yourself. I'm handsome and you hide. I'm okay with that. Are you?"

I thought about suggesting "Pretty" or "Beautiful" as a more flattering last name but caught myself when I noticed a hint of a smirk on his lips. He was probably baiting me into flirting with him. Too bad I wasn't going to bite.

"'Hide' it is then," I replied, feeling smug about outsmarting him.

We both laughed. It was a good feeling. It felt normal—laughing, exchanging numbers with a hot guy. It'd been so long, that I'd forgotten how good it felt. It sure beat sitting in a courtroom across from your mother's murderer.

Hunter never prodded me on my past the rest of the night. He probably figured I didn't want to talk about it. I didn't probe him about his past either. We just continued walking around and joking with one another. By the time I got into the cab to go back home, I found myself thinking that maybe this semester wouldn't be so bad after all.

Chapter Six

RUMORS

I woke up Saturday morning feeling pretty good. Last night seeing Hunter fight and going with him to the abandoned amusement park seemed like a faraway dream. Daniela gave me her notes for psych, and after lunch, I copied them into my own notebook. Some of the material was actually kind of interesting. Maybe Daniela was right: this class wouldn't be too bad.

I was almost done when my phone buzzed. I thought it would be Hunter and my heart skipped a beat. Glancing at the caller ID showed it was Aunt Caroline. A pang of guilt shot through me. We hadn't spoken since she'd dropped me off at the beginning of the semester over a week ago. I had visited my aunt and uncle regularly ever since Mom passed away but I'd been living with them just before Dad passed. After he passed, they practically adopted me. Although I sometimes took issue with Aunt Caroline's overprotectiveness, I was truly grateful for their care considering they already had their hands full raising two adolescent boys. I felt bad that I'd probably made Aunt Caroline feel neglected because I'd forgotten to call her.

I put my pen down and answered my phone. "Hi Aunt Caroline," I said sweetly.

"Hey! How's my college girl?" my aunt asked. "I'm guessing you've been pretty busy since we haven't heard from you."

I cringed. "Sorry about that. I've been busy, yes. I was actually just doing some homework when you called."

"Oh! I hope I'm not interrupting. Are you in the library?"

"No, it's fine. I'm in my room."

"That's good. So how are your classes? Do you like them so far?"

"Yeah, it's a little hard getting back into the swing of things but

63

I'm managing so far."

"That's good, dear. You know you can come back and visit anytime, or even take more time off if you need to. Just let us know and Uncle Stewart will pick you up."

"Thank you Aunt Caroline. But I think I'll be fine here. It hasn't been too bad so far. Actually, I think it's helped me take my mind off things."

I convinced myself I had to stay at Arrowhart because I needed a return to normality. The longer I put that off, the worse it was going to be for me. Dr. Schwartz had suggested that being around other people my age in a college environment could help and I agreed with her. These were supposed to be some of the best years of a person's life. So far, mine had been a nightmare. It was going to be tough getting back to feeling normal, but I had to get there.

"Good, I'm so glad to hear that. You know you can call me whenever, if you want to talk. Even if it's very late. It's been hard on all of us. The boys and Stewart are doing better but I'm still trying to get over it, myself. Your dad—my brother—was a good man. I know he loved you very much."

"Yeah, I know," I said sadly.

"But hey," she said brightly, quickly changing the depressing topic. "You're back at college now! I must ask, you do anything fun this weekend?"

My thoughts flew back to the craziness of last night. "Umm . . . I went out yesterday night on a double date with my roommate and two guys, but they were creeps. I did meet another guy though and gave him my number."

"Oh wow, look you at Lorrie," she said teasingly. "Already attracting boys in your first week. That sounds so exciting! What's he like?"

Let's see, he has tats, big muscles, he took me to an abandoned amusement park . . . Oh and he fights and girls are attracted to him like squirrels to acorns—you know, your typical college male.

Telling her what Hunter was like would give her the wrong impression. Knowing her, she'd probably freak out and insist on staying with me for a while to make sure I was all right. "I don't know, he's tall, he has short, dark hair. He's nice." I considered telling her about falling in the lake and how he saved me, but that would be too hard to explain and it would make her worry. It was better if I kept it vague.

"Are you going out on a date?" My aunt had a way of cutting straight to the point.

"Nah, I don't think I'm ready for that right now. I just told him we'd be friends. He hasn't called me yet though, I just gave him my number last night."

"Well you'll have to let me know how things go with Mr. Short-Dark-Hair." She chuckled.

"I'll be sure to let you know."

"Well, it sounds like you're doing okay." She released an audible breath. "I'm so relieved. I was worried you might have had a rough start."

"Nope, so far so good." No falling-into-frozen-lakes-and-almost-dying here. I gave a thumbs up sign though I knew she couldn't see it.

"Okay," my aunt said. "Well I'm glad to hear you're doing well. I'll let you get back to studying. Enjoy the rest of your weekend and let us know if you need anything."

"Will do. Bye Aunt Caroline."

"Goodbye dear." She paused for a moment. "We all love you, Lorrie."

"I love you too."

I ended the call and went back to Daniela's notes. My aunt—Caroline Perkins—was so good to me. When I thought about what life would be like without her, it made me shudder. The Perkins family and Daniela were just about all I had in the world at this point. Thinking about how close to alone I was scared the hell out of me.

Just as I finished with Daniela's notes, I heard my other two suitemates who shared the double—Kate and Petra—come in the suite. My door was open, so I called out a cheerful greeting into the common area.

Kate stopped in her tracks and peered into my room with Petra hiding behind her. "Hi Lorrie," Kate said. She shifted on her feet, apparently debating whether to continue walking by or to linger for a few more words. "Everything okay?" she asked delicately.

Petra leaned her head out from behind Kate to catch a peek at me but then jumped back behind Kate like a frightened child.

I narrowed my eyes. "Yeah, I was just copying Daniela's notes from lecture. Why wouldn't things be okay?"

"Sorry, no reason. You just surprised me. Anyway, me and Petra are going to the gym. Catch you later!"

As far as I could tell, Kate and Petra were pretty close to being literally attached at the hip. It was kind of annoying the way they always did everything together like they couldn't exist apart. Also annoying: the way Petra acted like I was a rabid beast liable to snap at any instant. Why did people like Petra have to be so awkward around me? All she had to do was say hi back. Instead, she acted like my eyes were red from crying all morning.

I took my stuff and went into the common area, plopping down on the futon. A few minutes later, Kate and Petra left for the gym. At least Kate waved goodbye. Ten minutes later, I was still stewing on why people couldn't treat me normally. Couldn't they understand it just made things worse for me?

Daniela came into the suite, smiling with a gym bag over her shoulder and her hair wet. I hadn't seen her since the previous night, which meant we hadn't caught up.

"Hi," I said brightly, as soon as the door had closed.

"Hey there," she said, a mischievous smile still playing on her lips. "Haven't seen you since last night."

"Yeah, I got home and crashed. Did you and Cody, you know . . ."

She shook her head. "We all left the bar and came home not too long after you went off with your fighter man. Cody got a little wasted so I came home alone, of course."

"Gotcha. I hope you didn't have too much trouble with my date. Justin or whatever. That guy was a douchebag."

"Yeah, sorry about that. I didn't know he'd be such a jerk. Speaking of guys though, it finally popped into my head who the guy with the hammer tattoo is."

I nodded. "The fighter guy I left with turned out to be him. Hunter Jensen." Just saying his name sent an unwelcome quivering to my belly.

She eyed me, amusement in her green irises. "Where did you go with him?"

I didn't like the look on her face, so I answered her question with one of my own. "Why?"

"You know that guy's reputation, right? Surely, you've heard of the rumors."

"No, I haven't. Remember? I've been gone a year and I try *not* to listen to rumors."

She shrugged. "That guy's a serious player. He has girls all over him. Like *all* the time."

The quivering in my belly turned slightly nauseous. My mind unwittingly recalled the condoms I'd seen in his bathroom trash. I narrowed my eyes. "Yeah, I figured as much when I met him. He has that kind of bad-boy-loner thing going on that makes some girls go crazy. I may be screwed up but I'm sane enough to know not to fall for a guy like that. We just went on a walk, that's all. There's nothing romantic between us."

She studied me carefully, not saying anything. The silence was killing me.

"I'm not stupid," I snapped. "Besides, he's not my type. We're just friends. I don't feel like explaining why."

She put her hands up in defense. "Okay, if you say so. Just saying, people saw you two together, and with his history . . ."

"What?"

"People are making assumptions. If you say you're not romantic with him, I believe you, but you should know that people already think you guys are a thing. Or at least were a thing last night. All night."

Blood rushed to my face and I ground my teeth. The last thing I needed was people gossiping about me more than they already were. Jeez, I couldn't catch a break. All I wanted to do was blend in at school and I somehow got involved with a super notorious cage fighter who apparently had a reputation for sleeping with any girl he wanted. Fuck my life.

"Well, we're not. I'm sure it'll pass." I waved my hand dismissively. "God knows I have experience with people talking shit about me."

Daniela grimaced. "Lorrie, I know it sucks when people

are gossiping about you, but you're at Arrowhart—gossip headquarters—and that was a super-crazy story. It's hard to blame them."

"I just want to be a normal student. Why is that so hard?"

She smiled slightly. "This *is* getting closer to normal, right? Boy-girl drama is what college is all about. Well, also studying but that's less important."

I looked at her for a second, but then I started giggling. It was all I could do, really. As crazy as my situation was, she was right about the drama. "I guess that's true."

"Just be careful, okay? I don't want to have to kick that guy's ass."

I nodded, smiling. "After watching him fight last night, I'm sure you could take him."

She flexed and we laughed. Maybe this *was* a little closer to normal.

That night I laid in bed, staring at my poster of a Japanese drawing of a wave and thinking things through. My first week back at school had been more eventful than I'd wanted, but all in all it had been good. Rumors aside, I was glad to have some connection with Hunter as a friend. It was like what I'd told Daniela: this semester was about getting myself right. I couldn't get too involved with anyone else's feelings. My best friend reminding me that the guy I had just become friends with was a huge player would only help with that.

I rolled over and closed my eyes. A friendship with Hunter could lead to trouble, but all I had to do was avoid getting into a romantic relationship with him. Although his romantic interests in me were clear, he wasn't overly aggressive in pursuing me. So I wasn't too concerned about him pushing things further than I was comfortable with. I just had to avoid developing feelings for him, myself.

Although I was used to feeling numb, being around Hunter made me feel alive. I could see how that would make it difficult to resist developing feelings for him. But I was strong. Dad had even said so in his letter. I was dealing with the tragedies in my past and moving on with life. Compared to that, how hard could it be to stop myself from developing feelings for Hunter?

Chapter Seven

ICE CREAM

I spent the next week settling into a groove with my classes. I stayed awake during psychology class and even took good enough notes that I didn't need to borrow Daniela's afterward. My drawing class was already a lot of fun; I was starting to think that maybe it could be my major. Daniela had been right, there were some rumors about me and Hunter, but the looks I was getting from people weren't too much different from what I had already been experiencing.

In fact, they might have been better. It wasn't pure pity anymore; these looks were more curious. *What's going on between that girl and Hunter?* I could hear them saying. That was a lot better than wondering about what it would be like to have both parents die from unnatural causes.

If people would have actually had the guts to talk to me and ask me what was going on between me and Hunter, I wouldn't have been able to tell them anyway. He didn't call me all week. I tried not to be disappointed, since I had made it clear that we were just friends. Obviously he wasn't going to pursue me as hard as if he were trying to date me—the rules of dating didn't even apply. We were just friends. Friends hung out whenever.

Friday rolled around, and this time I had no plans. Daniela had a cold and was going to stay in, and Kate and Petra were out at some date party. I had no one else to go out with. It was surprising how much this bummed me out. I could always entertain myself watching more *Grey's Anatomy* but I knew there would be loud, drunk people coming back to the dorm at two in the morning, and they would make me feel bad for missing out on a lively night.

I was sitting on the common area futon after an early cafeteria dinner thinking about what I wanted to do with the rest of my evening when my phone buzzed. My heart raced as I checked to see who it was, and then it began pounding in my ears when I recognized the name: Hunter.

"Hey," I said, a little too breathlessly.

"Hey Lorrie, what's up?"

His voice was smooth, like we'd just casually run into each other around campus. The fluttering in my nerves made me realize how much I'd missed hearing his voice all week. I tried to steady myself so I didn't sound too needy. "Not much, just ate dinner."

"Have any plans for tonight?"

My heart rose. "I was actually just figuring that out," I said. "Daniela and I were going to go out, but she's not feeling good, so now I'm free."

"Great! One of my buddies bailed on me, so I have an extra ticket for the hockey game tonight. Do you wanna come?"

I didn't know much about hockey, but hanging out with Hunter sounded more fun than hanging out with Meredith and McDreamy. "That sounds like fun! When's the game?"

"Game's at seven, but I like to get there a half hour early to get concessions, watch the guys warm up, and all that good stuff. Want to meet me at the arena at six-thirty?"

It was already a little after five, and I had no idea how far away the hockey rink was. How long did that give me to get ready? What did someone wear to a hockey game, anyway? I'd have to figure this out fast. "I can do that," I said, my mind racing.

"Do you know where the arena is?" he asked.

I stood up and started walking to my room to look it up. "I think so. Otherwise, I can figure it out. I'll see you then."

"Alright. Let's meet me out front. I'll see ya in a few."

I walked into my room and threw my phone on the bed before racing to my closet to figure out what to wear. I settled on a school sweatshirt, and threw that on my bed before racing to my laptop to look up the location of Barton Rink. It was at least a twenty minute walk across campus. I'd have to rush.

It took serious power-walking skills, but I made it to the area at six-thirty sharp. The people filtering into the arena were all dressed in red and white school gear: sweatshirts, hats, and even baggy hockey jerseys. I gave myself kudos for a good fashion choice. So far, so good.

I scanned the crowd looking for Hunter's short, brown hair and dark gray eyes for several seconds before we saw each other at the same time. He was standing by the doors and wearing a red and white hockey jersey that covered up his tattoos, but still hinted at his wide shoulders and huge chest. Even dressed in a baggy hockey jersey, he looked like someone you didn't want to mess with—in a fighting cage. A bed would be different.

He held up the two tickets and smiled as we walked toward one another. "Thanks for coming," he said, the low vibration in his voice flowing over me.

I smiled, both because I was glad to see him and to hide my antsiness. I hadn't seen Hunter in person all week and I had to admit I missed the charge I got from being around him. "Thanks for inviting me."

He handed me my ticket and I took it from him, careful to avoid brushing against his hand, knowing the effect a gentle brushing could have on the both of us. Then I thanked him graciously. "So have you been to a hockey game before?" he asked.

"Nope," I responded casually.

"Ever seen a game on TV?"

I shook my head. "But I know the basics: sticks, pucks, and touchdowns right?"

He lost his composure and laughed heartily. "I think you're mixing hockey with football, Lorrie. Hockey has goals and football has touchdowns."

"Oh, my bad," I replied, laughing along with him. I kind of felt silly for mixing up the two sports, but after the time we spent in Neverland teasing one another and joking around, I knew Hunter wasn't making fun of me mean-spiritedly.

He wiped a tear of laughter from his eye. "You're so adorable, Lorrie. But ya know, I'm surprised to hear you're a hockey virgin. You've just made tonight's game all the better. I'm looking forward to breaking you in."

I chuckled, amused by the flirtatious suggestion. Knowing

Hunter's reputation, my guard was already up, allowing me to let the suggestion easily roll off my shoulders. "Yeah, yeah, alright Hunter," I said sarcastically. "Unfortunately, I'm not much of a sports girl, so I'm not sure how much 'breaking in' is going to happen."

"We'll see about that." He grinned wickedly making my belly flutter in the way that it often did when I was around him. "But you're really not a sports girl? Given your throwing arm, I thought you would've been."

"Well, my dad and I would toss a baseball around when I was kid. I wasn't really good or anything, especially with accuracy— as you might have noticed. But I could throw it hard." I blew hot air on my knuckle and polished it on my sweatshirt. "Broke a few windows in my time."

I smiled and he chuckled. "And an amusement park booth. I'm impressed—you're quite destructive. Yet you've never seen hockey on TV?"

"I guess I'm more of a doer than a watcher. I think it's more fun that way, but I have watched a few basketball games, so it's not like I'm against watching sports. I mean, I'm certainly excited about seeing this hockey game."

He grinned. "I get it, you're more hands-on. I dig that. So you're not afraid of chipping a nail?"

I looked at my nails with amusement. "I guess I've always just kept them short . . . Never really thought about growing them out, figured it'd be annoying."

He chuckled. "Well I haven't grown mine out either. Glad to see we're on the same page. Anyway, you're in for a treat. I'll teach you the rules and you'll be a fan by the end of the game. C'mon let's get our seats."

Hunter insisted on getting nachos first, and by the time we got our food there were only fifteen minutes to go before game time according to the giant scoreboard on the wall. He explained the basic rules of the game as we made our way down the steps to our seats: there were three periods of twenty minutes apiece, and the players were trying to score goals by shooting the puck past the goalie into the net. The second part I already knew, which made me feel good. How complicated could hockey really be?

We were almost to our seats when we were approached by two short brunettes with red ribbons in their ponytails and the letters "AH" painted on each cheek. They were wearing matching white and red school t-shirts advertising the hockey season. "Hi Hunter! We're so happy to run into you!" one of them squeaked. The other one beamed at him.

"Hi Catelyn," Hunter said coolly.

Her skin was tanned golden despite the winter season, and her teeth were unnaturally white. "What are you doing after the game?" she asked, tossing her head to one side.

He shrugged. "Not sure, this and that. By the way, this is my friend Lorrie."

"Hi," I said semi-awkwardly, putting my hand up to give a small wave.

Catelyn glanced at me briefly before turning back to Hunter. Catelyn's friend didn't even acknowledge me, instead preferred keeping her attention on Hunter while flitting her hair. "Well, let us know when you're done . . . you know—" Catelyn looked at her friend who silently nodded back to her then Catelyn turned back to Hunter. "We can both come with you, wherever you're going. Maybe your place or our place. We'll *come* with you, anywhere you like." The way she looked and smiled at him was more than suggestive.

I blushed as I rolled my eyes and looked at Hunter to gauge his reaction. He gave me a quick glance but his expression was impassive. "Cool," he said evenly to them.

Both girls giggled. "Call whenever. We'll be up if you are." She winked and her friend nodded before they both bounced up the stairs.

Was that what I thought it was? Daniela had told me Hunter was a player but it hadn't occurred to me that I'd be seeing what that meant up close. I suddenly started feeling nauseous.

Hunter and I were silent the rest of the way down to our seats. When we finally got there, I was surprised to see the seats were in the front row, right behind the glass. The school's marching band was in the next section over with their trombones, trumpets, and drums. As we took our seats, I thought: this is going to be loud.

"So does that happen to you a lot?" I asked, more than a little curious.

"Does what?"

"Those girls were offering to have a threesome with you, weren't they?" I asked, never thinking that I'd ever be asking that question to anybody in my life.

He chuckled and looked at the ice for a second. "Probably, yeah."

"Does that happen a lot?"

He considered. "No, not *a lot.*"

I raised a brow. ". . . So you've had a threesome before?"

"I know you're curious Lorrie, but unfortunately I don't kiss and tell," he said, zipping his lips with his fingers.

"Oh yeah?"

"Yeah. If you hear anything about me like that, it didn't come from me. I can't control what other people say but I keep things like that to myself."

I recalled him protecting me by lying to Gary about how we met. He did seem to keep things to himself. Still, I had my doubts about whether he was telling the truth. Weren't guys always bragging about their sex lives? Plus, the idea of him even considering a threesome with Catelyn and her friend grossed me out. But the nausea I felt wasn't jealousy, I told myself; Hunter and I were just friends. And being friends gave me a unique opportunity to pick his male brain.

"So are you going to call those girls?"

He shook his head casually. "Nah, probably not. Not really in the mood."

His response somehow made me feel relieved. "Ah I see." I looked at the all the people trickling into the rink and taking their seats. Some were in large groups, some were by themselves, and a lot seemed like couples. I dimly wondered if people saw Hunter and me together and thought that we were a couple.

"Have you had a threesome before, Lorrie?"

Breaking from my thoughts, I erupted in a burst of laughter. "What do you think?"

"Yes." He smiled.

I smirked. "Well, you'd be wrong. I'm not interested in having one either. One guy is enough. Adding another guy would be too much. Way too much."

He smirked back. "What about adding another girl?"

I scoffed. "In your dreams, buddy."

He waved his hand dismissively. "For what it's worth, I don't think you'd be a good participant in a threesome anyway."

I was surprised at how much offense I took by that comment. "What? Why not?"

"You probably wouldn't get along with the other girl. You're kind of a lone wolf. You'd be either too selfless and let the girl have the guy all to herself or too selfish and take the guy all for yourself. There'd be no in between." He wagged his finger at me playfully.

I scrunched my brows, uncomfortable with how much his reasoning resonated with me. "That's quite a bold statement. And how did you come to that conclusion?"

"Just from our interactions . . . On the one hand, you're ridiculously nice by taking out my trash to repay me even though you didn't have to—that's the selfless part. On the other hand, you're kind of selfish especially with how much you share yourself with others—or even just information about yourself."

I shot him a wry smile. "A compliment and an insult all rolled into one. Remind me why I'm hanging out with you again?"

"Because we're friends." He flashed his boyish grin at me and I couldn't help but smile back.

"Alright, so what if it was another guy instead of a girl?" I asked, eager to turn this weird first-hang-out-discussion in my favor.

"You'd only focus on one guy. I don't see you wanting to please two at the same time."

"Fair," I said, thinking about the implications. "I don't think I can argue with you there, but I'm confused about something. Based on what you've said, you wouldn't be a good threesome partner either. You strike me as the lone wolf type yourself: clean apartment, solo walks, ignoring your adoring female fans. How do you do it then? How can you get along with people in a threesome?"

His eyes widened unexpectedly. "I'm shocked that you would even suggest I've ever had a threesome before!"

I rolled my eyes. I knew I wasn't going to tease any details out of him—not that I particularly wanted to hear them anyway. Hunter was certainly keeping to his word that he kept his private matters to himself. It was a good thing as far as I was concerned, and I certainly wouldn't have guessed he'd be that type of person based on my first impression of him.

Hoping to move onto a less awkward topic, I said, "These are nice seats, by the way."

Hunter popped a nacho in his mouth, chewed it, and swallowed. "Yup, one of the perks of going to games every year for four years. Best seats in the house."

"So they give you better seats if you've been to more games?"

"Pretty much. It kind of works on seniority, and this season it's my turn to have the good seats."

I nodded and eagerly took a nacho he offered me.

"We should finish these fast," he said. "Once the game starts, we won't be able to eat."

I squinted. "Why not?"

"We'll be standing the whole game."

"What? Why?"

"You'll see."

"That sounds tiring."

"It's more active that way—just the way you like it." He smiled and I returned the gesture, liking the way he paid attention to minor details I told him about myself. "But we do sit down between periods."

Hunter and I picked up the pace on eating the nachos. It seemed like Hunter was really into hockey and I kind of found it cute. We finished our nachos just as the arena lights dimmed. I looked around, but nobody seemed surprised, including Hunter. Instead, everyone was standing.

"Game time," he said, looking down at me.

I stood up and watched as our team filtered onto the ice, followed by several spotlights. They skated around the rink while the band played the fight song to our right. Hunter and the rest of the section sang the lyrics loudly. I didn't know the words to the Arrowhart fight song, so I just clapped along, making a mental note to learn the song in case I ever went to another sporting event.

When the song ended, the lights came back on. Hunter banged on the glass and screamed words of encouragement at the red and white clad players as they skated by. There were a few other people along the glass doing the same.

He turned to me to gauge my reaction as the players skated to the bench. I smiled at him and gave a thumbs-up sign, enjoying the lively pre-game ceremony.

The other team was already sitting on their bench, which was situated right next to our team's bench. Their jerseys were dark green and their coach, wearing a black suit, seemed to be already yelling at them already. Our coach was standing with his arms crossed as five guys and the goalie jumped over the short wall in front of the bench and onto the ice. Soon, the green team followed. The game was about to start, and everyone was yelling.

"This is called a faceoff," Hunter said. Even though he was right next to me, I could barely hear him above the clamor, but I nodded anyway. The referee dropped the puck and the game began.

It didn't take long to realize that hockey was a very fast game. The players seemed to be constantly chasing after the puck when it was against the boards. Whenever they crashed up against the glass, I was shocked at how much it shook. The way these guys kept skating after hitting each other so hard boggled my mind.

The first period was over quickly without anyone scoring any goals. The student section sat down for the first time since the game had started. It wasn't until I had taken a seat that I realized how sore my legs were.

"So what do you think?" Hunter asked.

"It's definitely fast."

He smiled. "Yeah, it keeps your attention."

"Is it normal for them to not score for a whole period?"

"Yeah, there's usually only a couple goals in a game. It makes it more exciting when they score."

I nodded. We were quiet for a while, recovering from the intensity of watching the game. Everyone in our section seemed to be resting before the next period.

"Did you ever play hockey?" I asked him.

He shook his head. "They don't really play much hockey in San

Diego. I didn't get into it until I came here for school, but now I love it. Kinda wish I played, actually."

"I guess doing cage fights is enough athletic activity for one person."

He laughed. "Yeah, probably. I'm sore enough after training that I doubt I'd have the energy for any other sports."

The second period and most of the third flew by. There were five minutes left in the game and we finally scored the first goal of the game. The entire arena erupted in cheers so loud the noise hurt my ears. Hunter high-fived everyone around us, including me. His palm made a loud slap against mine; it stung but I ignored the pain because his excitement for the game got me excited as well.

The band played the fight song, and everyone sang, then shouted a mean chant full of curses at the other team's goalie. Even though my ears were ringing like I'd just been at a concert, I found myself screaming and cursing along with everyone else. The energy was infectious.

"C'mon boys, hold on!" Hunter yelled during the third period.

"Yeah, fuck 'em up!" I screamed.

Hunter turned to me in surprise. "You're getting into this."

I flashed him a grin. "It's hockey."

His lips curved into a boyish smile. "Couldn't have said it any better."

Suddenly, a player was body-checked and slammed into the glass in front of us. Thinking he was going to crash through the wall and into us, I jumped into Hunter's protection.

Hunter put his arm around my shoulder and squeezed me to him. The hockey player shook off the hit, looked at me through the glass, grinned, and winked then he continued skating after the puck. Bold letters on the back of his jersey read "MASTERS".

"Focus on the game, you douche," Hunter yelled harshly then looked down at me tenderly. "Scared you huh?"

"Just surprised is all." His arm squeezing me against his hard body felt good.

"The glass might look weak since you can see through it but it's actually really strong. You don't have to worry about it breaking."

"Appearances can be deceiving," I said eyeing the glass gingerly.

"Did you know that player?"

"He's Caleb Masters, the star of the Arrowhart team. He's a bit of an arrogant prick but I have to admit he's good at hockey."

Arrowhart ended up winning the game, leaving our entire section in smiles. As we were filing out, Hunter asked me if I wanted to go to Clyde's for some ice cream so we could revel in our victory. I had a great time at the hockey game and could still feel excitement buzzing through my body like I'd actually been one of the players, so I agreed. Whereas Hunter preferred cooldown walks, I preferred cooldown ice cream eatings.

It seemed like everyone had the same idea he had, because the line at Clyde's was out the door and around the corner. We decided to wait it out. There were few things I remembered about Arrowhart from before I left, but one of them was Clyde's. They had some super delicious ice cream.

"So," Hunter said. "What's the verdict on hockey? Thumbs up?"

I put both thumbs up. "It was really fun. Thank you for inviting me." I actually couldn't remember the last time I'd been so excited about something. I recalled how Hunter looked at me weird when I shouted my support for our team. I thought that was pretty funny.

"Thanks for coming. It's been a fun night," he said giving me a brief hug and a rub on the shoulder. When he took his hand away, I felt strangely bereft, hoping for a longer contact.

"Agreed. I hope you didn't mind teaching me about hockey."

"My pleasure." The last word rolled slowly off his tongue or maybe it was just my imagination. "You picked it up pretty fast."

"Thanks."

We stood for a minute in the cold, staring ahead at the line. It was moving, but not very quickly.

"So you said you didn't play hockey," I started. "Do you play any other sports? Or is it just MMA?"

He looked off in the distance as if thinking. "Just MMA. I started boxing when I was pretty young and did wrestling in high school, but now it's just MMA."

"Those all sound violent."

He stared at me for a second, then laughed quietly. I felt like he was trying to figure out if I was being serious with that observation.

"Yeah, they're all violent."

"Why do you do it? You don't seem like a super angry guy. Or maybe I just don't know you well enough . . ."

"I'm not an angry guy."

"So why?"

"Why not?" His tone indicated his response was a genuine question.

It was my turn to laugh. "Most people don't volunteer to get punched in the face!"

He shrugged. "That's true. I guess I like training, I like the guys at the gym, and I really like testing myself against someone else. It's one-on-one, ya know? When you get into the ring with a guy who's been training just as hard as you and you beat him, it feels pretty awesome."

"There are plenty of other one-on-one sports," I said. "Like tennis."

"What, so I can get beat by some prick named Davis whose parents got him lessons at the country club when he was four? Fuck that." He looked at me, a fire in his eyes I'd never seen before. "Fighting's what I did growing up and it's what I'm good at. That's why I do it. Getting punched in the face sucks, but so do a lot of things." His chest moved in and out as he took a deep breath. "Plus the money helps with school and stuff."

The passion in his voice startled me; I would give a lot to care about anything as much as he cared about fighting. It felt like he thought of the world in terms of us versus them. For now, I was happy to be considered part of the "us."

"I guess it also gets you a lot of girls," I said, noticing that a few girls were stealing not-so-secret glances in our direction.

His eyes narrowed and a small smile crept onto his face. "Are you still thinking about Catelyn and Melissa?"

My chest tightened and I could feel my pulse quicken. "You know the other one too?"

He shrugged. "Yeah, she's just quiet most of the time. Why does it matter? You can't seriously be jealous of them."

"Of course not!"

"Then what?"

"I'm not jealous, Hunter," I said as convincingly as I could. "I was just noticing how there's girls around here that look like they'd be down for a threesome with you as well, maybe even a moresome. It reminds me of the fan girls I saw during your fight. It seems like you have quite a fan club."

"Does it bother you that girls watch me fight?" he tried once more, a sly grin on his face.

"No!"

He watched me for a moment as I tried to keep a straight face. "Okay," he said finally. "Yeah, girls like to watch me fight. I guess that's a perk."

I kept my silence since any interest I had in the subject seemed to be interpreted as jealousy. Why was it so hard to be just friends with a guy who was attractive? Okay, Hunter was a little more than *just* attractive and maybe that was the problem. The line moved until we were just inside the door. I rubbed my hands together to warm them up. It was cold outside and it was cold inside as well. I was beginning to question why we were getting ice cream in the middle of winter but then remembered that the taste of Clyde's ice cream was awesome in any season.

"I don't really get close with them, though."

I blinked. "What? Who?"

"The girls who watch me fight. I don't really get close to them."

Why would he need to? I wanted to say there was no point since he could sleep with whichever girl—or girls, apparently—he wanted, but I managed to bite my tongue. Instead, I kept it simple. "Yeah, I noticed you like to keep on the down-low. But why not get close to them?"

"I don't know, it all feels like bullshit. Like they just want to sleep with me so they can say they've slept with a cage fighter. I don't know, girls are complicated."

"I have to admit, sleeping with a cage fighter is not one of my fantasies."

He chuckled. "Yeah, you seem different."

My face heated. I put my head down and the hood on my sweatshirt up as if I was cold, hoping he wouldn't notice. He'd mentioned before that he thought I was different and a weirdo but

I didn't know what he meant exactly. "What do you mean?"

"I don't know, you just seem different."

"Like I'm not complicated?"

He scoffed. "I didn't say that. If anything, you seem even more complicated!" He chuckled lightly. "Maybe that's one reason why I find you so interesting."

"I guess I'll take that," I replied, musing his response.

Finally, we were at the front of the line. I ordered a banana split and Hunter got a milkshake.

"Together or separate?" the cashier asked, smiling at Hunter. She wore her hair back and had horn rimmed glasses.

"Together," Hunter said before I could speak.

I wanted to argue with him, but I didn't want to make a scene and hold everyone else up, so I just glared. He seemed oblivious as he gave the cashier a twenty-dollar bill and got his change back. We spotted a couple leave their table in the back and we dashed to take it before anyone else could.

"You shouldn't have done that," I said once we'd sat down.

"Done what?"

"Paid for the two of us like we're a couple. I told you, we're just friends."

"What? Friends can't buy each other ice cream? I just wanted to do you a little favor after you came to the hockey game with me on such short notice."

I thought of it more as him doing a favor to me by inviting me, but whatever. "Fine. I'm getting it next time, though. I know you're purposely trying to build up my debt to you."

He chuckled. "You're reading ulterior motives into my chivalry. I like that though. You're being honorable and you're also trying to keep me honest." He sipped on his milkshake. "It's cute."

My cheeks flustered from the compliment. I opened my mouth to protest but he spoke first. "I do love this place though."

Calming down, I took a bite of my banana split and my brain took a brief trip into flavorland. It was every bit as good as I remembered. "Yeah, Clyde's is definitely one of the highlights of this town."

"So," he said. "I feel like you know all kinds of stuff about me, but

I don't know that much about you."

I shrugged. "What do you want to know?"

"Well, you know I like training and fighting. What do you like to do when you're not learning about new sports?"

"I don't know. Watching trashy shows on TV, hanging out with my suitemate Daniela . . . I guess the latest thing I enjoy doing is drawing."

"Drawing?"

"Yeah, I'm in a class for it right now. It's my favorite by a longshot."

"That's cool. If I recall, you do have an active imagination—cats and all." He grinned.

"Dude, I totally saw that cat! I swear I wasn't making that up."

"*Sure*," he said, giving me a wink and taking another sip of his milkshake.

"You're really giving me a hard time about that aren't you?"

"If I was really giving you a hard time, you'd know it," he teased.

"*Sure*," I said with a smile, mimicking his sarcastic remark. I couldn't help but admire Hunter's ability to turn an objection into a flirtatious suggestion. I took another bite of my delicious banana split, half-wondering if I could keep my guard up around him the longer I spent with him.

He smiled, apparently pleased by my comeback. "So what do you like to draw?"

My mind flew to the drawing of the hammer I had been doing the previous week in Muller's class. "Lots of stuff. I don't know."

"The only art I know anything about is tattoos. Do you draw any designs like that?"

My brows shot up as I scrambled to decide whether I should tell him about the tattoo of *his* I had been sketching out last week. I kind of wanted him to roll up his sleeve so I could see how close I had come. "I think I've tried a few designs like that before."

"Do you have any, by the way?" he asked.

I shook my head. "Nope. Virgin skin over here."

He cocked an eyebrow and my face grew hot. "That's not what I meant," I said shrilly. I reached over the table to smack him on the arm.

He caught my hand before it could find its target. I gasped at both his quick reflexes and the warmth of his touch.

He squeezed my fist gently. "I have a lot of practice at that, ya know. MMA fighter and all."

I tried to pull my hand back but he held on.

"How are your hands, still cold?" he asked, bringing his other hand around mine and bringing them to rest on the table.

My chest tightened and I felt my face getting even warmer. "I don't know," I said. "Can I have my hand back please?"

"It's feels like ice. Don't you want to warm it up, just for a minute?"

I looked down and steadied myself. "No, I think I'll be okay."

He let my hand go and shrugged, leaning back. "Alright, just trying to help a friend out."

"It was appreciated," I said quickly then dug into my ice cream.

"So we were talking about your drawing," he said after a minute. "If you don't do tattoos, what kind of artist do you want to be?"

I looked up from my banana split, glad to have some time to think. What *did* I want to be? I didn't really know. The furthest ahead I would allow myself to think was the end of the semester. Getting to the end of the semester intact would be an accomplishment.

"I don't know," I said. "Still figuring that out. I'm really just focused on the present right now, to be honest." I had another bite. "What about you? What do you want to do? Did you always dream of being a cage fighter?"

He scoffed and looked down, then over my shoulder, eyes unfocused. I looked back but saw nothing that could have caught his attention, so I turned my gaze back to him. "Earth to Hunter," I said, waving my hand in his face.

As if coming out of a trance, he blinked and shook his head. "I'm focused on the present too. Just this minute, I think it's pretty great, actually." He smiled warmly.

Hunter and I finished our desserts then we got some root beer floats as an after-dessert dessert. I had a good time hanging out with Hunter. We laughed and teased one another a lot. It wasn't until I got back to my dorm at two in the morning, drunk on root beer floats that I realized I hadn't thought about my past the entire night. That damn immovable stone hadn't been anywhere in sight. For a few hours, I'd felt like a normal college girl hanging out with her guy friend on a Friday night.

Being friends with Hunter certainly had its perks, but I knew I needed to be careful that we stayed just friends. He'd teased me about being jealous of other girls and I'd emphatically told him I wasn't jealous. But when I thought about it further, I realized I might've been lying.

Chapter Eight

THE FLYMAN

I'd gotten in trouble. I was eight years old and it was Christmas morning. Dad had just started at Anderson & Partners PLC, though I didn't know its name at the time. We weren't wealthy by any means, but I was a kid and I didn't care. All I knew was that I was loved. Mom and Dad got along great those days. We were happy. We were a family.

I opened Mom's present first. It was a baby blue dress with sequins on it and it was the most beautiful dress I had ever seen. She had to help me put it on and afterwards I gave her a big hug and danced around the living room pretending that I was Cinderella. Then I opened Dad's gift.

If I thought Mom's present was amazing, Dad's was better. It was a giant box of art supplies. Maybe it was too much, but I didn't think it at the time. There were over a hundred crayons, a set of colored pencils, a packet of pastels, acrylic paints in small containers, and even watercolors. I was so excited that I forgot to even thank Dad for the present.

"Lorrie, you have to be careful not to get any of those paints on your dress or the carpet okay?" Mom said.

I nodded, only half listening to her. Dad handed me a sheet of paper and I set to work right away with the crayons. I drew us as a family. Mom, Dad, and me in my little blue dress.

The next morning, I thought it would be a good idea to redecorate the walls. I mean, they were so bland and white, I figured that my art would only improve them.

Mom was furious and Dad supervised me as I scrubbed the pastels and paint off the wall. For some reason though, they never took that art set away from me. But I was a good daughter, I learned my lesson and never painted on the walls again.

➤ ➤ ➤

It'd been a few days since the hockey game, and Hunter and I had maintained regular contact via frequent text messages. It was basically a continuation of the back and forth teasing and joking we did in person. I was glad for the banter, but it was sometimes distracting while trying to concentrate during class.

It was the third Thursday since the semester started, and I sat at a table in the back corner of the Wheatley Library cafe aptly called Husk Cafe. There were a handful of people sitting around, reading the campus paper, or fooling around on their laptops. It was still too early for people to be studying for midterms and if they really wanted to study, they'd be up in the stacks anyway. The cafe was for socializing and having coffee.

The girl I was sketching kept playing with her hair and I had to redo my sketch a few times. My pad was smudged with charcoal and eraser shavings. After she changed her position for the hundredth time, I decided to move on to a more cooperative subject.

Just as I was looking around the cafe, I spotted a familiar face waiting in line. Gary turned and waved at me. I gave him a small wave back. He looked younger in the afternoon light of the cafe but still looked just as ripped in a maroon v-neck sweater and jeans. After getting his drink, he headed over to my spot. I put my sketchpad and materials back into my bag.

"Hey Lorrie, good to see you!"

"Hi Gary."

"Whatcha up to?"

I shrugged and pointed to the coffee in front of me. "Not much, just hanging out."

"Mind if I join you? I gotta run to a class in a few minutes, but I still got some time."

"Sure, of course."

"How's life?"

I shrugged. "It's okay. Studying, drawing—the usual. Not too much else going on."

"Hey I never asked you the other night, what year are you?"

"Sophomore."

"Ah, right before the shit really starts to hit the fan. Let me tell you. Sophomore year is all rainbows and unicorns, but once junior year hits, all of a sudden you need to decide what you want to do with the rest of your life. And don't even get me started on senior year."

I laughed, "Wow, you're really making me look forward to the year."

"Hey, no problem, that's what I'm good for, that extra boost of motivation." He took a sip of his drink before continuing, "I heard you and Hunter went to the hockey game a few nights ago."

I narrowed my eyes. What had Hunter told him?

"Oh," I said, trying to keep my voice as neutral as possible, "he told you?"

"Yeah, I had to bail on him last minute because something came up at my frat house. Glad you were able to make it though. Hunter really loves those hockey games. If he hadn't found somebody else to go with him he would've really been pissed at me." Gary laughed. I could tell why Hunter was friends with him.

"What happened at your frat? Is everything okay?"

"Yeah, yeah, everything's fine. I'm the social chair of the house which sounds pretty cool, but really it means I have to take care of whatever bullshit that comes up."

"Isn't that the president's job?"

"Yeah, but our president was outta town, and a lot of the other guys on the board were already out partying. I swear, sometimes I think I'm the only responsible person there. Anyway, a toilet was clogged up and the idiot sophomores didn't know how to fix a toilet or call a plumber, that was the emergency that ruined my night." He looked at me. "I mean, no offense to sophomores. You're much smarter than those clowns anyway."

I smiled. "None taken."

"Don't get me wrong, I love Phi Kappa Delta and the brothers are all good guys, even the younger ones, but some of them just need more life experience."

I chuckled shaking my head in disbelief. "Nobody there had any idea how to fix a toilet?"

Gary shrugged, "Who knows, hopefully the older brothers can set a good example for them. Anyway, enough about my *shitty* night. How was your date with Hunter?"

I froze, did Hunter tell him that it was a date? "It wasn't a date," I said icily.

He held his hands up in surrender. "I didn't mean it that way, sorry. I just meant to ask if you had fun at the game."

Unclenching my fists, I relaxed a bit. I guess I was getting a little too sensitive about that topic.

"It was fun, I guess. It was my first hockey game so there was a lot to take in. I think I'll have to watch a few more to really get the rules." I didn't want to keep talking about my time with Hunter, so I changed the subject. "How do you know Hunter?"

"We met freshman year, but we only became friends during our sophomore year. Hunter started coming around the gym more often and we'd train and spar together. I don't know anybody that works as hard as he does in the gym."

"Do you guys ever have to fight each other?"

"Naw, the league wouldn't make us do that, and we wouldn't take those fights anyway. Not to brag, but I'm a pretty good fighter myself. If they put the two of us into a ring together, one of us is bound to get hurt. Besides, if there's one person I don't want to ever face in the ring it'd be Hunter."

Gary nodded and started getting up. "Hey, I gotta head to my class soon. I guess it was a good thing I had a *crappy* night then, if that meant you had a good one. Sorry about earlier. I didn't mean to call it a date. I know you and Hunter are just friends."

"It's okay. I guess I'm just a little sensitive about that. It must've looked like a date to a lot of people huh?"

Gary looked pensive for a second and then filled his cheeks with air. After he exhaled, he said, "Look Lorrie, you're a cool girl and I like you. I know it's none of my business to tell you what to do, but I wanted you to know that you should be careful around Hunter. If you guys are just friends, then it's all good, but don't let his charm get to you."

"What are you talking about? Why are you saying that?"

"It's no secret that Hunter's a hit with the ladies, and I just don't want you to get hurt that's all."

"Are you saying I'm not good enough for him?"

"No, Lorrie, not at all. I just know that by the way he treats you, he would never want to hurt you."

"If he would never hurt me why are you telling me this?"

"Hunter . . . Hunter doesn't always do things that make sense. There was another girl and . . . well . . . Look it's really not my place to tell you the details. Whatever you do with him, just know that he's got a lot of baggage okay? He's all swagger and tattoos on the outside, but the real Hunter is more . . . complicated."

"Whose team are you on anyway? Aren't you supposed to be *helping* him get laid?"

That got a laugh out of him. "I guess you can call me the referee. Trust me, I know Hunter and I know that you're not just some other girl to him. I don't want to see either of you hurt."

I nodded cautiously. "I'll keep that in mind. Thanks Gary."

"Yeah, no problem. Take care Lorrie, I'm late for class. I'll see you around."

After Gary left, I just sat there looking outside for a while. What had that been about? Whatever it was, he didn't tell me that offhand. With the things he did for his frat house, it was unlikely that Gary was the irresponsible gossiping type. If he told me to be careful about Hunter, he must've really thought it through. What had he meant that Hunter was complicated?

I mean, it didn't really surprise me. Hunter was cocky and flirty, which was to be expected given the attention he got, but some of the things that Hunter said made it clear he wasn't just some dumb musclehead cage fighter. Hunter had told me his parents were druggies . . . was that why he was complicated? And who was the girl Hunter had a history with? Thinking about it made my heart ache with jealousy, but I quickly talked myself back to my senses. Hunter and I were friends. I had to stop getting jealous every time I heard him linked with a girl.

I supposed that Hunter didn't have a lot of female friends

without benefits, but that didn't suddenly mean that he was in love with me. Even if he was, so what? I could admit that I was attracted to Hunter without acting on it. Like Gary said, Hunter already had some baggage, add my baggage on top of that and it'd be a recipe for pissing off airport security.

Gary may have been trying to be helpful but he just raised more questions than he answered. I took my sketchpad out again to distract myself and spent the better part of an hour sketching the campus view just outside the cafe windows. A light layer of snow covered the bare trees that stood in a row by the walkway.

When the sun was starting to set, I decided to head back to my room. It would get too dark to sketch anything outside soon and I had to do some reading anyway. The campus was shades of orange and purple as the sun hung over the west side of campus.

I was halfway back to the dorms when I passed by the campus health center. I almost didn't notice him at first, but then when I looked again I recognized Hunter, wearing a leather jacket and black jeans. He was walking out of the doors of the health center, he stopped to hold the door for another student leaving behind him.

"Hey," I said, waving to him.

Hunter's eyes brightened when he saw me."Lorrie!" He flashed me a smile and raised an eyebrow "You stalking me?"

"You wish. Just heading home. Everything okay? Why were you in the health center?"

"Huh? Oh yeah. Had some injuries from a fight last night, they patched me right up."

He didn't look injured, but maybe the injuries were under his clothes or they were internal or something. His eyes did look a bit sunken and his gorgeous face didn't have its usual brightness.

"Oh my god, are you okay?"

Hunter waved away my concerns. "Come on, don't fuss over me or I'll stop telling you about my fights. It's no big deal. What are you doing right now?"

"Uh . . . heading home?"

"Want to watch a movie with me?"

"What?"

"C'mon, we'll go to the movie theater by the mall."

I looked down, my face getting heated. I was getting too excited about watching a movie with Hunter.

"I don't know . . . I wanted to catch up on my Psych 102 readings."

"Professor Muller? I aced that class."

I laughed, a puff of steam rose in the air between us. "Wow, how humble of you. Some of us have to study you know."

"Don't worry about it, I'll help you with it." He tilted his head toward the direction of the theater. "It'll be fun."

"Wait, how do you manage to do so well in your classes if you're busy training all the time?"

"Well, I took Muller's class freshman year and I didn't start fighting until sophomore year so I devoted a lot more time to studying back then. My grades still aren't that bad now. I don't spend as much time studying but I'm passing all my classes at least. So what do ya say?"

I sighed, but seeing a movie did sound like fun. Even though I had planned on going back to my room and cracking open the psych textbook, I knew that I'd probably end up vegging out in front of the TV anyway.

"Okay, but if I fail the class I'm blaming it on you."

Hunter pumped his fist in victory. "You got it. It's all my fault. Alright, now let's go!"

We walked to the bus stop but didn't have to wait long before we caught one. The mall was only a ten minute bus ride away and we were let off right in front. We made our way through the mall, chatting about what movie we wanted to watch, until we were in front of the movie theater.

There was no one in the box office and the lights were all off. "What the . . ." Hunter said, putting his hands on his head like he had just received some terrible news.

When we got closer to box office window, we saw the notice taped onto it.

Closed for Renovation. Reopening Next Week.

Hunter walked to the doors, peering into the dark theater. "This is crazy! When did this happen? They don't need to be renovated!"

I tried to hide my laughter as Hunter dropped to his knees, pulling at his hair in mock despair. It was becoming more clear to me why Hunter had referred to himself as a 'weirdo'.

"Hunter, you're going to draw attention, and then mall security will kick us out. We'll just come back next week." A few shoppers were already looking over at us.

He quickly got up, and brushed the dirt off his knees, shrugging as if it had never happened. "They can kick us out, this mall sucks anyway. Without a movie theater this place is lame."

"Sorry, I know you really wanted to see a movie. Guess it's back to studying tonight."

Hunter nodded grumpily, until his eyes suddenly widened. I leveled my gaze at him, it looked like he had an idea, hopefully it wasn't crazy. "I know, let's drop by the video rental place in town. We'll rent something and watch it on my TV. We can even make popcorn."

He tugged my sleeve like he was a kid asking if he could have ice cream. I tried to imagine Hunter as a goofy adolescent boy but had trouble ignoring the fact that he was a towering badass alpha male.

"You're really determined to prevent me from doing any work tonight aren't you?" I asked him.

"Don't try to deny it Lorrie, it's a great idea. Even better than watching something in the theaters. Let's get some scary movies. You're not scared are you?" He wiggled his fingers in front of my face like he was a conjurer or magician. God, who knew that Tattoos and Muscles would be such a goofball.

"Psh, I eat horror movies for breakfast. Nothing's gonna freak me out." Hunter didn't know that I had a phase in high school after my parents had divorced when I watched a ton of scary movies and wore only black. It wasn't a phase I was really proud of, but I did have the advantage of no longer being easily scared by ghosts and gore.

"Wanna bet?" He looked at me in challenge.

"You're on." I playfully poked his stomach with my finger. It was like poking a brick wall. He grabbed my hand in his and shook it like we were solidifying a business deal. His hand felt warm and soft against my palm making my heart skip a beat.

"Come on, let's go, no time to waste. I don't want everyone to rent out all the good movies," he said as we walked over to the bus stop by the front of the mall.

"Um. Are you serious? There's only one video rental place in town and no one ever goes there anymore."

"Who knows, maybe everyone else who came to the theater got the same idea and all the really scary movies are already checked out."

I was skeptical of that unlikely scenario ever happening but followed him quickly to the bus stop.

We took the bus to "Mad Mike's Movies" and Hunter picked out a stack of DVDs of old classic horror films. A lot of them looked really cheesy, but Hunter kept trying to psych me out and tease me about how scary they were going to be. I just rolled my eyes and went along with it. It felt good to just tease and have fun with someone. Although Daniela and I had that kind of relationship, I hadn't had that with a guy in a long time.

By the time we got to Hunter's place it was already a bit past eight. I paid for the popcorn we picked up from the supermarket, since Hunter had paid for the movies. His place looked the same as when I was last here. Once we had made the popcorn and settled in on the couch, Hunter presented the movies to me.

"Alright, what'll it be first? 'The Girl with No Eyes', 'Flyman', or 'The Vampire Bride'?" he said, holding out the DVDs in front of me so I could see the covers.

"How about 'Flyman'? That sounds pretty interesting."

Hunter nodded. "Good choice, I would've picked that too."

He got up, turned off the lights and put the disc into the DVD player before joining me on the couch again. The popcorn bowl nestled between us, providing just enough distance so as not to be inappropriate. Hunter patted me on the arm during the opening credits.

"Don't worry Lorrie, if you're scared, I'll protect you with my muscles."

"Gee thanks Hunter," I said remembering how I jumped into his muscles at the amusement park and at the hockey game. He was probably planning on a hat-trick—a hockey term I learned from him—with these scary movies. "What would I do without you and your chiseled abs?"

He smirked, grabbed a handful of popcorn and then turned back to the TV.

The movie was predictably cheesy. The Flyman was just an ordinary man who, as a result of secret government experiments, developed the head of a fly. Of course, the experiment also turned him insane, so he started wreaking havoc soon after his unfortunate transformation. It was entertaining but nowhere near as scary as some of the movies I watched as a teenager.

Whenever the Flyman would pop out from behind a corner though, Hunter's eyes would widen and he'd shriek while grabbing my arm. I laughed it off the first time, but then I couldn't tell if he was just teasing me or if he was actually getting freaked out. There was no way a six foot, two inch brawler like him who regularly fights other freakishly huge guys was afraid of some horror movies.

"Wait, wait, Hunter, you're just teasing me right? You're not seriously scared are you?"

He turned to look at me, wide-eyed. He shook his head back and forth quickly. I watched him carefully, my mouth half-open, unsure of what to make of it. I would've sworn he was actually scared if I hadn't seen the hint of a smile playing at the edge of his lips. I slapped his arm.

"What happened to all that big talk of protecting me with your muscles?" I teased.

Hunter smiled, all suave nonchalance again. "Seems like you don't need any protection from the Flyman, you didn't even blink when he jumped out from behind the lab door."

"Come on Hunter, you can't possibly think that I'd be scared of black and white special effects from the sixties."

"I don't know, it looks pretty convincing to me. Next time I'm in the biology building, I'll be checking all the corners."

I laughed and we turned back to the movie.

When the movie finally ended with Flyman jumping into an incinerator to save the woman he'd loved when he was still a human, we had already finished an entire bowl of popcorn. I yawned, stretching out my arms. Hunter looked at me, holding up the disc for "The Vampire Bride."

"One more?"

"I don't know Hunter, I'm pretty wiped out."

"Aw, come on, it's Thursday night. It's practically the weekend."

"Fine, just one more. But let me text Daniela and use the bathroom first."

"Great! I'll make some more popcorn."

I knew his bathroom was situated across from his bedroom, having showered there the first time I came to his apartment. On my way, I noticed his bedroom door was closed and had a sign that said "Uno Ab Alto". I shrugged at the mysterious phrase and moved on. I texted Daniela when I was in the bathroom, letting her know that I'd be back to the dorms late. When I was finished, I could still hear Hunter in the kitchen microwaving the popcorn.

I was about to return to the living room when I noticed the door on my right was cracked open a slit. Curious, I pushed it open slightly. It was dark but it looked like it was a closet. The floor was covered in cardboard boxes, filled with irregular shapes. I struggled to make out what they were for a second, and then I recognized the shapes. They were model airplanes. There were maybe a hundred model airplanes of various types covering the floor.

"Lorrie, the popcorn is ready!"

His voice made me jump. Why did he have so many model planes? And why in this closet? He didn't have any on display in his apartment. If he had them hidden away, it was probably something I wasn't supposed to see. I pulled the closet door closed again and then went back to the living room to join him.

Hunter offered me the bowl and I popped a small handful into my mouth. He smiled at me brightly. I was relieved he hadn't heard me snooping around. We returned to the couch and turned the movie on, thoughts of the contents of Hunter's closet still swirling through my mind.

Halfway through the movie, my eyes started to droop. I looked over sleepily at Hunter, but he was entranced with the bloodsucking on screen. My eyelids grew even heavier. I couldn't fight the tiredness anymore. I gave in and let my eyes close.

I opened my eyes and the bowl of popcorn that had formed the barrier between us was on the coffee table. I was leaning right on Hunter's shoulder, a blanket covering us.

If I was less sleepy I would have freaked out, but I just looked up at him. "What happened?"

"You started snoring, and your head was lolling back. I figured you'd be more comfortable this way. Also those vampires got scary so I needed your protection."

I smiled against his chest, suppressing a yawn. His chest was so warm and welcoming. He smelled faintly of aftershave and leather.

"Go back to sleep, Snorrie," he said softly.

I grinned at the stupid name and nodded sleepily.

He leaned his head back to look at me. I squinted my eyes open and saw he had a serious expression on his face. "Hey Lorrie?"

"Yeah?"

"Thanks."

"For what?" I yawned.

"For coming to the movies with me."

"Thanks for inviting me Hunter," I said, before drifting off completely.

$$\textbf{\textit{ϟ ϟ ϟ}}$$

Sunlight flickered against my face, bringing me slowly to consciousness. I felt completely content and satisfied. Then I realized I wasn't in my dorm room.

My eyes shot open. I was leaning right against Hunter's chin. His eyes were closed, and he was snoring gently. We were both laying on his couch together, my arms around him, his arms around me. My heart pounded erratically, and a cold sweat started breaking out on my skin.

Had we . . .

The previous night's events came back to me slowly and I realized I'd fallen asleep on his shoulder while watching vampires. *Thank god.* We hadn't gone that far, but it was still a mistake. We were supposed to be just friends. Friends didn't casually fall asleep nestled together like lovers on the guy's couch. I was supposed to be strong. I wasn't supposed to fall for Hunter, yet I'd fallen asleep in his arms. This was bad. I gently unweaved my limbs from

Hunter's, careful not to disturb him. Then I grabbed my bag and snuck out of his apartment.

Why was I always sneaking out of his place?

Chapter Nine

LESSONS

Rushing across campus from Hunter's apartment, I got back to my dorm around ten in the morning. It was Friday and I had to get to swim class. I climbed the four flights of stairs to my suite and gingerly unlocked the door, hoping that Daniela wouldn't notice that I was away all night. Otherwise I'd owe her an explanation, and I did not want to have to explain that I'd slept over at Hunter's place last night.

I opened the suite door and saw Daniela sitting on the couch watching TV. She slowly twisted her head in my direction and her wide green eyes locked onto me making me jump. Her movement reminded me of the movie *The Exorcist*. Damn horror movies last night.

"Well, well, well," she said with a sly grin.

"Hello to you too. I was just grabbing breakfast in the dining hall." It was a good excuse and I was pleased with myself for thinking quick on my toes.

"No, you weren't."

Shit.

"I knocked on your door two hours ago to go eat breakfast. I've been sitting on this couch, waiting for you to get up and here you come walking through the front door. You were out all night weren't you? Hm?" Her eyes were mischievous yet probing.

Shifting nervously on my feet, I answered, "I got up at seven and went down early."

"And ate a three hour breakfast?" She swiped her hand as if batting away my excuse. "I'm hungry and irritable. Admit it. I caught you, Lorrie. Spill."

101

I put my hands up in surrender. "Alright, alright." I sighed heavily. "I slept over at Hunter's place."

Her eyes widened and seemed to become possessed. "No way. I know I warned you to be careful around him, but what's done is done. Tell me everything. Was he big? Small? Was he rough? Tender? Spare no detail. I want *everything*."

"Whoa, whoa." I was tempted to make a cross sign with my fingers to ward her away but ended up just shoving my hands in the air in front me. "We didn't have sex. We didn't even kiss. I just went over to his place to watch some movies we rented and I fell asleep on his couch. It wasn't even intentional, I was just tired." I then remembered that Hunter was supposed to help me with studying for my psych class but that clearly never happened. *Dammit Hunter.*

"Oh." Daniela deflated. "Well I'm happy for you Lorrie. Sounds like you've made a new friend in Hunter."

"I don't know, it's really awkward. It was a mistake. We were supposed to be just friends and I think I might've given him an unintentional signal. He might think I want to take things further."

"How do you feel about him? Do you want to be just friends?"

"Of course I just want to be friends!" I said, trying to convince her as much as myself. "Like I said before I'm not ready for a relationship. I'm having a hard enough time getting back into the swing of things and keeping up with my classes. I just want a normal, drama-free life."

She looked at me skeptically as if me telling her I was only interested in Hunter as a "friend" was a bold-faced lie. "Not to be a nagging-nanna but I already told you he's got a reputation for shagging and tagging girls all over campus. I'm glad you and him are friends but I don't want to see you getting hurt by him. He's broken a few hearts before."

"Thanks Daniela, but you don't have to worry about me. I'll be careful."

Daniela asked me a few more questions about Hunter and I responded as agreeably as I could. The conversation could've gone on for a good hour but I had to cut it short when I noticed the time on the clock in our suite.

"Well, I have to go to class," I said. I hurriedly packed my backpack with my swimsuit and left the dorm.

It was the first day of my swim class which started later in the semester than the other classes. Since there was a lake around campus, students at Arrowhart were required to either pass a swim test or take a swim class. I had planned to take the swim test but there was some administrative mix up and they didn't register me in time for it. I ended up being signed up for the swim class, which I didn't mind. After that debacle with falling into the lake, I figured I could use the practice.

On my way past the student union, I received a text from Hunter. *Why did you leave?*

I thumbed a quick response. *Had class in the morning. Sorry.*

You forgot to take my trash with you :).

I knew he was trying to be funny, but I didn't find it particularly amusing. Sleeping over at his place was a mistake, not a joke. To drop the issue, I responded with a simple smiley.

Walking across the arts quad, I arrived at The Annex, which was a large glass building used for athletic activities. Among its various amenities, it had a state-of-the-art gym and an Olympic-sized swimming pool. I navigated the hallways, following the signs posted for the swimming pool, and found the women's locker room. I changed into my swimsuit and went to join the swim class.

The instructor introduced himself as Mitch McHenry. He was an older man with gray on the top of his head matching his neatly groomed mustache and beard. His posture and the commanding tone of his voice reminded me of a military officer.

"All right, guppies! Who here already knows how to swim?"

About half the class raised their hand, myself included.

"Good. You guys can help out your fellow classmates. Since it's everyone's first day, I'm going to go over the basics: the doggy-paddle and treading water. Then you guys are going to do laps back and forth on the shallow end of the pool."

One by one, each student entered the pool. Some dipped their toes to test the water before hopping in, some took the steps down, and some cannonballed right into the pool. Once everyone was up to their necks in chlorinated water, Mr. McHenry spent the next ten minutes demonstrating how to do the strokes properly then he ordered us to practice.

I already knew the basic strokes so practice was a breeze. It was apparent half the class felt the same way but the other half were borderline drowning in five feet of water. Mr. McHenry spent the next half hour helping the worst cases.

I was in the middle of helping a redheaded female freshman with her doggy paddle, when I glanced over and saw a student through the pool's glass entrance walking toward the men's locker room. He briefly passed by the entrance but then doubled-back. I recognized him. Hunter narrowed his eyes at me then waved in my direction.

My pulse leaped. The moment was beyond awkward—particularly because I was trying to avoid him—but I managed to wave back. Just when I thought he'd walk over and we'd have an uncomfortable conversation about why I bolted from his apartment this morning in front of the entire swim class, he turned around and continued toward the men's locker room. I was left with both relief and regret.

"Focus your attention on your partner, Ms. Burnham," a gruff voice said behind me, making me jump out of the water.

I twisted around to see Mr. McHenry helping the redheaded freshman stay afloat. Her face was as bright as her hair. I was supposed to be helping her but I'd been distracted.

"Oh I'm so sorry," I said, apologizing to both Mr. McHenry and the redhead—who now had a scowl on her face.

"Just because you know how to swim, doesn't give you the right to let your fellow classmate drown," Mr. McHenry said, more as a statement than an accusation. He assigned the freshman to a different partner and then turned back to me. "So you know Hunter?"

I found the question odd coming from Mr. McHenry so I paused a moment before answering. "Yeah . . ."

"Are you guys friends?"

"Um . . . yeah I met him a few weeks ago and we became friends . . . Do you know him from somewhere?"

He glanced at the entrance where Hunter had been then

returned his gaze to me. "I run the ROTC program here. Hunter was a member two years ago."

"He wanted to be in the Army?" Just as I asked the question, the image of the shirt he'd given me and the model airplanes in his closet popped into mind.

"Air Force, actually. He was dead set on making it. I put a lot of effort into training and helping him. I hoped he'd make it but unfortunately he's no longer in the program."

Curious, I asked, "Why not?"

"It definitely wasn't because of his performance. With evaluations like he had, he was a shoo-in for any branch... but well ... it's his story to tell, not my place to discuss details." He scratched his neatly trimmed beard. "He's a good kid but a bit troubled. Anyway, I have to go make sure nobody drowns. Although you're a bit irresponsible, you seem like a nice girl. Just thought you ought to know. If you get the chance, keep your eye on Hunter. Make sure he stays out of trouble."

Mr. McHenry swam away to help another student, leaving me to think about what he'd just told me. He'd asked me to watch over Hunter implying that Hunter, for some reason, needed watching over. Gary had mentioned something similar. Could it have been a coincidence? I didn't know what to make of it except that Hunter seemed like the kind of guy who could take care of himself. Between Hunter and myself, I was probably the one who needed help.

Chapter Ten

FRIENDS?

The weekend passed as well as the beginning of the next week. I'd been trying to avoid Hunter but he'd been texting me at least a few times per day. I had to tell him I'd gotten sick over the weekend to gracefully turn down his requests to hang out. It was getting harder to make up excuses to avoid him without appearing suspicious.

I'd just finished art history class learning about how Van Gogh cut off his ear and was in the hall preparing to head to my next class when I received a call. Nervous that it was Hunter, my heart started beating faster as I reached into my pocket for my phone. It was one thing brushing him off via text, it was another saying it out loud. Talking made it more difficult to come up with excuses. I took a deep breath and looked at my phone. I released a long sigh when I saw that it was my aunt.

"Hey Aunt Caroline!" I answered as I went to a private corner in the Arts building to talk to her.

"Hey hey! How are you doing?"

"Good. Just got done with my art history class."

"Oh, sounds like you're keeping busy. How's your semester going so far?"

"It's been a little difficult, but I think I'm getting used to it."

"Sounds wonderful. Hey, what do you think about me visiting you next week? The boys are going on a field trip to D.C. and Stewart's going on a business trip. Plus it's been a while since I've visited Studsen."

My heart leaped. "I'd love it if you came and visited."

"Perfect. I'll see you next week!"

Just as I hung up, I noticed an icon at the top of the screen telling me I had a voicemail. It was from Hunter.

"Hey Lorrie, haven't heard from you in a while. Just wondering if you're doing all right. You want to get together and hang out this week?"

An electronic voice asked me to press seven if I wanted to delete the message and nine if I wanted to save it. I thought about how I needed to have less complications in my life and at a tap of a digital button, I could do that. I pressed seven.

I had a good hour and a half until my economics class. It was a short enough break that it made going back to my dorm impractical. Instead, I found a bench outside and whipped out my sketch pad just as the sky started sprinkling snow. I became entranced by a lone blue bird perched atop a branch of one of the large trees that lined the arts quad. The color of his feathers reminded me of Hunter's fighting trunks. Most of the birds had flown south by now, but this little guy was an exception. He wasn't normal, just like me.

"Nice doodle."

Startled by Hunter's sudden appearance, I nearly poked a hole through the paper with my pencil. Looking over my shoulder, he exhaled a warm breath against my neck, raising goosebumps on the skin.

"Thanks," I replied coolly, giving him only a quick glance before returning to my drawing. I did my best to ignore him though I knew it was futile.

"Are birds your favorite thing to draw?"

"Not really. This weird one just happened to catch my attention, that's all. I'm not particularly attached to it or anything."

"Are you trying to avoid me?" he hummed in my ear, making me realize I hadn't said 'hi' to him.

"What?" I laughed nervously. "Don't be silly. I've just been busy with classes."

"Are you busy now?"

"I'm busy drawing my picture."

"Can you draw in a place where it's a little warmer? Maybe at the cafe? I'll buy you a latte, my treat."

I grumbled because I wanted to avoid Hunter and him showing

up and asking me to hang out at a cafe didn't mix. But then I remembered I had a debt to repay him. "Alright, let's go. I'll buy though since you got the ice cream last time."

We went to Huck Cafe. Upon my insistence, I ordered him a latte and he thanked me for the kind gesture. Then I ordered a black coffee for myself. We found a table and sat down across from one another.

Hunter took a long sip of his drink. "Mmm yummy. Want a sip?"

"No thank you, Hunter," I said politely.

"So, Lorrie—" He looked at me seriously. "—Is it because you stayed over at my place after we watched those movies?"

His direct question caught me off guard. "Uh . . . no."

He shook his head. "Why are you freaking out about staying over at my place? Just because you stayed over doesn't mean anything."

I was prepared to agree with him about me staying over not meaning anything but the "not meaning anything" part upset me, when I knew it shouldn't.

"Why would you say it doesn't mean anything? It does mean something. It means we went further than we should have as friends."

"We didn't do anything though. I didn't even kiss you when you fell asleep. Are you saying that having my arm around you is inappropriate?"

I sighed. Hunter didn't understand the implications of the situation. "When you hang out with Gary, does he fall asleep nestled in your arms after you guys down some beers?"

"What? No! Of course not. That's different."

"How is that different?"

"Gary's a dude. Man Code doesn't allow that."

"Okay, well what does Man Code say about falling asleep with girls that are friends?"

"It says it's acceptable if neither of them are attached to anyone else. Therefore, what we did was acceptable. You might even say normal. Unless . . . you are attached?"

"No, I'm not," I clarified, hoping Hunter took the cue that I was including my feelings toward him as well.

"Good, then there's no issue."

"I hate to tell you this, Hunter, but I don't abide by Man Code. I abide by Girl Code."

He lifted one brow. "Alright . . . then what does Girl Code say?"

I took a sip of my black coffee enjoying the sobering bitter taste. "First rule of Girl Code: don't talk about Girl Code."

He narrowed his gaze at me. "So you're already breaking the first rule?"

"I referenced it. I didn't talk about it."

He rolled his eyes. Although I'd done that plenty of times to him, it was the first time I saw him do it to me. "I'm pretty sure you referenced *Fight Club* rather than an actual rule."

"Does it matter?"

"Yes, it matters! Dammit, Lorrie. Talk to me. I'm okay with you not telling me some things about yourself but please, don't avoid me. I told you before, I don't bite."

I sighed. "Hunter, this—" I referenced to the space between us. "—is drama I don't need right now. I have enough problems already. This is what I was concerned about in terms of us becoming 'friends' and now it's come true."

"Lorrie," he sighed. "My dick's not coming out. My lips are keeping to themselves. My hands aren't roaming. You wanted that, and I've been following through. You want me to keep *you* accountable now? You want me to kick you outta my place when you fall asleep on my couch? You want me to be an asshole?"

"No . . . yes. I mean, no. I can handle myself just fine, Hunter. I just want you to know that us sleeping together last night wasn't a signal for you to move forward."

He put his hands up briefly in defense as if I was going for a takedown attempt on him. "Consider it known."

"It was a mistake on my part," I added. "And it shouldn't have happened in the first place."

"It wasn't a mistake. Nothing happened beyond sleeping. I haven't forgotten our 'friend'—" He put his fingers up and wiggled them to indicate quotes. "—friend agreement. But honestly, I'm a little pissed off you didn't talk to me about this upfront. Avoiding me is such a drama-queen thing to do. I thought you were different from other girls. Maybe I was wrong."

"Ugh, I hate to disappoint you, Hunter, but even if I'm cool with watching hockey with you and talking about threesomes, I'm still a girl. I have emotions you know." I was beginning to see cracks in our friendship and as much as it sucked to consider, I wasn't sure if we were going to work out. Maybe we didn't understand each other as well as we'd thought. "If you still want to be friends, you're just going to have to deal with that fact. Besides, didn't you say yourself that I was both selfless and selfish?"

He grumbled. "And just because I'm a guy, doesn't mean I don't have feelings. Just because you see me getting punched in the face doesn't mean I don't get upset when you do shit like avoid me. Man, when I woke up and found out you weren't there, I got worried."

"Why would you get worried? I told you I had to go to class."

"That was after I texted you first asking where you went. Even when I made that joke about you forgetting to take my trash with you and you responded with a smiley, I knew you were faking it. You usually respond to my jokes with L-O-L and then some snarky comeback that makes me laugh. I knew you were hiding your true feelings. They don't call you Lorrie Hide for nothing."

Hunter knew some of my habits better than even I did. "Only you call me that, Gunther." I stuck my tongue out at him and he did the same to me.

"I know you have some personal issues you're dealing with, Lorrie. I don't know what they are and I haven't asked you about them because I know you don't wanna talk about it. I'm fine with that. I got my own issues and I'm more than happy to leave our skeletons in their closets. Just don't leave me hanging especially since I care about you."

After a few moments, I realized how poorly I handled the situation and decided to take responsibility. "Alright, fine. I'm sorry for being a bitch to you, Hunter. I care about you as well. I just sort of freaked out and didn't give you enough credit. I'm actually surprised you're being so level headed about this."

His shoulders relaxed and he smiled. "I humbly accept your apology. And I'm sorry for being such a comfortable pillow for your face that I made you fall asleep on me."

"Apology accepted," I puffed.

He grinned. "That wasn't so hard was it? I'm glad that we talked this out and got it resolved. Aren't you?"

"I suppose so."

"So are we still friends?"

My lips betrayed a small smile. "Yeah."

He returned the smile and gently put his palm over my hand. "Am I allowed to put my hand on top of yours?"

"I suppose," I said, relishing the warmth from his skin more than the warmth from the coffee in my other hand.

"Are you going to stop blowing me off?" His dark gray eyes were wide and fiercely tender.

How could he attack me with such adorable puppy-dog eyes?

I felt myself becoming immediately disarmed. "I can't promise anything," I grumbled, taking a sip of my drink to hide the smile on my face. "But I'll try."

"Good enough."

He pulled a folded piece of paper out of his pocket and handed it to me.

"What's this?" I asked.

"A flyer. It's for an art portfolio competition. I saw it hanging up on the student board in the Barnyard and thought about you."

I took the paper from him, dimly musing about how silly it was for the school to name the main cafeteria as "The Barnyard". I unfolded the flyer and scanned the details. The winner would get featured in a major art gallery in Chicago and a good chunk of cash.

"Thanks, Hunter. It sounds exciting but I don't think my stuff is exactly a fit for this kind of competition."

"What are you talking about? You're a great artist! Don't sell yourself short."

I pointed at one of the example pieces in the flyer. "This is 'high art'." I pulled out one of my previous sketches from my backpack and showed it to him. "This is not."

He looked at the sketch and jolted backward nearly falling out of his chair. "Whoa."

"See? I told you."

His eyes narrowed. "No, this is good! Like really good. It's so realistic. Man the shading and everything. Scared the hell outta me when I saw it."

I looked at the drawing again. It was a giant fly head with a human body like the one in the movie Hunter and I rented.

"It was just a quick sketch," I said a little bashfully. I'd never really shown people my sketches before because I didn't think they were that good. Hunter's positive reaction surprised me.

"How quick?"

"Like ten minutes."

"No way you did that in ten minutes. Lorrie, is your real last name Picasso? Is that why you haven't told me it? Because that's some serious talent you've got there. "

"If you like it so much, you can keep it. Here." I handed him the drawing, feeling it to be an appropriate gesture since he'd thought of me when taking the flyer.

His eyes lit up. "Are you sure?"

"Yeah."

"Awesome."

I giggled.

"But really, Lorrie. I think you should enter that competition. Submit your portfolio. Worst that can happen is you don't win. But you'll kick yourself if you didn't at least try."

Feeling a little excited by Hunter's encouragement, I looked at the sketch again and found myself having a greater appreciation for it. "Alright, fine. I'll have to do some more pieces but I'll enter the competition."

He grinned. "Sweet. You going to give me a portion of your winnings? Don't forget I was the one who convinced you and brought you the flyer. Consider it the manager's cut."

"How about if I win, I'll cheer for you at one of your fights?"

His grin became wider. "My very own cheerleader? Even better. I could use the support during my fights."

"I think you get plenty already."

"You can never have enough support from 'friends.'"

"True that."

He offered his coffee cup out for a toast. "To Snorrie and Gunther. May their friendship be filled with miscommunication and drama."

"—Or not." I smirked and met his latte with my black coffee.

Hunter stayed with me in the cafe until we finished our drinks. Then we parted ways to go to our classes.

Chapter Eleven

CURIOSITY

I went out Saturday and picked up some art supplies at the school bookstore. Watercolors, pastels, and some charcoal to go along with the pencils I already had. I was thinking about mixing media by coloring in some of my pencil or charcoal drawings with the paints or pastels. It would take some experimentation, but maybe the results would be portfolio-worthy.

I spent the next few days messing around with coloring in sketches. Thursday came, and I went dutifully to Econ in the morning, then killed some time before my drawing class at one. By the time I got back to my dorm, it was about three. I sprawled out in my bed and started coloring in some sketches I had done between classes in the coffee shop. I was considering whether to use pastels or watercolors on a sketch of a steaming mug of tea when my phone started vibrating on my nightstand. Startled, I got up and picked up my phone.

"Hey Hunter," I said brightly.

"Hey Lorrie, are you busy?" There was a combination of loud music and men's voices yelling in the background, so I could barely hear him. I put my hand over my other ear to concentrate on what he was saying.

"I was just working on my portfolio," I said. "Why? What's up?"

"Oh cool, you'll have to show me what you have when it's ready. Anyway, I was wondering if you could come down to the gym to help me out with something."

He was being vague and I couldn't tell why. "What is it?" I asked.

Someone yelled in the background wherever Hunter was, which I was guessing was his gym. "It's a surprise. Can you come?"

"A surprise? What kind of surprise?"

"A good one, I promise. If you're too busy it's okay, but I'd really appreciate it if you came by."

I thought about it. Tomorrow was Friday and that was pretty much the start of the weekend since I didn't have any classes other than swimming, and it wasn't like I was in some super groove on my art. I could spare an hour or two to find out what Hunter's surprise was.

"Okay, I'll come by."

"Great! The gym's called Bigg's. I think it's like a ten or fifteen minute walk from your dorm."

"I'll figure it out. Should I just walk in?"

"Yeah there's a woman at the front desk. Just ask for me and I'll be right there."

"Okay, see you in a few."

"Thanks so much. See you soon."

He hung up. I opened the maps app on my phone and typed in Bigg's Gym. Hunter was right: my phone said it would take twelve minutes to walk there. I put on my coat and headed out, curious what he had in store for me.

I had to look at my phone to make sure I was at the right address. The place had darkened windows and no sign I could see. The address above the door matched the one I'd punched into my phone, but this building seemed deserted and the sidewalk was strangely empty.

What is this sketchy place? Should I call him? It would be embarrassing if this was the right address and I didn't just walk through the door. I cupped my hands above my eyes to block out any other light and pressed my face against the glass of the door. The glass wasn't just tinted black: it was actually covered. *Very sketch.*

I stepped back and was considering trying the door when it popped open and caught me flush in the face. My hands shot up to my nose and over my eyes as I stepped back, praying I wasn't bleeding.

"Oh my god, I'm so sorry!" a woman's voice said.

My nose was throbbing, but I didn't feel any blood, so I lowered my hands. "It's okay," I said. "Not your fault." She looked to be in her mid forties and had brightly dyed bottle-blonde hair.

"I heard you outside," she said, eyeing my face. "Are you here to meet someone?"

I rubbed my nose gingerly, but the pain was already going away. "Is this Bigg's Gym?"

Her eyes brightened. "It is. Are you here to see Hunter?"

How had she guessed? "Yes, actually."

She smiled wide. "Oh, good! Come in, I'll go and get him."

I stepped inside after her and took a seat in what seemed like a waiting area. There was a desk and a computer where I presumed the receptionist—the women who had hit me in the face with the door—did her work. On the wall behind the desk was a sign that read "Bigg's Gym: Get Bigggg!!!" in red block letters in front of a cartoonishly muscled guy that would make even Popeye the Sailor Man say "Damn, that's ridiculous!" To the right of the sign was a large black curtain, behind which I heard the sounds of loud music and leather hitting leather. Old black and white pictures of fighters littered the beige walls around the waiting room. Every picture had the same pose: a shirtless guy with big muscles stood with his right hand in a fist just under his chin and a scowl on his face. I looked for a picture of Hunter, but didn't see one.

Hunter came through the curtain a moment later, followed by the receptionist. They both wore big smiles. He was shirtless and breathing hard, wearing the same small gloves he had worn when I saw him fight at The Bearded Squirrel. When he exhaled, the hard lines of his six pack popped. The way he was sweating made the muscles in his shoulders and chest even more defined as they glistened under the harsh gym light.

Seeing Hunter half-naked, my heart felt like it was bouncing back and forth between my stomach and my throat. "You look happy with yourself," I said, my voice high.

He nodded and gestured over his shoulder with his head. "Come on, you're going to love this. Thanks for letting her in, Kristy."

Kristy beamed. "My pleasure Hunter." She took her seat at the desk and watched us as we walked into the gym.

I got up and followed him past the curtain. Punching bags were against the wall to my right, and there were several guys practicing wrestling moves on foam mats. In the back was a ring where two guys wearing red foam helmets were sparring with one another.

"Come on over here," Hunter said as he led the way through the gym. He gestured to the corner of the gym. "Alright, just back there in the corner. There's Gary, actually."

Gary was standing over a large cardboard box and grinning like an idiot. We locked eyes as I approached and he gestured me over before pointing to the box.

"Ok, Lorrie," Hunter said. "This is what I needed you for."

I peered down into the box and gasped. There were at least six kittens squirming inside, all in different shades of brown with white patches. They were all cuddled up with each other, some awake, some sleeping, and looked as soft as a cloud. I was unwittingly reminded of the black cat that had scared me and made me fall into Lake Teewee. That was when I met Hunter for the first time.

Despite my unluckiness with cats, I broke out in a big smile and squealed at the sight of the cute little creatures. So *this* was why everyone was grinning like an idiot. Now that I knew, I couldn't blame them.

"Kittens! Where did these come from?" I said excitedly.

Gary looked at Hunter, who shrugged. "I was on my jog before coming here and they were just sitting along the side of the road in that box. They had a blanket, but it's really cold outside and I was worried they'd freeze to death before anyone found them, so I picked up the box and brought them here."

An MMA fighter with tattoos on half his upper body who had such a soft heart he rescued a box of kittens—Hunter was an odd one, I had to give him that.

"Thing is," Hunter said. "Now I don't know what to do with them."

"What do you mean?"

"I've never had a pet before, to be honest. Growing up there's no way my parents were responsible enough for that. Do you know anything about cats?"

My heart sank. "Not really, no. I didn't have any pets growing up either."

Hunter's face fell. "You see imaginary cats but never had one yourself? Odd."

"Imaginary cats?" Gary asked.

I looked at Gary then glared at Hunter. He was going to let the cat out of the bag—so to speak—about my lake swim.

"Nah, I'm joking," Hunter said quickly. "It's nothing. I just thought Lorrie had a bit of cat lady in her, that's all."

I put my hands on my hips. "Apparently it's less than you thought."

"I mean, how hard could it be?" Gary said. "You feed them and change their litter box, right?"

"Do you want them?" Hunter asked.

"I told you man, I can't have pets at the frat house. Plus I wouldn't trust these cute little things around those guys. They're pretty irresponsible," Gary said.

"I can't have them in the dorms," I said. Even if I was allowed to have them, I wouldn't want to care for cats with my suitemates. Things were awkward enough with Kate and Petra.

"Okay, fine. I'll take them," Hunter said. "But we need to get food and stuff for them because I don't have anything at my place. Where do I get those?"

"I think there's a pet store next to the GUESS at the mall," Gary said.

Hunter and I looked at Gary quizzically. We'd been to the mall that one time when we discovered the theater was closed but it was a big mall and we almost got lost even finding the theater.

"How much time do you spend at the mall?" Hunter asked.

Gary looked between the two of us. "What? I've got to look fly for the ladies!"

All three of us laughed.

"Lorrie, want to come with me to the mall?" Hunter asked. "There's a bus stop like two minutes away. I'm pretty sure that line goes to the mall."

"It does," Gary said quickly.

Hunter chuckled. "Okay. Want to come?" he asked me.

Homework could wait when there were kittens that needed care. "Sure, I'll come." I said.

"Great." He turned to Gary. "You can hang out with the kittens for a couple hours, right?"

Gary nodded. "You bet."

"Okay," he said, turning to me. "Let's go."

We arrived at the mall about a half hour later. Hunter had showered and changed into jeans and a hoodie, his usual nondescript attire. He never failed to look good in anything I'd seen him wear. Neither of us had much of an idea how to get around, so we found a directory kiosk and navigated our way to the pet store from there. The store was as big as a department store and had row after row of supplies for just about any animal you could imagine. We walked over to the aisle labeled CATS and started figuring out what we needed.

"Thanks for helping me with this, Lorrie," Hunter said. "I'm sure you have other stuff to do with your day."

"No problemo. But if you were concerned about me having other things to do, why did you make it such a surprise?"

"I wanted to see your face when you saw the kittens." He grinned. "It was a very cute face by the way."

His warm tone made me feel fuzzy inside. Maybe it was just the pet store. "Well, thank you. I'm pretty excited about these kittens. How long do you think you'll keep them?"

He shrugged. "Haven't thought about it. I have to get them home and settled first, then I'll decide."

I nodded. Even though I didn't have any firm future plans, I would maybe think twice about adopting six kittens, but Hunter was apparently barreling ahead.

"Will you help me take care of them?" he asked.

What kind of commitment was he asking for here? I decided to keep my answer vague. "Sure."

"Great." He picked up a food bowl. "They probably need one of these, right?"

I nodded. "Yeah, I think they need to eat."

He threw two in the cart and some water bowls too. "What do kittens eat, do you think? As opposed to cats. Is the food different?"

I shrugged, having no idea. Hunter had already picked up a bag of cat food and was reading the back. "This says for cats over one year old. What do you feed kittens, then?"

He scanned the aisle. Someone who worked at the store came over to talk to us. He had dark hair and glasses, and was only a few inches taller than me. Hunter towered over him. "Can I help you with anything?" he wheezed.

"Yeah. I'm looking for food for my cats," Hunter said.

The guy was wearing a nametag that said TODD. "How old are your cats?" Todd asked.

"I don't know," Hunter answered.

Todd looked exasperated. "What do you *mean*, you don't know?"

"I don't know."

"Well," he said. "Do you know if they're older or younger than a year old?"

Hunter looked at me over Todd's head and smiled. "Yeah, they're definitely less than a year old."

"Well then you need kitten food, obviously," Todd said, emphasizing the last word as if Hunter was a buffoon.

I laughed silently, noting the plight of the tall and muscular. Hunter could pretty much snap Todd in half if he wanted to, but he was putting up with Todd being a jerk to him anyway.

"Okay," Hunter said gamely. "Where is the kitten food?"

Todd stomped down to the other end of the aisle and held up a yellow bag of food. "It's the one that says 'For Kittens.'"

Hunter nodded. "Okay, but these are really little kittens. Can they eat that?"

"Where did you get these kittens?" Todd asked.

"I rescued them."

"How small are we talking?"

Hunter used his hands to show how small they were. I would have just said "super tiny."

Todd's eyebrows shot up. "And there's no mother cat?"

"Nope."

"Well, you should really get them to a vet as soon as possible, but at the end of the aisle you'll find kitten milk, syringes, and bottles. There's a little manual with the supplies that should teach you what you need to feed the kittens."

Hunter nodded and looked over at me. "This is going to be a lot of work," he said.

Was he thinking about giving them up for adoption? "They're *really* cute, though."

"Are you going to help me with them?" he asked.

"Sure," I said, shrugging. Who didn't want to play with kittens?

"No, I mean are you going to really help me? Like co-raise them."

What was he talking about? I looked at Todd, who was standing there dumbly.

"They're going to be staying at your apartment, right?" I asked.

"I'll give you a key. I'm just saying, if we need to be feeding these little guys constantly, having some help in case I have to be gone would turn this from being impossible to being a fun challenge."

I took a deep breath. It felt like no matter what I did, I was getting closer to Hunter. "Okay, that does sound fun actually. But you're not afraid I'm going to snoop around your apartment and find things I shouldn't?" I teased.

He grinned. "Nah, I trust you."

Todd cleared his throat. I had totally forgotten he was there, and my face grew hot. Why was I constantly managing to do embarrassing things?

"Yeah dude, thanks," Hunter said. Todd scampered away as Hunter turned back to me. "Lorrie, thanks for agreeing to help me. I think this will be fun."

We picked out our syringes, bottles, rubber nipples, kitten milk, and manual. I began flipping through the guide to feeding newborn kittens as we walked to checkout. There was a lot to make sure you got right. I was already feeling a little intimidated by it all.

The cashier that checked us out eyed Hunter flirtatiously from under her dark bangs as she rang up our kitten formula, but then her eyes caught the sight of his tattoos and her expression changed.

"You're bottle-feeding kittens?" she asked.

"Yup," Hunter said. "Just rescued them."

She nodded, her lips a thin line. "Well, make sure you get them to the vet," she said. "Kittens are very delicate at that age."

"Thanks for the advice," I said as politely as possible. Why did everyone treat Hunter like he wasn't capable of taking care of some kittens? People seemed to love jumping to conclusions about others so quickly. Like people assuming I was depressed and suicidal, or assuming I was having sex with Hunter. Why couldn't people just give you the benefit of the doubt and assume the best?

"Yeah, thank you Stephanie," Hunter said, reading her name tag. "We'll be sure to get them into the vet as soon as possible." He flashed a smile. I was glad that at least he could take the way people treated him in stride even if I didn't.

We finished checking out and left the mall. The muscles on his tattooed arms stretched against his black t-shirt as we walked to the bus stop. It made me feel strange to admit it, but being seen with such an attractive guy made me throw my shoulders back and feel more self-confidence than I had in years. Even if we were just friends.

We didn't get back to the gym until after five-thirty. The people training changed from younger, college-aged guys like Hunter and Gary to older guys in their late twenties and older. I couldn't help but notice that there were no women training in the gym. The smell of man sweat was everywhere.

Gary was holding a sleeping kitten with a big white spot right between its eyes as we approached. He put one finger up to his lips telling us to be quiet.

"These things do nothing but sleep," he said. "But wow, are they cute when they sleep."

The kitten fit into his hand easily. "Check it out," he said. He used a finger on his other hand to tickle its stomach softly. The kitten squirmed and grabbed at the finger with all four paws without waking up. My heart melted.

"How cute is that?" Gary said.

I looked over at Hunter, who was smiling. "Pretty cute," he said. "These little guys are probably super hungry by now, though. We have to figure out how to feed them."

"You don't just give them regular cat food?" Gary asked.

"Nope. There's a whole manual on how to do it. I guess you have to bottle feed them when they're this little."

Listening to them talk about feeding the cats snapped me to

attention and I whipped out the kitten manual. "Yup, and we need to get going on that. The manual says we need to weigh them to figure out how much to feed each kitten."

"We have a scale in the gym," Hunter said.

"And we'll need to warm up the milk," I added.

"We have a microwave in the office," Gary said.

I held up the manual and pointed to the warning printed in bold font. "It says not to microwave the formula."

"Then we'll just run it under hot water until it's the right temp. Can't be that hard," Hunter said. "Let's go."

Preparing the formula was quite an ordeal, but we managed to get it in the right amounts and the right temperatures. Hunter had the bright idea of weighing himself with and without the kitten rather than placing the little creature on the dirty scale, demonstrating practical use of his physics knowledge. He might've been a tough MMA fighter, but he was also pretty smart.

We had three bottles and three people, so we fed the kittens in two shifts. Even in my hand, the kittens felt small; they practically disappeared in Hunter's and Gary's. As powerful as they were, though, they were gentle with the little kitties, especially Hunter. He took particular joy in tickling the kitten's tummy after feeding it so it would burp.

"I think it farted!" Hunter said, laughing.

I looked over and narrowed my eyes.

"What? You said that was good!" he cried.

I shook my head. "You're such a little boy," I teased.

"Yeah, but you love it."

Gary took the kitten he was feeding and set it back down on its blanket in the box. "Okay guys, I gotta bounce. Get the kittens home safe."

"Will do," Hunter said. "Later dude."

We put our kittens back in their box shortly after Gary left. They all fell asleep almost immediately after being fed. Apparently kittens had to sleep *a lot*. I got a little sketchpad out of my purse and decided I would sketch them. Maybe the kittens could be a subject I could use for my portfolio.

"What do you want to name them?" I asked.

"I was thinking of naming them after MMA fighters. You know, Rampage, Iceman, that kind of thing."

"You want to name a kitten Rampage?"

"Yeah, after Quentin 'Rampage' Jackson. Then another one could be Iceman for Chuck 'The Iceman' Liddell, and then maybe Bones for Jon 'Bones' Jones."

"Hunter, they're kittens."

"Yeah, and they would have awesome names."

"I'm not taking care of a kitten named Rampage."

"Come on! How about this: there are three boys and three girls. I'll name the boy kittens and you can name the girl kittens. That's fair, right?"

I sighed. "Sure."

"Awesome. So those are my three names, what are yours?"

"I don't know, give me a minute to think."

Since Hunter chose fighter names, I figured I'd choose painter names. "Okay, I'm going to name one Georgia after Georgia O'Keefe."

"Ah, the woman who paints flowers that look like vaginas."

I chuckled. "Yeah, she's a good artist. Then I'll name another one Frida after Frida Kahlo."

"Is she a painter too?"

"Yeah, haven't you seen that movie with Salma Hayek? You know, the one where she has that unibrow thing going on?"

"Oh, that's right! I remember it now."

I struggled for a third name but couldn't think of another famous painter. Why did men have to be such dicks throughout history and not let women paint? After a minute, I gave up and decided to go another direction. "And then the third I'll call Taylor."

"Which painter is that?"

"It's not a painter. I'm naming her after Taylor Swift."

"The singer?" He looked genuinely perplexed.

"Yup. Got a problem with that?"

He laughed. "Other than the fact that she always blames the guy for screwing up the relationship— never taking responsibility for her own part—no I don't have a problem with that. I just didn't realize you liked Taylor Swift. Isn't she kind of for middle school and high school girls?"

I playfully stuck my tongue out at him. "Taylor Swift is universal, damn it! Her songs are catchy and fun. Plus, she does take responsibility. She's just never the one at fault."

"Fine, fine," he said, still laughing. "So Georgia, Frida, Taylor, Rampage, Iceman, and Bones. I like it. We'll figure out which kitten gets which name later. I'm gonna go find a bag to put all this stuff in."

He went away and I sketched the kittens, thinking about which one would get which name. It was only a couple minutes before he came back. He started putting the supplies into the gym bag he'd found.

"Ya know, you should come down to Bigg's to train with me sometime," Hunter said with a smile on his face. "I'll show you the ropes."

I shot him a wry grin. "I don't think I'm interested in a sport where I have to wrestle with gross sweaty guys."

"You think I'm gross?" he teased, taking mock offense.

"No, no, that's not what I meant." In fact, I loved the way he smelled when sweaty but I'd never tell him that. It would be too weird. "I guess I just don't want to get injured that's all."

"Don't worry, I won't hurt you. Since it's your first time, I'll be gentle," he crooned.

I slapped him on the arm playfully. "Shut up, Hunter. Why don't you just offer to show me the ways of the Kama Sutra while you're at it?"

"Whoa there! I never suggested that. You've got a filthy mind."

"*Sure,*" I replied sarcastically.

"But if you want me to show you how to do the 'rear naked choke', I can certainly do that." He wiggled his brows.

I laughed and rolled my eyes. "Is that even a real move?"

He laughed. "Real move, unfortunate name. No, but in all seriousness, it's fun and it's also a good workout."

"Yeah, I can imagine. But I've already got swim class to give me a good workout. Oh speaking of which, my instructor for my swim class is Mitch McHenry. He said he knows you."

Hunter paused for a moment then scoffed. "Yeah, he knows me."

The change in his tone was weird. "He said he was your ROTC

instructor."

"Yup."

"But you quit or something, right?"

He stopped. "Or something," he said after a moment.

It sounded like it was something painful, but I couldn't imagine what. "Were you kicked out or something? Mitch said your evaluations were excellent."

He took a deep breath. "Something came up and I couldn't do it anymore, so I stopped. Listen, we have to get these kittens home. Want to help me with the bag while I get the box?"

It was obvious he didn't want to talk about it, so I let the subject drop. His reluctance to share the whole story made me wonder, though. What was he hiding? Something that would stop him from doing ROTC had to be pretty big. The possibilities ran through my mind as we walked back to his apartment. I'd hidden things about my personal life from Hunter, but apparently he was hiding things about himself as well. Druggie parents, kicked out of ROTC despite top scores—it sounded like Hunter had a fucked up past like I did. I decided not to prod him on it though. He hadn't questioned me about my past even though it was clear I was hiding something bad from him.

Instead, I focused on the prospect of taking care of six adorable little furry babies with Hunter. It was going to be an adventure.

Chapter Twelve

HOME

Friday marked the end of the fifth week of classes. I stood outside the Floyd Hall parking lot, eagerly awaiting my aunt's arrival. She had called me asking if it was okay to park in the lot for the weekend or if she needed some sort of permit. After checking the signs posted on lamplights around the lot, I told her that she didn't need a permit on weekends.

I looked at the rows of cars and saw Aunt Caroline step out of the driver-side of a white minivan with a bumper sticker that said "#1 Soccer Mom."

"Aunt Caroline!" I waved at her to catch her attention as she pulled out a small suitcase from the trunk.

She turned around and smiled. "Lorrie!"

I walked over to help her carry her suitcase.

"You're looking good!" she said. "It's been what . . . a little over a month since I last saw you."

"Thanks! Yeah, it's been some time."

"I can see you're eating well at the dorms." She grinned.

My face heated as I laughed. Aunt Caroline was a good observer and wasn't afraid to call it as she saw it. But she wasn't mean-spirited or critical. She was in decent shape considering she had two boys, but by no means a Jessica Alba getting a six pack a few months after delivering. "Yeah, maybe a little too much."

"Hey if it feels good, it can't be wrong right? Bah, I wish I was your age again with your metabolism. I remember I'd be able to eat almost a whole pizza from the dining hall and not gain a single pound." She sighed. "Now, it's all about eating salads and dieting just to stay somewhat in shape. Ah, youth."

"Well, you look great Aunt Caroline."

"You're too sweet!"

We went back to my dorm room. Aunt Caroline opened up her suitcase and presented me with a gift bag filled with cookies and other delicious treats.

"I wasn't sure if you were eating enough, being busy with studying and everything, so I brought you this just in case," she said.

I laughed. "And here you were making fun of me for eating too much!"

"I know, but you can eat these guilt-free because it contains Auntie's love. Think of it as aspartame for cookies."

"Ah, Diet Cookies. Don't mind if I do then." I took a bite of a chocolate chip one and the cookie crumbled in my mouth in all its gooey glory. I could taste the love.

"So," she said, taking a bite of one herself. "How's everything going? Are you adjusting to student life again?"

"Yeah, it was kind of hard in the beginning but it's gotten easier. I'm getting into the groove, doing a lot more art."

"That's great to hear! Sometimes it takes a little while to adjust, it can be hard coming back from a long break. Classes going well?"

"So-so. Classes are tough but I'm passing at least. Psychology is kind of hard. Economics is harder. My other classes like sociology and art history aren't too bad though."

Aunt Caroline put her hand on my shoulder. "Don't feel bad, Lorrie. College isn't all about grades. Half of it is meeting new people and enjoying your experience. You should be making fond memories that you can look back on when you're older. When it comes to grades, what's important is that you're doing your best. Have you made any new friends besides Daniela?"

I thought about Hunter. Suddenly I remembered that I had to feed little Rampage and Taylor. Otherwise they'd get grumpy.

"Yes, actually. Speaking of which, I have to go over to his place to feed his kittens."

"A boy?"

I thought about correcting her by referring to Hunter as a 'man' but decided against it because no 'man' would be afraid of a black-and-white fly monster. "Yes, a boy."

"Ooh, tell me about him and the kittens."

I told Aunt Caroline a little about Hunter beyond him having short, dark hair—but not too much more. Certain parts—like girls propositioning him for a threesome—were definitely left out of the explanation. Having nothing else to do, Aunt Caroline joined me in going over to Hunter's apartment. I was wary of my aunt meeting Hunter and getting the wrong impression, but he was usually at the gym around this time. On the way, I asked her about how Uncle Stewart and the boys were doing and she said that Stewart was keeping busy with his job as a salesman and the boys—Billy and Joel—were keeping busy with soccer practice. It seemed like the Perkins household was as stable as always.

I began bottle-feeding the cats and Aunt Caroline helped out as well. When we were almost done, the door opened and Hunter stepped inside. He was wearing a black sweater with the hood up and jeans and was carrying a gym bag in one hand; he looked like he'd showered recently.

Oh no.

"Hey Lorrie!" He waved at me kneeling in the kitchen, kitten on my lap. "Oh, hello," he said, noticing my aunt beside me.

I put Bones down and stood up. "Hey Hunter. Oh this is my aunt, Caroline." Hunter smiled and extended his hand. Aunt Caroline got up and shook it, and returned the smile. "I didn't expect you to be back from the gym already."

"Yeah, I got done early with training today," he said as he set his bag down and removed the hood of his sweater. "So you guys just feeding the kittens?"

"Yep," I replied, giving Bones a pet on the head as he mewed at me.

"So Hunter," my aunt chirped. "Lorrie's told me a lot about you. It sounds like you two are good friends."

He grinned. "Yeah, I'd say so. Wouldn't you agree, Lorrie?"

I tried to hide my smile by rolling my eyes at Hunter. "I'd say decent friends. We get on each other's nerves sometimes."

"Maybe not enough," he replied.

Aunt Caroline was too busy admiring Hunter's appearance to pay close attention to our banter. "Hunter, you're very tall and handsome. You even have tattoos I see." She pointed at the collar of his sweater. "Has anyone told you that you look like Tom Hardy?"

Oh no, Aunt Caroline noticed his tattoos.

Hunter laughed. "Yeah, I get that a lot. Thank you for the compliments."

I was expecting Aunt Caroline to promptly pull me back to the dorm or even back to Indiana and lock me inside my room, so what she said next came as a surprise. "Have you considered dating Lorrie?"

"A-Aunt Caroline!" I spluttered. "Why would you ask such a thing?"

Hunter smiled widely. A little too widely. "We've had a discussion or two about it but we're just friends at the moment."

"I see." Aunt Caroline looked at me gauging my reaction. She must've noticed how red my face was. "So tell me more about those tattoos you have," she said to Hunter, changing the subject.

Hunter pushed up his sleeve showing us his bulging biceps and the tattoos on his arm. "I don't have anything too crazy. Just some simple designs."

"That's some cool ink! I really like that hammer!" Aunt Caroline then lifted up her sleeve and showed us a tattoo on her arm. "The reason I ask is because I got one recently myself." I looked at her arm and saw an etched soccer ball with big letters in front of it that said 'MOM'.

"Awesome!" Hunter said, smiling.

"Whoa, Aunt Caroline! I never knew you had a tattoo. How come you never showed me?"

"I just got it recently, Lorrie. Well, me and a few other moms on the team got tattoos. We wanted to show our support for our boys."

I stared at her, dumbfounded. A bumper sticker was one thing, but a tattoo? When I thought about it further, I realized that Aunt Caroline did have a bit of a wild side so I shouldn't be too surprised. She was probably the one who suggested it and got the other mothers on board.

The rest of the evening went by without anymore shocking surprises. Aunt Caroline and I stayed at Hunter's a bit longer to play with the kittens and hang out with Hunter. Hunter was being uncharacteristically flattering and entertaining to Aunt Caroline and me, taking every opportunity to flash his tattoos and biceps.

It wasn't until dinner time that we got back to my dorm.

"I'm happy that things are going well for you Lorrie. Hunter seems like a nice boy. Seems like he really cares about you." She had a sly smile. "I know you're reluctant to admit it, but I know you have feelings for him, Lorrie. I can tell. Maybe you should think about talking to him about those feelings sometime. A guy like him is probably not going to be available for long, you know."

"Thanks," I said sarcastically. I was still a little annoyed by Aunt Caroline asking Hunter if he wanted to date me. "I'm actually surprised you're pushing me to date. I thought you'd be wrangling me back to Indiana once you saw Hunter's tats."

"Oh Lorrie. I know I'm sometimes a little overprotective of you but I also want you to live your life. As long as you're not drinking or doing drugs or sleeping around with guys left and right, I think it's good for you to have some fun."

I raised a brow skeptically. "I'll keep that in mind."

"I'm just saying, I know you're still adjusting to school but I don't want you to be afraid of taking chances. Worst comes to worst, it doesn't work out. Have some fun." She grinned. "You've always got me and Stewart and the boys behind you. You've got our home you can always come back to when things get tough. So feel free to spread your wings. I just don't want you to regret not seizing the opportunity when it's there, that's all."

I sighed. "Yeah, yeah. I know Hunter's a nice guy. I just want to go at my own pace with things though."

"Sure, sure, Lorrie."

We spent the rest of the night hanging out. On Sunday, I showed her around campus and we had fun getting ice cream from Clyde's. Then she went back home Sunday night. It was a bittersweet goodbye. Although she had embarrassed me in front of Hunter, I was really glad she visited. With her surprising approval of Hunter as a potential boyfriend, I began to think that maybe that wasn't such a bad idea.

Chapter Thirteen

THE SCAM

I dropped by Hunter's apartment regularly the next couple days to feed the kittens. They were growing by the day but still so tiny. Even though feeding them by bottle was cute, I would be glad when they could finally eat solid food. Hunter and I had taken the kittens to the vet yesterday and they said it would still be a few more weeks of bottle-feeding.

The way Hunter and my Aunt Caroline had interacted still puzzled me. She had always been so overprotective, but Hunter and his tattoos seemed to impress her. I still couldn't believe she'd gotten that soccer mom tattoo.

Thinking about all this made it hard to concentrate on psychology. Wednesday had come around and I had managed to drag myself to class with Daniela, but that didn't mean I was really there. I was sketching Georgia's adorable furry face in my notes when Daniela elbowed me.

"You should pay attention, this is interesting," she whispered.

"Sorry, I've been distracted. What's up?"

"Muller's talking about how our emotions during an event affect our memory of it."

"Oh, that does sound cool. Can I borrow your notes?"

"Sure. What's bugging you, anyway?"

People were starting to give us dirty looks for chatting during lecture. I debated in my mind whether I should tell her I was developing feelings for Hunter. "I'll tell you later," I whispered.

She nodded. I spent the rest of class doing my best to pay attention, but it was hard to follow after missing the first part. Guess I'd have to copy Daniela's notes again before the midterm. I went back to sketching Georgia. At least that was turning out well.

Daniela had to rush to meet with her group before a presentation in Geology, so I said goodbye and headed to the bathroom. I was hanging my purse up in the stall when I heard two girls enter with noisy footwear. They were chatting excitedly and quickly. I was preparing to ignore their gossip when I caught two words: "kittens" and "Hunter."

"Did you see how little they were?" the girl with flats said.

"Oh my god, I know! And he looked so cute holding them. He's *so* hot," her friend wearing boots replied.

"I knowwwww!" Flats gushed.

"I've never seen that side of him before. He always seems so tough. He's like an M&M: hard on the outside but soft on the inside."

Flats laughed. "Maybe. But I like to think of him as a Snickers: long and hard." They both laughed.

These girls were talking like they knew Hunter intimately. I started to fear the worst.

"Yeah, it's too bad we didn't get a chance to have sex with him," Boots said.

I carefully released a breath of relief. Hunter had a reputation for being a player with women. Daniela had warned me multiple times and I had my own suspicions. But after becoming friends with Hunter, I realized he was a good-hearted guy who liked to be alone most of the time or only with close friends like me and Gary. Other than the threesome proposition at the hockey game—which he turned down—I hadn't seen any signs of him living up to his reputation. Gossip could be stupid. These girls were stupid.

"Do you think he uses the kittens to pick up girls?"

"I wonder if he's trying to be ironic with the whole using pussy to get pussy you know?" She laughed. "That's so Hunter's sense of humor! He doesn't need to but I don't see how any girl could resist him after seeing him with those kitties. I mean, it definitely worked on us. I was like so ready to scratch his pants off!"

"Yeah, me too." They both laughed.

God, these girls made me want to hurl. Fortunately—but unfortunately for them—I couldn't see Hunter ever going for these bimbos. It's because of these types of girls that Hunter often wore hooded sweaters to hide his identity in public.

"At least we got to give him a blowjob," Flats said.

My stomach dropped. Did I hear that correctly? Hunter got a blowjob from them? *What the fuck.*

I suddenly felt light headed. Surely I misheard her or she was joking. I had to have misunderstood her words. "Blowjob" could mean she'd been cutting his hair and had blow-dried his head after a rinse. Maybe these girls were part-time hair-stylists. Misinterpretation and jumping to conclusions was how rumors got started in the first place.

Boots chuckled. "Yeah, his cock has literally got to be the biggest on campus! I didn't think it was possible but it was somehow long enough for both of us to suck on it at the same time!"

I fought against the urge to retch. The sordid details were too damning to ignore. How could Hunter be using his kittens to pick up girls? Our kittens, really. I was over there just about every day taking care of those things. And he was using them to get girls to suck his cock? I was so disgusted I wanted to vomit.

"Oh, and did you hear their names?" Flats giggled. "Rampage? How funny is that?"

"He said that girl Lorrie named the females. Are they like together?"

My heart pounded as I tried to steady my breathing.

"They have to be, right? I mean they have kittens together. Even still, Hunter's never really 'with' girls. I mean, he let us give him a BJ."

"Yeah. So weird. He must like the tragic emo type. I guess he's probably as much with her as he ever is with anyone?"

Her friend laughed. "Well, now that I think about it, that's not entirely true. He was with Ada for a while during freshman year and I don't think he ever cheated on her."

"Oh right, I never heard anything either, but who knows with him? It's been a pretty long time since they dated, anyway."

Who's Ada? I was tempted to ask them what Ada's last name was so I could look her up but decided against blowing my cover.

"Okay, how do my eyes look?" Boots said.

"Great! Let's go before we're late."

I heard footsteps, and then the door opened and closed. Bending down to look under the stall, I scanned the room for feet, but there were none. They were gone. I finished up in the bathroom and headed out. My face was hot with rage; it took all of my effort to try and fix my face in an expression that didn't make me look like a deranged person. How could he do that to me? How?

Hunter texted me just as I entered my dorm after my drawing class. It was a little after three.

Hey are you coming by later to take care of the kittens? Rampage misses you ;-)

I stared at my phone, angry that he still thought he was tricking me into taking care of his kittens for him. How long would he have kept it up if I hadn't found out? Months? I thought about giving him the typical avoidance treatment but decided I was going to be slightly more mature this time.

Find some other girl to take care of them.

Right as I hit 'send', I realized I should've made myself clearer so I sent another text immediately afterward.

Asshole.

Seconds later, my phone buzzed, but I put it on silent. I didn't want to deal with his bullshit just then. If he wanted to try and explain his actions, I was going to make him think *long* and *hard* about what he had to say—like a fucking Snickers bar.

As soon as I got to my suite I threw my bag down on the futon and began to cry. I knew Kate and Petra were probably at the gym at this time so I didn't care about letting loose. It was the first time I'd cried in a while and it surprised me that I was having this stupid reaction to what I'd heard earlier. Just when I opened myself up to someone, he stabbed me in the back with a smiley in his text message.

Daniela came out from her room and saw me. Her face fell as her eyes tracked the tears falling down my cheeks.

"Oh my god Lorrie! What happened?"

I took a deep breath and sat down on the futon. She took a seat beside me and took my hand in hers.

"So I was in the bathroom today and I heard some girls gossiping . . ." I sighed deeply.

"Oh no," Daniela said. "They weren't talking crap about you were they?"

"No, worse. They were talking about how they went over to Hunter's apartment to play with the kittens."

She looked at me as though she were expecting me to go on. "Umm . . . am I missing a part of the story? Kittens are kind of made to be played with."

"They were saying how cute the kittens were and how it made Hunter so much hotter. Then Hunter got them to give him a blowjob . . ."

"Oh Lorrie, I'm so sorry . . . Wait, did he use the kittens as bait to get him a blowjob?"

The reasoning sounded ridiculous when I heard it out loud, but it was a difficult conclusion to ignore. "I . . . I don't know!"

"Oh my god!"

I opened my mouth to respond but was interrupted by a knock at the suite door. Daniela got up from the futon and cracked open the door.

"Is Lorrie here?" I heard the voice behind the door say. It was Hunter. He must've come to my dorm since I refused to answer my phone.

Daniela looked at me, eyebrows raised. I could tell her to shut the door in Hunter's face, but I decided that I should at least hear him out. Maybe he had a good explanation for what those girls said and I was just overreacting. I begrudgingly nodded.

"Yes, she's here," Daniela said.

"Can I come in?"

Daniela checked with me. I raised my brows.

She looked back at Hunter.

"Please?" he said.

I nodded and Daniela opened the door for him. "I'm going to leave you two alone," she said. She turned to me. "I'll be in my room."

She walked out of the common area and closed her door.

Hunter entered the suite, lacking the usual swagger in his step. He was shuffling his feet like a zombie. I couldn't be sure but I interpreted it as the distinct walk of a guilty man. He eyed me carefully, confusion on his face, his mouth a thin line. He was wearing a brown leather jacket over his usual gray hoodie, dark jeans that hinted at the powerful legs beneath, and tan winter boots with traces of snow clinging to the laces. The backpack slung over one shoulder seemed full of books.

"You sure came over here quickly," I grumbled. Seeing his gorgeous self in person made me think about how those girls must've felt when they were giving him head. I grabbed a futon pillow and squeezed it angrily over my chest.

He squinted to get a better look at me almost as if he'd just woken up from a nap. "I came as quick as I could."

Hunter shifted on his feet, adjusting his balance. Although his speech seemed fine, I was beginning to suspect he was inebriated. "Have you been drinking Hunter?" I snapped. "It would certainly explain a lot."

"No, no . . . I'm just tired that's all." He sighed. "I was studying in Wheatley when I texted you," he said, sounding frustrated. "Lorrie, what's the matter?"

God, I could barely even look at him. Hunter wasn't just a weirdo; he was a sick person. "It's hard for me to even look at you after what you did."

"Huh? What the hell? What did I do?" His shuffling feet came to a stop near the TV. He kept his distance.

"Don't pretend like you don't know. I fell for your bullshit before, I tried not to listen to the rumors about you. Maybe I was just stupidly naive to think you were a decent guy despite all the red flags, but now it's all clear to me. Congratulations, Hunter. You're a fucking asshole."

"What the hell, Lorrie. If you're going to accuse me of something, say it for god's sake!"

I threw my pillow at him but he casually swatted it away. "You used kittens to get a blowjob!" I screamed.

His sleepy eyes widened. "W-What?!"

"I heard two girls saying you invited them over to pet the kittens and they gave you a blowjob."

"Dammit, I thought you said you didn't listen to rumors," he snapped. "Who did you hear that from anyway?"

"It wasn't a rumor Hunter!" I shouted. "It was a first-hand account! I was in the bathroom and I heard them talking about how they went over to your place to see the kittens and how hot you looked with Rampage. They said they both went down on you at the same time—I don't even know how that's possible!" Just saying it almost made me gag. "Go ahead, tell me it's not true. Tell me I'm being delirious and creating imaginary cats and imaginary blowjobs in my head. Tell me I'm wrong."

His mouth was a thin line. "I told you I don't like talking about that kind of personal stuff. I keep my sex life private."

His obvious deflection made me seethe. "Jesus Hunter! If that's not an admission then I don't know what is. You make me sick! To think you were using them . . . using poor Taylor, Georgia, and Frida to get your cock sucked. Somebody should send you to prison where you can fight all day and have your balls rot off."

"Lorrie!" he yelled. He leaned an elbow on top of the TV to brace himself and rubbed his forehead with his other hand. "Let's get one thing straight: I did not use the kittens to get me a blowjob! And I never would. It's so ridiculous, are you even listening to yourself? It pisses me off to even think about it, let alone have you accuse me of it. I don't need kittens to get me a blowjob. Girls would give me head even if I had a fucking pet rock!"

"Oh wow. The true Hunter shows his colors. So that's what you've been hiding in your closet huh? You're an egomaniac and a sexaholic. The compassionate-loner-weirdo thing you have going on was all a facade."

"Dude, Lorrie. I'd never tell anyone details about my sex life. I just told you that because we're friends and you're accusing the hell outta me! What's your deal anyway? Why are you so worked up over me getting a blowjob? You were the one who wanted to just be friends. Are you telling me you're jealous?"

"You wish!" I yelled, my face heating from embarrassment. "I admit I might've been attracted to you before Hunter but after this . . . after this I don't even know if I want to be your friend."

"You don't mean that," he said somberly.

I threw my hands up in frustration, beginning to realize that I was more mad about the fact that Hunter got a BJ than the silly idea that he exploited the kittens. "Goddammit Hunter! Why did you get a blowjob from those two girls? Jesus, it wasn't even just one girl, it was two at the same time!"

"Lorrie... what they did wasn't really... it didn't mean anything to me. They don't really mean anything to me. Not like you mean to me."

"Wow, now you have two accolades: Not only do you apparently have the biggest cock on campus, you're also the most insensitive guy on campus! I was pissed off at those girls before, but now I'm starting to feel bad for them. You used them."

"It isn't like that!" he shouted but then his voice softened. "They knew what they were getting into. I've always been upfront with girls about any arrangement we have. We were all consenting adults. There were no mixed signals."

"Whatever," I scoffed. "How many girls have you seduced since the beginning of the semester?"

"... I've only been with two girls—Lauren and Teri—they were the ones that came over and saw the cats. And to be clear: we didn't have sex. I knew it would upset you, so I didn't have sex with them. God, I can't believe I'm even telling you their names. I'm breaking my rules for you, Lorrie."

"You can break your dick while you're at it." Seeing no other pillows around, I settled for crossing my arms over my chest. "You thought having sex with them would upset me and so you settled for a BJ? Seriously, what goes through that fucked up brain of yours Hunter? You think I see imaginary cats? Well, I think you see imaginary logic."

"I'm sorry, Lorrie. I needed to feel something . . . I wasn't in a right state of mind. I'm a bit of a mess right now. It's stupid but it's the only thing I know that helps . . . I'm just trying to put myself back together."

"What are you talking about? You seemed fine just a few days ago when you met my aunt. How could you go from flexing and making jokes to a Danny Downer? You know what, nevermind. I don't know and I don't wanna know. We discussed it before: we both have issues that we don't want to share. And that's fine. All I'll say is this: I don't care who you sleep with or who you don't sleep with but get BJs from. We're just friends, so why should I care?"

"Well I care! I care about you. I care about what you think. I consider you more than just a friend, Lorrie. You're a close friend. You mean more to me than any other girl. You're like the female version of Gary to me."

"What does that even mean?"

"It means that you being upset with me is not something I can brush off. I can ignore the gossip about me, I can take the rumors. But I can't take you being mad at me. How can I make this right, Lorrie? I fucked up big time. How can I make it up to you?"

Although I was still mad at him, my heart broke to see him so distressed over things I said. I sighed, realizing I really cared about Hunter and didn't want to lose him as a friend. "Okay, I admit hearing you getting a BJ from two girls pissed me off. It still pisses me off. But that's my own issue. Even though we're just friends, I can't help being a little jealous. It's irrational, I know, and that's my fault . . . I'm sorry for that. I have to find a way to get over it. You're entitled to do whatever you want in your private life." I exhaled deeply. "I'm sorry Hunter, I'll try to keep my jealousy under wraps."

He shook his head. "Alright, check this out, Lorrie. First thing I'm gonna do is make it up to the kittens by buying them Tiki Cat Gourmet. I'm also gonna get them one of those running waterfall dispensers. I'm gonna pamper the hell outta them. Just watch me. And second, I'm gonna cut that shit out with girls. It's as much for you as it is for me." He sighed. "I've been fucking up a lot, way before I even met you, and I need to get my shit together. I'm glad you're here to give me a kick in the ass."

I took a deep breath, trying to digest Hunter's admission that he was a messed up person. I felt bad for causing to him to admit that. I also felt bad that maybe Hunter was being overly hard on himself. "Those ideas for the cats sound good. As for what you do with other girls, really it's your decision. I don't want to be a terrible friend to you. I'm sorry I said all those nasty things. Maybe I'm just getting stressed out about midterms coming up."

He walked over and put his arms around me, squeezing me tightly. I squeezed him back just as tight. "You know what I bet will cheer us both up?"

I knew his answer but played along anyway. "What?"

"Rammmmppaaaaagggee!" he bellowed, his muscular arms spread wide and his voice deep.

Despite still being a little upset, I giggled; Hunter loved to pretend like Rampage could talk, but he always did it in that voice. The contrast between the little kitten and Hunter's booming voice never failed to make me laugh. Rampage was definitely Hunter's favorite.

"Do you think your roommate would want to come?" he asked.

I shrugged as Daniela's voice came from her room. "Yes she would!"

Had she been listening to the whole thing? I turned and saw her emerge, purse in hand. Hunter looked at me.

"Okay, let's go," I said, eyeing my best friend suspiciously.

"Yay!" Daniela squealed. "Oh my gosh, I bet these things are so cute."

"You have no idea," Hunter said, standing up. "Get ready to have your chest explode."

The squeal Daniela made when she saw the kittens was higher pitched than I thought was humanly possible. Hunter's hands shot up to cover his ears, but I wasn't so lucky. They stayed ringing for what felt like several minutes.

"Oh my god look at the little kittens!" she cooed. "They're so tiny!"

She got down on her knees and tapped the rough wood floor. "Come here kitty!"

One of the kittens crept up to her unsteadily. They had just started being able to walk with any success a week or so prior. Before that, they had mostly squirmed, slept, and pooped. Now they'd added wobbling around on their feet to that list, and we were trying to get them to start using the litter box.

I looked more closely at the pattern on the kitten's back. It had a little white patch on its brown fur shaped a little like a heart. That one was Taylor.

Taylor came up to Daniela's outstretched hand and purred as she stroked her back. Some of the other kittens began to creep out from their sleepiness to see what all the commotion was about.

"How old are they?" Daniela asked.

I looked at Hunter, who shrugged. "We think they're like five weeks," I said.

She nodded. "They're the smallest kittens I've ever seen. Can I hold her?"

"Sure. If she'll let you. Taylor can be a little feisty."

Daniela stuck her lip out and made a pouty face at me, then she turned her attention back to Taylor and picked her up. Taylor meowed in protest but didn't scratch.

"See, she's fine!" Daniela said.

I smiled, skeptical how long that would last. When I looked over at Hunter he was focused on his phone.

"Hey Lorrie, Gary wants to come over. That cool?"

"Why not?" I said.

He shrugged and tapped a reply on his phone. "I don't know, just checking." He put his phone in his pocket. "Now where's Rampage?"

I shook my head and laughed. "If I didn't know better I'd swear he's the only one you ever pay attention to."

Hunter walked over to the box and found a kitten with a white patch that went from between its eyes all the way to the base of its neck. He was a little sleepy but crawled up to him anyway and rolled on his back. That was typical Rampage.

Hunter scooped him and up and held him in his hand, the kitten's head cradled in his fingers. He tickled Rampage's belly and the little guy squirmed in approval, trying to grab onto Hunter's finger with its tiny paws.

"I have enough love to go around," Hunter said. "But just look at him? He's just so adorable." He held the kitten up for us to admire. Then Hunter's face fell and he rushed to the litter box.

"God damn it Rampage!" he said.

"What?" Daniela asked worriedly. I already knew the answer .

Hunter plopped Rampage into the litter box, then got up to go to the kitchen sink. "He pooped on me!"

I giggled when Daniela turned to me in horror then down on Taylor. "They aren't trained?" she asked me.

"Daniela, these kittens are little babies. Of course they aren't trained. They've only been able to use the litter box at all for a few days."

"So she could poop on me at any moment?"

"Yup," Hunter said from the kitchen. "I don't know how kittens so small can poop so much, but they do."

Daniela wrinkled her nose.

"Hey Lorrie," Hunter said, "can you come help me with the kitten milk? It's just about time for them to eat."

"Sure," I said.

I got up at the same time as Daniela, who was gently putting Taylor into the litter box. Apparently she didn't want kitten poop on her hands. I walked into the kitchen, opened the fridge, and pulled out the kitten formula while Hunter finished washing his hands. When I closed the door I saw Hunter had pinned a drawing to his fridge with a magnet.

It was the sketch I had done of a man with a fly's head. He had said he liked it, but I didn't realize he liked it enough to put it up in his apartment. The fact he had put it up made me feel good, both about my artistic abilities and about Hunter's feelings toward our friendship.

As I stood looking at the drawing, I felt him come up behind me. The warmth from his body made the light hairs on my arms stand on end. I felt my skin prickle at his presence.

"We didn't leave any syringes in there, did we?" he asked.

"No, I think those are in the cupboard with the bottles."

"Okay. Are you alright?"

I blinked and turned to him. His eyes were narrowed in concern. "Yeah, I was just admiring this awesome drawing on your fridge."

His face relaxed into a smile. "Oh. Yeah, the artist is really something. I look forward to seeing more of her work."

"I think she's working on a series involving kittens."

He grinned. "Sounds cool."

"But if she's going to continue that series, these kittens need to be fed," I said, stepping around him and going to a cupboard to look for a sauce pan. We needed to boil some water to warm up the kitten milk and sterilize the rubber nipples.

I found one and got the water going on the stove. We returned to the common area to find Daniela gingerly petting another kitten. Judging by its fur it looked like Bones.

"Good lord," I said. "It's just kitten poop. You're petting that thing like it might sting you."

She turned to me and frowned. "I don't want to get it on my sweater! This is dry clean only."

Hunter scoffed. "I can get you a hoodie if you want to wear it while feeding them. Or a blanket maybe."

"You're the one who yelled when he pooped on you!" she said.

He shrugged. "Yeah, it kind of sucks when something poops on you. I do stuff all the time knowing it's going to suck every once in a while. Doesn't mean I don't do it for the awesome parts." He walked over to where Rampage had plopped down next to the litter box and picked him up. "Isn't that right Rampage?"

He held the kitten and walked over to Daniela, waving Rampage around like he was flying. Rampage didn't seem to mind. "Raaaammmmmpppaaaaggggggggeeee!"

He tried to set Rampage onto Daniela's head, still holding onto him, but Daniela shot up and ran away. Hunter chased after her laughing. "Rampage is going to get you!" he yelled then turned to Rampage and softened his tone. "Aren't you Rampage?"

Rampage meowed and we all laughed. He looked a little annoyed that he was flying instead of sleeping.

Gary came over while we were waiting for the water to boil, then he helped the kittens. Daniela eventually braved the potential for kitten poop and fed one of the cats too. She came away poop free. Gary wasn't so lucky, but he was a champ about it.

The whole evening ended up being a very pleasant time. Hanging out with the three of them was so comfortable and fun in a non-stressful way. I was beginning to look forward to enjoying the rest of the semester with both old and new friends.

Chapter Fourteen

CUPID

The beginning of February came and went. Before anyone knew it, we were at that dreaded mid-February holiday. I sat at a table by myself on the second floor of the Barnyard looking idly over the railing at the bustle of student activity below, trying not to gag from seeing all pink and red Valentine's Day decorations around me. I'd finished my lunch and was waiting for Daniela to meet me after class.

I spotted her in jeans and a forest-green sherpa jacket through the fifty-foot glass windows long before she reached the entrance. I waved to her and she came up the stairs with a smile. "Hey girl, what's wrong?" she said, setting her backpack down and taking a seat across from me. "You don't look so hot."

"Yeah, sorry. I'm just allergic to Valentine's Day."

Daniela flipped her sandy-blonde hair back and removed her jacket. "I know what you mean. Valentine's Day is lame." She put her finger up. "Hold on, I'm starving. Lemme get some food first. Otherwise, my belly's gonna revolt." I waited a few minutes and she came back with a tray containing a large cheeseburger topped with all the fixings and a huge plate of fries.

I noticed that we were the only two people in the cafeteria not wearing a shade of red. It was kind of surprising that Daniela wasn't decked out in hearts and arrows, actually.

"You know Daniela, I was kind of expecting you to be wearing a pink tutu and one of those heart shaped tiara's on your head."

She scrunched her face at me. "Meanie. Just because I wanted to celebrate Valentine's Day in style two years ago doesn't mean that I feel the same way about it now."

I raised an eyebrow, skeptical. "Really? What's changed?"

She shrugged, "Valentine's Day is just a construct of the media-entertainment complex, designed to keep the poor girl down."

Whatever answer I was expecting from her, it wasn't that. "Uh … what?"

She looked at me waving the fry in her hand for emphasis. "Think about it. The entire day is designed to make you feel shitty if you're single. It's even worse if you're seeing someone, because then you feel obligated to spend money."

"Um, I take it things aren't going well with Cody?"

"Cody is old news," she puffed then rolled her eyes. "Turns out he was a total loser. You win some, you lose some." She shrugged then dipped a fry into a dish of ketchup.

"You don't seem too broken up about it."

"You know how it is, easy-come, easy-go."

She didn't seem too eager to talk about it, so I didn't ask her to elaborate. A few tables behind Daniela, a bulky guy in a tight frat t-shirt was going around table to table with a basket in his hand. After chatting with a group of starry-eyed freshman, he started coming our way. He got to our table and smiled at Daniela, his cheeks dimpling. A red heart had been painted on his left cheekbone.

"Hey, ladies, want to buy some chocolates for your Valentines? P-K-D is raising money for heart disease."

Phi Kappa Delta? Wasn't that Gary's frat?

Daniela finished chewing her mouthful of cheeseburger, before wiping the corner of her mouth daintily with a paper napkin. She looked up at him, her eyes glinting mischievously. Uh-oh. That was her tiger-stalking-her-prey look. I had a feeling I was about to get a demonstration of "easy-come". I leaned back, looking forward to the show.

"Hey cutie, what's your name?" she said, batting her eyes at him.

Nice Daniela, real subtle.

The guy licked his lips before answering. "Jeff. I'm Jeff."

"Hi Jeff, I'm Daniela, and this is Lorrie. Unfortunately, us two ladies don't have Valentines to give chocolates to. Now I might be interested in getting some chocolates for myself, but … I think I'll need a little extra sweetness with my chocolate."

He stared at her dumbly. "Uh . . . you can sprinkle some extra sugar on top of them I guess."

I rolled my eyes and shot a look at Daniela. Was she serious? What could she possibly see in this guy besides his dimples and muscles?

Daniela put her hand in front of her mouth and mock whispered to him, "Put your number on the wrapper and I'll buy one from you."

The frat guy scrunched his brow, seeming to consider it for a second, before realizing that he was being hit on. His eyes suddenly lit up in realization, and he nodded quickly with a smile.

"Yeah, oh yeah. Okay." He scribbled something on one of the chocolate bars before handing it to Daniela. She rummaged a dollar out of her purse and handed it to him with a wink.

After the guy walked away to a different table, we both erupted in giggles.

"Oh my god Daniela, you're impossible! You were just telling me about how you hated Valentine's Day!"

"I still hate Valentine's Day, but that doesn't mean I can't use it to my advantage." She picked up her burger again, taking another big bite.

I shook my head still laughing softly. "So are you going to call him?" I asked her.

She chewed thoughtfully. "Maybe, I don't know yet. I like to keep my options open. Besides, what if someone hotter comes along selling flowers before the end of the day?"

I wanted to say something back to her, but the alarm on my phone played its melody reminding me that it was time to feed the kittens.

"That's the sound of kittens crying for their Mommy," I said, turning off the alarm and putting my phone back into my pocket.

"Feeding time at Hunter's?"

"Yep."

"Hey you know, what if Hunter was your Valentine? Or if you were his? I know you guys have been pretty chummy lately taking care of the kittens and all." She nudged me.

I rolled my eyes. "There's only one problem: there's nothing romantic going on between us. Also, what happened to you warning me to be careful around Hunter?"

"I've been brainwashed by the Hunter-bad-boy complex," she confessed. "Behind his reputation, he's actually been a good guy. I'm thinking I misjudged him."

"Yeah, I might've misjudged him as well—although being friends with him has had its rough spots, it hasn't been the trouble I thought it'd be."

"Have you considered moving further with him?"

"Eh . . . we're two friends jointly caring for six furry babies. We could be Valentine's Day Buddies but that wouldn't be true to Saint Valentine's spirit. It'd be like if you took your brother to prom as your date."

Daniela opened her mouth and put a finger inside to simulate gagging. "Yuck! On the other hand, if my brother looked like Hunter. . ." She grinned. "I'm not going to say what would happen but I'll just suggest that there might be some incest going on in the Stauffer household."

"Ewww. Aren't there laws against that?"

"Not even the law can stop love," she said playfully.

"What about your parents? Knowing your dad, he'd probably kick the both of you out of the house. Lack of a home can certainly stop love."

"Well, of course the hypothetical Hunter Stauffer and I would keep our relationship on the down-low. On the outside, we'd seem like a normal brother and sister pair; we may or may not kiss each other on the lips in public—depends on social norms. Beyond that though, society wouldn't be ready to accept us."

"Okay, well Hunter is basically like an older brother to me. And I hate to disappoint you by not jumping on the incest train but I ain't a 'ho that has sex with her bro.'" I nudged her back.

"Whatever," she scoffed as if I was acting pretentious then took a sip of her drink.

"Besides, I'm sure Hunter has his pick of Valentines. Girls probably give him roses and chocolates instead of the other way around. It's not hard to believe considering you'd go as far as to break state laws for him."

She laughed. "I was just joshin ya, Lorrie. Hunter's all *yours*." She gave an exaggerated wink that made me uncomfortable. "But you're probably right about girls wanting to woo him. Anyway, it's fun to dream about opportunities that'll never arise."

"Maybe. But it's also fun just being buddies."

"To each, her own. Anyway, I don't want to keep you from the kids. I'll see you back at the dorms."

I left the Barnyard feeling better about Valentine's Day. Despite the odd direction the conversation took, it raised my spirit. Somehow Daniela always knew how to make me feel more upbeat. The walk across campus to Hunter's place was quick, even with the two inches of snow crunching beneath my boots. When I reached his apartment, I unlocked the door, and stamped my boots on the welcome mat.

I could hear the kittens meowing already in their box so I quickly opened the fridge for the formula and started heating it up. I spent the next half hour feeding them. It wouldn't have taken so long if Taylor hadn't kept trying to climb out of the box after she had already been fed. They were already growing so big, I could barely hold their entire bodies in my hands.

The six little monsters finally fell asleep in their box, and I started cleaning up. Just then, Hunter came through the front door.

"Hey Lorrie, Happy Valentine's Day!" I heard him yell as he came in.

Shit, I almost forgot. If it was Valentine's Day, Hunter might have brought a girl back. My heart beat faster. How awkward would it be to meet his Valentine? I turned around quickly, blood rushing to my face, but it was only Hunter standing in the doorway, letting in a blast of winter air.

He was wearing a black sweatshirt and thick sweatpants: he must've just come back from the gym. I let out a slow breath of relief. He wasn't with anyone.

"Hey Hunter. Don't even remind me."

"Oh, okay. I don't really care, but I figured girls liked Valentine's Day. How are the kittens?"

"Just fed 'em, they're all sleeping now."

He walked through the apartment to his bedroom. When he

emerged again, he was shirtless. His body glistened with a thin sheen of sweat sending an unwelcome surge of awareness through me.

"Come on Hunter, do you always need to show off your muscles?"

He laughed, "Hey sorry, I wanted to get out of my sweaty clothes ASAP. You have any Valentine's Day plans?"

"Why? Are you trying to ask me to be your Valentine?" I crossed my arms, ready for whatever he was going to try to throw at me next. It would be difficult to top being half-naked, but I wouldn't put it past him.

Hunter held his hands up in surrender. "Whoa whoa, slow down there Lorrie. I was just going to ask if you wanted to stick around and hang out. Gary is coming over in a bit. We were just going to have some beers and watch TV."

I wasn't expecting Hunter to be lacking dates for Valentine's Day so I was surprised that he wasn't going out.

"Really? You're hanging out with Gary on Valentine's? Are you sure there's nothing going on between you two?" I teased him.

He smirked at me. "Well you'll have to stick around if you want to find out. So what do you say?"

I giggled at the thought of the two of them wrestling naked like ancient Greek combatants. "Sure. Sounds like fun."

Hunter went into the bathroom to take his shower, and I plopped down on the couch to watch TV. Bridezillas was on—an appropriate show for the occasion. I watched the brides for a while, but I couldn't stop thinking about why Hunter wasn't going out for a date on Valentine's Day.

After he finished his shower, he walked over to the couch. He was wearing a tight white t-shirt and a new pair of gray sweatpants. His hammer tattoo peeked out beneath his sleeve when he took a seat beside me and my heart did a pitter patter. I wanted to shift further away on the couch but I was already squeezed against the armrest.

"What are you watching?" he asked, his eyes fixed on the TV.

"Bridezillas."

He remained silent while watching a group of bridesmaids console the bride who was crying over being unable to squeeze into her dress on the last fitting because she had gained weight from tasting too many wedding cake options.

"You like this kinda stuff?" he asked casually.

"Uh, yeah!" I chimed.

He continued watching, seemingly mesmerized. "Why?"

"It's a guilty pleasure. It's like you know it's bad, but you can't stop watching. It's kind of like watching a train wreck."

He hummed to himself in thought as the bride began sucking on her thumb like a toddler to ease her anxiety. "Yeah, I can see the appeal. I wanna stop watching but I'm not sure I can. You think you'd ever be like that?"

"What? No. No way. I'd be way more reasonable . . . I think."

"You think?"

"Well, they say there's a 'Bridezilla' in everyone. I'd like to think I'm better than that but it's easy to believe you're better until you're actually put into a similarly stressful situation. A lot of people enjoy watching trashy reality shows because deep down it makes us feel good about ourselves. But maybe we've all been lying to ourselves and Bridezillas is a true reflection of human nature."

"That's deep," he said softly.

We sat together in silence, watching the show and pondering the philosophical implications of Bridezillas.

During a commercial break, Hunter shrugged then went to the kitchen and came back to the couch with a large heart-shaped box in his hands.

My pulse skipped a beat. "Is that . . . for me?"

He narrowed his brows and looked at me funny. After pausing for a second, a light flashed across his eyes, and he grinned mischievously. ". . . Maybe."

"No, it's not," I said, realizing the ruse. "Dude, did you forget it was Valentine's Day already?" I asked, annoyed that he led me to assume he got me a V-Day present.

Hunter ran his hand through his wet hair and a few drops of water fell onto his shirt, forming dark spots. I caught a faint trace of his body wash and it smelled really good. As weird as it was, I found he smelled equally good sweaty as he did fresh.

"My stomach forgot." He opened the box, picked out a chocolate and popped it into his mouth. "Mmm yummy. Nothing like some post-workout carbs." He chewed a few times then handed me the open box. "Want one?" he said, his mouth full.

Just looking at the assortment of chocolates made my mouth salivate, dimly reminding me of Pavlov's slobbering dog from psychology class. Thanks to Daniela's joke at the beginning of the semester, I couldn't remember the real reason Pavlov's dog was famous. "Are you sure I can have one?"

"Sure, of course. I can't eat 'em all myself anyway. Someone gave them to me this morning."

"Who gave them to you?" I asked curiously, pinching a circle-shaped milk chocolate with an almond on top.

"This girl came up to me in the Barnyard, gave me a box of chocolates, and invited herself over. I said no but kept the box of chocolates." He popped another caramel-drizzled candy in his mouth and continued chewing. "Mmm soo good."

"I've seen a proposition for a threesome and now a chocolate bribe." I thought about the sordid implications. "Have you ever thought of becoming a male gigolo instead of a fighter? You could make some good money."

"Nah, I don't often get material bribes. It's one of the perks of Valentine's Day," he said casually. "Besides, I don't like the idea of being used for sex, so being a gigolo is out of the question."

I wrinkled my forehead. "But you're okay with using girls for sex?"

"No, I'm not okay with that. Like I said before, I'm always upfront about the arrangement."

"I see."

We continued eating chocolates for a minute, wet chewing noises filling the silence between us. It still made me uncomfortable to think about Hunter getting a blowjob from two girls.

"Speaking of receiving V-Day gifts," he said. "Don't you have guys doing the same to you? You know, random guys coming up to you and giving you chocolates? I thought that was what Valentine's Day was all about."

I groaned at his teasing. "I hate to break it to you, Hunter, but I'm not exactly as popular with the opposite sex as you are."

"Hmm? Why not?"

"I don't know. You're the guy, you tell me."

"I don't see why you wouldn't be popular with guys. You certainly are—" He looked me up and down. "—titillating. Have you had a boyfriend before?"

Feeling comfortable enough with Hunter to discuss my dating history, I gave him an honest answer. "Yes, I've had a boyfriend before. Well, three to be exact."

His eyes widened. "Three?"

"Yeah, why does that come as such a surprise? Are you showing your true opinion, that you really think I'm unpopular?"

He swallowed the contents in his mouth and got started on a third piece. "No, I just don't really like hearing you've been with other guys. I'm a little jealous, that's all." He smiled at me and rubbed my thigh briefly.

I laughed at the thought of Hunter being jealous. "Yeah, sure," I said sarcastically, affectionately slapping his thigh in return. It was hard to tell if he was teasing or being serious. "Fortunately, you have nothing to be jealous about. I'm single on Valentine's Day. Yay!"

"That makes the two of us. We can celebrate together, Snorrie." He held a caramel cube up and I clinked it with my butterscotch square for a toast. Then we both popped them into our mouths.

"How come you don't have a Valentine's date?" I asked, mouth full like Hunter's. Our friendship had apparently matured far enough that manners were out the door.

He shrugged. "Nobody wanted to be my Valentine." He gave me that adorable puppy-dog face he'd given me before at the cafe—the one that made me want to reach out and pet him on the head.

"You got chocolates from someone though."

"That doesn't count." The bride on TV fretting about her dress size was getting obnoxiously loud so Hunter picked up the remote from the coffee table and turned down the volume.

"Sure seems like it does. You probably just turn down all your Valentine's dates. We both know you have a lot of fans that like to watch you fight."

"You know me Lorrie, if I spent Valentine's Day with one of them, it would give them the wrong idea."

"What's the wrong idea?"

"That I want to date them, hang around with them. You know I pretty much only like hanging around with you and Gary."

"Won't people get ideas if I'm here with you?"

"Sure, other people can think whatever they want about you and me hanging out. Are you okay with that?"

"Well, I don't like the gossip, but I don't let it bother me. Usually. That time about the kittens was different."

"That's fair." He looked at me earnestly. "Hey, you got some chocolate on the edge of your mouth."

I tried wiping it with my finger but wasn't confident that I got it.

"No, you missed it." He reached his finger up and gently brushed the corner of my lip. I was uncomfortably aware of his body being so close to mine. I could feel the heat from his legs through the layer of clothes separating us.

I cleared my throat and pulled away.

"What's wrong Snorrie? Afraid of touching me?" He sucked the chocolate that had been on my mouth off his finger.

"No," I said casually. I didn't trust my voice enough to say anything further so I just stayed silent and looked at the TV. It was stupid, but maybe Valentine's Day was getting to me too. I felt lonelier than usual, and being this close to Hunter wasn't helping.

I saw Hunter flash a wicked smile at me from the side of my vision. He lifted his hand to the side of my neck and brushed away a strand of hair. His hands were warm and soft against my skin, I flinched back, afraid of him seeing the effect he had on me.

Hunter kept dragging his fingers against my neck using just a feather-light touch. I rolled my head, trying to avoid his touch. I knew where this was going.

"Wait, you're not ticklish, are you Lorrie?"

"No! Of course not!"

"Okay, I guess then you don't feel anything when I do this right?"

Hunter tickled my neck and I squealed before grabbing his arm and pushing it away. He laughed heartily to himself.

"No fair!" I cried. Reaching my arm over, I decided to go on the offensive by tickling his ribs. He didn't react at first and I watched his face for any sign of a reaction. Just when I thought he wasn't ticklish at all and that I was at a terrible disadvantage, he guffawed loudly, and wriggled away. I knew he was being nice and could have stopped me at any point, but he let me continue tickling him a bit longer as he tried to squirm away on the couch.

My fingers felt only hardened muscle everywhere they went, and Hunter kept trying to get away from me. I was breathing heavy from the exertion, laughing along with him when he suddenly grabbed my wrist.

We paused for a second, both of us panting slightly.

"That wasn't fair, you took advantage of me when I wasn't ready!" Hunter protested.

I opened my mouth to argue. "What?! You were the one who started it!"

"Hm . . . you do have a good point, but now I'm going to finish it!" Before I could break away, he was on top of me, his fingers tickling my ribs. I giggled, taking short panicked breaths, but I couldn't get away from his fingers torturing me.

Finally when I couldn't take it anymore I squealed, "Stop, Hunter! Stop! You win!"

My face felt hot and my stomach hurt from laughing. I was afraid if he tickled me any more, I'd die from laughter.

He finally stopped, but still held my wrists firm in his hands. I let out a few more panicked laughs before sucking in deep breaths for a second, a layer of sweat on my forehead. We were both horizontal on his couch. Hunter was lying on top of me, his muscular chest pressed heavy against my breasts. I could tell from the way he was breathing that I had made him work for it too.

Hunter looked down at me, victory in his eyes. "I win, Lorrie. Defeating you makes me the heavyweight-champion of tickling."

I rolled my eyes. "Whatever, Mr. Overly-Competitive." I looked to my side and spotted the chocolate box that was nearly empty. "Last chocolate!" I frantically grabbed at the lone raspberry truffle, knocking the box off the coffee table in the process.

"Hey, no fair! Wait!" he cried.

I laughed. "Too late, Hunter, I'm the Chocolate-Champion. You gotta work on your hand speed."

"I just gotta work on my mouth speed," he growled. His jaw

swooped in on the truffle in my hand and tried to bite it but I quickly pulled it away at the last instant.

Giggling, I continued moving it away each time he tried chomping at it like I was dangling a chocolate covered carrot in front of him. Sensing he was getting better at anticipating my movements, I hurriedly brought it to my mouth and bit down on the delicious truffle. An instant later, Hunter had bitten down on the other half that had been sticking out of my mouth.

Our lips touched.

We locked eyes. Neither us moved for what seemed like an eternity. Anticipation coiled in my stomach. My skin prickled. I exhaled heavily and slowly through my nose, flickering my eyes down to where our lips made contact. His light breathing through his nostrils blew across my eyelashes. My pulse thundered in my veins as a heated flush rose to my face. I gazed deeply into his gray eyes, feeling the chocolate melting between our lips. I stared, watching him watch me, watching his eyelids grow heavy, feeling my own lids falling. We both bit down on the truffle at the same time our lips locked.

I arched myself up into his mouth. His lips felt damp and hot. The melted raspberry chocolate swirled between us. I kissed him needily, wanting to feel every surface of his mouth against mine, wanting to taste every inch. Our tongues darted in and out of each other, exploring each other fully. His knee pressed against the crotch of my jeans and I ground my hips into him, needing to feel more. Something long, thick, and hot pressed against my thigh. I knew what it was. I'd seen it before when he was just wearing a towel and sitting on the coffee table in front of me, but now I felt it. Our tongues entwined, I felt his mouth begin to pull away—perhaps he had momentarily come to his senses—but I reached behind his head and pulled him back to me. Our mouths wrestled and our tongues tangled passionately.

Then there was a knock on the door. I pushed Hunter off of me, my skin suddenly clammy with a cold sweat.

The door opened and Gary's voice drifted in. *Shit.* Hadn't Hunter locked the door? No, of course not, he was probably expecting Gary.

We quickly disentangled ourselves from each other and sat

upright.

"Hey boys and girls! Party's here!" Gary said, setting something down on the kitchen counter that clinked loudly.

I could sense Hunter's eyes on me, trying to gauge my response. *Shit.* How did it ever come to this? Stupid. Stupid. Stupid. And on Valentine's Day no less. We were supposed to be friends. Just friends. Of course Hunter was going to get the wrong idea now. And if Gary saw us . . .

Turning around on the couch I saw Gary's back was to us. He unpacked what must've been the beer.

"Hey Gary," I said, trying to keep my voice steady.

Hunter didn't say anything but I could tell he was still watching me. *Damn it Lorrie, what's wrong with you? You knew that hanging around Hunter on Valentine's Day was a bad idea.*

Hunter grunted something and Gary turned around to look at us. If Gary thought something was up, he was certainly a good actor. He walked over and then handed Hunter and me each a bottle of Miller Lite. We took our bottles and then Gary clinked his bottle against mine first, then Hunter's.

"To being single," he announced, beaming at us. I couldn't tell if he was trying to be funny or if he was just oblivious.

I nodded and took a long swig from my bottle, before turning back around in the couch, trying to avoid Hunter's gaze.

"So, Gary, I saw some brothers from Phi Kappa Delta selling chocolates today, did you sell any too?" I asked, trying to mask the awkwardness between Hunter and me.

"Sure did. I just unloaded two boxes at the gym this morning. Those guys crave the carbs you know." He winked at me before settling down on the lounge chair next to the sofa.

Hunter hadn't said a single word since Gary arrived and it was making me nervous. I couldn't tell if it was because he was mad at me or what. Surely Gary would notice something was wrong. I was antsy in my seat, both because I couldn't talk to Hunter immediately about what just happened and also because I was worried about Gary catching on soon.

Gary switched the channel on the TV and we all watched a few rounds of a breakdancing competition sponsored by Red Bull.

Hunter grunted a few words here and there, but he wasn't his usual self. Sitting there next to him, and not being able to talk about it was painful.

After an hour, I made an excuse about needing to hang out with Daniela and took my leave. Hunter didn't protest and just nodded slowly. We could barely meet each other's eyes. We'd already admitted our attraction to one another and now we had kissed. It was easier to pretend a sleepover never happened and move on but how could we pretend that a kiss never happened?

Chapter Fifteen

HURT

The next day I sat in Psych 102, trying not to zone out while Professor Muller droned on about something to do with marshmallows and Harvard. I didn't know what to make of the kiss between me and Hunter. Whose fault was it? What did Hunter think about it? Things between us were a mess and I had no idea how we were going to fix it. Even though we had become much closer over the past weeks, I still had my baggage. And Hunter had his as well—Gary and Mitch had practically pointed to it with a neon sign.

It was one thing to be friends, it was another to be in a relationship. Two unstable people like us shouldn't get together.

I looked over at Daniela, who was as focused on the lecture as she had been every other. Hopefully she would end up becoming a psychologist; I couldn't think of anyone who loved any subject as much as she seemed to love psychology. It made me a little jealous that she had found something she loved so much. So far all I had was drawing, and that was more of a hobby than my life's passion.

She looked over at me and seemed to read my expression. "What's up?" she whispered.

I shook my head and looked down, but saw her watch me another few seconds out of the corner of my eye. She eventually turned back to the front of the class and paid attention to the rest of the lecture. Twenty minutes later, the class ended. I was packing my stuff up when she grabbed my arm. "Something happened," she said matter-of-factly. "We're going to Starbucks."

"You don't have to meet your group early for Geology or anything?"

"Nope. Come on, let's go."

We chatted idly on the walk over and continued chatting while waiting in line at the Starbucks next to the Barnyard. I got black coffee as usual; Daniela went for a mocha. Our drinks came, and we found a seat on an open couch.

"Okay, what's up?" she asked.

I looked out the window at the snow falling lightly to the ground. Where should I start with that question? My whole world felt upside down.

"This has to do with Hunter doesn't it?"

I nodded. "Yeah, I was at his place to feed the kittens on Valentine's Day and . . . well . . . something happened between us."

Her face lit up. "Holy shit, you guys kissed, didn't you?"

I blinked and looked back at my friend. Was I that easy to read? Looking around to see if anyone was listening to our conversation, I pressed my lips together into a thin line and nodded. It looked like people were minding their own business.

Her eyes widened. "I knew it!" She smirked. "You said you thought of him as your older brother and now you kissed him. Not so high on your moral-horse now aren't you? But I can't blame you, it's Hunter. Tell me everything. How did it happen?"

"We were sitting on his couch watching TV and he started tickling my neck. After that we were kind of going back and forth in a tickle fight for a little while, and he ended up on top of me. Then we bit down on this chocolate together and somehow that turned into making out."

"Was it hot?" she asked breathlessly.

I felt myself blushing fiercely as I remembered the warm, smooth feeling of his lips locked on mine. When we kissed, I hadn't resisted at all. I'd wanted more. What would have happened if Gary hadn't come through the door at that moment?

"It was a mistake," I said through my teeth.

She pursed her lips and shook her head. "What happened after he kissed you?"

I grimaced. "Gary came in."

She gasped.

"But I don't think he saw anything," I added quickly. I took a sip of my coffee. It was so hot it burnt the roof of my mouth. I swallowed it painfully, feeling it travel all the way down to my stomach.

"Whoa, you okay?" Daniela asked.

"Yeah, sorry," I choked. "Coffee's just a little hot, that's all."

"Okay, so what happened after Gary came in?"

"Nothing. It looked like he was watching me to see how I would react, but he didn't say anything. I hung around for a little while after Gary came, then left."

"So you have no idea what he thinks about it right now?"

I shook my head.

"Were you drunk?"

"No! And neither was he."

She tilted her head in apparent thought. "So he was hanging out with Gary on Valentine's Day?"

"Yeah, I thought that was weird too."

"Maybe he wanted to hang out with you on V-Day rather than Gary," she said before taking a sip of her mocha.

"I don't know, I guess. Does it matter? I'm not going to get romantically involved with him. You were there when I yelled at him for exploiting the kittens. He's used to getting BJs whenever he wants from anyone he wants. I'm not that kind of girl."

She shrugged. "What if he wants to be exclusive with you?"

I remembered Hunter asking me for a date back when we walked through that abandoned amusement park together, and I had declined. Although Hunter and I had admitted our mutual attraction for one another since then, dating was one thing, exclusivity was another. "Like boyfriend and girlfriend?"

"Yeah. I mean, hypothetically, what would you think?"

I took a deep breath. Most of the girls at Arrowhart would think that question was a no-brainer, but I wasn't sure. Hunter was gorgeous, there was no denying that. Plus, we had a lot of fun together just goofing off and hanging out. Still, I wasn't sure if I was ready to have a romantic relationship with anyone, let alone Hunter.

"I don't know," I said finally. "When I decided to come back this semester, all I wanted to do was make it through without having a breakdown and failing any of my classes."

"Those are good goals."

I laughed. "Yeah, and I'm not sure dating someone is going to help. I don't know if I'm emotionally ready for that right now, you know?"

"I hear you, but I'm kind of wondering if that ship's sailed. At this point you're already emotionally involved with him. If you break it off now, it's still going to hurt."

"Maybe a little pain now is better than a lot of pain later . . ."

She shrugged and looked at her phone. "Shit, I have to run to class. Keep me posted though, okay? We can talk more tonight."

I nodded and watched her pack up. She left with a wave, leaving me alone to think. Talking with Daniela had confused me even more. I had been assuming that Hunter was seeing lots of different girls, but the fact that he was alone on Valentine's Day made me question that. What if he did want to be my boyfriend? Did I want that? Could I handle that right now?

I didn't know. Sighing, I packed up my stuff and headed outside. Maybe the cold air would help me clear my mind.

After walking for a few minutes, I took a seat on a bench in the Arts Quad and pulled out my sketchbook. The snow had eased up, leaving a thin layer on the landscape. It was one of those beautiful winter scenes you could put on a Christmas card. I scanned my surroundings hoping for inspiration to sketch something.

Nothing was coming. It was such a beautiful day, but I couldn't find the right subject to focus on. I inhaled a deep breath and put my pencil down. As I exhaled, I watched my breath in the cold winter air disappear.

Hunter and I hadn't been in contact since the kiss yesterday. It was an unusually long time for us to not at least exchange a text message. Barely thinking, I picked my pencil back up and began sketching Hunter from memory. The lines came easily: his hard gray eyes, pronounced cheekbones, and strong jaw came from my pencil as if they were meant to. I quickly had a workable sketch of his face. The pensive expression I gave him in my sketch reflected what I was feeling. After completing the shading, I realized I didn't know how Hunter felt about our kiss. Was he as confused as I was?

I decided to break the silence and send him a message.

Hey Hunter, you wanna talk about what happened yesterday? Maybe later?

Before I could hit send, I received a message from Hunter. *Hey Lorrie, just wondering what you're up to.*

I deleted my original message and typed out a reply. *Just sitting on a bench outside Wheatley. It's cold. Brrr.*

I hit 'send' and waited for a reply. It came seconds later.

I'm at the Engineering building now. Sit tight, I'll see ya in a bit!

I waited a few minutes but didn't receive a reply. Shrugging, I put my phone back in my pocket and turned my attention back to my sketchpad.

"Hello," a voice called from directly behind me.

I jumped in my seat and crumpled up the sketch. "Hunter, stop sneaking up on me while I'm drawing!"

He came around the bench and took a seat next to me. "Why'd you crumple up your sketch? You're gonna ruin it that way. Can I see it?"

I shook my head. "It's not ready."

"Okay. Well, you know I like seeing the drawings you do. I think you have a lot of talent."

I turned to him and saw he had a rose in one hand and a box of chocolates in the other. My heart skipped a beat.

"What are those for?" I asked.

"Brought you some gifts," he said brightly. "I messed up, Lorrie. I wasn't sure how you felt about me so I didn't get you anything for Valentine's Day. I thought about it, but then I figured you might get pissed off or feel awkward if I got you something."

A bit confused, I tried to put a smile on my face as I took the gifts from him. "Hunter, this is really sweet, but you didn't have to do this."

"Of course I did." He sucked in a deep breath, his large chest expanding. "Lorrie, you mean a lot to me. I know you're afraid that I'm gonna hurt you but I hope you know by now that I'd never do that. After that kiss, I was thinking that we should give dating a shot."

My eyebrows raised. "Wait, what? Who said anything about dating?"

He smiled and laughed. "We kissed yesterday. It meant a lot to me, and I know it meant a lot to you too."

Suddenly feeling uncomfortable with the whole situation, I offered the rose and chocolates back to him. Knowing Hunter's casual relations with other girls, I hadn't anticipated him interpreting the kiss as seriously as he did. "Hunter," I said soberly. "I really appreciate all of this. But a kiss is just a kiss. It doesn't mean I'm ready to date you."

He furrowed his brows, ignoring my attempt to give him back his gifts. "Why are you trying to give me back your presents? Are you saying it didn't mean anything to you?"

I brought the rose and chocolates back to my lap. "No, that's not it at all. I'm just saying I'm not ready to move beyond friendship. I don't want that kiss to change anything between us." I took a calm breath, expecting him to be as understanding as he had been when I got angry about sleeping over at his place. As sweet as Hunter was, and as much as I enjoyed hanging out with him, being 'just friends' had enough stressful moments—gossip, drama, being distracted from school work. Dating would only multiply that.

He paused for a moment. "I can't accept that. Not after what happened yesterday."

My eyes widened. "What? Why?"

"I felt the way you kissed me back. I was fine being just friends if you didn't have romantic feelings for me. But now I know you do, and you already know I have feelings for you."

Was he really going to argue with me about how I felt? I fished for an appropriate response. "My feelings for you are purely platonic," I said evenly. "I think of you as an older brother, not as a romantic partner. One kiss doesn't change that."

"Platonic?" he asked, his eyebrows high. "Do you even know what platonic means? The way your hips moved against mine was anything but platonic. Dammit Lorrie, I even tried to pull away. I wasn't sure you wanted it, but you pulled me right back in."

Blood rushed to my face as I remembered the sensation of his leg against my crotch and his hair between my fingers. I looked around to make sure no one was listening. "So I let myself get caught up in the heat of the moment and now we can't be friends?"

I asked, my voice rising. "You of all people shouldn't be making assumptions off of one kiss."

He narrowed his eyes. "What's that supposed to mean?"

Did I really have to spell it out for him? "Those girls gave you a blowjob and you didn't think anything of it."

"That's different," he said, his own voice rising. "Those girls don't mean anything to me. You do."

"You mean something to me too," I said sternly. "As a friend."

"I don't see how you can't tell the difference between kissing someone purely for pleasure and kissing someone who really means something to you. Kissing for us is something special."

My jaw clenched. He was treating me like an idiot. "Trust me, I do see the difference. That kiss is looking like it might cost me a close friend, and that's very disappointing." I paused to let that sink in. "Like I said, I don't want anything to change between us. But it seems like you won't let that happen."

He kicked a small rock on the ground, sending it tumbling in the distance. "I don't get it. What's the matter with you? I'm spilling my guts here and you're turning to stone."

"You might say 'those girls' mean nothing to you, but at least you respect 'those girls' enough to be upfront about the arrangement," I snapped. "Frankly, the longer this conversation goes on, the more I feel like you've just been biding your time waiting for things to become romantic between us. Did you ever even want to be friends?"

"Lorrie, come on," he said with a sigh. "I was totally cool with being friends. But I like you. You're different. I know you like hanging out with me, and last night shows you're definitely more than just attracted to me. So now I can't understand why you're denying your feelings. Especially when I'm being upfront with mine."

"Here are my feelings," I said, my fists balled up in frustration. "I don't want to be in a romantic relationship with you, and I wish you would respect that. Maybe I got confused because we spend too much time together, and it was Valentine's Day, and I was caught off guard. I don't know, but it won't happen again."

"Lorrie—"

"Hunter, stop. I'm sorry, but we can't. I told you before and I'm telling you again: I'm not ready. Maybe we shouldn't be spending so much time together. It seems like things are getting confused."

"We need to spend *more* time together."

I looked into his gray eyes. "You're willing to jeopardize our friendship for a chance at a relationship?"

His eyes became big and round. "We can be friends *and* in a relationship, Lorrie. We can have it all."

"No," I said, pursing my lips, my heart thumping in my chest. "I can't do that. I really think we should have some distance."

He looked at me carefully before standing up. "Fine," he said. "You want to spend time apart. That's what we'll do."

He turned and walked away. Halfway to the corner of the Social Sciences Building, he kicked a trash can over in anger. Empty bottles and cans tumbled across the ground.

My stomach churned as I watched him turn the corner out of sight. When I was sure he was gone, I took out the sketch I had been working on and uncrumpled it. The eyes were all wrong. I had drawn them sharp like they were when he was fighting, but I knew there was also a softer side to him. A vulnerable side.

I looked at the box of chocolates and rose in my lap. Sighing, I put the box in my bag to share with Daniela—no sense in wasting perfectly good chocolate —and left the rose on the bench. Once I packed up, I got up from the bench and fixed the trash can that Hunter knocked over. Then I crumpled up the sketch again, threw it in the trash, and went to my next class.

Chapter Sixteen

THE STUNNER

I spent the next few days praying I wouldn't see Hunter. Every time my phone jingled its reminder to feed the kittens, I had a mild panic attack. When I would go to his apartment, I would check the windows to see if his lights were on or if I could see some other sign he was home, but he never was. The most I heard from him was the notes he left on the whiteboard above the kittens' bed: "need to get formula" or "Bones wouldn't eat make sure he gets enough" or "has Georgia been sleepy for you too?"

He was giving me time apart, that was for sure. The more I didn't see him, the more I wasn't sure if that was what I wanted. I had dreamed about kissing him twice in four days, each time waking up with an annoying ache between my legs and my lips pressed against my pillow.

The situation was on my mind as I walked into the dining hall with Daniela on Thursday night. All I had was swimming on Fridays, so this was practically the beginning of my weekend. That meant I should've been happy, like a normal college student when the weekend rolled around. Instead I was a nervous wreck. All I could think about was whether I would run into Hunter over the weekend.

"Hey, cheer up!" Daniela said as we stood in line for the cafeteria. "Let's go out this weekend and do something fun. Go to a house party or something."

I shrugged. "Yeah, maybe."

"Lorrie, I know you're trying to give it time because you guys said you'd give each other space, but you've been really bummed out the past few days. If it's really bothering you, you should talk to him again. From what you told me, it sounds like he would want that."

Maybe she was right. I didn't want to admit it, but maybe it was time to admit my feelings for Hunter were more than platonic. No matter how hard I tried, I couldn't get him out of my mind.

We handed our student IDs to the cashier to allow her to scan them, took our trays, and got in line for food. The Barnyard was serving chicken broccoli bake, an Arrowhart favorite. Once we got our food, we searched for a place to sit. The cafeteria was buzzing with excitement for the approaching weekend. All around us I heard people making plans, gossiping, complaining about the upcoming midterms, and generally getting ready to relax for a couple days. It was then that I saw Hunter on the other side of the cafeteria.

He was sitting at a table and talking to a girl with shoulder length blonde hair and a perfect tan despite the lack of sun in winter. Her black coat hanging on the back of her chair, she was wearing a lilac colored cotton tank top that showed off her ample breasts, and looked *very* comfortable with Hunter.

They were eating off of one plate. I felt sick as I watched her lean over and whisper into his ear, tracing her fingers along the muscles under his tight-fitting navy t-shirt. He looked over at her and smiled, making suggestive movements toward her lips with a peeled banana in his hand. She playfully slapped his arm but then lunged for the banana with her mouth, taking a bite. He laughed and took a bite himself. I was starting to feel dizzy. Daniela looked at me, then followed my eyes and gasped.

"Come on," she said pointing to a table away from Hunter. "Let's go sit over on this side."

She walked to the side of the cafeteria opposite from Hunter and sat down. I followed her numbly, barely able to process what was happening.

I'd been hungry when I was in the food line but when I sat down, I couldn't even look at my plate. Who was that girl and why was she so cozy with Hunter? Had he moved on that quickly? Just a few days ago he'd been baring his soul about his feelings for me, bringing me a rose and chocolate. Now he apparently had feelings for someone else. I wanted to pretend that it didn't bother me but the bundle of coils in my stomach made that impossible.

Noticing Daniela studying me carefully, I decided to break the silence. "I don't know if I can eat," I said.

She nodded but stayed silent. I stared at my food thinking about how stupid I was for feeling jealous that Hunter was flirting with another girl. I'd told him my feelings for him were strictly based on friendship but it was becoming increasingly clear to me that I wasn't being entirely honest.

Finally Daniela spoke. "Do you know who she is?"

I shook my head. This was so humiliating, even in front of my best friend. I wanted to turn around and curl up in bed until Spring came.

She grimaced. "Okay. We can leave if you want."

"No, you should eat." I gestured to her food, which was as untouched as mine was.

"I'm not leaving you here, Lorrie. If you want to leave I'm going with you."

I felt like I was pinned flat on my back by a giant boulder. Overwhelmed, I felt tears welling up in my eyes. "Thank you," I said, trying to smile.

"You're welcome. I know you'd do the same for me." She speared a forkful of chicken and broccoli. "I'll try to eat fast," she said, chewing. "Like a chicken broccoli bake eating contest."

I looked down at the spread on my plate and took a fork full of food. Knowing from experience that neglecting food was just going to make me feel worse, I decided to take a few bites. The food tasted bland, but I didn't feel like I was going to throw up, so I continued eating.

Chewing my food, I was tempted to look at Hunter. I turned and found him staring right at me. His gray eyes opened wide in surprise and then narrowed. He tapped the girl sitting next to him on the shoulder, fed her another suggestive bite of his banana then looked at me for my reaction. I glared at him for a second and then turned back to Daniela.

"This is ridiculous. He's taunting me! I have to go," I said, my heart racing as I stood up.

"Lorrie wait!" Daniela cried.

But I was already heading out of the dining hall. It felt like everyone in the Barnyard was staring at me as I rushed out, but I didn't care. I wasn't going to talk to Hunter when he was consciously trying to piss me off.

Stepping outside into the night, the cold winter air stung my bare arms. As I walked down the steps, I realized I'd forgotten my coat in the rush to get out of the cafeteria. Rather than go back in, I hugged my arms to my body and powered forward, figuring Daniela would bring it back to the dorm when she finished eating. There was no way I was going back in there and embarrassing myself even more. I hurried down the last few steps and started in the direction of Floyd Hall.

I'd gone three paces when I heard Hunter calling from the top of the steps. "Lorrie, wait!"

I continued walking, ignoring Hunter's cries. He knew how I reacted to hearing about him getting a blowjob from those girls. Deciding to feed that girl a banana in front of me made him a huge jackass. After resolving the blowjob incident, this felt like huge betrayal of my trust.

"Wait! You forgot your coat," he called.

Feeling the cold biting through my thin layer of clothes, I stopped and turned. "What are you doing?" I said harshly.

He held up my coat from the top of the stairs. "Apparently saving you from freezing to death—again."

"I'll be just fine, thanks. Leave my coat with Daniela." I turned to walk away.

"Lorrie, what the fuck?" he yelled. "How are *you* mad at *me*? You rejected me, remember? I'm the one who should be mad at you. And frankly, I am." He descended the steps and offered the coat as I turned to face him.

I stomped my foot. "What do you have to be mad about? I said I wasn't ready and needed a little space, and you responded by running into the arms of another girl immediately! Who is she, anyway? One of the girls who would suck your dick even if you had a pet rock?"

"Dammit Lorrie!" he roared, nostrils flared. His anger surprised me. He looked like he was going to keep yelling but pursed his lips together and ran his free hand through his short brown hair. "No," he said in a measured tone. "She's an ex that I'm still friends with."

"Ada?" I blurted.

His brows shot up in surprise, but he nodded. "Yes. Ada. So you've heard about her. Well, now you've seen her."

"Have you been hanging out with her a lot?"

His mouth opened to speak but then he shook his head. "Look, Ada and I ... are not exactly friends, it's just ... complicated between us."

"You think I'm blind, Hunter?" I said angrily. "You guys sure *looked* friendly."

"Things between Ada and I aren't romantic or sexual. We still hang out every once in a while, but nowhere near as much as I hang out with you."

Now he was changing his story. I wondered if he was just telling me what he thought I wanted to hear. "So she's not your friend, and things aren't sexual between you, but you still suggestively feed her bananas?"

"What do you want from me, Lorrie?" he yelled. "First you push me away because I want you, now you get jealous when I'm hanging out with another girl. This is ridiculous!"

"Ridiculous? Jumping into your ex's arms days after saying you have feelings for me is ridiculous! I thought you would at least keep it to a quiet hookup."

He sighed. "Listen, I'm sorry I fed Ada that banana to piss you off. That was immature, but I swear to you there was no hookup."

"Why would you use a friend—or whatever she is— to try and get back at me when I've done nothing wrong?"

He scoffed. "Nothing wrong? Lorrie, you're playing with me like a yo-yo. You push me away then get jealous and pull me in. Over and over."

I snatched my coat from his outstretched hand and backed away. "Hunter, you can't force me to date you, even if we did kiss. But you're right, maybe I have been unfair. Maybe we should stay away from each other."

"Come on, don't say that!" He took a deep breath. "I'm sorry. What can I do to make this right?"

"I don't know!"

I turned on my heel and hurried away, expecting him to chase after me. When I realized he wasn't following, I put my coat on and quickened my pace toward the dorm, the crisp night air chilling my tear-stained cheeks. *Goddammit.* Why did things always have to turn out so horribly?

I got back to my room and checked my phone. Daniela had texted me several times asking what happened and how I was. I texted back and told her I was going to the library to study. I knew it would be hard to be productive, but I had to do something. Sitting in my dorm would drive me crazy.

Daniela texted back and said the two of us should meet up when I was done. I agreed, grabbed my books, and headed to Wheatley Library.

Once I got to the library, I had a hard time focusing. It was emptier than usual, and the people that were there were mostly chatting first and studying second. There was too much swirling through my head. I stared at my psych textbook rereading the same paragraph over and over. I needed to know this material soon or I would fail my midterm. *Dammit this is all because of Hunter.* Frustrated, I tried focusing on just the pictures and diagrams, but nothing stuck.

I took a break and stared out the window at the student union. Why did I think that being just friends with Hunter would work out? I'd been warned multiple times by Daniela to be careful and not fall for him. I'd ignored her warnings, and here I was, trying to study in the library on a Friday night so I didn't fail my midterms.

Looking down at my notebook, I saw the only words I had written were "Psych Notes" at the top of the page. This was hopeless. I texted Daniela to ask if she wanted to watch some Grey's Anatomy together. She responded with an enthusiastic message: *Hell yeah :).* I packed up my stuff and headed back to my dorm.

Chapter Seventeen

SPECIAL

A few days passed without word from Hunter. I was beginning to wonder if I had made a mistake by suggesting we stay away from each other. Was this the end of our friendship?

Still, those damn dreams of kissing his lips didn't stop, if anything, they only intensified with his absence. I'd tried taking Benadryl hoping for a dreamless slumber, but it ended up twisting the dream, turning a kiss into some bizarre situation where Hunter was bottle-feeding me across his lap like a little kitten while stroking my sex at the same time. When I woke up, I immediately tossed that bottle of Benadryl into the garbage. We'd been talking about Freud and the interpretation of dreams in psych class the other day and I shuddered to think what that dream had meant.

Finally, Saturday evening arrived. Daniela decided to forego partying in favor of studying for midterms and I didn't feel like doing anything either so I decided on enjoying a quiet night in my dorm room.

My phone alarm chimed, notifying me I had to go feed the kittens soon. I hated the idea of having to go over to Hunter's apartment. The thought of seeing him again pissed me off. After debating it over in my mind and considering other options, I decided I was going to go over a little earlier to feed the kittens, hoping it would give me a greater chance of avoiding him in case he decided to come back from the gym early to catch me still at his place. Those poor little creatures didn't deserve being caught in the crossfire of whatever was happening between Hunter and me.

I put my jacket on and walked over to Hunter's place.

As soon as I opened the door, I heard adorable high-pitched mews coming from the kitchen. I walked inside, took off my snow boots, and hung my coat on the hanger beside the door.

"Where's my little kitties?" I said in my best babying voice.

The mews grew louder in response and I heard tiny paws scurrying across the tile to the pet barrier. I could distinctly hear Taylor's sweet—but loud—voice above the others. As much as I didn't want to play favorites, if some sick person put a gun to my head and asked me to choose my favorite kitten of the litter, I'd have to say it was Taylor.

"There's my kitties!" I exclaimed.

"Lorrie?"

I paused. *Kittens aren't supposed to know English, let alone speak it,* I thought. Grasping the situation, I turned and saw Hunter on the other side of the kitchen counter with a towel around his waist and damp hair. His bare muscular torso snapped me to attention and a heated ache moved through me.

"Hunter!" Recovering from surprise, my mood immediately turned sour. "I thought you'd be at the gym."

"I was," he said evenly as he dried his hair with a second, smaller towel. "I went earlier today so I could have more time to relax in the evening. What are you doing here so early?" Although his question indicated otherwise, his tone seemed like he'd anticipated I'd be coming early.

Dammit, he outsmarted me.

It was apparent Hunter had altered his clockwork routine because he wanted to talk about the recent drama between us. Unfortunately, I was too pissed at him to want to do the same. I put my hands on my hips. "Oh. Well, I've got plans later so I came earlier to feed the babies and give them some attention. Once I'm done here, I'm out."

He ran a hand through his dark hair, pushing wet strands away from his forehead. "You need help?" he said, lacking his usual enthusiasm. "I'll feed the boys and you feed the girls?"

I was about to decline his help but then a kitten began gently grazing my leg with his paws. I turned to identify the rascal and saw it was Rampage—Hunter's favorite kitten. A petty thought ran through my head and I couldn't resist. "Oh look who it is! Rampage wants me to feed him. I think he likes me better," I said smugly.

Hunter was visibly taken aback. "What?" he grunted. Hunter came over to my side, kneeled down, and began petting Rampage. "C'mon Rampage, I'll feed you."

Rampage closed his eyes and tilted his ears down enjoying the pets against his back but he didn't stop kneading my jeans.

Stooping to pet Rampage on the head, I eyed Hunter. "You might play with Rampage a lot and give him affection but the little guy wants my affection too."

Hunter narrowed his eyes. "He's a naive kitten. He probably just likes that peachy perfume you always wear."

"What are you talking about? I'm not wearing any perfume."

He grumbled. "Or lotion, or shampoo. Whatever it is you always wear."

I rolled my eyes. "Whatever."

Hunter's attention diverted to something at his side. "Oh, who is this?" he said smugly.

Glancing over and seeing Taylor pawing at Hunter's leg, I became further irritated. "Taylor, come here, let me feed you," I commanded. I tried coaxing her over by tapping the floor with my hand and calling her name but she remained fixed on Hunter.

Hunter looked at me and grinned wickedly. "She can't resist," he said pleased with himself. "Looks like Taylor likes me better."

"Whatever," I snapped. "You just got out of the shower so she's probably just trying to mark you with her scent."

"Whatever."

We spent the next twenty minutes sitting on the kitchen floor bottle-feeding the kittens over our laps and burping them in awkward silence. I ended up feeding Rampage and Hunter ended up feeding Taylor. I tried avoiding eye contact with Hunter and I could tell he was trying to do the same but somehow we always managed to check on one another at the exact same time, making brief, incredibly awkward eye contact. When the awkwardness became too much to bear, I decided to speak up.

"Hunter—"

"Lorrie, we need to talk."

I waited a beat before responding. "Yeah," I said, gently taking a drowsy Georgia off my lap and placing her in the cat bed next to the other four sleeping kittens.

"We're both upset with one another." Hunter put a tired Bones in the bed next to Georgia who was already falling into dream land.

We both stood up and faced one another. I folded my arms across my chest. "Yes, we are."

He puffed air from his lungs and ran hand through his hair. "Look, it's not easy for me to say this . . ."

I watched him carefully, wondering if this was the going to be the end of our friendship.

"I like you Lorrie. I really do. You make me laugh, I like hanging out with you. You're strong and you call me out on my shit. I feel good when I'm around you . . ."

I took a second to digest all the positive words, nodding slowly in acknowledgement. "But . . .?"

"But—" He locked his gaze with mine and I could see his expression had changed from irritated to pained. "—I have feelings for you, Lorrie. Feelings beyond friendship."

I remained silent.

"You knew that I was attracted to you before we even became friends. But that was a while ago, when we were just getting to know one another. You were this beautiful, quirky girl that fell into my life—literally, you fell into a lake and I saved you—and I haven't been able to stop thinking about you since. I have real feelings for you now, Lorrie. Strong ones."

My chest tightened at the raw intensity of his gaze and voice. Hunter was baring himself to me in a way he never had before and the anger I had held since stepping into the apartment began to disappear.

"I'm not even sure I want these feelings for you because now you have the ability to hurt me. And you did. You pushed me away. You're not like other girls to me, Lorrie. I can't just shake it off or ignore it."

Hunter's passionate words and the pain in his voice touched me deeply. I could feel my emotional walls cracking. He was a badass and a goofball but right now he was a hurt little boy. And it was all because of me.

I hurt him.

My eyes began to prickle and my throat started constricting. I briefly glanced away to compose myself before looking at him directly. "I'm really sorry that I hurt you, Hunter," I said trying to control the shakiness in my voice. "But what did you expect? Did you think I was going to be your girlfriend because you gave me flowers and a box of chocolates?" I stumbled over the pet barrier and headed toward the door, hoping I'd make it there before the inevitable tears came.

As I slipped my foot into one boot, he caught me by the shoulder and spun me around to meet his forceful gaze. "I know you have feelings for me, Lorrie! Don't push me away."

"I can't do this, Hunter!" I exclaimed, trying desperately to be strong, to resist him when I knew I didn't want to. "You're sweet, but I just can't do this . . ."

"What do you have against us? Haven't you known me long enough now to trust me? We can take it slow. Lorrie . . ."

"Hunter." I released a shaky breath, preparing to end this discussion before it went too far—before either of us let our emotions get the best of our composure. "I like you," I admitted. "I really do. You're this lovable goofball that also happens to be a badass MMA fighter. Or maybe it's the other way around, I don't know. You're almost too good to be true . . ." I paused to swallow a lump scratching at my throat.

"Then what is it, Lorrie? Please, tell me." His eyes began to glisten. It was something I'd never seen before, not even after witnessing him get punched in the face. Seeing his vulnerability emboldened me to continue.

"I have feelings for you beyond friendship as well, Hunter. And that's the problem. That's what I'm scared of. You can hurt me. Whatever you're going through now, I don't want to experience that."

His jaw tightened but his tone remained controlled. "Dammit, that's selfish—I put myself out there and you can hurt me while keeping yourself defended."

I exhaled a shaky breath. As difficult as it was, I persisted in meeting his gaze. "It's self-preservation, Hunter. It's just like you using girls for blow jobs. As much as I care about you—and I do care about you probably more than I'm willing to admit—I have to take care of myself first. I know it's fucked up, Hunter. I know it's bad and it makes me a terrible person. But guess what? I *am* fucked up. I'm a fucked up girl who can't get her life right. I already told you my parents are divorced and dead . . . I'm fighting just to feel normal." Tears began streaming down my cheeks and I hurriedly wiped them away with my hand. My lips began to quiver and my throat started constricting but I forced myself to continue.

His gaze softened. "Lorrie . . ."

"I can't lose, Hunter! This isn't like one of your fights where if you lose, you can get back up again and fight another day, fight another opponent. If I lose this fight, I may not ever get back up again. I'm going to be dead. If not completely then at least on the inside, which isn't much better. And it's always the same damn opponent! It's like I'm fighting to roll this gigantic boulder up a hill every day, hoping to god that it doesn't crush me."

Hunter's lips tightened as if he wanted to say something but was holding back to let me finish.

Blinking away tears, I swallowed another lump in my throat. "I know it sounds ridiculous. I know it sounds like I'm just being a quitter, that I don't have that eye-of-the-tiger never-give-up attitude that you might have, but real life isn't the movies. There's no Rocky montage for overcoming obstacles in life. Not for me. Or anyone else. I've seen the best fail, I've seen my own dad lose after fighting so hard, struggling for so long. Can't you see, Hunter? It's not that I don't *want* to get hurt. It's that I *can't*. If I do, it's over. It's all over for me." I started to feel a familiar numbness creeping into my chest again. It was my body's way of protecting me from intolerable pain.

Hunter stared passionately into my eyes even as the tears rolling down both our cheeks threatened to distance us. "Then let's stop hurting each other! You make me feel alive and I make you feel alive. Let's save each other."

I cupped my hand over my mouth to stifle an unexpected laugh, choking back sobs in the process. "You're too sweet, Hunter. Really, you are. I don't deserve you as a friend. As much as I want to believe it, you can't save me, Hunter. Deep down we're both fucked up selfish kids just trying to make it to the next day. We both know that. All we can do is try to survive on our own."

I tried turning my head away but he gently placed his hand against my cheek and returned my gaze to his. The comforting warmth of his palm heated my face as he wiped tears away with his thumb. His gaze was intensely tender. "I don't care how selfish we are because I know we can be selfless too! I've seen your kindness. You care about others. You care about me. You're just drowning right now, Lorrie. I saved you once, I can do it again."

"We're both drowning, Hunter," I sobbed, trying to push him away but he held me tightly. "I'm flailing like an idiot and I'm just going to pull you down with me! We're both going to drown, can't you see that? I can't do that to you, Hunter..."

He tilted forehead to rest against mine, his eyes squeezed shut. Wet droplets fell softly from his face onto my cheeks. He tenderly kissed the tip of my nose. "I won't let it happen. I'm gonna save us both. But I can't do it by myself. I need you with me, Lorrie. I need you to give us both strength." His voice was pained and he spoke with his lips inches from mine.

"Hunter..." His hands slid down to grip my waist, ensuring I wouldn't leave him. Trembling, I briefly touched my lips against his to feel something. To feel him here, with me. To make sure I wasn't imagining it. That I wasn't alone this time. "I've already hurt you, I could do it again. I could hurt you beyond what you can handle, you're not invincible, Hunter. And you could do the same to me. We could be the death of one another."

He kissed my lips back, letting me know he was here. "I know how much you care about me, Lorrie. We all make mistakes. You're here with me now, that's all that matters."

He wrapped his arms around me and I fell into his embrace. All thoughts of struggling flew from my mind as I buried my face into his bare chest and cried. Feeling the heat of his skin and smelling his fresh masculine scent, I did what I wanted to do the moment I first saw him half-naked in this apartment: I kissed the soft skin of his hard pecs. I kissed him again and again, the word "sorry" tumbling from my lips repeatedly, uncontrollably.

He cupped my face with his hands and his lips collided with mine. He kissed me, his tongue running gently over my lips at first then over my tongue melting away my anxiety. I wrapped my arms around him and squeezed, our hips pressing tightly together. Suddenly, Hunter dipped and lifted me into the air with strong arms, our mouths never breaking contact. I faintly registered movement then heard the sound of a door being kicked open. A moment later, my back settled against soft sheets.

Hunter moved his lips from my mouth to my cheek, following along the trail of tears, softly pecking away the damp traces. A fresh wave of tears flowed and he diligently kissed each one, never letting them fall to the bed.

I gazed at his beautiful face hovering above me. Tears were flowing freely from his eyes as well. "Hunter," I said softly, another wave of tears forming. "Don't leave me alone, tonight."

"Lorrie, we're going to be together tonight. And tomorrow, and the day after, and the day after that. We're going to work things out together."

He carefully unbuttoned my jeans and slipped them off me with my help. He kissed me tenderly then moved lower, planting his lips on the skin of my neck down to my stomach, removing layers of my clothing in between passionate kisses. Soon I was left only in my bra and panties. I exhaled a shaky breath as I watched him look me up and down like he did the first time I came out from his shower dressed in his clothes. Back then his gaze had made me uncomfortable, but now his fiercely tender gaze made feel desirable.

"You're so beautiful, Lorrie."

I admired his dazzling bare torso through blurry eyes. Passionate kisses and tender caresses had quelled the tears for both of us. We pressed our heated bodies together as if we needed to. "You too, Hunter."

"I have to kiss you again. I have to feel you, Lorrie."

"I don't want to fight it anymore, Hunter," I breathed. "I want you. Kiss me."

"Oh *Lorrie.*" He leaned down, crushing my body deliciously with his weight and crushing my lips with his.

I opened my mouth and his tongue slipped inside. He gave long, leisurely licks even as I grabbed at his damp hair and pulled him greedily into me. Our tongues tangled and wrestled, leaving both of us gasping for air. I closed my eyes as Hunter unhooked my bra and sealed his mouth over a breast, continuing his leisurely licks against the hardened tip.

"Hunter," I moaned.

I squirmed beneath him, pushing my chest up into his mouth as he flicked the tip of his tongue over my nipple. His fingertips trailed soft caresses down my neck and across my chest, sending tiny shivers of pleasure across my body. I pulled one of his fingers into my mouth and began sucking on it, pulling a sexy groan from his lips that vibrated through my chest. His lips tightened around the tip of my breast and he sucked the point as I sucked his finger. Filled with need, my hips bucked impatiently into his. He responded by growling and clamping my nipple with his teeth.

"Ohhh." I exhaled a shaky breath.

The sharp sensation pierced through the fog clouding my mind, erasing lingering feelings of despair and numbness. It was an exquisite mix of pleasure tinged with an edge of pain, and it was even better when he soothed the spot with tender, placating licks afterward. Deep down I knew he could this; he could strike away the pain that haunted me even if it was for only a brief moment. I knew it because of the charge I got every time I was near him. Only he could make me feel this way. Only Hunter could make me feel truly normal—no, not normal—better than that. Alive.

I could feel him growing hot and hard through the towel around his waist. He began slowly, softly grinding himself against my thigh even as he gently caressed me with his hands and kissed my breasts.

"Hunter," I whispered. "Your towel."

"I know," he groaned softly. "I'm sorry. I'm getting a boner around you again. I can't help myself . . ."

I cupped his cheek and gently tilted his gaze up to meet mine. "I don't want you to help yourself."

I slipped my fingers into the waist of the towel and slowly pulled it away. His cock fell heavily against my thigh with a dull slap, the heat of the engorged flesh searing my skin.

His hand tightened around my waist. "Are you sure?"

I stared deeply into those dark irises. I didn't know what troubles laid behind them that caused him so much pain but I didn't need to. I knew I wanted to make him forget about them. I knew I wanted him to do the same for me. My hands fumbled for the burning rod against my thigh and I stroked the head gently with the pads of my fingers. Butterfly touches stuttered his breath.

"Jesus, that feels so good." He winced, pained by the pleasure of gentle touches. I continued massaging him delicately—without lubrication—and a tear fell from his eye onto my cheek. "The way you touch me, Lorrie . . . I've never felt anything like this before. I can't explain it."

"I care about you, Hunter. Can you feel it?" I took his palm and placed it against my heart. "I'm so sorry for hurting you. I'm sorry for avoiding you, pushing you away." A tear of my own rolled down the side of my face onto the pillow. "I'm sorry for being so selfish. I'm sorry for being such a fucked up person and complicating your life."

"Shhh shhh." He hushed me softly. "You don't need to apologize." He wiped the tears from my eyes with his thumb then wiped his own. "It's behind us now. The past doesn't matter when we have tonight and the future."

I took his thumb and kissed it dearly, tasting the salty pain of both of us on my lips. It was all coming out. The tears. The pain. The emotions. Everything we'd held back. Everything we hid away to appear strong on the outside. I'd never seen this wave of emotions from Hunter before and the force of it was enough to shatter everything I thought I knew about him, about me, and about us. We were bare physically and emotionally. Without needing words, for the first time we were being completely honest with one another.

I tenderly wiped his eyes and then mine. With my palm damp with tears, I wrapped my hand around his cock and began stroking the length of it. He had said we could do this together, that we could be strong together. I wanted him to know I understood that the pain we endured—the tears we shed—could be used to heal one another.

He groaned from the sensation. "Your hand . . . " he stuttered. "It's too much, Lorrie. It feels too good."

I stroked him slowly but insistently, feeling him growing hotter, witnessing the need in his eyes becoming stronger. He gently but urgently thrust his hips into my firm grasp, softly grunting with each drive. I watched his pleasure-tortured expression with fascination, feeling a swelling ache developing between my thighs.

Hunter slid himself smoothly from my hand as he ducked below my waist. He dug his fingers into the band of my panties and looked up at me. "I want these off."

I nodded silently and wiggled my hips to help him, my belly fluttering with heated anticipation. Slipping the small fabric from my feet, he cast them to the floor where my other clothes lay haphazardly. Then he lifted my legs onto his broad shoulders and planted his lips against the inner flesh of one thigh.

He kissed along my leg, his mouth edging dangerously close to my sex. I clenched against the urge to hide from him even as he firmly held my legs apart. "I'm not going anywhere, Lorrie. You can't avoid me or push me away this time. I'm gonna be right here, giving you what you need."

Growling, he dove down and began flicking his tongue against my clit. I balled the velvety sheets in my fists trying to hold on as a flood of sensations and emotions overwhelmed me. I hadn't had sex in almost two years but the long absence of partner stimulation couldn't fully explain the waves of pleasure coursing through my body. Hunter's expert tongue was just that good.

"Hunter, it feels too good . . . Don't stop."

The pace of his fluttering tongue quickened. My legs shook as I struggled against his restraining hands to squeeze my thighs against his head. He groaned into my depths, vibrating my folds with his yearning. Then he began sucking on the sensitive flesh of my clitoris. My head arched back against the pillow and my lips parted to release fervent moans. As he alternated between firm suction and feather-light licks, I could feel a fire growing in my sex. His confident movements had just the right amount of pressure and friction to drive me wild. I'd never experienced oral sex this good before let alone half this good. It wasn't long before I shattered. I came harder than I ever had—either by myself or with someone else. I closed my eyes and pressed the back of my head into the pillow as a string of obscenities sputtered softly from my lips.

I faintly heard Hunter's voice through the roaring in my ears. "God, you're so adorable when you come. I could watch you come all night."

He kissed my thighs tenderly as I hovered in post-climax bliss. Moments later, he inserted the tip of one finger into me and gently thrust it in back and forth.

"Want more?" he asked, teasing me with shallow penetration.

"I *need* more," I breathed. "Much more."

His thrusts came deeper and faster, firing sensitive nerves in their wake. The rhythm was quick and steady, further fueling my desire instead of satisfying it. I'd been barely able to resist Hunter before we'd even kissed, and now that he was pleasuring me, I could scarcely contain myself. My hips bucked into his finger in tune with his thrusts, eager for more.

"I feel it again . . . I'm coming, Hunter."

I looked down to see him watching me intensely. "Don't fight it, Lorrie. Let go. Let me see you come."

I came again. The world turned dark for a moment and my body trembled from the aftershocks. I panted for my breath and struggled to recollect the pieces of my mind. "Oh god Hunter, you make me come so hard . . ."

"We're not done yet, Lorrie," he grunted, desire oozing from his voice making me want him even more.

He reached into a bedside drawer and brought out a shiny packet. After sheathing himself, he pulled back the covers and we curled up beneath his sheets. He wrapped one arm across my chest holding me tightly as we lay sideways with my back to him. I felt him nudging at my entrance. Realizing how big he was, I was suddenly grateful for the orgasms loosening me in preparation to receive him.

"You ready?" he whispered into my ear.

I bit my lip and nodded, eager to feel him inside me.

Hunter pushed his hips forward slowly, parting my folds with his cock and beginning to slide in gently. "Ah, god. You're so tight, Lorrie."

I sucked in a deep breath as the head cleared. "It's been a while since I've been with someone," I answered softly.

"You're so gorgeous. I'm so glad you're with me." He pushed in to the hilt and I moaned from the sensation.

He started with slow, gentle thrusts allowing me to accommodate to his size and the feeling of impossible fullness. I reached back to grip his buttocks, encouraging him. His drives came harder and quicker, pulling cries of pleasure from both our lips. After an extended period, I came for a third time. As I contracted around him, he growled painfully. He thrust a few more times then I felt the condom fill with his hot seed.

I didn't know how long we lay there, our bodies fit together like spoons. I was so exhausted from all the crying and all the climaxes that I had lost track of time. As I listened to Hunter's steady breathing in my ear—vaguely musing on the orgasm hat trick he had performed—I dozed off.

Chapter Eighteen

SHUT-IN

Sunlight flickered against my face, bringing me slowly to consciousness. I woke to find myself nestled beneath Hunter's chin. My arms were around him and his arms were around me. My heart beat steadily, calmly. The moment was like when I fell asleep on his couch while watching horror movies. Except this time, there was no question about whether we had sex. I vividly remembered the tears and multiple orgasms from last night. I remembered the connection we'd made and the feelings that had poured out of both of us. I didn't want to run this time. I wanted to stay in his bed and hoped I'd never have to leave.

I knew Hunter and I weren't friends anymore. Friends didn't fall asleep nestled together naked like lovers.

I shifted my leg which was wrapped over Hunter's and realized his cock was still inside me though no longer hard. I silently watched his chest rise and lower steadily with each breath, wondering how I ended up in this situation. This wasn't a dream—there was no way I could dream up something this good.

Hunter's eyes opened lazily. "Lorrie?"

"Morning, sleepyhead." I ran a hand through his hair, tousling dark brown strands; the soft, silky strands slipping between my fingers was even better than I'd imagined it'd be.

He smiled. "You stayed."

I smiled back. "Yes, I did," I said softly.

He gently pulled me to him and we kissed.

"God, it's so good to see you laying beside me," he said. "If I woke up and found you weren't here, I probably would've lost it."

"It would take a major catastrophe to keep me away from you." I nuzzled my nose against his, finding the hard edge soft and pliable. Gentle butterfly kisses stuttered our breaths as I ran my fingertips along his arm where the hammer was etched. I could hardly believe someone with such savagely beautiful muscles could be so tender. Hunter was unlike any guy I'd ever met—or probably would ever meet. He was a walking contradiction: fierce yet tender, strong but damaged. Soon our nuzzling became a mini-makeout session.

"Mmm I like kissing you," he said. "Your lips are so soft, you're so soft everywhere." He gently squeezed my hips. "You're like my favorite body pillow." He wrapped his arms around me and crushed my breasts against his chest.

"Your lips are soft too." I touched his lips gently with my finger. "But everywhere else, you're hard as a rock." I poked his abs and he surprisingly giggled like the Pillsbury Doughboy. "So you really are ticklish?" I said, stunned. "You weren't faking it last time."

His expression was mock serious. "That's my weakness. Please don't tell my opponents."

I laughed. "I can just imagine 'Mr. Hyde' taking you down and then tickling you in the ribs. 'Goochy goochy goo!' The ref would have to end the fight because people would be booing and throwing tomatoes into the ring."

He chuckled and brushed my hair behind my ear. "You wouldn't want to see two half-naked muscular guys tickling one another?"

I thought about it for a second. "Nah, I think that would be more silly than sexy. It just wouldn't be very manly."

"Ya know, one time I was sparring with Gary and he accidentally grabbed one of my ticklish spots and I started laughing. He thought I was making fun of him and he got pissed. Broke a punching bag and stormed off."

"Gary did say you had a shitty ground game."

"Did he?" Hunter chuckled again. "That sounds like him."

"I could take you." I smirked.

"Mmm . . . that sounds like a challenge. Well, Ms. Hide, shall we have a sparring session?"

We sparred for a long time, breaking all the MMA rules by using licking, biting, and deliberate groin attacks. By the time the sun had risen to its peak, we'd blown through four condoms and half a bottle of lube. But we were still without a winner. We were about to keep going but the kittens began mewing for their food.

"Ah, we should take a break and feed the babies their breakfast," Hunter groaned, moments after filling up the fifth condom.

"Agreed," I panted. I rested the back of my hand against my forehead noting the faint traces of sweat there. "We can continue this afterward."

After putting on a pair of athletic shorts Hunter supplied me, I grabbed one of his infamous hoodies laying on the back of his desk chair. I slipped it on, zipped it up, and took a moment to inhale his manly scent lingering in the fabric.

He looked at me and frowned. "Why do you have to look so good in my clothes?"

I eyed him. He was wearing a white v-neck that stretched against his muscles and gray sweatpants that hung loose around one side of his waist exposing the fact that he wasn't wearing any underwear beneath. "Why do *you* have to look so good in your clothes? And without your clothes . . ."

"Don't tempt me, Lorrie," he said darkly. "It's already taking every bit of willpower to go on this break."

I blushed. "Me too. I can't wait to get you back in the sack—after we feed the babies."

We went into the kitchen and found the kittens awake and lively. Rampage and Taylor were playing with a plush mouse together. They were usually fighting, so the sight of them enjoying one another's company was remarkable. Twenty minutes later, we finished feeding the kittens. We both affectionately looked at all six of them sleeping together in their bed.

"Do you think they think of us as their parents?" I asked, sitting on the kitchen floor with my head resting against Hunter's shoulder and both of us leaning against the bottom cupboards.

"Probably," he said. "We've been taking care of them almost since they were born." His arm around my shoulder, he kissed the top of my head.

"But we're not cats," I offered.

"It doesn't matter; they don't have their real parents. The kittens are fortunate that they're so young—they won't know what it's like to lose their parents, or be neglected by them. To them, we've always been their parents. And I think we've been doing a pretty good job so far."

I murmured approval, dimly pondering the implications. It was hard to deny our affections for the kittens and the kittens' affections for us. Rampage loved Hunter and Hunter loved him.

"Want something to eat?" Hunter asked, moving his arm affectionately around my waist as we stood up from the kitchen floor.

"Sure, I could use a little more energy," I said, looking up at him. "I could also use a shower."

"What's the point when you're just going to get hot and sweaty again?" He grinned.

I smiled. "I have to set a good hygiene example for the kids," I said jokingly. "Especially if you don't."

"So responsible. Ya know, if you really want to teach them proper grooming, I can help you with that."

"How would you help me, when you're the one who's making me need a shower in the first place?"

"Cats lick one another. So if you'll stand still . . . I know just the spot too."

I laughed and playfully slapped his rock-hard chest. "Aren't you a silly one? Humans don't do that."

Hunter smiled wickedly. "Alright fine, I'll have to show you later. In the meantime, I'm gonna cook us some breakfast. Eggs, sausage, and toast okay?"

"Sure, I'd love that. Thank you," I said as I began moving toward the bathroom.

"Oh, and Lorrie—"

I halted my gallop and turned to face him. "Yes?"

"Don't lock the door," he said. "I'm gonna join you and we're gonna pick up where we left off."

The way he looked at me and said those words sent a surge of desire between my legs. I wanted to jump on him right there and tear off those sagging sweatpants with my teeth. Instead, I took a deep breath to calm myself and simply smiled at him innocently. "Okay Gunther, I'll be waiting."

I could feel Hunter's eyes burning a hole in the back of my athletic shorts as I strolled back into the bedroom. I pulled my phone out of my jean pocket and sent a quick text to Daniela letting her know I was hanging out with Hunter, so she wouldn't worry. Then I skipped to the bathroom. Breathing in the familiar clean smell of the bathroom, I looked at myself in the mirror.

Wow, I look like a mess.

Although there were no bits of algae and ice caught in my hair this time, my hair was disheveled, having that just-been-fucked look—except ten times over—and the light amount of mascara I wore was smeared across my cheeks. I should've felt self-conscious but instead I felt confident and secure. What had gotten into me?

Hunter. That's what.

Tattoos and Muscles made me feel beautiful and desirable. Humming Taylor Swift's *Love Story* merrily, I slipped out of my clothes and stepped into the shower. Noticing the loofah I'd avoided using before, I picked it up and began brushing it sensually across my body. The thought of Hunter soaping it up and rubbing it across his naked body turned me on. It was amazing to think about how so much had changed since the first time I came over to his place. I'd been cold, numb, and on the verge of freezing to death. Now I was hot and needy, aching to have more mind-blowing sex with Hunter. His bathroom trash can was filled with condoms—many more than before—but this time I knew where they had come from. It was as if my sexual desire for Hunter had been held back by a dam built from the tragedy of my past and the uncertainty of my future. And now that dam had broken.

Still humming, I was preparing to begin pleasuring myself—a warm up before Hunter joined me—when on the other side of the shower curtain I heard the bathroom door open.

"Breakfast is served," Hunter called.

"Mmm I can smell it already," I answered. "Smells so delicious. I'll be out in a jiffy."

"No need. I brought it in here." I heard a clink as he placed the food on the bathroom counter. Then he pulled the shower curtain back and marveled at my body. "How's the shower going?" he purred.

"Good, but a little lonely. All I have is this loofah to keep me company."

"That loofah is a bastard." He growled. "Lemme keep you company." He tore off his clothes and hopped into the shower with me. I held the loofah idly by my waist but he took it and tossed it into the trash; he dipped to his knees and began kissing the skin where the loofah had been.

"Mmm," I hummed as hot water poured over our bodies. I'd never showered with a guy before and my excitement for the idea was heightened by the fact that the guy was Hunter.

"Now lemme lick this sweet cunt of yours, Lorrie."

His filthy words made my body thrum with desire. Before I could react, he grabbed my waist and closed his mouth over my sex. Instinctively, I leaned back against the tile, one hand holding onto the ceramic soap dish affixed to the wall, the other hand grabbing Hunter's hair. He wasted no time sucking on and flittering his tongue over my clit as if starved for the taste of it. I curled my toes against the tub, desperately trying to remain standing even as I felt my legs turning to jelly.

He growled into my folds and dipped his tongue into my depths, spearing me with a back and forth movement of his head.

"Oh *god*, Hunter. That feels *so* good."

"You *taste* so good," he grunted.

Because of the water, my fingers were beginning to slip from the soap dish. I was afraid I was going to fall and crack my head open mid-orgasm. Feeling a balance-shattering climax dangerously approaching, I tried to wiggle free but his large hands firmly grasped my waist. "Hunter, we shouldn't stay in the water too long," I managed to utter between moans. "We'll end up looking like prunes."

He stopped, leaving me bereft of pleasure. I wanted him to quell the gnawing ache between my legs he had started but I also wanted to finish my shower and eat breakfast. If only we could multitask.

"Good point," he said casually.

I turned off the shower and Hunter guided me out of the tub by hand like a bad boy gentleman. While he began drying my body with a towel, sneaking kisses against my skin here and there, I spotted a tray on the bathroom counter with a plate of eggs and sausage, another plate with toast, a jar of grape jelly to the side, and a tall glass of orange juice. I was impressed not only by the demonstration of his culinary skills but also by the presentation.

"Aw, you're so sweet, Hunter." I turned to him, lifted on my toes, and affectionately kissed his lips. "You're so sweet you're going to give me cavities."

"I've got an extra toothbrush you can use." He winked. "Don't worry about it."

"Are you going to have any food?" I asked smiling, my mouth watering at the feast before me.

"I already ate a little bit. All this is for you. Dig in."

I turned to the food, rubbed my hands together, picked up a sausage link, and bit off a piece. "Mmm so yummy," I murmured with my mouth full. "So juicy and tender."

Hunter slid his hands across my waist from behind. I wiped the condensation from the bathroom mirror and saw ourselves in the reflection. Enjoying the surreal sight of both of us naked together, I reached up to cup his cheek and he smiled. "You're so gorgeous, Hunter. I love it when you smile."

He locked his eyes with mine in the mirror as he tugged me to him, the small of my lower back pressing against his formidable erection. "It's 'cause you're here with me. But look at yourself. Look at these gorgeous tits," he said as he began plumping my breasts in the reflection. "I could play with them all day."

"I like you playing with me," I said, feeling the ache in my sex swelling from his hands at my chest. "Can we multitask?" I took another bite of the sausage in my hand and backed my ass into his erection teasingly, which pulled an erotic groan from his lips.

"Brunch sex huh? I guess there's a first time for everything." He reached into the pocket of his sweatpants that were lying on the floor and pulled out protection.

"Never had brunch sex before?"

"I've never had this much sex in such a short time, period." He grinned as he finished wrapping his cock. "You ready?

"Wait Hunter, I've got to eat this sausage," I said flirtatiously, preparing to take another bite.

"I got your fucking sausage right here." He growled.

He shoved himself into me, hips crashing into my backside. I was already primed since stepping out of the shower, so his entrance came easily. I gasped and instinctively leaned over the bathroom counter for support, eager for him.

His strong hands firmly gripping my waist, he continued thrusting into me, steadily, needily but without hurry. I watched our bodies colliding in the mirror, saw how my hair and breasts jostled each time he drove into me. We performed our own song with him grunting and me moaning in response. It wouldn't be a billboard hit, but I found I enjoyed it more than *Love Story*.

We'd already had sex half a dozen times in the last sixteen hours. Sex with Hunter was quickly becoming as frequent and necessary as breathing. Finding myself adjusting to his demanding pace, I casually reached over to open the jar of grape jelly. I tried to unscrew it but my hands were wet; the vigorous thrusting quaking my body didn't help either.

"Can you help me with this?" I asked, holding up the jar for Hunter.

"Sure, no problem." His pace persisted even as he casually moved his hands from my hips to the jar and unscrewed it. "Here you go."

I backed into him, taking his cock to the hilt as a way of offering my thanks. "You're so helpful, Hunter."

I saw his reflection smile. "I do what I can."

After spreading some jam onto the pre-buttered toast, I bit off a piece, and licked my lips. "This is really good toast. You want a bite?"

"Sure."

I raised it up for him and he leaned over—penetrating me deeper—and chomped on the toast. "Mmm yummy. I need the energy to keep fucking you," he said as another thrust pressed my thighs into the counter cabinets.

"Then maybe you should have some more energy." I dipped my finger into the grape jelly and held it up for him. "Here have some sugar."

He took my finger and inserted it into his mouth, sucking it the delicious way he'd sucked my clitoris. Then he licked the tip clean, making my sex clench around him from the teasing. In a flurry of lust, he growled and flipped me around to face him. We locked desire-lidded eyes. He plucked the jar of grape jam from my hand and poured the contents all over my breasts. I arched my neck and gasped from the cold sensation, fingers desperately clutching the edge of the counter for balance.

"You're getting me all dirty again!" I cried.

"Just the way I like it." He growled before dipping and taking one breast into his mouth. His hand swirled the jelly around the other breast. He swirled his tongue around the tip, spreading the sticky substance over my skin before sucking it up into his mouth. "Now that's a good breakfast."

I popped the last of the toast into my mouth. "I agree. Best breakfast I've had yet." Missing his cock inside me, I said, "I could go for some more of that Hunter sausage though."

There was a momentary smile on his lips before he slammed his cock into me, pushing me from a standing position into a seated position on the bathroom counter.

We continued going at it until long after the steam had dissipated from the bathroom. Eventually, we finished breakfast with two orgasms and a side of orange juice.

After another quick rinse in the shower, we dried off, neglected to put on clothes, and plopped onto his bed, crawling back into the warm blissful haven beneath the sheets. Light beamed in through his bedroom window. It was one of those unusual days where the ground was still covered in snow but the sun shone brightly in the sky.

"Do you have any plans the rest of the day?" he asked, propping himself on an elbow beside me. "I know you said you had plans last night, I'm sorry I made you miss them."

Laying on my back, I turned to smile at him. He hadn't shaved and I found the light stubble on his face made him even more alluring. "Well, I didn't really have any last night. I was just saying that as an excuse to avoid you."

He gave a lopsided smile. "I figured as much."

"But to answer your question, no, I don't really have any plans today. I might have to do some studying for midterms coming up, but nothing really pressing. You? You going to train today?"

"I usually do on Sundays but I don't really feel like going today."

He groaned then smiled at me. "I just wanna stay inside the apartment all day long and hang out with you. What do ya think?" He squeezed me to him. I loved it every time he squeezed me and crushed my body against his; the pressure was invigorating.

"Don't you train like every day though? When's the last time you missed a session?"

"Umm . . . I think I missed a day about two years ago because I got sick."

"Wow, so dedicated. I feel bad, I don't want to be the reason you skip again if it's that important to you."

"You're what's important to me. I just wanna be with you and that's what I plan on doing. So what do ya think about hanging out with me all day?"

I giggled. "I'd love that actually. I was kind of thinking the same thing: staying in all day. I don't want to leave the apartment either. I wish we could just stay in and have sex all day every day."

He laughed. "I like that idea. Why *can't* we do that?"

"Because we have responsibilities and stuff," I offered as a suggestion.

"Eh, we can blow those off."

I smiled in agreement. "I mean we have classes and midterms, you have matches to fight, we have to eat—we'll eventually run out of protein bars you know."

He kissed me and brushed my hair behind my ear. "We can order delivery. I got some extra money from my fights. That should last us a while."

"Mmm . . . delivery. I like the sound of that." I giggled. "We can be like the cats—they're happy never leaving the apartment. It's scary and dangerous outside, there's fast cars and feral cats." I briefly thought about that feral black cat again and how it had almost caused me to drown. It terrified me to think what would happen if Taylor got into a fight with that cat. "Plus, I'm sure other cats gossip. And I don't want anyone talking shit about Taylor."

"That's right," he murmured against my cheek before pecking it with his lips. "Well, the kitties need more food too. So we may have to get them some more from the mall. Unless we can order it off of Amazon."

I nodded. "Amazon rocks."

He glanced at my breasts. "We also need to get more condoms and lube. I think we're almost out. I can't believe we blew through so much. I can't get enough of you."

"Yeah, I don't know what it is, but I can't get enough of you either, Hunter. It's like you're turning me into a sex kitten," I teased. "You make me feel so good."

"You're not sore yet right?"

"I'm a little sore but I like the feeling. It's like having an itch but when you scratch it, it feels so good. It's kind of good to feel something all the time, you know? I want to be even more sore. How are you holding up?"

"I'm so sore right now." He grinned. "I don't think I'm gonna be able to walk tomorrow. But I can't stop fucking you, Lorrie. Everytime I look at you, feel your body against mine, I'm hard again. It's painful, but goddammit does it feel good. It's like I have to be inside you. I've never felt this way before, ever. I don't care if my dick falls off."

I giggled, wondering if such a thing was possible. "Is it possible to have too much sex? Maybe we'll go blind."

"Who cares? As long as we have each other, we'll be good. You ready for round ten?"

I nodded eagerly. "Bring it on, Hunter 'The Hammer' Jensen!"

🪓 🪓 🪓

I woke up with my head against Hunter's chest. I must've fallen asleep. There was still a little bit of light outside. Hunter was gently stroking my hair, his eyes closed.

I grumbled softly. "Mmm . . . what time is it?"

"Dunno," he murmured lazily.

"How long was I asleep?"

"Mmm . . . maybe an hour, half an hour?"

"Really?" I rubbed my eye and yawned. "Feels like I was out for a while."

A buzzing on the bedside stand woke us from our stupor. Hunter reached over and picked up his phone. "Damn, Gary just sent me a text. I was supposed to spar with him today." He showed me the message on his phone.

"Uh oh," I replied. "Will he be mad?"

"Busy hanging with Lorrie," Hunter said, prolonging the pronunciation as he typed out the words. He sent the reply to Gary and returned the phone to the nightstand. "Nah, there's plenty of other guys at Bigg's that can help him train . . . now what were we talking about again?"

I smiled from Hunter's attentiveness and leaned my head against his chest again. Light hairs tickling my cheek were a fresh reminder of his raw masculinity. Although his chest was firm, it was the best pillow I'd ever slept on. ". . . I was just wondering how long I'd been asleep."

"Oh yeah, I think you dozed off after that last orgasm. You were probably exhausted." He yawned and closed his eyes again.

"Ah, right." A montage of riding Hunter and being ridden by him came back to me. I didn't know how it was possible after all the energy I'd expelled, but I felt myself getting aroused again. "You sleepy?"

"Umm . . . a little. Why?"

I fumbled for his cock beneath the sheets. Finding it soft, I began gently stroking it. "I don't know. I was just thinking if you want to go for another round. Which one would this be?"

"Hmm . . . I lost count." He chuckled. "Yeah, of course I'm up for it. Just be a little gentle until it gets fully hard. I'm so numb and sensitive right now. It feels like it's raw. It's so weird."

"Well we're weirdos aren't we?" I flashed a smile at him even though his eyes were still closed.

He smiled back. "Snorrie and Gunther. Two sex fiends."

"Sex fiends, and sex friends."

"That's right. We can have it all, Lorrie."

It took a few minutes of gentle massaging before Hunter became fully erect. During that time, he was stroking my sex with his hand, heightening my arousal to match his. When we were both ready, I straddled his waist and rode him until we both came.

$$\text{↗ ↗ ↗}$$

When I woke up again, night had fallen, and Hunter was snoring gently. We had fed the kittens, snacked on some powerbars for dinner and came back to the bed to nap. The bed was fast becoming a home within a home.

I watched him sleep peacefully. I was amused at the irony of him calling me Snorrie when he snored as well. It felt so surreal being with him now, in this moment. We were snuggled up naked together like we were in our own little world. Just him, me, and an ocean of blankets. It was so simple compared to the chaos happening outside this apartment. Everything out there—the rumors, the homework, the deaths, the stress, the sadness—seemed to disappear when I was with Hunter in this bed.

Eventually he woke up.

"What do you think about the future, Hunter?" I said softly.

He blinked away his drowsiness and smiled warmly at me. "Hm? Like what about it?"

"I dunno. Like end of this semester when you graduate. What are you going to do?"

"Haven't really thought about it." He chuckled. "I'll probably get a job somewhere, work. There aren't a lot of jobs related to physics but I'm sure I'll find something. What about you?"

"I haven't really thought about it much either. It's so confusing: the future, real life. I wish I didn't have to face it."

"Me too, Lorrie." He kissed my forehead. "You're a sophomore, so you still have a few years to figure it out. Whereas for me, I got a few months." He laughed.

"I don't want us to break up because you graduate," I said softly.

His expression became serious. "We won't. We can face the future together. We're both good with our hands—you got the drawing skills and I got the punching skills. We can team up and start an art gallery. You'll do the art pieces and I'll knock out the competitors."

I laughed. "Mmmhmm. I like that idea. But what if the competitors start hiring their own muscle?"

"I'll take 'em all down." He kissed my nose. "Anything for you."

"You're so sweet." I beamed, returning the kiss. "Hey, do you have a pencil and a piece of paper?" I said, suddenly inspired. "I kind of want to draw you."

He grinned. "Sure." We both emerged from the blankets, naked. He flicked on the bedroom lights and retrieved the requested items from his desk beside the dresser. As I took his desk chair, flipped it around to face him, and sat down, he made the bed neatly and stretched across it. "Alright, how do you want me?"

"How do I want you? Umm... I want you... all over me, actually," I teased as I reached for a thin physics workbook on his desk and used it to prop up the piece of paper Hunter gave me.

Hunter narrowed his eyes then eagerly jumped off the bed, his cock bouncing as he walked over to my side, a seductive smile on his lips. My pulse leaped. As often as I'd seen Hunter without clothes over the past twenty-four hours, I was certain I'd never get tired of seeing him naked. He was too beautiful.

"I was just joking," I said with a smirk. I playfully slapped his semi-erect cock by my shoulder making it wobble back and forth. "I mean, I do want you all over me... but after I finish this drawing."

"Of course," he said, grinning. He left my side and settled back on the bed. "So what kind of pose do you want?"

I thought about all the pictures hanging on the wall in Bigg's Gym where the fighters had the same aggressive pose. I had enough drawings of Hunter looking intimidating. I wanted to sketch the vulnerable side of him, the side I'd only seen recently. "Why don't you choose a comfortable position. Sitting or laying. It's up to you, whatever's relaxing enough that you can hold it for like twenty minutes."

He smiled. "Okay." He shifted around on the bed, trying out different positions. Eventually, he settled into a dramatic laying pose with his finger outstretched toward me. One knee was raised while the other leg lay on its side, and his outstretched left arm supported him from the bed.

Even under the bedroom's soft lighting, the sharp lines of his naked body contrasted boldly with the smooth sheets beneath him. I'd always drawn parts of Hunter from memory—his hammer tattoo, his face—but now I had him as a live subject. All of him. An excitement swelled inside of me as I began to scan the length of his exposed figure.

My gaze started from his large feet and my pulse began beating faster as I moved toward those powerful legs that were used to drive vicious punches against his opponents. My breath hitched at the sight of his savage cock draped lazily over the side of one thigh. I felt my thighs become heated as I thought about how the expert use of that one part of him could pull mind-shattering orgasms from my body. My gaze snagged on his pelvis and I bit my lip, following the hard lines up to his trim hips and then to his pack of ab muscles that were so cut they appeared flexed even when I knew he was relaxed. They looked so yummy that I wanted to lick them slowly all the way from the bottom to base of his pecs. His chest was composed of two chiseled slabs of flesh, expanding and contracting with each of his calm breaths. I reached his face and was mesmerized by those dark gray eyes filled with depth and mystery. Behind those irises hid a past that I didn't know about. What was it like to have drug-addict parents? A thread of doubt twisted through me. Could I really capture the essence of Hunter in a drawing?

He smiled at me. "How's this?"

"Umm . . . that's a classic pose from the Sistine Chapel." I giggled, recalling the fresco painting titled *The Creation of Adam.* "Unfortunately, my name's not Michelangelo and this isn't the 1500s."

He narrowed his eyebrows. "Michelangelo? I was going for the scene from E.T. with the glowy-healing finger."

I giggled again. "Ah, I see. How about we try something less dramatic? Something more natural. I want to see the *Hunter* in his natural element."

"Hmm . . ." His body remained in the same pose but he rested his right elbow on his one raised knee and put his forefinger to his lip in thought. "Lemme think about it."

"There that's it! Hold that if you can."

He turned toward me. "Huh? You like this?" He tilted his head to examine himself.

"Yeah! Don't move!"

He knitted his brows. "What's so special about this position?"

"I think it suits you well. It's kind of like you're exposed and vulnerable... but not fully since you still have that one knee up. You also look relaxed but also concerned—like the weight of the world is on your mind. It seems like a natural pose. Hmm it's still missing something though..." I picked up one of his gray hoodies from the floor and threw it to him. "Here put this on. Leave it unzipped so I can see your six pack but put the hood up."

With his brow raised skeptically, he caught the hoodie with one hand and carefully put it on while maintaining his position; the hoodie was the only thing he was wearing. He left the sweater unzipped like I'd asked, leaving his chest and abs deliciously exposed. His cock was still draped over his thigh carelessly.

"How does this look?" he asked.

"That's perfect," I hummed, feeling a thrill from the added sexiness the sweater brought to the pose. "Now just hold that while I work."

I began drawing him starting with the basic contours of his body then refined the lines with small details here and there—the round curve of his shoulders, the slight jutting of his developed obliques.

"You keep doing that and we're not gonna finish this drawing," he said.

Breaking out of my intense concentration, I lifted my head from the paper. "Doing what?"

"Biting your bottom lip like that. If you keep doing that, we're gonna have to work off some tension."

I glanced at his leg and saw his cock becoming unabashedly erect.

I smiled pleasantly, returning my focus to the drawing to avoid seeing the lust in his eyes that I knew was there. The throbbing between my legs made me unsure whether I'd be able to resist him if I saw his hunger for me. "I'm trying, Hunter." I grumbled. "It's difficult though. I'm just getting really into this drawing."

"I can see that. Your tits are so hard right now. It's all I can think about. How can I lay still when I know they're so suckable."

My smile widened. "Patience, my dear Hunter. I'll be finished soon."

Once I completed the shading on his body, I began working on the details of his face. It was difficult to capture his eyes just right.

I kept looking at his eyes, comparing him to what I had drawn, but something was always off. It took every ounce of concentration, but I finally finished the drawing. Releasing a satisfied exhalation, I put down my pencil and fingered him over. He eagerly hopped off the bed and returned to my side.

I handed him the completed drawing and waited for his reaction. "This is amazing." he said, his voice intimately low and filled with admiration.

"Well, the figure is you after all, Mr. Humble," I teased.

"No, aside from that . . . I've never seen anything like this before. Somehow you've captured every little detail about me. How did you do it?"

I pointed at the picture in between his hands. "Well, first your body was a challenge. There were a lot of subtle contours and a wide range of hard and soft shadows. Most people aren't even close to being as muscular as you so they generally have a lot of light shadows and simple lines. Your lines and shadows were much more complex."

He nodded, listening to my words and scanning the picture carefully.

I directed his attention to particular spots on his torso. "You've also got all these scars, bumps, and bruises on your skin that I take you got from fighting. Some of them are more faded and some are fresher. I spent a lot of effort trying to capture each of them." I recalled Aunt Caroline telling me before that the scars we have— both on the inside as well as on the outside—are part of what makes us who we are. I wondered at how Hunter had changed after receiving each of his scars.

" . . . The detail is incredible. It's even better than a mirror."

"Sometimes it takes another person to see us for who we really are."

"You're right, I'd even forgotten I had some these scars, I'd seen 'em so often in the mirror. They're supposed to be reminders of the mistakes I made in my fights. But it's easy to overlook things you see often until you see them from a different perspective."

"Mmhmm." I nodded. ". . . So after I finished your body, I had to fill in the details of your face. This was the hardest part. I was able to get the shape of your nose and the curve of your lips pretty easily but when it came to your eyes, I had to redraw them at least a dozen times."

"What was wrong with the eyes?"

"I don't know. You've got these stunning gray eyes . . . every time I drew them they came out too flat or one-dimensional. So I had to keep redoing them—you can still see some of the eraser marks here." I pointed to the rough texture of the paper where I'd erased multiple times. "Even now, I don't think I've quite captured them."

"No, this looks amazing," he said, mesmerized.

I grinned. "Thank you, it's my best work to-date. Couldn't have done it without such a capable model."

"It's even better now that you've explained it to me. I didn't realize you put so much thought and effort into every line. I thought art just came naturally for you."

"Well, it's probably similar to fighting for you. Some of it comes naturally but a lot of it is practice and thinking."

"You're so smart and talented." He kissed me on the top of my head. "We make a good team, don't we?"

"The best team. Now that we're finished, let's get back to business." I took the drawing from his hands and placed it on the desk then I ripped off his hoodie and we tumbled onto the bed, lips locked in passionate embrace. We curled up beneath the sheets and remained there the rest of the night.

$$ \nearrow \nearrow \nearrow $$

I woke up Monday morning to light kisses against my neck. I squirmed and softly squealed.

"Did I wake you?" Hunter crooned.

"A little bit."

"Sorry, I couldn't help kissing you, you're so beautiful in the morning. You look so peaceful when you're sleeping."

"I like you kissing me," I said sleepily. "There are certainly much worse ways of waking up." I cupped a hand over my mouth and yawned. "Was I snoring?"

He smiled, brushing a strand of hair out of my face. "Yeah, you were, Snorrie. But I think it's cute. I could make an mp3 of it and listen to it while I'm jogging."

I squealed from his embarrassing comment and curled into him. Hunter could say some embarrassing things that made him even more endearing than he already was.

"It's still early, ya know," he said. "We have time to go to our classes . . . if we want."

I ran a finger gently along the tattoos on his shoulder and chest, admiring the art there. "I really don't want to go."

Hunter grinned. "Me neither."

We lay together in silence for a moment while I continued tracing the inked lines on his skin and he traced the curve of my hips with his fingertips.

"You wanna stay in again?" he asked, looking at me carefully.

After an amazing weekend, I dreaded the thought of it ending and having to return to the world outside. I knew Hunter was thinking the same thing. I bit my bottom lip and nodded slightly. He smiled and I did as well.

"Let's do it then," he said. "I don't have anything too important going on. We can even study in the living room if we need to. I still have my psych book from freshman year. You can use that."

"That sounds like a good idea."

After lounging in bed for an extra hour, we got up, put on some clothes, fed the kitties, and ate breakfast. We did the dishes together with me washing and Hunter rinsing. It was an oddly domestic experience and I found it to be fun and relaxing. At about eleven we both finished showering.

"Ready to hit the books, babe?" Hunter said as I came out from the bathroom with a towel around my waist and another around my hair. He was seated at the living room table with a physics textbook and psychology textbook on the surface.

Feeling a thrill from him calling me *babe*, I approached him and gave him a peck on his cheek. As endearing as *Snorrie* was, I considered this new nickname an upgrade. "Mmhmm but first . . . I think we have a morning class we need to attend together."

He cocked one brow. "And what is that?"

"Sex Ed 101. And you're the professor."

He looked surprised but then a flash crossed his eyes and he grinned mischievously. "Well then." He cleared his throat. "Welcome to class, Ms . . ."

"—Burnham. Lorrie Burnham." I smiled at him, feeling at ease with telling him my last name for the first time.

His eyes widened for a moment then he smiled warmly. "Of course Ms. Burnham," he said, pronouncing my name with a silky voice. ". . . It's always a pleasure to see you. You're my favorite student you know."

"Well Professor Jensen, you're my favorite professor. I always love the assignments you give. I can't wait to do them."

"The lesson today is going to be very hands-on. We'll be learning about the human body and sexual pleasure. I hope you've come prepared to learn."

"Ooh, I like the sound of that."

We went through a rigorous hour and a half lesson. It was the most demanding class I'd ever attended. The professor and I masturbated in front of one another then we pleasured each other to demonstrate our learning. At several points, I failed to follow instructions so Professor Jensen ended up spanking my naked rear while I was sprawled across his bare lap. It was a new experience for the both of us and we both found it thrilling.

"So what's my grade?" I panted after we had both orgasmed.

"Definitely an A," he groaned, still recovering from his climax.

Despite the failure to follow instructions a few times—some purposely—I thought I had performed quite admirably. "Just an A? Why not an A+, Professor Jensen?"

"If you want an A+, Ms. Burnham, you're going to have to do some extra credit," he purred.

"What do I have to do?"

"We'll save that for another lesson," he said with a wicked grin.

We decided to take a break. Hunter went to the kitchen to snack on a protein bar and I went to the bedroom to put on some clothes. Just as I finished dressing, my phone rang inside my pocket and I saw it was Daniela.

"Hey Lorrie, what's up girl? Just wanted to call to see where you were. I missed you in psych today."

With the excitement of this morning's activities still buzzing through my body, I'd almost forgotten I had a real class to go to today. "Oh I've just been hanging out at Hunter's place. What did I miss?"

"Muller was talking about sex!"

"What? No way." I couldn't imagine Professor Muller—an old guy with a German accent—talking to a bunch of nineteen-year-olds about sex. That sounded like an awkward lecture.

"Yes way! He was talking about the pleasure-reward system in our brains and how the chemical dopamine makes us feel good. A lot of it gets released whenever we do something enjoyable like gambling or having sex, which is often the basis for addiction."

It occurred to me that I could tell Daniela I'd attended my own lecture on sex and how my brain was probably drowning in dopamine at the moment, but I quickly dismissed the idea, preferring to play it cool instead. "Oh that sounds interesting."

"Yeah, definitely. You gonna be home tonight? Wanna get dinner at the Barnyard?"

I thought about how Hunter and I had a lot of studying to accomplish tonight. If the last hour and a half was any indication of the type of 'studying' we were going to do, our textbooks might never get cracked open. But I was more than okay with that. "Umm ... I'll give you a call if I get back?"

"Okay." She sounded a little disappointed since we ate dinner together nearly every night. I felt slightly bad for brushing her off but not bad enough to change my mind. Having more fun with Hunter dominated my mind at the moment. "I guess I'll see you whenever you get back."

"Yep, bye Daniela."

She said bye and we both hung up.

"Hey, Lorrie," Hunter said wrapping his arms around me from behind. "Someone call?"

"Yeah, it was just Daniela, checking in on me," I said sweetly.

"There's certainly a lot to check out," he said running his hands up and down my legs and in between them, making me bite my lip in excitement. "That's for sure. Ready to talk about that extra credit?"

I nodded and voiced my excitement.

It was approaching evening by the time we finished Sex Ed 101. The class took a lot longer than both of us had anticipated. There was just so much for him to teach, and for me to learn. We sat down at the living room table, sore and fatigued, but strangely energetic.

"Alright, let's study for real this time," I said.

"For real, babe," he agreed.

"Are you going to help me with psych?" I offered. "I recall you promised you'd help me last time."

He seemed perplexed. "When was that?"

"When we went to the theater and ended up watching horror movies instead, Hun." I decided to call him 'hun' since he was calling me 'babe'. I found it to work as both a shortening of his name and an affectionate term for 'honey'.

"Oh right." He laughed. "Sorry, I totally forgot about that. That was when you ended up sleeping on me."

"That's right."

"Okay, let's do it."

I was a little surprised to find Hunter as knowledgeable about the material as he had claimed. I knew he was smart but it was still unusual to see a muscled brawler be brainy. We hit the books with determination, and I intended to soak in as much material as I could. Studying was helpful for about an hour before we got distracted again. Jokes about classical conditioning turned into teasing, which turned into kissing. And from there things escalated. We were in the middle of having sex in the bedroom with me on top when Hunter's phone buzzed on the nightstand. He ignored it at first, preferring to focus his attention on the way I was bouncing my hips against him but the noise became a growing distraction. He groaned, reached for his phone, and checked it.

"Who is it?" I asked, my breaths heavy.

"Oh, it's just Gary again." He showed me his phone with a text message that said: *Yo, you still hanging out with Lorrie? C'mon man, these punching bags ain't gonna punch themselves.*

"So you going to train at Bigg's today?" I asked Hunter breathlessly, as I continued rocking my pelvis.

"Nah, Gary's just giving me shit. Besides, I'm getting more than a workout right here," Hunter said, thrusting up into me teasingly. He pecked at his phone a few times then became frustrated and handed it to me. "Why don't you reply to Gary. I gotta take care of this greedy little pussy." He gripped my hips and continued driving himself upward.

"Okay," I said. I tried typing a quick response but found it nearly impossible because it's difficult to hit small virtual buttons with your thumbs when a gorgeous guy is thrusting his cock into you. The message ended up saying: *Sowwylm'bizzzzyy*. It was a garbled mess but I hit send anyway.

Satisfied with my work, I handed his phone back to him. He briefly glanced at the message, smiled then shut it off before setting it back on the nightstand. "No more distractions."

I nodded and we continued "studying" well into the night, uninterrupted.

$$\textbf{\textit{r r r}}$$

I woke up naked lying next to Hunter in his bed Tuesday morning, feeling an easy contentment I was becoming accustomed to feeling whenever I woke up beside him. I was beginning to suspect we spent more time naked at his apartment than we did clothed unless comforters counted as clothes. Hunter woke up shortly after, as if our bodies were attuned to the same bizarre rhythm. Watching him open those stunning eyes after a deep slumber was something I always looked forward to.

"Hey Hunter," I said quietly. As great as the moment was, something had been on my mind since the using-kittens-for-blowjobs incident and now that our relationship had progressed beyond friendship, I wanted to talk to him about it. I considered it an opportunity to clarify some misunderstandings so our relationship could continue to grow. "Can I ask you something?"

"Sure, what is it?"

"Umm . . . this isn't an accusation but I kind of need to know— since we're more than friends now . . . Are you seeing anyone else?"

The sleepiness in his eyes immediately disappeared. He

narrowed his brows. "I'm only seeing you, Lorrie. I promise. Why do you ask?"

"... I've been burned before, Hunter," I admitted reluctantly. "I believe I already told you I've had a few boyfriends in my past..."

"Yeah, I know," he grunted, registering his displeasure as he did anytime I mentioned being with other men.

"Well, my first boyfriend cheated on me in high school. I caught him walking out of a movie theater with his arm around this girl who was my best friend at the time. I found out they'd been seeing each other for weeks behind my back. I felt so betrayed. After I cut off ties with them, It was so difficult for me to trust anyone that I didn't date for a few years."

He narrowed his eyes in concern. "I'm sorry to hear that," he said softly as he kissed me tenderly on the forehead. "You don't have to worry, babe. I'd never cheat on you."

"What do you think of Daniela?" I asked matter-of-factly. Daniela had more success attracting men than I did and I attributed it to her good looks and outgoing personality. I wondered what Hunter thought of her.

He chuckled at the suggestion. "Well, I don't really know her. There was really only that one time you and her came over to see the kitties. I guess my impression is: she's cool but there's no way I'd date her."

"Oh? Why not?"

"Well for one—and no offense to her—she seems kinda like one of those pushy go-getter types. Like she knows what she wants and isn't afraid to say it or go after it. It's an admirable trait but not really my preference. You're much more down-to-earth and relatable."

"Hmm ... I thought that's one of her more endearing qualities— her strong personality." I recalled how Daniela was the one who set up the double-date at the Bearded Squirrel and how she hit on that Phi Kappa Delta guy on Valentine's Day. When it came to men, she was often the one to make the first move.

"Maybe to other girls it's endearing. I mean, I do know some guys at the gym that are attracted to that kind of personality, at least initially—it's a thrill to be around a feisty girl—but after a while it can get tiring."

"Umm . . . isn't that kind of an insensitive thing to say, Hunter?" I remarked.

He shrugged. "There's a thin line between being a go-getter and being pushy just as there's a thin line between being arrogant and being confident. You're confident and sassy without being pushy. I dunno how you do it."

I furrowed my eyebrows. "I mean . . . I get what you're saying. It makes sense, but I'm not sure I'm liking it for some reason. It's almost like you're saying I'm meek or passive."

He chuckled. "Nah, babe. We both know you're anything *but* meek." He rubbed my arm affectionately. "You're funny, sweet, polite, you call me on my shit, and you draw awesome pictures of human-fly hybrids. I'm crazy about you. You're complicated but somehow it's like I get you and vice-versa. You're unlike any girl I've ever met—when you're being hard, you do it in a way that doesn't push me away. Maybe it's because I feel that strongly about you, or maybe you're good at being hard but soft. Maybe it's both."

"Hmm . . . I guess I'll take that."

"Good. Also Daniela's afraid of kitten poo. That's a deal breaker for me."

I laughed even as I suddenly felt bad for Daniela. "She's actually pretty smart you know and she's probably not as pushy as you think."

"Yeah, I'm sure she's a great girl. She's just not the one for me. You are."

I blushed and curled into his chest, inhaling his masculine scent.

"But while we're on the topic," he said, "what do you think of Gary?"

I spluttered a laugh. "Wow, I didn't think you would ask me that in return."

"Well, I did. And it's a serious question."

"Don't worry about it, Hun," I said patting his chest lightly. "Gary's a cool guy but he's got nothing on you. He doesn't ooze raw sex like you do."

He grinned. "I'm more than just a piece of meat ya know."

"You're so much more than that. But as a piece of meat, you're

Prime Grade." I reached down to play with his cock and I licked my lips to signal to him my arousal. "I want some more of this meat you've got here."

After having sex, we spent the rest of the day hanging out with the cats, watching Bridezilla, and trying to study in between dopamine-inducing sex bouts. It was another perfect day—one where I felt wonderfully alive and safe. But as night fell and we finally ran out of condoms, we realized we couldn't stay nestled inside the cozy apartment forever. We had responsibilities to the outside world: classes, training, friends. The pressures of the real world were growing and we both felt it. After a heartfelt discussion, we finally decided to go to our classes in the morning. It was time to face the real world again. As boyfriend and girlfriend.

Chapter Nineteen

NEW BEGINNINGS

Daniela would not stop staring daggers at me in Muller's class Wednesday morning. It was the first time I had ever seen her not paying attention to the lecture. I did my best to take notes, but it was hard with my best friend staring at me.

When class finished, I hadn't even gotten my bag out to put my stuff away before Daniela was on me. "Someone didn't come home for four nights straight," she said, her green eyes expectant. "Quite a vacation you've been on."

"Yeah," I said casually, packing my notes and books into my backpack.

"Did you at least bring me a souvenir?"

I handed her a pencil I'd stolen from Hunter's place. It was the same one I'd used to sketch him and I'd been using it take notes during class. "Here you go. A souvenir from the illustrious land of apartment 2E."

She pushed the pencil back to me. "Alright, Lorrie. Cut the crap and spill the juicy beans."

I took a deep breath, trying to refrain from smiling. "Let's save some time. Yes, Hunter and I are dating now."

She squealed and hopped up and down. I look around, embarrassed. Several people were staring at us trying to figure out what was going on.

"I knew it!" she whispered excitedly. "That's so amazing Lorrie!"

"Keep it down," I whispered back. "People are staring."

She nodded and looked around, gradually wiping the smile off her face. The lecture hall gradually emptied out as I continued to put my stuff away.

"So are you guys like keeping it a secret or something?" she asked, this time keeping her voice low.

Were we keeping it a secret? We hadn't really talked about it, but I guessed it would get out soon enough. Still, I didn't want to broadcast our involvement to the world immediately.

"I don't know," I answered. "I guess not. But I still don't like people being in my business."

"I can understand that. People are going to find out eventually though." She finished packing up and slung her bag over her shoulder and I did the same. We left the lecture hall and headed over for our usual post-psych Starbucks mini-date.

I walked behind her and out into the cold winter air. The sky was the kind of brilliant light blue that only comes around in a cold place during winter. Seeing the sun for the first time in a few days cheered me up even more.

"So," Daniela said, breaking me out of my spell. "There's this party I'm going to Friday night. You should come! Oh, and bring Hunter."

I thought nervously about going to a party that weekend. All I really wanted to do was curl up with my new boyfriend and hang out with him and the kittens—maybe for four more days or even four weeks. "I don't know . . ."

"Oh c'mon! I haven't seen you in almost a week and you're gonna bail on me just like that?"

I suddenly felt bad for wanting to ditch her; she was a good friend and the eagerness in her expression indicated she really wanted me to go with her to this party.

"Alright, alright," I said, yielding to her guilt trip. "I think I can go, but I don't know about Hunter. We only just started dating, I don't feel like I can drag him to parties yet."

"You have to set the rules early!" she said, smiling mischievously. "Plus I bet he'll love it. Free drinks and hot music. Who wouldn't love it?"

"I don't know. I'll ask him, but I'm not promising anything."

She turned to me and shrugged. "Okay, just let me know. When are you seeing him next, anyway?"

"He actually wants to see me tonight. We're having dinner in the dining hall together."

She smiled. "You guys were together twenty-four seven for four days straight and don't need a break from each other? He must really like you. Lemme guess, then you're going back to his place to hang out with the kittens?"

I blushed. "I think we're going to my room, actually."

Her eyes widened. "Even better. Get ready, because I'm going to ask you details about how he 'hangs out,' if you get my drift." She winked. "I'm just giving you a pardon for a few days because I know you'll clam up."

"Daniela!" I yelled, my face even hotter than before.

"What? If my best friend is dating a guy as gorgeous as he is, I'm getting the details!"

The righteousness of her expression made me laugh. I'd have to deal with her inquiries about Hunter's sexual prowess when the time came, but at least she was giving me a momentary reprieve. Her interest in the "details" made me think of them myself. The truth was, I couldn't wait to get him back in bed.

We parted ways at Starbucks. I opted against getting a coffee, realizing I had time for a nap before my drawing class. When I got back to my dorm room, I went straight for my bed. It felt kind of strange to be back in my room after sleeping somewhere else the previous few nights. As I dozed off, I thought about seeing Hunter that evening. It was the only thing on my mind.

My phone alarm chimed and I dragged myself out of bed just in time for class, which went smoothly. Drawing was just about the only class that was going well, schoolwise. I'd intended to get work done at Hunter's but we ended up studying Sex Ed more than for classes we were actually taking. I decided to spend some time studying at the library before dinner so I could begin to dig myself out of the rut I'd gotten into with my classwork. After grabbing my first coffee of the day, I walked into Wheatley Library ready to get to it.

The best place to study when you really needed to get stuff done was the cubbies located in the stacks, so that's where I went. The strong stench of old book smell greeted me; I knew a lot of people liked the aroma of book paper, but I wasn't one of them. I found a cubby, put my bag on the desk, and checked my phone. It was five-fifteen—I had almost two hours before meeting Hunter at the Barnyard. After putting on my headphones and starting my Taylor Swift mix, I got to work.

I'd been at it for almost an hour when my mix ended. I put my headphones on the table, wanting a break before moving on to another playlist. It was then that I heard my name from somewhere in the stacks. Putting my pen down on my page of notes, I remained motionless, listening quietly.

"They have to be dating now, right? I mean she's *always* over there. I heard she was even there on Valentine's day," a girl with a high-pitched voice said.

"Yeah," said another girl with a lower voice. "I don't get it though. I mean I guess she's cute, but she's not exactly super hot or anything, and she is such a debbie downer. Sure, I get it, your parents are dead, it's really sad. I'm not blaming her, but come on! He deserves better than that."

My jaw tightened as I listened to these two faceless girls gossip about me. Apparently it hadn't gotten out that Hunter and I were dating. If it had, these two girls would certainly know.

"I'll bet she just gives really good head," the high-pitched girl mused.

"I don't know, I'm sure Hunter can get a blowjob anytime he wants."

"Yeah, but maybe Lorrie can do special tricks with her tongue or something." She paused. "Or maybe she's just willing to do absolutely anything?"

"Like what?"

"I don't know, just think about it. Like really dirty porn star stuff."

The lower-pitched girl giggled. "I haven't really seen much porn."

"Use your imagination then."

There was silence. I felt my heart pounding in my ears and my stomach wringing itself out. Listening to these two girls talk about me was excruciating.

"I guess," the second girl said finally. "Doesn't really matter. I bet he'll lose interest soon."

"I agree."

That was it. I had to get out of here or these girls were going to drive me crazy. The way these girls were talking about me like I wasn't worth Hunter's attention was pissing me off. I packed my stuff up hastily and walked out.

As I walked toward the exit I saw the two gossiping girls. One was blonde, the other brunette, and they were both sitting down in front of a book shelf. The blonde locked eyes with me and did a double-take. "Hi," she said. I scowled and kept walking, trying to ignore what those girls said about me.

I got to the elevator and hit the button to go down to ground level, thinking I'd just spend the rest of my studying time in a study room at the Student Union. In the back of my mind, I guess I'd known that Hunter was well-known on campus so going out with him would have people talking, but coming face-to-face with it had made me feel sick. People could be so awful to each other.

I got another coffee at Starbucks and tried to study for the next hour, but it was very unproductive. I couldn't concentrate. All I could think about was the tone those girls had taken talking about me. It didn't even sound like they were trying to be nasty; they just sounded confused. They were wrong about why Hunter was dating me, but it shook my confidence all the same. Seven o'clock couldn't come soon enough.

Eventually, evening came. I left the Student Union and walked over to the Barnyard to meet Hunter for dinner. As I stood in line for a tray, my appetite disappeared, replaced by nervous energy. Should I talk to Hunter about what those girls had said? How would he respond if I did? We had an argument before about me listening to gossip, and I tried myself not to listen to it, but dammit did gossip always seem to follow me and then linger on my mind afterward. My pulse starting to quicken, I ground my teeth and took a deep breath.

I grabbed a tray and put a modest serving of potatoes and turkey on my plate along with a dinner roll. It was probably more than I'd be able to eat, but I could give it a try. After grabbing a soda to drink, I looked around to see if Hunter had beaten me here. When I saw him, I was lucky to hold onto my plate.

Hunter was sitting with the same girl who had been cozy with him the last time I'd seen him in the Barnyard. *Ada*. This time, however, she was sitting across from him. Did Hunter invite her to *our* dinner? Or did she invite herself? I wanted to turn and run, but instead put my shoulders back and walked as confidently as I could toward the open seat next to Hunter. I had nothing to be ashamed of. I approached and she locked eyes with me.

Hunter followed Ada's stare. His face lit up when he saw me, causing a warm bubbly feeling to emerge in my midsection. I felt myself relaxing immediately. Being around Hunter was so comfortable and felt so right. I took a deep breath and sat down next to him.

He smiled at me. "Lorrie!"

"Hey Hunter," I said cheerily, returning his smile.

Hunter gestured to Ada and me, in turn. "Ada, this is my girlfriend Lorrie. Lorrie, Ada."

The fact he'd immediately called me his girlfriend boosted my confidence. He knew how to make me feel good. Ada plastered a big fake smile on and tilted her head. "So nice to meet you, Lorrie."

"Hi," I said politely.

"Sorry it was last minute," Hunter said. "But I saw Ada at another table and invited her over so you guys can meet. Clear up some confusion."

"Yeah, sorry about that whole banana thing," she said, waving her hand dismissively. "It wasn't serious. We were just goofing around."

"Ah, I see," I replied awkwardly, unsure what the proper response to that was. I noted a subtle hint of insincerity in her voice but I wasn't certain enough to address it. "No worries."

"Well, I already ate and now I'm gonna go study," Ada said, clearly uncomfortable with the situation. "It was nice to meet you, Lorrie."

"Oh, you don't have to go," I offered, trying to be nice.

"No, no, it's okay. I have to be somewhere and I'll let you guys enjoy your dinner. Bye Hunter." Ada got up and left.

"Yeah, sorry about that, she can be a little cold. I also want to apologize to you again for the banana thing."

"It's alright, Hunter. I was pissed off before, but I think I'm over it now. I know how much you care about me."

He smiled warmly and hugged me to him. "Good, I'm glad to hear it."

I paused to consider Ada's odd tone. "Does she still have feelings for you, Hunter?"

"Nah, we dated for a little over a year up 'til sophomore year. We have history, but that chapter's closed," he reassured me. "Remember how we had that discussion about Daniela and pushy-types? Well, Ada pretty much fits that description."

"Really? She seemed kind of nice . . ."

"Trust me, we've had some bitter arguments." He shook his head. "But whatever, we're cool now."

Feeling better about the awkward start to our dinner and the whole Ada situation in general, I began eating and so did Hunter. I was in the middle of taking a bite of my turkey when I spied him looking at my food longingly. His own plate was filled with basically just meat. Where were the carbs?

"You want a bite of my potatoes, Hunter?"

He smirked. "It's not in my training diet, but oh do you know how to tempt me Lorrie."

He kissed me on the cheek then took a bite of my potatoes and chewed. I leaned into his warm chest and he put his arm around me. He was wearing a very plush, red Arrowhart hoodie that I wanted to melt into. Maybe I could steal it from him sometime. I told him about the gossiping incident in the library and he did his best to comfort me. "The whole thing just made me feel shitty. Why do people have to be so mean?"

"I don't know. All you can do is ignore them and eventually they'll stop. Everyone needs something new to gossip about sooner or later."

"I know," I said, burrowing into his chest. I lifted my gaze up to his. "It still hurt, though. I mean, none of it's true, right?"

He squeezed me tighter to his chest. "No, none of it's true. I'm with you because I'm absolutely crazy about you. Our relationship is nobody's business but ours."

I smiled and felt the muscles in my shoulders and back relax. Hunter's confident tone made me feel better. I finally picked up my fork and began to pick at my food. We ate in silence for a few minutes. Just being close to him made me feel warm, like I was tucked tightly into bed under my covers.

"Daniela told me about a party she's going to on Friday night," I said after a while. "I told her I wasn't sure if you'd want to go but I'd ask anyway."

"Do you want to go?" he asked

"I don't know. Do you?"

He shrugged. "Why not? If you decide you want to go, let me know. I'm flexible: wherever you are, I want to be."

His perfect words made me smile. "Okay, let's go."

"Great."

We finished up eating and went back to my dorm to watch a movie. One of the benefits of living with three roommates was pooling together all our movies. Daniela was especially useful because she liked action movies. I ended up picking *The Dark Knight Rises*, which I hadn't seen before. We put the disc into my laptop and watched while cuddled up in my bed.

It was an extra-long twin, which made it way too small for two people, especially someone the size of Hunter. I ended up lying against him with the laptop on my lap as he propped his back against the wall. The huge muscles in his chest were like a warm, comfy pillow, made all the better by his sweatshirt.

About half way through the movie he decided to take his sweatshirt off revealing a fitted black t-shirt underneath.

"Aww, I like that hoodie," I said, twisting to face him.

He cocked a brow. "Watch it Snorrie. If you keep complaining every time I take a piece of clothing off, you're going to destroy my confidence."

I smiled. "I doubt that, Mr. Tattoos and Muscles."

He grinned wickedly. "Maybe you're right. But we better make sure, don't you think?"

My heart began racing in my chest at Hunter's suggestion of sex.

"We can't," I said softly. "My suitemates will hear."

He took the laptop from my lap and set it down beside my bed. "That's why we keep the movie playing."

"You don't want to finish it?"

His eyes locked on mine. "I want a lot of things right now."

Heat rippled through my core as he took my chin between his thumb and forefinger and kissed me passionately. His tongue slipped in with mine and probed my mouth with lush slides. I took his mouth greedily, desperate for more contact with him.

He moved me, switching our positions so that he was on top then helped ease my shirt over my head and let me back down to the pillow. My body quivered with excited energy as he lowered his huge frame onto me and slipped a muscular arm under my back. His free hand traced a line down my collar bone to my bra and slipped under to tease my nipple. The contact made my skin prickle, making me eager for every bit of pleasurable sensation.

His lips sealed over mine again as he used the hand under me to unclasp my bra. Our tongues wrestled playfully before he pulled away, taking the bra with him and exposing my breasts. I put my hands around his waist and slipped them under his t-shirt, eager for access to the beautiful body beneath. Even with my jeans still on, I felt myself getting wet.

Hunter trailed small kisses from my cheek to my jaw and down my neck as he crushed my breasts with the weight of his chest. "Mmm it's been too long since I've felt you naked. "

It had only been a day since we last had sex but it felt like an eternity. I tugged at the hem of his t-shirt wanting to expose him as much as I was exposed. "Same here."

He sat up and took off the shirt in one swift movement before bringing himself back down to me. My eyes traveled over his body hovering above me, taking in the strong lines of his shoulders and chest. Then he slipped out of his jeans, leaving just his black boxer briefs. Seeing his cock stretch against the thin cotton of his underwear made my pulse quicken.

His hands were on the button of my jeans. "Want help?" he asked, his voice low and husky.

I nodded. He unbuttoned and unzipped my jeans and pulled

them off. The sudden rush of air on my legs made me feel cold. I squirmed and curled up, covering myself with my arms.

"Cold?" he asked.

"Hurry up so we can get under the covers. I'm freezing."

He smiled and came back to the head of the bed. We slipped beneath my comforter. The warmth coming from his body made him my favorite personal heater.

We lay side by side and kissed each other playfully with little kisses, then longer and more passionately. One of his legs slid between mine and up my thigh toward my aching sex. I wanted him inside me desperately.

He kissed my neck at the same instant his thigh pressed up against my soaked panties, making me shudder. Smiling against my lips, his hand eased between my legs and around my underwear. The light flick of his finger on my sensitive folds sent bolts of pleasure through my torso. I closed my eyes as he eased my slick panties down my legs and threw them on the floor.

His next touch made my back arch toward him in pleasure. The way his fingers danced around my pussy, alternating between touching my clit and pumping in and out of me, made me flushed and needy. I felt an orgasm steadily building inside me and realized I wanted to pleasure him too, so I reached down and grabbed his hard cock through his underwear.

He responded by plunging his fingers even deeper inside me, curling them so they touched my g-spot. I used my free hand to grip his short hair and bring him closer, kissing him as hard as I could.

"God your pussy is so tight," he growled. "I want to feel you around my cock."

My heart sank as I had a grim realization: I didn't have any condoms. Or any other sexual stuff, actually. I'd been so dead set against causing drama in my life by hooking up with boys that I hadn't bought supplies. It was supposed to be a way of stopping myself from being tempted.

I took a deep breath and squeezed my legs together. "Sorry, but I don't think we can do that tonight."

He narrowed his eyes. "Why not? Is something wrong?"

"I don't have any condoms," I said quietly.

He smiled. "Okay, we can fix that problem later." He kissed me and opened my legs back up. " But I don't need to be inside you to get you off."

I let out a breath I hadn't realized I'd been holding and relaxed. My pussy felt on fire as his fingers quickly found their rhythm again. The orgasm building up in my core was rapidly approaching release.

I didn't want to let him get me off without giving him anything, so I reached toward his waistband and peeled his underwear down his muscular thighs. His cock sprang up, huge and heavy. I wrapped my fingers around the smooth skin and stroked my hand up and down its length.

Feeling his cock respond to my touch took me to the edge. I closed my eyes and continued to stroke him as he fingered me. We continued pleasuring one another as the movie played, the sound of explosions and bad guys grunting making for an interesting background track. When he touched my clit with the pad of his thumb, my climax came in a burst.

I bit back a cry, moaning from the back of my throat as my core tightened deliciously and released in spasms. My hand fell away from his cock and I gripped the sheets hard. When I opened my eyes I saw his face focused on mine. He wore an expression of masculine triumph.

"You look like you enjoyed that," he said.

"I did," I murmured, curling up into him.

His cock, still hard, brushed against my leg. I reached down and began stroking him again. He relaxed his face and threw his head back. Feeling like it was my turn to please him, I trailed kisses down his neck to his hard chest.

He ran his fingers through my hair to my nape. "That feels good."

"I don't have any lube . . ." I said, trailing off.

"That's okay, just keep doing what you're doing."

"I don't want to hurt you," I protested.

I lightly grazed his balls with the tips of my fingers and he exhaled sharply from the sensation. "You won't. I trust you."

I quickened my pace, making sure to keep my touch light so

my hand I didn't catch on his skin. His grip on my hair tightened and he uttered a throaty rasp like he was struggling for control. I squirmed, excited to see the effect my touches had on him.

"Don't stop," he panted. Despite my hand becoming fatigued from stroking him through an entire fight scene, I spit some saliva in my palm and continued jerking him quickly but lightly.

"Oh god, I'm going to come," he cried.

His cock twitched then erupted, shooting hot, thick semen through my fingers and against my stomach. He arched himself against me, bucking with every spurt. The guttural moan of agony mixed with pleasure that escaped his lips filled me with triumph.

"You look like you enjoyed that," I said smiling.

He let out a long breath. "Hell yeah I did. I hope you have Kleenex."

I giggled and got up to clean myself off. "I do."

"And detergent for your sheets," he added.

"Check on that as well."

After wiping myself down, I tossed the kleenex to him so he could clean himself up too. An explosion from the movie playing on my laptop made me realize Batman was still fighting to save Gotham. I laughed again.

"I guess we'll have to catch the end of *The Dark Knight Rises* another time," I said.

"What?"

"The movie. We didn't finish it."

"Oh. I guess you can pause it now."

I did so with an enormous smile on my face, then got back under the covers with him. We cuddled for a while, his fingers tracing circles on my back, my nails gently exploring the outlines of the tattoos on his firm chest. Being with Hunter made me feel safe and alive. I reflected on how hard I'd fought to prevent something like this from happening—from being in a sexual relationship with Hunter. It seemed so silly now.

Chapter Twenty

PARTY

On Thursday during psych class, Daniela reminded me she'd been invited to a Tau Beta Pi party by Cody. Even though Daniela wasn't "seeing" Cody anymore, they had made up and were now back on friendly terms. I had given her an uncertain answer earlier in the week but after asking Hunter and him telling me he wanted to go, I notified Daniela that we were game to join her. I figured it would be a fun experience for both Hunter and me.

After classes, I texted Hunter. *You ready for the TBP party tonight?*

Moments later, he responded. *Sure, am. I'm looking forward to showing you off :)*

I responded with two smiley faces and he texted back. *Well, as long as they look and don't touch :).*

I was looking forward to our first appearance as a couple at a public event.

Daniela was excited to meet Cody's frat buddies so she took an extra long time in picking an outfit and applying her makeup while Hunter and I waited in the suite. She came out from the bathroom with frizzy hair wearing a denim jacket over a pastel polo, a short white skirt, pointy-toed flats, and big, gaudy sunglasses. The party had a spring break Miami-Vice dress theme and Daniela took it very seriously. I wore a pair of dark jeans and a maroon-checkered button down, and Hunter traded his usual training sweats for an olive polo and jeans. He looked mouth-watering with his muscles stretching against whatever fabric he wore.

"So, how do I look?" Daniela said striking a pose.

I laughed. "Wow, you look awesome!"

Hunter laughed as well. "Definitely."

"Thanks! Hopefully, the fratdaddys at the party will think so as well!"

We left Floyd Hall around 10:30 and by the time we arrived at the TBP house, it was almost eleven.

"Did you go to any TBP parties freshman year, Lorrie?" Daniela asked, as we approached the front porch where a couple of guys and girls were smoking and drinking.

"No, I went to like one frat party and I don't remember what the house was," I said.

"Oh yeah," she said. "We went to that one Phi Kappa Delta party together but all the boys there were pretty immature so we left early."

I recalled the event and how some drunk guy spilled beer all over both our shoes. Then I realized that had been Gary's frat. His story about having to skip the hockey game with Hunter because the guys at PKD couldn't unclog a toilet made a lot more sense now.

Hunter chuckled. "If any guy does that to you tonight, Lorrie, I'll teach him a lesson."

"Oooh, so protective," Daniela said. "Wish I had me an MMA fighter boyfriend."

I smiled at her, slightly blushing.

"I can introduce you to a few of the guys down at Bigg's Gym," Hunter said. "Although, I gotta warn ya, they've got some rough edges."

"Even better. I like a guy who's a little unruly. Makes it all the more fun to change 'em."

Hunter and I both laughed.

We walked up to the porch and Hunter held the door open for both of us as we went inside. The house was full of people. *Wagon Wheel* was blaring from a stereo somewhere and people—especially the girls—were singing along with the chorus: "Heyyyy mama rack me!"

"Banjos, man," Hunter said, shaking his head as he watched a group of drunk girls slurring words off-pitch, drinks held high in the air. "They're like catnip for Midwest girls." He looked at us. "Thirsty? I'll get us some drinks."

"Thanks, Hunter," I said.

Like a true gentleman, he went to get Daniela and me drinks while we hung out in the living room watching an overly competitive group of people play beer pong.

"So how have Hunter and you been? You guys look so cute together!"

"We're doing great. I actually feel like we're kind of obsessed with each other," I mused. "Not sure if that's a good thing or a bad thing."

"It's a good thing from what I can see. You've got this glowy aura going on. I haven't seen you look so happy in a long time, Hunter has quite the effect on you. To be honest, I'm actually kinda jealous . . ."

I flustered at her compliments and giggled. "Yeah, I guess I'm pretty lucky things have worked out between Hunter and me. We've certainly had our ups and downs before getting to this point. But now that we're dating, I'm glad he's in my life."

Daniela nodded and smiled. We exchanged a few bits about Hunter's awesomeness and began to scan the room for a potential guy for Daniela when Hunter returned, balancing three drinks with two hands. "Here ya go ladies!"

Just as we offered our thanks to Hunter, the music unexpectedly changed to a rap song.

"Awww yeahhh. Now this is what I'm talking about! I love this song!" cried Daniela, shaking her hips and waving her drink around in the air to the hypnotic beat and explicit lyrics. "Make it nasty! Make it nasty!"

"What song is this?" I said.

"You haven't heard this?! Jesus, Lorrie. It's *Make It Nasty* by Tyga. Duh! Please at least tell me you've heard of twerking."

"Of course I've heard of twerking!" I said, slightly offended by the accusation. I turned to Hunter to see if he was judging me and he was simply smiling. "Everybody knows about Miley Cyrus and that VMA performance."

"Well, this is like THE twerking song. You can't listen to it and not want to shake your butt. It can bring out the slutty side in any good girl! It's gotta be like some form of subliminal messaging or something."

I listened to the lyrics, noting that there was nothing subtle about the chorus: *Make it nasty! Make it nasty!*

"I'm gonna find a guy to grind on. I'll see you guys in a bit," Daniela said before grabbing a random guy nearby and tugging him to the open dance area.

Although this wasn't my kind of music, I began warming to the song from seeing everyone having fun. I was considering dancing as well but didn't think Hunter was the dancing type.

"C'mon, babe. Let's dance too," Hunter said with a mischievous grin. "I wanna see your twerkin skills."

He led me by the hand over to where Daniela and her dance partner went.

"You like dancing?" I asked Hunter.

He gave me a lopsided grin. "You know what they say about fighters: they're good both on their feet and off."

I smirked at him. "I agree with the 'off' part. I guess we'll find out about the 'on' part."

I began swaying to the beat, dancing in front of Hunter. I wasn't the best dancer in the world, but I knew how to move my body to at least *look* like I knew what I was doing. I was surprised to see Hunter actually moving his feet and dancing instead of just nodding his head like I saw most of the guys doing. Most of the guys were just shifting side-to-side with a drink in one hand while their girl did all the work. I noticed that during the chorus, the girls would bend over and vigorously shake their butts in front of the guy's crotch.

As we continued dancing, I saw a few girls eyeing Hunter. It would've bothered me before but after everything that's happened between Hunter and me in the past week, I felt confident shrugging it off. I was enjoying myself and having such a great time with Hunter that I decided to be adventurous and try twerking on him. I bent over and began shaking my booty. I looked back to gauge his reaction and saw his eyes wide and filled with lust.

"Jesus, Lorrie. That's so sexy."

Encouraged, I bent further until I was parallel with the ground, continuing to shake my bottom like a salt shaker.

"Yeah, you go girl! Make it nasty!" I heard Daniela shout over to me. She was twerking on her man too but that guy looked lost, like he couldn't handle what Daniela was shaking.

I bent down until my hair was touching the ground then I slapped the floor and arched my back as I came up slowly. Curious, I glanced back and saw Hunter looking borderline ready to ravage me on the dance floor in front of everyone.

I glanced at the other girls admiring Hunter and noticed their expression had turned from jealousy to disdain.

Yeah, that's right. Hunter's MY man, I thought smugly.

Hunter lightly slapped my backside. I turned around and playfully tapped my hand against his chest. "Cool your jets, Hun, you're burning up."

"My jet's on fire. I wanna crash into you so bad, it hurts."

"Save it for later tonight. We'll crash and burn together," I whispered into his ear seductively.

By the time the song ended, I'd worked up a sweat and was breathing hard like I'd ran five miles; I desperately needed a glass of water. Who knew booty-shaking could be such a workout?

I had a lot of fun dancing and letting loose with Hunter. After Daniela remarked on how she's never seen me so lively before, I went to the kitchen to get myself and Hunter another drink, a smile on my face knowing that Hunter and I were going to have some amazing sex tonight.

A curly-haired frat guy wearing a striped polo over a noticeable beer gut approached me, cheeks rosy from a few drinks. He face seemed familiar but I couldn't place it. "Lorrie Burnham, out partying."

"Hey . . . what's up?" I smiled at him, my mood chipper. "Do I know you?"

"Name's Jimmy." He leaned against the kitchen island, taking up the space beside me. "We've got the same art history class together."

"Ah, nice to meet you Jimmy. I'm Lorrie—err but you already knew that." I laughed.

"You're like the talk of the campus," he said casually as he popped an orange cheese ball into his mouth.

"Oh. . ." I continued smiling but suddenly felt uncomfortable.

"Let me guess, it's because of Hunter?"

"Yeah, that and what happened in the news. Man that's crazy stuff."

The smile on my face disappeared. I stood there silent, dreading where this conversation was headed.

"Hey, you know I've been curious—" He chuckled. "I saw you on TV when they read the verdict. I was like 'wow, that girl's pretty cute'. But man, what was up with your reaction? You were like stone-faced." He made an exaggerated blank-faced expression. "Totally emotionless." He chuckled again. "Did you even *like* your mom?"

My jaw tightened. I blinked a few times, hoping the situation wasn't real. "What?"

"You know, when you were in the courtroom and the judge was like 'guilty'!" He pounded his fist against the island like a mallet. "I woulda jumped outta my seat and been like 'hell yeah!' Give that fucker what he deserves!" He laughed.

"Stop," I murmured softly, in a daze.

"What?" He leaned closer, tilting his ear to hear me.

My hands became cold. I remained silent as my past crawled back into my mind drowning out the ruckus of the party around me.

"Helloooo?" He smiled as he waved his hand in front of my face. "Earth to stone girl." He chuckled again.

I slapped his hand away. "Fuck off, douchebag!" I yelled.

He took a step back. The chattering around us halted; I could feel everyone's gaze on me. My pulse pounded and my ears roared.

"Whoa, chill out. What the hell's your problem?"

"You," I shot back, too angry to care about the onlookers.

He looked around at the people staring at us. His jovial expression became serious. "I was just trying to be nice and talk to you. Then you act like a stupid loner, bitch," he spat. "No wonder you don't have any friends."

"She's got one right here," Hunter snarled coming up behind Jimmy. He grabbed the Jimmy by the shirt and shoved him, making him stumble out the back door and tumble across the backyard lawn. Hunter followed him and I followed Hunter. Everyone else in the kitchen followed as well.

"Jesus, dude. What the fuck's your problem?" Jimmy barked at Hunter, getting back on his feet.

"Don't fuck with Lorrie," Hunter warned, his tone serious and cold.

"I wasn't doing shit to your girlfriend. That bitch is the one who started it!" He pointed an accusing finger at me.

"You better watch that mouth of yours," Hunter threatened. "Apologize to her."

Jimmy looked at all the people watching the spectacle. "What? Hell no! You think I'm scared of you, you stupid musclehead. I didn't do anything wrong! She's the one who should be apologizing to me!" He gestured to his sleeve that had been torn from tumbling across the ground. "Look you ripped my fuckin shirt, bro! That's NOT cool!"

Hunter was approaching Jimmy, his hands balled into tight fists and I ran over to stop him. "Hunter!" I cried trying to keep my voice controlled despite feeling frantic. "Come on, let's get out of here, I don't want to be here anymore . . ."

As I wrapped my arms around his waist and hugged him tightly, Hunter seemed to cool off, vibrating rage pacifying. He turned to me and his gaze softened. "Okay, Lorrie. Let's get outta here . . ." His arm protectively around my shoulder, we began to walk back into the kitchen.

Behind us, Jimmy scoffed. "That's right, get the fuck outta here. Neanderthal and his stupid stone-faced bitch." I heard Jimmy laugh and a few people around us gasped.

My arms around Hunter's waist, I could feel every muscle in his core tighten. I tried restraining him even as I felt him turn around to face Jimmy. "No, Hunter! Don't!"

He broke from my grasp, stomped over to Jimmy—who was now scared shitless—and lifted him a foot into the air by his shirt collar. "Don't you ever fuckin talk about Lorrie like that!" Hunter tossed Jimmy backward like a ragdoll, making him crash through a wooden fence. Broken splinters flew across the grass. A few onlookers cried "Holy shit!" as Hunter approached Jimmy who was dazed and trying to recover.

"Hunter!" I cried desperately, panic taking hold.

Hunter picked Jimmy up and socked him across the jaw. Jimmy crumbled to the ground, out cold. Hunter was about to mount him but I ran over and grabbed Hunter and screamed into his ear, "Stop! Stop! Hunter!" Tears streamed down my face.

He turned to me, his expression changing from anger to a mixture of confusion and concern. "Lorrie . . . I'm sorry . . . I . . . Let's get outta here." He put his arm around my shoulder and guided me through the house. We asked Daniela to leave with us but she suggested she would stay behind to assess the fallout.

Most of the people in the Tau Beta Pi house were still bumping and grinding to the music, sipping liberally on their drinks as if nothing had happened in the backyard. But for Hunter and me, the party had ended.

After ten minutes of walking with Hunter's arm around my shoulder and us looking out for campus police, we arrived at Hunter's apartment.

"Lorrie, it's okay. We're at my place, we're safe now." He pulled my coat from my shoulders and hung it up on the rack along with his own.

"I'm sorry I got you involved in this," I said, hugging him tightly. "This is all my fault."

"No, you have nothing to be sorry about. It's not your fault," he consoled me.

"Yes it is. It's because of my past, Hunter. . ." I began to cry into his chest, emotions newly resurfaced since the party getting the best of me.

"What are you talking about?" His voice was soft and filled with concern.

I took a step back and looked into his eyes with uncertainty. "Haven't you heard about me by now? About Lorrie Burnham?"

He furrowed his brows. "I haven't heard anything other than what you've told me."

". . . I'm messed up, Hunter." I exhaled deeply as a tear rolled down my cheek. "I told you my parents are divorced and dead but I didn't tell you how it happened."

He paused. ". . . How did it happen?" he asked softly.

My throat tightened and I had to swallow a few times before speaking. "My mom . . . she . . . oh god—"

A tear fell down my cheek as I recalled the details of her death and Hunter quietly consoled me. "Shh, you don't have to tell me, Lorrie. Nothing's gonna change the way I feel about you." He kissed my forehead and rubbed my shoulders.

"You deserve to know, Hunter," I said, feeling strengthened by his words. "My mom . . . after her and my dad got divorced she married this guy and he . . . he murdered her a year and a half ago." Another tear rolled down my face. ". . . Then my dad took his own life a few months ago. The story was in the news. All of it was . . ."

"Lorrie . . ."

"I loved my parents!" I sobbed. More tears rolled down my cheeks. "To think that asshole would accuse me of not caring about them . . ."

Hunter clenched his jaw. "That asshole got what he deserved." He growled. "I made sure of that. I'll make sure of it for anyone who hurts you." His muscles tightened again the way they did when Jimmy had called me a bitch. "Lorrie, where's the murderer?"

Realizing Hunter probably wanted to go after him to do what he did to Jimmy or worse, I started crying. "You can't do anything, Hunter! He's in jail."

"I'll find a way," he grunted.

"No Hunter! Please, I don't want to talk about this anymore . . ." I pleaded. "Can we just go to bed?"

His body relaxed as he looked at me. He took a deep breath then hushed me softly by sealing his mouth over mine. It was just what I needed. I parted my lips and his tongue slipped inside placating my quivering tongue.

When we broke the kiss, he tilted my chin and stared deep into my eyes. "I love you, Lorrie."

My heart stopped for a moment. His words flowed over me washing away all the stress in my life. Hunter was the most amazing person I ever met. "I love you, too, Hunter."

We fell asleep in his bed, the one place where everything was right—where the world couldn't touch us. All through the night we kissed and touched each other like we were the last two people alive.

Chapter Twenty-one

THE LETTER

The weekend passed along with the beginning of next week. There'd been no sign of campus police showing up at Hunter's apartment, which meant Jimmy probably had kept quiet about the incident to protect his own pride. I was surprised by how supportive Hunter was after hearing the details about my past. I'd been reluctant to tell him, afraid of how he'd react, but now that I had it felt like a burden had been lifted from my shoulders.

After finishing another study session with Hunter at the library, I returned to Floyd Hall and decided to check my student mailbox before dinner. Most of the mail I got was from the college, but sometimes my aunt and uncle would send a care package.

Although there had been incidents of drama here and there—particularly with Hunter—I couldn't imagine the semester going much better than it was. My relationship with Hunter was amazing; I felt more alive with him than I ever had since the trial. The sex was even more amazing. I'd been worried he would destabilize me, but instead he made me feel safe and secure. Hunter was my anchor.

Being so happy with Hunter, I didn't care that I was doing bad in a few of my classes. In the three days since the party, I'd tried to study but always got distracted thinking about Hunter. It was always a welcome distraction though. Spending so much time with him at his place, I had time to work on art pieces for the portfolio competition. The pieces I was doing on the kittens were coming together nicely.

The kittens had finally graduated from being bottle fed to eating hard kitten food, which was a relief. That meant Hunter and I could just feed them once a day rather than having to give them a meal every few hours.

Smiling from musing on the positive developments in my life, I opened my mailbox, grabbed the stack of mail, and took the stairs up to my floor. When I got to my room, I began flipping through the envelopes. Most were from the college as usual, but when I saw the last piece I nearly dropped everything.

It was from the Cook County Penal System.

Possibilities raced through my head. My heart began to pound and my skin started breaking out in a cold sweat. What the hell was going on? Was *he* really trying to contact me?

Sitting down on my bed with my fingers shaking, I tore the envelope open and pulled out the contents. The name on the cover sheet sent a fresh wave of queasiness to my stomach. I had to look away to avoid throwing up.

Marco Peralta. The man who murdered my mom and threw my dad into such a depression he took his own life.

My entire body went numb. My brain felt frozen. I looked up and stared at the wall for a while, unable to move a muscle. My breath was shallow, but it was still coming. I was still breathing—I was still alive. Just me.

Finally, I pulled out the letter Marco had written and began to read.

Dear Lorrie,

I am very sorry for the pain of you and your family. Kelsey's death is something I regret every moment. It hurts me to think about you and how much your mother's death has hurt you. I hope you are recovering well.

I'm sure you are very angry with me, but I hope that you can eventually find it in your heart to forgive me. If you could write me a letter back, I would be very grateful, even if it is angry.

With much love,

Marco

Finishing reading the last two lines—*With much love, Marco*—I looked up and found the room spinning. Tilting precariously on the edge of my bed, I gripped the mattress to steady my balance. The queasiness in my stomach suddenly became severe nausea. For a second I thought the letter could've been written by someone else, but the awkward English made me certain the words had come from Marco. *Maybe I'll wake up*, I thought. Maybe this hadn't happened in real life; it felt like a nightmare where every bit of my good mood was being devoured by a ravenous monster who, unsatiated from killing my parents, was now coming after me.

I rolled onto my side and curled my legs into my chest to protect myself, dropping the letter to the floor.

Despite my best efforts, the past came rushing to the present with disturbing clarity. Marco had blindsided everyone. Growing up with Marco had been as normal as living with a stepfather could be. He treated my mom well and they seemed to love each other. Unlike my dad, Marco hadn't even had much of a liking for alcohol. He would be the hundredth person you would pick out of a hundred to commit a grisly murder.

But that was what had happened. The forensics experts said there were no signs of resistance. It looked like Marco had come home one night, stabbed my mom to death—maybe in her sleep—and left early for a business trip scheduled to start the next morning. It took them days to find the body. When they found it and notified Marco, he was still in Iowa for business and pleaded ignorance.

It was summer after freshman year when it had happened and I'd been staying with my dad in Chicago. My dad was never the same from the moment he got the call from the police notifying him of his ex-wife's death. He had never stopped loving Mom, even after the divorce. Dad had always enjoyed having a beer or two after work, but after he heard about my mom's death, two became six or more. At first, neither of us could believe the murder had actually happened. If it were an accident, or Marco had been drunk, or even if he were trying to steal money, anything at all, it would have been easier to accept. But there was no motive.

"Why?" That was a question I—no, all of us—asked ourselves afterwards. We just couldn't understand why. Was Marco mentally ill? That was the only thing that could even somewhat make sense. He had shown no signs of violent tendencies before, no drug abuse or alcohol abuse. He and my mother hardly ever argued. So why?

But that was a question that I stopped asking myself long ago. It was only a slow poison that ate me up inside. Maybe it was even worse than the loss of my mom—not understanding why something like this could happen.

The lack of motive had not only made it difficult for the prosecution to proceed in the trial, it also made the trial interesting for the media. I shuddered in my bed as I thought about the frenzy of cameras that surrounded the court room. The trial was so public and dragged on for so long that I had no choice but to take time off from school. That was the first of three semesters away from Arrowhart.

Finally, the verdict came in. The forensic evidence was enough: Marco was found guilty of first degree murder. Cameras flashed in my face as the words were delivered—the journalists were probably expecting tears and smiles at justice being delivered but they got none of that.

All they got was the numb expression of a girl who had stopped feeling. From the pictures, you might have thought I'd been the one convicted. Even after the sentence of life in prison was delivered and everything was finally over, I felt nothing. My life had been damaged by an act so senseless lawyers couldn't even come up with a bad reason for why the murderer did it. All I could do was stare into space.

And sit. After the verdict I did a lot of sitting and staring into space. When the anguish became too much, I'd curl into a ball on my bed and lay there for hours until I fell asleep from exhaustion.

Marco's letter was bringing it all back. Just when I was finally beginning to feel again, my mother's murderer had forced his way back into my life—for who knows what reason—making me numb to the world again.

Laying on my bed, I did my best to steady my breathing. The letter hadn't mentioned my father. Had news gotten back to Marco about Dad's suicide? Was he aware of just how much damage he'd done? That his pointless action had driven a good man to kill himself?

I managed enough strength to pick up the offending letter, ball it up, and throw it in the trash. The words "*With much love, Marco*" echoed through my head. How dare he write that he loved me? He had no right to pretend he had any connection with anyone.

There was no way I was writing him back. Although Dr. Schwartz had told me that I needed to forgive him if I was ever going to completely move on, I couldn't. Not yet. He wouldn't even take responsibility for what happened. He was sorry "for *the* pain of my family"—not the pain *he* had caused.

It wasn't that I wanted something bad to happen to Marco. I just wanted to erase him from my life. I thought I'd managed to shut the closet door on my skeletons but one had managed to escape. I propped myself up and got under the covers of my bed, burying my face in my pillow. But even under the covers, I still felt cold.

Chapter Twenty-two

THE FALL

"Lorrie, get up! You can't skip today. We have an exam!"

Daniela's muffled yelling stirred me from a dreamless sleep. I reached over to my night stand and looked at the time on my phone: 8:00 AM. I had slept a long time, but I still felt exhausted. What the hell happened? What day was it? Why didn't my cell phone alarm go off?

My friend burst into my room, making me realize I neglected to lock the door. "Your alarm was going off forever. Are you feeling okay? I wasn't even sure you were here last night until I heard your phone beeping."

I was aware of her words but couldn't form a response. It felt like my jaw was glued shut. Something bad had happened. There was a reason I was supposed to be unhappy that I couldn't quite put my finger on. Something in the back of my mind.

The letter.

My stepfather had sent me a letter begging forgiveness. Slowly, it came back to me: Marco, the letter, the murder, his dead eyes in the courtroom when he'd been sentenced. I had fallen asleep after I'd read it.

Daniela was staring at me, confusion on her face. "Lorrie, wake up! What's wrong? You're white as a ghost."

I threw my covers off and sat up, rubbing my eyes. "Go on, I'll be there," I said quietly. I scanned my room, thinking of what I wanted to wear.

My friend watched me for another minute, then spun and left. I sighed as I watched her hurry back to her room to finish getting ready. As I absentmindedly packed my backpack, dropping books and papers in the process, I realized this exam was going to be a disaster.

The walk to the exam had been a daze. It felt like my head was a balloon loosely attached to the rest of my body. The sensation was familiar—I'd felt the same way when Dad told me with tears in his eyes that Mom passed away.

Daniela and I made our way through the crowded aisles of the auditorium, until we finally found two empty seats. One of the teacher's assistants handed us test packets. Moments later, the professor at the front of the auditorium explained the exam was scantron multiple choice; eighty minutes for a forty question test.

I breathed a sigh of relief when I heard the exam would be multiple choice, figuring it wouldn't be too bad.

But I did not anticipate using every ounce of concentration just to focus my eyes enough that I could bubble in the letters of my name. Every thought that flickered through my brain felt like it was traveling through mud. Holding my pencil correctly took effort. My muscles did not want to listen to what my brain was trying to make them do.

I stared at my test blankly:

1. *What anxiety disorder—characterized by its link to one or more specific events—is said to affect over 6% of women in the United States at some point in their lives?*

The words seemed to pass in and out of my mind without processing. I closed my eyes and focused on my breathing, trying to follow the technique Dr. Schwartz had taught me to manage my anxiety.

Gradually, I became aware of being kicked in the shin. I opened my eyes and turned to see the coffee brown eyes and receding hairline of my stepfather, Marco.

My heart slammed into my chest, knocking the breath out of me.

I blinked. It wasn't Marco. It was Daniela, and she was looking at me out of the corner of her eye suspiciously. I turned to study her. What did she want? How long had she been watching me? As I tried to put together the pieces, there was a cough at the front of the classroom.

Startled, I nearly jumped out of my seat. Did Muller think I was cheating? I looked at the front of the classroom and saw he was sitting at the table, reading a newspaper like he always did during exams. Nobody was looking at me. *I had overreacted.*

My heart still pounding, I went back to my test and realized I had lost my pencil. It must have flown out of my hand in my panic. I looked at the floor and saw it had rolled under the feet of the girl in the row in front of me. Why had I ignored Daniela's advice to bring an extra? *God, this sucks.*

I stared at my fallen writing utensil in despair, knowing it was too far away to reach it with my foot. Suddenly, I felt a kick at my shin again. I turned my head and saw a pencil on the table. Daniela met my eyes briefly, then went back to her test. I smiled at her, but she was already focusing on her exam. That girl wasn't letting anything get in the way of an A in this class.

My case was different. I looked at the exam and tried to answer the first question. The words might as well have been in a different language. The sound of a metal chair grating against the floor from the front of the room caused me to jump again.

After an hour of futilely reading and rereading the first damn question, I realized that it was hopeless. I bubbled in C for every question just so I'd have something, then struggled through the rest of the exam period trying to find some question that I had a clue on. It didn't work. I had studied for this exam the previous day, but even understanding the questions was too much to handle at the moment.

After the exam ended, I told Daniela I wasn't feeling well after all. She looked at me quizzically, but nodded and let me go without asking any questions. I headed back to my dorm and to the comfort of my bed. As I slid miserably under the covers, I thought about what was happening. Why had he picked now to contact me? Why not when I was taking time off school? How had he found my address, anyway?

I stared at the ceiling and drifted off to sleep, hoping I would feel better when I woke up.

A friendly hand shook my shoulder, jarring me awake. I turned over lazily and looked up. It was Daniela again. Even in the darkness of my room, I could see she looked worried. I smiled and closed my eyes again. It was dark out. People were allowed to sleep when it was dark out.

"I hope you're recovering well," she said.

The words were the same ones used in the letter. *Marco.* I jolted up and looked around, my heart racing in my chest, my skin covered by a thin film of sweat. Daniela stared back at me, wide-eyed.

"Lorrie," she said. "You're starting to scare me. Are you sure you're okay?"

My chest heaved in and out heavily as I worked to catch my breath. Adrenaline poured through my veins. "Sorry, bad dream," I said unsteadily. I did my best to smile at her, but it was hard to even meet her gaze.

She put the back of her hand to my forehead. "Jesus, you're having cold sweats. You should go to the health center."

I shook my head. "I'll be fine, just need to sleep."

"Didn't you have an Econ exam this afternoon? Did you go?"

My heart felt like it had been mashed into little sinews. In my rush to get over what had happened during my Psych exam, I had totally forgotten about the Econ exam I had later in the same day. A few hours ago.

"No, I forgot," I said softly.

Her face didn't move as she studied me. She just nodded slowly. "Okay . . . Well, I'll let you sleep. When's your next exam?"

It took a long time to remember, but eventually it came to me. "I have sociology tomorrow morning."

"What time?"

"Ten."

"Okay, I'll come wake you up. Get some rest. I'll see you tomorrow."

Daniela woke me up on Thursday to make sure I went to my exam. As I got dressed and ate a granola bar for breakfast, my head still felt like it was filled with a hazy cloud. All the muscles in my body were tensed in frayed knots. Dammit, I felt awful—why couldn't I just put the letter out of mind long enough to take my exams?

Backpack over my shoulder, I left Floyd Hall with my mind swirling. Everything on campus looked slightly off; I kept asking myself if the campus always looked this way. The detailing on the street lamps, the flyers on the bulletin boards, even the way the sun looked—everything seemed to belong to a strange photograph rather than real life. I kept waiting for a tug at my shoulders to pull me out of this nightmare, but it never came.

Passing the student union, I sighed. After bombing a test yesterday because I was so upset I couldn't read properly, it was looking like the same thing would happen again. A storm was still thundering inside my head. I had a hard enough time with sociology when I was at my best so I knew that taking the midterm in this condition was going to be a disaster.

Hot tears welled up in my eyes before rolling in thin lines down my cheeks. I tilted my head toward the ground and wiped them away, hoping no one would notice.

Dammit. It was unfair how he could ruin my life again, and this time by a simple letter. I just wanted a fair shot at being normal and not having to deal with something awful for a while. A few months of a normal college life: passing my classes, figuring out my career, working on my relationship with Hunter. Being in my twenties in college was dramatic enough without fresh reminders of the dear loved ones I had lost.

I looked up at the clear blue sky as I entered the arts quad. The sun reflected painfully against the tears in my eyes; I shut them and turned away. My chest heaved as the tears began coming more freely. My life was taking yet another shitty turn. What was I doing even taking this test when I knew I had no prayer of passing?

I tried wiping my eyes with my sleeve but I couldn't stop the fresh waves of tears from flowing. I was forced to stop near a large tree to collect myself. As I unslung my backpack and sat against the tree I noticed people were staring at me. I covered my eyes with my hands and cried harder. Each choked sob led to another one I didn't have the strength to stop. I could try as hard as I wanted, but the crying continued no matter what. Too much was pent up inside.

I reluctantly peeked through my fingers and saw students craning their necks, trying to get a glimpse of my face.

Yes, I thought, *that girl is really crying in the middle of the quad. Uncontrollably.*

Groaning in frustration, I picked up my backpack and turned toward Floyd Hall instead of the exam building. Who was I kidding? There was no way I was passing that exam. I decided to spare myself further embarrassment by going back to my room.

As I dragged myself back to Floyd Hall, something that had been in the back of my mind since I failed my psych exam came to the front: I might have to withdraw from the semester.

I spent the rest of the day Thursday locked in my room. Daniela knocked on my door that night to check on me, but went away after I called out that I was still sick. I was thankful she left me alone. There was nothing to say about how I was feeling. I didn't want to talk to her about the possibility of withdrawing from another semester. Not yet.

Friday was more of the same. I skipped swimming, deciding that there was no point in splashing around in a pool when I already felt like I was drowning. As I lay in bed I realized with more and more certainty that I would have to withdraw from Arrowhart again. The thought depressed me: I had been doing so well, but then that damn letter derailed me, causing me to already fail two classes. Now there was nothing I could do.

I texted Hunter in the afternoon asking what he was up to before rolling over for a nap. It was weird we hadn't been in contact since Tuesday, but we both had a lot of stuff going on. Maybe he was just extra busy with exams.

Daniela came in that night and made me swear that if I still felt bad the next day that I would go to the health center. I agreed, wanting to placate her so she would leave. When she did, I rolled over and checked my phone. No response from Hunter. I wrinkled my brows finding the situation strange. Frustrated and tired, I burrowed into my pillow and tried to sleep, hoping I would somehow feel better in the morning.

I woke up Saturday and sat in my bed thinking about how I could recover. Even if I was going to withdraw, I couldn't stay in bed forever. I had to get up and eat, shower, and try to pull myself together.

I looked at my phone on my night stand. Still no reply. It was weird that Hunter hadn't responded to the text I sent him yesterday afternoon. What was he thinking about the way I'd disappeared? Where had he disappeared to?

I thought about calling him, but decided I wasn't ready to talk to him about the letter yet. The first person I wanted to talk to was my Aunt Caroline. I dialed her number and put the phone to my ear. It rang four times before I heard her voice.

"Hello?" she answered. She sounded sleepy.

I did my best to make my voice perky. "Hi Aunt Caroline. Did I wake you up?"

"Lorrie? You did, yes. It's five o'clock in the morning!"

I looked out my window and realized it was still dark outside. A glance at my phone's clock proved Aunt Caroline had been right about the time—it had totally escaped me. I put the phone back to my ear, trying to think of what to say next.

"Is everything okay?" my aunt asked. She sounded very worried.

It started with a single tear escaping from my right eye and falling warmly down my cheek. As it fell from my face, the dam broke and I cried hard, my chest convulsing with powerful sobs. Tears poured from my eyes as if they'd been saved up since I'd walked home from my econ exam.

Why had Marco sent that letter? Why now? The effort of crying so hard was exhausting and yet the release was such a relief that I couldn't stop.

"Lorrie talk to me. What's wrong?"

"I'm sorry," I choked out.

"You're sorry?" she asked. Her voice had raised a pitch, indicating her concern. "What are you sorry about?"

I tried to get words out, but blubbered instead. My aunt stopped asking me to speak. I could hear her breathing tense on the other side.

Several minutes passed as I tried to gather myself. The prospect of telling her about the letter kept bringing fresh sobs. I couldn't imagine what a mess I'd be trying to talk to Hunter about this.

"Lorrie, do you need me to come get you?" she asked carefully.

I swallowed a hard lump in my throat. ". . . He sent me a letter," I said quietly.

"Who sent you a letter?"

I tried to say the name but it made me too scared, too angry, so it came out as a mumble.

"No!" she yelled. It was so loud I had to pull the phone away from my ear. "That monster?"

I said nothing. There was silence on the line for several seconds.

"What did it say?" she asked quietly.

I breathed in and out several times, trying to steady myself. "He wants me to forgive him."

"Bastard," my aunt spat. I was surprised to hear her swear. That was unlike her. "He has some nerve sending you something like that."

"He also said he loves me," I added.

"*What?*" she screamed, even more loudly than before. I heard my uncle grumble in the background.

I closed my eyes and tried to steady my breathing. "I couldn't believe it either."

"How did he know where you live?" She sounded panicked.

"I don't know . . . I don't think he does, it was forwarded from the Cook County Penal System, they must have our records."

"Those idiots need to get it together, how could they forward something like that to you? Haven't we suffered enough already? I'm going to get a lawyer to give them a call."

"No Aunt Caroline, forget it," I pleaded. The thought of interacting with more lawyers and making the situation bigger than it already was made me sick.

She paused. "When did you get the letter?"

"A couple days ago."

"And you're just calling me now about it? What did you do when you got it?"

I sat up in my bed. "I'm sorry. After I saw the letter, I was so shocked . . . it . . . brought back everything I've been feeling since Mom died. I thought I was starting to do better but now I don't know . . ."

There was a long pause on the line until my aunt broke it. "How are your classes going?" she asked, concern heavy in her tone.

"They were going okay before I got the letter," I answered truthfully. "Now I'm not so sure."

"Is it exams time?"

"Kind of," I said, grimacing.

"Lorrie, I've seen you do this before. You need to come home."

"No! I'm not going to let him win again. Not this easily."

"Lorrie," my aunt said delicately. "It's not about winning and losing. It's about surviving. Remember how you wandered off into the woods after hearing the news about your father? Uncle Stewart and I were worried sick."

I'd told them I needed to take a walk after getting the news about my dad's passing. My walk had turned into a several hour ordeal after I got lost in the woods behind their house. Uncle Stewart eventually came looking for me; they had never said it, but I was pretty sure they thought I'd gone the same route my dad did.

"I know, Aunt Caroline, but I have to take some time to see if I can figure this out. I'm not going to forgive myself if I run away unless I absolutely have to."

"Lorrie, I'm not asking," she said, her voice turning hard. "I'm sending Uncle Stewart to pick you up tomorrow."

My stomach soured. "What? You can't make me come home!"

"Then I'll come with him so we can at least keep our eyes on you. I'm worried sick, and I know Uncle Stewart will be too the instant I tell him what happened."

"No, you don't have to do that!" I said hastily. "I'm fine! Just give me a couple days. I promise I'll keep you in the loop."

"We need to at least see you, Lorrie," Aunt Caroline pleaded. "And I'm going to have a very hard time leaving you there unless I feel one-hundred percent certain that you really are fine."

"Okay, okay. Maybe I can take the bus back to Indiana for a few days."

There was silence on the line as my aunt was thinking. "Is there a bus available tomorrow?" she asked tentatively.

I stood up and went to my desk. "Let me check."

Once I was at my desk, I did a search for the buses leaving for

Indiana the next day. My aunt waited on the line.

"Yeah," I said, "looks like there's one for nine a.m. tomorrow."

"Okay, dear. Buy that ticket and I'll give you the money when you get home. If you don't get on that bus, I'm sending Uncle Stewart to pick you up on Monday."

"You won't have to do that," I said.

"Good . . . Is everything else going okay? What's going on with that boy I met with all the tattoos? Hector?"

"Hunter," I said, a small laugh escaping my lips despite the tear rolling down my cheek. "We're actually dating now. Since last week."

"Oh! That's exciting," she said, apparently trying to change the depressing tone of the conversation to a brighter one. "I'm glad you two finally shared your feelings for each other."

"Me too," I said, a smile on my face for the first time in what felt like forever.

"What does he have to say about this letter?"

My smile turned to a frown. "I haven't talked to him about it yet. I think I will later today."

"Okay. Well I'm going to get up and start on breakfast for the boys before their soccer practice."

I grimaced. She was going to be a nervous wreck until I decided to go home. "Okay. Bye Aunt Caroline."

"Goodbye dear."

I ended the call and stared out the window. How long was I going to stay in Indiana? I really needed to talk to Hunter and fill him in on everything that had happened. This had quickly become a situation we needed to work through together. Where the hell was he?

I was a little worried about our relationship. We'd confessed our love for each other on Friday, and I knew I still felt that way about him. Hopefully his feelings hadn't changed either. Still, not being able to get in touch with him when I really needed to made me uneasy. Could I count on him to be my anchor through thick and thin?

I bit my lip, suddenly feeling more uncertain than ever. It upset me that a rough patch had come so early in our relationship, but it had, and he wasn't off to a good start in helping me through it. He hadn't answered my texts for days. What would make you ignore someone you love for days? Could anything? Did he really love me?

I looked at my phone again and sighed. Five in the morning was too early to call, but I needed to talk to him today. After setting an alarm for eight o'clock, I rolled over and tried to fall asleep. My plan was to go down to breakfast and get some food in my system, then talk to Daniela and Hunter.

I had to get this situation figured out soon.

Chapter Twenty-three

MISSING

This time, when my alarm rang I turned it off and sat up in bed. Throwing my sheets aside and getting out was literally painful. My legs felt like jelly after surviving on granola bars for a few days. Once I walked around and stretched for a minute, I changed into some new pajamas and went down to the Floyd Hall dining room for Saturday morning breakfast. I loaded up on carbs like I was about to run a marathon: two bagels with cream cheese, Cinnamon Toast Crunch, melon, and blueberry pancakes drowned in syrup. After cleaning my plate, I walked back to my suite, hoping a hot shower would help me feel slightly more normal. I opened the door to my suite and nearly bumped into Daniela.

"Hey!" she said brightly, her hair a bed head mess. "Did you go to the health center? You look a lot better."

I shook my head. "No, I was just down at breakfast."

"Oh. Why didn't you come get me? I would have gone down with you."

I shifted back and forth on my feet. Now was as good a time as any to talk to her about it. "I just . . . we should talk."

Her face scrunched up in worry. "Is something wrong?"

"No. Not with you, I mean. Let's go to my room."

We walked over to my room and sat down on my bed. Once we were settled, I took a deep breath and started. "I wasn't really sick the past few days."

"Really? I saw you though. You looked white as a ghost."

"I didn't feel good, but I wasn't really sick."

Her eyes narrowed. "I'm confused."

I pressed my lips together. It was so hard to talk about something that upset me so much, even to my best friend. "My stepfather sent me a letter a few days ago," I said, choking on the last couple words. Tears were welling up in my eyes again.

Daniela watched me blankly for several seconds before realization appeared to click in and her jaw dropped. "Oh my god, you mean the one in jail?"

"I don't have any others."

She shook her head, bug-eyed. "But how? Is he allowed to do that?"

I thought of my aunt's anger when I had told her about the letter earlier that morning. "I don't know. It doesn't really matter, I guess. It happened."

She nodded. "What did it say?"

I told her about the letter and cried into her shoulder. Why did this have to happen now?

After I'd calmed down I told her about my conversation with my aunt. Daniela listened attentively, her face wrinkled in thought.

"Guess this came at a bad time with exams and stuff," she said when I was done.

I scoffed. "That's an understatement."

"You looked like you were feeling awful during that psych exam."

"Yeah." I sighed. "I just filled in bubbles on the answer sheet. My brain was so foggy I couldn't even understand the questions."

"Oh wow, I'm so sorry, Lorrie."

"It's okay." I tried to smile reassuringly but my mouth barely responded. "Not your fault, obviously."

We sat in silence for a couple minutes. Then Daniela's eyes widened as if she'd had a realization. "I don't mean to pry Lorrie . . . but did your therapist ever mention you might have PTSD?"

I thought back. "Yeah . . . It was one of the first things she said, actually."

"I guess having it doesn't help you take an exam about it, right?" She smiled uncertainly. I knew she was trying to cheer me up and I felt better knowing she cared.

I forced a small smile and shook my head. Leave it to Daniela to do some amateur diagnosis. "Whatever is going on with me, it didn't help on that test."

She watched me for a second then her head dropped back

down."So what are you going to do now?" she asked quietly.

I tapped my nervous fingers on my legs. My small dorm room began to have the same oppressive feeling the courtroom had.

"I don't know," I said. "My aunt wants me to go back to Indiana tomorrow for at least a couple days. "

"Do you want to go home?"

I pursed my lips. "Yeah, at least for a couple days. I think it'll help me get my head straight."

"Fair enough. What does Hunter think about all this?"

My face felt hot. It was embarrassing that I didn't know the answer to that question. "I haven't heard from him since I got the letter, actually. I texted him last night before bed but he hasn't responded."

"That's weird," she mused. "Did you guys have a fight or something?"

I shrugged, feeling even more bewildered now that I was talking about it out loud. "Nope."

She bit her lip. "Huh. I have to say, that is pretty strange. When are you going to talk to him?"

"I don't know," I said truthfully. "I was going to take a shower then give him a call and see if I can go over there or something."

"What are you going to say? I mean, are you thinking you want to try and stay here? Go back to Indiana? Am I going to see you anymore?"

Her questions were making me feel overwhelmed. "I don't know," I said, my voice breaking. "I love Hunter and I want things to work out, but I don't know how we can do that."

Daniela's eyebrows shot up. "Have you told Hunter that you love him?"

"Yeah, that night of the party."

"And he loves you?"

"That's what he said," I rasped, trying to stop from crying. "But I don't know why he hasn't contacted me in days. This decision is going to drastically change things for us and I can't even get ahold of him. He's letting me down."

She grimaced. "You didn't text him before last night, right? Maybe he'll respond soon."

"Yeah, that's true."

"I say give it some time," she said with a shrug. "Once you do talk to him, if you really love each other then you'll find a way to make it work."

I took a deep breath, thankful for my friend's level-headedness. "Thanks Daniela."

"I guess what you have to decide is whether you're staying or going. Everything depends on that."

I nodded. "Yeah. I'll definitely keep you in the loop."

"Thanks," my friend said. "Let me know if I can do anything, okay?"

I smiled at Daniela as she stood up and walked out of my room.

After she left, I sat and stared out my window. Was there some way Hunter and I could stay together? I sent another text asking where he was. After waiting a minute to see if he would respond, I grew impatient and went to take a shower in the suite bathroom. The sensation of the warm water hitting my shoulders and chest helped me feel a little closer to normal. After a few days of being alone in bed with my thoughts, I was looking forward to just being around other people again.

When I got back to my room the first thing I did was check my phone. Still no response from Hunter. This was getting weird.

I stared at my phone, deciding whether to call. *Screw it,* I thought. Even if he was being a jerk by not responding to texts, I still needed to talk to him. I found his number and put the phone to my ear. The phone rang a few times—which meant it wasn't off—and went to voicemail. I left a message asking where he was and threw the phone on my bed.

An idea dawned on me as I looked at the keys sitting on my dresser. I could go over there to see if Hunter was there. Seeing the kittens might also make me feel better.

I grabbed my keys, put on my coat, and left. Part of me hoped he would be at his apartment. Part of me had a bad feeling about his reason for not picking up the phone.

Hunter wasn't at his apartment. As I kicked off my boots and hung up my coat, I heard the kittens eagerly mewling, excited to have a new friend to play with. All six of them came running to me as I walked into the kitchen. As I gave them loving pets, I noticed dirty dishes filled the sink. Judging by the brown line ringing around one of the pots, it looked like the sink had been filled up with water and left to sit for days.

Had he not been home for a while? Afraid that the kittens hadn't been fed, I looked to their food and water bowls and was relieved to see they were reasonably full. Even if it wasn't Hunter, someone had been in the apartment within the last few hours, because the kittens went through food and water like locusts.

The more I thought about it, the more likely it seemed that it hadn't been Hunter who fed them. Life got crazy for everyone sometimes, but things would have to be pretty hectic for a clean freak like him to ignore his dishes for days. My guess was he hadn't been home.

At the same time, it was hard to imagine why he would be sleeping somewhere else. Was he hurt? Sick? The more I thought about it, the less sense it made.

Then an ugly thought flashed through my mind: there was no way he was cheating, right?

I shook my head and brushed it aside, afraid to even consider the idea. After writing a note on the fridge's whiteboard asking him to call as soon as possible, I left his apartment and walked over to Huck Cafe. I had just spent several days alone. Being around people sounded a lot better than going back to my dorm room and staring at the wall.

I got my usual large black coffee, found a table, and sat down with my sketch pad in my lap and my phone on the table. When was Hunter going to get back to me? The messiness in his apartment increasingly worried me the more I thought about it. It was so out of character for him to leave things as untidy as he did. There was no way he would allow that if he were home for more than a few minutes at a time.

I looked around from my seat, hoping to find something or someone to sketch. As I scanned, I heard Hunter's name above the general buzz in the shop. I found the source of the conversation after a moment's search: two girls wearing pink sorority t-shirts sitting a couple tables over from mine. The girl on the left had her blonde hair in a sloppy ponytail, the one on the right had wavy shoulder-length hair.

"I thought he was dating that girl whose mom got murdered," Ponytail said.

"Me too," Wavy answered. "But Shannon said she saw him and Ada walking into the health center, and he didn't look right, like he was really stunned or something."

My spine straightened and I nearly dropped the coffee in my hand. I subtly tilted my ear to listen more closely.

"That's weird," Ponytail said. "Why would they be at the health center together?"

"I don't know. They used to be a couple, right?"

Ponytail took a sip of her iced coffee. "Yeah, but that was like two years ago."

Her friend twirled her hair. "Maybe they never totally stopped sleeping together."

All the air left my lungs at once. I suddenly wished I was back in bed. This was rampant speculation, but I still hated it.

"I don't know. Even if they still hook up sometimes, they wouldn't go together to the health center. Unless—"

"What if she's pregnant?"

My skin prickled and the hairs on my neck stood on end. This was getting ridiculous.

Ponytail's eyebrows shot up into her bangs. "Oh my god, no way."

Her friend pounded the table, leaning forward. "Come on. How many explanations could there be?"

"I don't know, that sounds crazy."

"Then what could it be?"

"I don't know," Ponytail said, shaking her head.

"I mean it would make sense. I'm not saying it's for sure, but it would make sense, and I'm not hearing any better explanations."

"I guess."

I couldn't listen to any more. Hearing that Ada and Hunter had been seen together when I couldn't even get ahold of him was bad enough. I didn't need to listen to these two girls speculating on *why* they were together. They would always go for the craziest explanation. That's how gossip was.

Still, as I packed up my stuff my stomach felt like I'd been punched repeatedly. Even if Ada wasn't pregnant—and who knew, anything felt possible at this point—it was still pretty shady that they'd been together at the same time he had been impossible to get ahold of. I searched my brain for more reasonable explanations for why he'd been going with her to the health center. Maybe they'd just been having a great conversation and he'd wanted to continue it, so he walked with her while she picked up a prescription or something. Maybe he went with her to get the results of a test. Not a pregnancy test. Like a test for cancer, maybe. Shannon, whoever that was, could've also been lying.

Thinking about the possibilities wasn't making me feel any better. Trying to figure this out without more information would only drive me crazy. I just had to add it to the already long conversation I was going to have with Hunter, whenever that fucking happened.

I finished packing up my sketchbook and headed for my dorm. Maybe being around people wasn't so great after all.

Chapter Twenty-four

THE CONFRONTATION

Ponytail's words echoed through my ears as I trudged through the snow toward Floyd Hall in my black winter coat and matching pom pom beanie. The sky was gray and snowflakes were falling lightly down. The weather guy on TV called this a "dusting," if I remembered right. I had paid a lot of attention to the local weather when I was taking a break from school and living with my aunt and uncle. It was just the right amount of stimulation to get my mind off my mom for a couple minutes. That had been a relatively pleasant couple minutes at the time.

Walking, staring at the snowy ground, I realized Ponytail had been right about one thing—Hunter *was* dating that girl whose mom got murdered. That girl was also seriously wondering where the hell he was. I needed to talk to Hunter as soon as possible. Pondering what had happened to him was driving me crazy.

Why had he left his apartment a mess? Why hadn't he tried to contact me for days? What was he doing with his ex-girlfriend? I didn't expect him to be a mind reader, but hanging out with your ex-girlfriend when your current girlfriend couldn't get in touch with you was obviously going to piss your current girlfriend off. Especially when she was trying to deal with something terrible.

Why, of all places, would he be with her at the health center? It was attached to the college hospital; maybe he was going for a follow-up from some fighting injury. But why would he be with her? Why not ask *me* to go with him?

Trying to shake away the worst of my thoughts, I looked up to see the giant metal and glass complex that was the Arrowhart Medical Complex. I'd been so wrapped up in my head that I hadn't realized the complex was on my way back to the dorm.

When I looked up, I saw a familiar figure. And an unwelcome one.

Hunter was walking toward me in a weathered brown bomber jacket. Stubble on his face indicating he hadn't shaved in a few days and mussed up hair didn't compromise his attractiveness. Ada was by his side wearing a black North Face winter coat that went down past her knees.

She had her arm around him.

My jaw dropped as I stopped in place. I was unwittingly reminded of my first boyfriend coming out of the movie theater with his arm around my best friend. How could something like this be happening again? Could this day get any worse? A million questions flew through my mind as I stood there, feeling my limbs freeze over. Every cold breath in my lungs made me feel closer to throwing up. I wanted to curl up in a little ball right there in the snow and not move.

Hunter's eyes widened when they found mine. He brushed Ada's arm from his back and hurried toward me, arms out. "Lorrie, I was just going to text you," he said. Ada was trailing a few steps behind him.

"Where have you been?" I asked, my voice unsteady.

He came closer and stopped a few feet from me. "Listen, this isn't what it looks like."

I'd barely been able to keep myself together the past week; I'd been crying, sleeping, failing my classes, missing Hunter when I needed him most . . . So the sight of Hunter—the man I loved, or thought I loved—threw my emotions into turmoil. He had been my anchor but now . . . I didn't know what to think. Overwhelmed, tears burst from my eyes. "What's going on Hunter? I needed to talk to you! Where were you?"

His features softened further as he looked at me pleadingly. "Lorrie please calm down."

My fists clenched and I stomped my feet, blinking away tears that fell down my cheeks. "Calm down? Now? Why should I be calm? You've disappeared for a week, didn't respond to my texts or call, and now I see you with her! I thought *we* were supposed to be a team, why are you with *her* when I don't know what's going on?"

Hunter opened his mouth to respond, but Ada jumped in front of him before he could get the words out. "Shut up," she spat, pointing her index finger at me. "How dare you? You barely try to find your boyfriend when he's been gone and then yell at him the instant you see him? Seriously, a couple of texts? Give me a break. I would have called the police! You have no right to be screaming at him. He should be mad at you!"

Mad at *me*? What? I could barely leave my room for days and just flunked three exams, how was it my fault? How did she know about the texts, anyway? Was she checking Hunter's phone?

"What are you talking about?" I responded angrily. Knowing that Ada and I had barely interacted, I struggled to make sense of her aggressive accusations. The time we'd met at dinner might've been awkward but this was ridiculous. Was this what Hunter was referring to when he said Ada was pushy? "Are you jealous?" I shot back.

She reared back for a second before laughing bitterly and turning toward Hunter. "Oh my god. Are you serious right now? Hunter, what the hell do you see in this girl? Is it her ability to be a thick-headed moron? Is that what you relate to?"

Hunter looked conflicted. "Ada, please stop," he said, his eyes getting softer by the minute. "Lorrie, we can talk—"

"Stop?" Ada screeched. Her eyes were darting between Hunter and me wildly. "Stop what? Trying to look out for you? This girl's crazy, Hunter. Anyone can see it in two seconds. I get that you feel sorry for her and everything, but it's okay to leave the rescue job to someone else. You have your own shit going on."

Feel sorry for me? What was she talking about? My face was burning. "Crazy? You don't even know me! You think I'm crazy because I want some answers from Hunter?"

She turned to Hunter—whose face was an uncharacteristic combination of panic and confusion—and shook her head. "This is impossible."

"What?" I snapped, furious heat coursing through my cheeks. "That you're the other woman?"

Her jaw fell open. "Good lord, now this? I should fucking slap you."

Several people stopped to look at the source of the commotion we were causing. This was quickly becoming a scene.

"Ada, please stop," Hunter pleaded, looking around. Deep concern was etched into his expression but he lacked the fervor he had when he knocked out Jimmy for talking shit about me. Was Ada that important to him? More important to him than me? "You're embarrassing all of us."

I stared, dumbfounded and in shock. Why wasn't he defending me? Why was he still by her side?

"What were you doing in the health center in the first place?" I asked, trying to regain my composure though I was on the edge of hysterics. "Did you get hurt from a fight? Why didn't you tell me?"

His eyes were frantic as he looked around at the people who had stopped to gawk—some didn't even bother hiding their interest, having their camera phones out and recording the scene. "I'm sorry, I promise this isn't what it looks like."

I threw my hands up in the air. "I don't even know what this looks like Hunter! What is it?"

"Just wait," Ada spat. "You're going to feel like such a bitch when you find out the truth. You think you're the only one with problems, Ms. Sob Story? I'm going to tell her, Hunter. I swear I'm going to tell her."

"NO! Ada, you can't do this to me! Not now!" Hunter yelled at her.

Tell me what? What was Ada going to tell me?

Ada shook her head in disgust before stomping past me, her shoulder knocking mine in the process. I stumbled back a few steps, barely keeping my balance on the slippery concrete.

Hunter's eyes looked panicked as they darted between me and Ada. "Lorrie, listen, we need to talk, but just—just wait okay? I need to talk to Ada first, but I want to talk to you okay? I—I love you, nothing's changed, everything's gonna get back to normal, just let me talk to Ada first."

My vision was blurry with the hot tears flooding my eyes. "Give me something, Hunter. Please, don't leave me with just this."

I don't know if he heard it or not, but Hunter was already hurrying after Ada.

He left me to go after Ada.

People were staring at me, waiting to see what I'd do next. *What the hell just happened?* This was a nightmare that I couldn't wake up from. I adjusted my beanie and put my head down, walking the way I'd come, which was the opposite direction Hunter was walking. My face was already streaked with tears and my eyes were brimming with fresh ones, but I had to hold it together. Just a little longer Lorrie. Just a little longer.

I felt the eyes of the people who had been gawking bore into my back as I hurried away. My face was flushed with embarrassment; whatever I'd been expecting when I saw Hunter, total humiliation hadn't been it. I could practically see the text messages being sent by onlookers as I slogged through the snow. This was a gossip gold mine.

Ada had acted like I'd done something terrible to Hunter. Why did she sound like she was so sure she had the moral high ground? Instead of her, it was Hunter who appeared to be panicking. The image of his expression as he snapped his head around, staring at the people who had stopped to watch, burned in my memory. He looked like a cornered animal. But why would *he* be so scared when Ada wasn't? Was it as simple as him having a conscience and her being born without one? Why on earth had they been at the health center anyway? Was Hunter sick? Then why didn't he tell me?

My jacket vibrated. Pulling out the phone with fingers that were numb from the cold, I pecked at the screen angrily to input my password. Suddenly, the phone slipped out of my hand; I fumbled but couldn't save it.

I cringed as I watched it splash into a slush pile. Even though I bent down and snatched it up immediately, fingers freezing, I knew it was too late. I pressed the power button repeatedly, but the screen wouldn't turn on. My precious phone was toast.

Dammit. This is fucking great.

What was I going to do now?

I stopped in my tracks on the sidewalk and stared out across campus. Tomorrow I would be on a bus to Indiana. My phone was dead but I still really needed to talk to Hunter. Instead of heading back to my dorm, I decided to head for his place. He had to come home eventually, and when he did we could have our conversation. We had a lot to talk about.

We had been doing so well. How did things get so messed up?

Chapter Twenty-five

GOODBYE

My heart in my throat, I walked into Hunter's apartment and greeted the kittens. At first glance Hunter wasn't here. He was probably still dealing with Ada. I took a big breath and crouched down to the kittens' level, wondering how long it would take him to get home. The incident in front of the health center still had me shaken up.

Taylor ran up to me and rubbed the length of her body against my leg. Her large blue eyes looked up at me affectionately. I gave her some pets on the chest, her favorite spot, and her eyes closed as she purred her approval.

I scooped her up and walked to the living room. Taylor looked around curiously at her new surroundings. The two of us plopped down on the couch and waited.

And waited. And waited. I kept feeling for my phone before remembering it was dead. Taylor squirmed around a bit before falling asleep on my lap. After I'd sat there for around thirty minutes I reached for the remote control—careful not to wake up the sleeping kitty on my lap—and turned on the television. Bravo was running a marathon of *The Millionaire Matchmaker*, and I watched that for a couple hours. Taylor continued to sleep in peace, blissfully unaware of the shit going on between me and Hunter.

As the episodes and hours piled on, confusion turned to frustration. It was ten o'clock and the light outside had turned dark. I'd been sure he'd be home by now. My stomach was starting to growl, having not eaten for hours. Where the hell was he? He couldn't still be with Ada, right? What did "I want to talk to you" mean to him, anyway?

I felt isolated sitting in his living room while he wasn't there. For the hundredth time, I wished my phone was working. Not being able to get in touch with people made me feel helpless.

I couldn't sit waiting forever, and I definitely wasn't falling asleep at his place—my bus was leaving tomorrow morning. If he didn't come back to the apartment soon, I was going to have to leave. *Leave Studsen without having talked to Hunter.* My stomach dropped. The frustration that had been building inside of me began to turn to dread.

What if I had to leave before he came home? It was unlikely that I'd have time to track him down tomorrow; I didn't have a phone and my bus was leaving at nine in the morning. Besides, even if I wanted to track him down, would I even be able to? He had disappeared for a week before I saw him today and now he was nowhere to be found again when he promised me that we would talk. Hunter was getting more unreliable every minute he didn't show up at his own apartment.

I was petting Taylor in my lap when a sudden wave of nausea hit me like an oncoming bus. *If I leave Studsen, I may never pet Taylor again. Hunter had been with Ada; I was in his apartment, maybe for the last time; my stepfather had sent me that letter; I failed my semester; my parents were dead; the man I loved was flaking out on me again and everything was turning to shit. Again.*

The weight of everything came crashing down on me like a pile of heavy stones. I suddenly felt incredibly nauseous. After hastily putting Taylor to the side, I sprinted on shaky legs for the bathroom so I wouldn't vomit on the living room floor. Thankfully, I made it to the toilet. I held my hair back and threw up until my guts were empty.

Sitting on the floor hunched over the toilet, ragged, I had a moment to think. *This is awful.* I couldn't handle this. No matter how much I wanted to, I couldn't keep burying my problems and hoping they would go away with time—it would kill me.

A sound came from the bathroom door as it slowly creaked open. Hunter?

Taylor popped her furry head through the door and entered. She stood there, looking at me wide-eyed as I sat there breathing heavily, still trying to steady myself. She approached and nuzzled against my leg. Tears of frustration welled up in my eyes and I stood up to wash myself off in the sink.

After cleaning myself up and walking out of the bathroom with Taylor following close behind, I realized I needed more than a few days stay in Indiana to recuperate. I had dreaded the idea before, but I wasn't sure what else I could do now. I needed an anchor in my life. Something to stabilize me. I thought Hunter had been it, but the past few days were proving that wrong. I needed to be with Aunt Caroline and Uncle Stewart for more than just a few days.

How was I going to tell Hunter? I needed to get out of here, but he was nowhere to be seen, and I had no way of knowing when he would get home. One thing I didn't want to do was what he had done to me by disappearing. I couldn't leave Studsen with this conversation hanging over my head.

Maybe I could leave him a note. It wasn't perfect, but at least I could explain the situation. Resigned, I rummaged through my bag, seeing if I had a notebook to write Hunter something if he didn't get back soon. No luck. All I had was my sketchpad and charcoal from earlier in the coffeeshop. It would have to do.

I scratched out my opening: *Hunter.* Warm tears beaded up in my eyes and rolled down my cheeks. I remembered the things he had said to me when we spent those four nights holed up in this apartment.

"I'm gonna save us both."

When he said those words, I'd believed him. But he was wrong. He could barely save himself from whatever he was dealing with, and if I added my problems on top of that, it was just going to pull us both down. I had to save myself or I wouldn't make it. Neither of us would.

I took a deep breath and kept writing as tears streamed down my face, pausing now and then to think of my next sentence.

Hunter—

I want to start by saying I'm sorry. After the past few days, I came to your apartment hoping we could talk about everything, but you never came back. I don't know where you are, but I hope you're okay.

So now I'm leaving this note. Some stuff happened and there's no way I can continue with my classes, so I'm withdrawing from the semester. I don't know if I'm ever coming back to Arrowhart.

I'm writing this to tell you we're over. I'll be leaving Studsen early tomorrow morning.

It kills me to do it this way, but since you didn't come back home I have to. Waiting around any longer than I have isn't an option. I can't function with the way my mind is right now. Look at this note. My hand is shaking so badly, I can barely write these words.

I don't know what's going to happen to me if I don't find something solid in my life. I want to believe that we had something real Hunter. Maybe if things hadn't happened this way we could have worked things out, but I have to leave now. If I stay here any longer I might not make it.

I'm so sorry I can't explain more, but it would be unfair to involve you in this now. I'm not going to do that.

Please don't think this is about you. You were the happiest thing in my life, and I'm sorry I have to hurt you like this.

I wish life had treated us differently.

-Lorrie

I read over what I wrote as best I could through the tears blurring my vision. A warm bead dropped down onto the note. I dabbed it away with my finger, and read again. He wouldn't be happy when he read the note, but hopefully he would understand with time.

Note in hand, I went into the kitchen. A small body brushed up against my leg. I looked down and saw Hunter's favorite kitten, Rampage. He was looking up at me with eyes wide, his ears down.

I crouched and gave him some pets behind the ears, still sniffling, but it didn't seem to cheer him up. It was like he knew I was leaving.

After taking a deep breath and looking at the letter one more time, I folded it in half, wrote Hunter's name on the outside, and set it on his kitchen counter where he could see it easily. Once I was done, I packed up, said one last goodbye to the kittens, and walked out feeling emotionally exhausted .

The cold winter air stung my tear-stained face as I left the apartment. I hurried down the forest path toward Floyd Hall. It was the same path Hunter had given me a piggyback ride through after he'd saved me from drowning. That happened on the day we first met.

That day seemed so long ago now.

Chapter Twenty-six

TIME

By the time I got back to the dorm, it was almost eleven. Daniela was sitting on the futon watching TV when I came in. She turned around and muted the TV.

"Where have you been?" she asked, concern tingeing her voice.

I shut the door separating the suite from the hallway. "What do you mean?"

"You didn't return my calls. What happened?"

"Sorry, I dropped my phone and it broke," I said weakly. "Can I sit down?"

She scooted over to make room for me on the futon, and I collapsed into it. "I broke up with Hunter today," I said somberly.

"Why? What happened?"

I took a deep breath. "I went to the coffee shop to do some sketching and overheard these two girls talking about how one of their friends had seen Hunter and Ada together recently. The girl said they were going into the health center. I told you before that he'd gone totally missing since last week, and I didn't know where he was so I didn't know what to think."

Daniela tilted her head to the side. "Okay, that sounds crazy. What did you do?"

"I was frustrated and left to get away from them. You know, I just don't have the energy for gossip and everything. But sure enough, as I was walking by the health center guess who comes out?"

She recoiled. "Hunter?"

"And Ada."

"No way. What did you say?"

I told her the story of how I'd confronted Hunter and the fight with Ada. She gasped as I related the details of the screaming

277

match and the people who had stopped to watch. Remembering the experience made me feel queasy.

"And Hunter did nothing?" she asked when I was done.

"Not until Ada bumped me as she walked away. Then he said he wanted to talk to me, but he chased after her instead. Before that he seemed kind of not all there."

"Wow. I didn't think Ada was such a psycho. So what do you think was going on with him and Ada?"

"No idea. I went over to his place to wait for him so that we could talk, but he never showed up. My bus is leaving tomorrow and I couldn't call him, so I left him a note." I bit my lip in frustration. It wasn't supposed to happen this way, but now it was done. I'd be on my way to Indiana tomorrow morning and I'd probably never come back.

Just thinking about the fact that I would probably never see Hunter again brought fresh tears welling to my eyes.

Daniela's eyes widened. "Wait, why does that mean you had to leave a note? I thought you were only going back to your Aunt's for a break. Does this mean you're not coming back?"

I shook my head. "I'm sorry Daniela. You've made this semester as good for me as you could; I couldn't have asked for a better friend." She reached over and squeezed my hand. "—but I think I have to withdraw from the semester. With everything going on, the letter from Marco, me flunking all those exams, and this thing with Hunter . . . I—I don't think I can stay here."

She patted my hand to console me and gave me a tissue. I blew my nose into it.

"So what now?" she asked.

"I don't know, I might take another semester off? Maybe take classes online when I feel ready? Obviously what's happening right now isn't working."

"Do you think you'll ever talk to Hunter? You know, to get closure? You guys were crazy about each other."

"I don't know. I don't even know what to think about Hunter anymore. Maybe he did something with Ada, maybe he didn't, but it's clear that he's hiding something serious from me. I don't know what he's dealing with, but my mind is so messed up right now that

I just can't sort everything out. I wish we could have talked, but I couldn't keep waiting for him."

"Yeah." She nodded. "You have to take care of yourself first. Even if Hunter has some stuff going on, he could have at least found some way to explain things."

I nodded, wiping my nose. "Thanks Daniela . . . for everything."

"Hey, don't worry. You should get some rest for your trip tomorrow. I'll see you off in the morning."

"Okay, thanks."

"Okay. Good night."

I got up to go back to my room.

"Hey Lorrie?" she said. "Can I come visit you over Spring Break?"

I smiled, "Yeah, of course. I think Aunt Caroline would like to see you too."

"Great!"

I went back into my room and started packing my clothes thinking that maybe this was a blessing in disguise. I'd be safe with Aunt Caroline and Uncle Stewart, and Daniela would be coming by to visit. Maybe all I needed was just some more time to sort myself out.

Chapter Twenty-seven

SECOND TRY

The bus station was depressing. Its concrete walls were painted a bland beige, and the mix of wood-panel benches and mustard-colored vinyl seats—that might have been modern in the eighties—looked like relics now. I had said my tearful goodbye to Daniela in the morning and caught a cab to the bus station.

I was sitting on the bench trying to keep my mind blank instead of wondering if Hunter had read the note I left him. At 8:30AM, half an hour before the bus was scheduled to leave, I heard an announcement crackling over the intercom.

"Attention please. Attention. The bus from Springfield to Indianapolis, traveling through Studsen is delayed due to a mechanical malfunction. The bus company is working to send a backup to our location, but expect a delay of three to four hours."

A collective groan rose from the handful of people scattered around the station. *God. What else was going to go wrong in my life?* I slumped in my seat, feeling miserably defeated. Studsen was kind of in the middle of nowhere, and that was the only bus that came through the town.

I sat there for another few hours, frustrated. Another announcement over the intercom told us that it would be yet another "two to three" hours before the backup bus would be there to pick us up. I could feel the tears beginning to well up in my eyes again.

This is so stupid. Am I seriously going to cry over a late bus?

Taking a few deep, shaky breaths, I tried to calm myself down. It was going to be okay. The bus would come soon and then I'd be away from all this. Away from the gossip, the failed classes, and the dirty looks.

Away from Hunter, the one happy thing I found at Arrowhart.

What was Hunter doing now? Had he gone back to his place last night? Had he read my note? Was he looking for me to talk to me? I'd only left him that note because I didn't think there'd be enough time in the morning to find him and talk. Now, it looked like I would be stuck in Studsen until the late afternoon at the earliest. Maybe it would give me an opportunity to talk to Hunter one last time. Maybe we could figure out where we went wrong.

Even though there were so many things in my life I could never get closure on, maybe my relationship with Hunter was something I still had a chance to understand. Daniela was right, it would be nice if I could have a second chance to talk to him, before I left Studsen for good. It sure as hell beat sitting in this bus station and thinking about what could have been.

I sat on the bench and stared out the window as a cab approached, dropping off a passenger at the station. As I watched the cab's passenger get her luggage out of the trunk, I made my decision. I had to try to talk to Hunter. I had to know what had happened the past few days.

After leaving my luggage with the station attendant—who assured me it would get on the bus even if I wasn't there—I ran out waving my arms and managed to get the cabbie's attention. I got in and told the driver to take me to Hunter's apartment.

I sat and watched Studsen fly past the window, hoping Hunter would be at his apartment this time. The cab arrived at its destination and I paid before hopping up the steps to Hunter's unit. I took a deep breath and walked in.

The kittens greeted me like I still belonged there. Taylor and Bones ran up to me together and hopped up on their hind legs to paw at my shins. I gave them affectionate pets and ran my fingers along the two tiny bodies. When I looked at the kitchen, I gasped. *Good god, what happened here?* The place was a mess. The cabinet next to the sink—or what was left of it—had a giant hole in the door, and one of the hinges had come off.

Had Hunter read my note and gotten angry enough to destroy his apartment?

An ill feeling settled in my gut. I called out Hunter's name, hoping he might be in another room, but the apartment was silent. Frustration welled up inside me when I realized Hunter wasn't home. I'd gotten my hopes up for nothing. I needed find Hunter. Where could he be now?

After saying a last goodbye to the kittens, I walked out of the apartment. If he wasn't home at this time of day, the gym was the next best bet. Maybe he was blowing off some steam. I decided to walk over there and check it out.

Ten minutes later I strode into the gym and was met by Kristy at the reception desk. I was surprised to find the normal frenetic commotion of the gym was subdued to almost nothing. It didn't sound like there were more than a few people training today.

"Hey you," she said, brightly. "How are the kittens?"

"Good," I replied, barely keeping in check my anxiousness to find out about Hunter's whereabouts. "They're getting big fast."

"I bet. Those little guys were so cute here in the gym. Seems like yesterday Hunter came in with that box."

I smiled even though I was feeling more nauseous by the second. "Yeah. Is Hunter here?"

She shook her head. "Of course not. Didn't he tell you? He has a fight right now."

"A fight? Where?"

Her penciled-in eyebrows furrowed in thought. "The Squirrel, I think."

"The Bearded Squirrel?"

She nodded. "Yeah, that one."

"Was it scheduled?" I asked.

"No. Dan has the flu, so he had to cancel, and Hunter is filling in. I only have afternoon shift today, so I just heard about it from the guys."

My head spun. What the hell was going on? "Oh. Do you know what time he's fighting?"

She shrugged. "Usually they start these things in the afternoon on weekends, maybe at one? But they don't always run on time. He's probably fighting right now."

Right now? From the condition of Hunter's apartment, I was starting to get a very bad feeling about this fight that I couldn't shake. I had to talk to Hunter right away. I borrowed the gym phone and called a cab. Ten minutes later, a cab came to pick me up. Fifteen minutes after that, I was at The Bearded Squirrel.

The bar was a little less crowded than last time, but the guitars of the hard rock music playing on the jukebox were still as loud as I remembered. Most of the tables at the front of the bar were empty, along with most of the stools. A poster on the wall next to the entrance advertised the fight of the day: Walter Morris vs Dan Evans. That was the guy Kristy had said Hunter was filling in for: Dan Evans. This was definitely the right spot.

There was a crowd gathered out back—just as there had been the last time I had seen Hunter fight. I walked to the crowd's edge. People were standing shoulder to shoulder, making it hard to see the cage. There was an anxious tension in the air. Something wasn't right.

"Dude, this guy's taking a beating," I heard a man say. "What did you say his name was?"

I turned to find the voice and located it a few feet away. The man was tall and wearing a white fraternity baseball cap backwards over his long brown hair.

"I didn't," the guy next to him replied. "But after this fight it won't matter because nobody will be able to recognize him. Holy shit, his face! How can someone take so much punishment and not go down?"

Who were they talking about? I felt a sick dread beginning to coil in my stomach before I could even glimpse the ring. Desperate to see the fight, I eased around the crowd's fringe, looking for a clear line of sight.

As I frantically shuffled around the crowd, I came across two girls huddled together. One girl with wavy blonde hair had her hand to her mouth, shocked.

"He looks like he's dying out there," she gasped.

Her friend, a straight-haired dirty blonde with a mousy face, rubbed her friend's shoulder. "I'm sure he'll be fine. It's the last round. He'll make it."

"But just look at him!"

The dread that had formed in my stomach began to swallow

my entire midsection. I needed to see Hunter right now. My palms were clammy and it felt like my chest was being crushed.

I left the two girls to themselves and hurried around to a gap that had been left in the crowd. A roar erupted as I got there and I had my first glimpse of the cage.

The men inside were wrestling with each other and pressed up against the side closest to where I stood. I didn't recognize the guy with his back to me, but the face that popped up over his shoulder made my legs go soft. Even with his left eye swollen nearly shut and cuts on his cheekbones, I would recognize those dark gray irises and that mussed up brown hair anywhere.

It was Hunter.

A sharp pain knifed through my chest. He looked beyond exhausted. His chest heaved and his mouth hung wide open, gasping for breath. There was blood dripping down his face from one of the cuts on his right cheek and the bruise on his left eye was a stormy mix of gray and purple. It seemed to be getting darker and swelling bigger by the second.

A violent shiver ran through my body, and my mouth opened in horror. I'd never seen Hunter like this before. I'd never seen someone so broken.

Finally, the other fighter managed to push Hunter away. The two began circling each other again. Hunter's hands were down by his stomach and his legs wobbled with the effort to remain standing. My heart squeezed in my throat as I watched him struggle.

Something was horribly wrong.

Chapter Twenty-eight

SECRET

Hunter

Three years ago

I'd always hated the doctor's office. The chemical smell reminded me of the cleaner we used on the wrestling mats after practice. We used it for the same reason they used it in a hospital: to kill things. Sure, they were microscopic things, but still, it wasn't a healthy smell.

I was just halfway through my freshman year at Arrowhart. I'd gotten a scholarship to be in the Reserve Officer Training Program—something I'd wanted to do ever since I met an Air Force recruiter in high school. I was going to be a pilot. I was going to fly. But first I had to get through this doctor's visit.

I sat on the thin paper covering the exam table, nervously studying the the various anatomy charts posted on the walls as I waited for the doctor to come in. This particular visit was even worse because I had no idea what the fuck was wrong with me.

When I first came in, the doctor had been worried I might have a neurological issue. I'd been fighting and getting bumps and bruises my whole life, but this was different. This was my brain.

Just as I was about to get up and check on the doc, the door opened, and the doctor came in with his clipboard. I studied his expression, trying to get a read on what the news was, but he was poker-faced.

"Hello, Hunter," the doctor said, carefully neutral. He was gray around the temples and wore silver-rimmed glasses. "How are you feeling?"

"Fine," I answered. "Did you find out what's wrong with me?"

Taking a seat on a stool by the counter, he double-checked the chart, flipping carefully through to the last page. Then he removed his glasses, placed them in his coat pocket, and looked at me. I swallowed and gritted my teeth but said nothing.

He paused for a moment to take a deep breath. "Looking at the MRI, we have all the data we need. It appears you have suffered exacerbations from a condition called relapsing-remitting multiple sclerosis, or RRMS."

My pulse leaped and my stomach churned. *Did he just say multiple sclerosis?* I'd heard about the condition before but all I knew was it was a neurological condition and it wasn't something to fuck with.

I exhaled heavily and looked back up at the doctor. "How did I get it?"

Growing up, there were always dirty syringes and used crack pipes littering the "home" I lived in. I didn't remember ever touching them, but it couldn't have helped to be around that.

The doctor shook his head, "You didn't catch it from anyone else if that's what you're asking. MS isn't contagious. As for the cause, even the best researchers don't know yet."

The doctor continued. "We found two lesions on your brain in the MRI. At this point it looks like it's RRMS because you've recovered pretty well. You're on the young side to be diagnosed with this, but at this point we've ruled out everything else."

"So what happens now? You write me some drugs and it's back to action, right?"

He looked at me seriously for a moment before continuing, "Not exactly. It's not curable. But we can manage it with treatment. What you had recently was a flare-up, after the treatment starts your symptoms will likely get better; they might not even be noticeable. In between flare-ups you'll likely only have minimal symptoms."

"So, my vision will be a bit fuzzy but I'll be okay?" I asked. That didn't sound so bad. I could live with that. But a sinking sensation in my stomach told me that I wouldn't get off the hook that easily.

He frowned. "The nature of the disease is that it's progressive. It will gradually get worse and worse. You'll lose your sense of touch first, then your sense of balance, then you might start losing control of your muscles. Eventually your brain stops telling your heart to beat, or your lungs to breathe. We can slow it down, but we can't stop it."

Growing up like I did, not much fazed me, but right now I could feel a cold sweat on my forehead and a helpless fury expanding in my chest. "How long have I got?"

He sighed. "Hard to say, but with proper management and modern treatment, some patients live full productive lives."

"Some patients? What happens to the ones that don't?"

"In the most severe cases, hospice care is required within a couple of years, maybe months."

"Jesus Christ, months? In a few months I'll be waiting to die?" I felt hollow, like I should vomit but there was nothing inside of me. I'd faced difficulties before but this thing was different. This thing wasn't real. It came out of nowhere. It wasn't something I could grab, punch, or knockout. I had no idea how to fight this.

The doctor shook his head. "The prognosis largely depends on how severe of a case you have. As for you, it's too early to tell how aggressively the disease will progress. The good news is that we caught it fairly early, so we can plan a course of treatment. "

I clenched my fists, my insides roiling. *Fuck this shit.* Why did this have to happen to me? I thought I had done it. I'd finally gotten away from the drugs, the filth, and the petty crimes that were forced on my childhood. Even though I still got in trouble sometimes, I busted my ass in school so that I could get into college and go somewhere far far away from the negativity and bullshit of my parents. School, wrestling team, boxing club—that was my routine throughout high school. My life was fucked up, but at least there were things that I could control.

But now this. Now I had a death sentence hanging over my head, just waiting to crush me.

༓ ༓ ༓

Two and a half years ago

After receiving my diagnosis, I threw myself one-hundred percent into ROTC. The doctor couldn't tell me how quickly my MS would progress, but from what he said, I figured worst case scenario was I would still have a few years. Maybe ten, definitely five at least. I was young, and other than the MS, pretty healthy. I could still do it, I could still get into the Air Force.

I'd work my ass off even if I could only fly one mission. I just wanted to fly, to be up in the air, free and away from it all. That was all I needed, all I asked for.

The doctor gave me some resources for cleaning up my diet and pointed me to some alternative therapies I could try, like yoga and meditation. He also encouraged me to continue my exercise routine. Leading a healthy lifestyle in general was something I could do to manage my condition.

Living a disciplined and healthy lifestyle fit well with my goal of being an Air Force officer, so that's what I did. Everything I read about dealing with MS said the worst thing you could do was feel sorry for yourself and dwell on it, so I threw myself into training. I felt pretty shitty when I first found out, but I wasn't big on long pity parties. This thing wasn't going to stop me from doing what I wanted to do.

After training hard all summer, I was a beast in Physical Training when school started. I finished first in every drill, and the supervisors were noticing. It made me feel good to be recognized for all the work I'd done. I was beating these guys even with my condition. It proved to me that there was still plenty in my life I had control over.

I was still sweaty from another session of dominating PT in the late summer heat when Captain Mitch McHenry called me into his office. It was September of my sophomore year. I was a little worried that he was calling me in. Most of the time, unscheduled visits to McHenry's office were a bad thing.

"Sit, Jensen," he said pointing to the chair in front of his desk when I entered. His face looked grim, but I couldn't think of anything I'd done wrong.

He grimaced before he spoke. "There's no way to put this lightly. I've seen how hard you've worked, both last year and the beginning of this year, so I know how much you want this. But the Air Force is going to have to release you from the ROTC program."

I bolted upright in the chair and caught myself before I stood up. This couldn't be happening. McHenry could be a hardass, but he was always fair.

"What do you mean?" I asked, racking my brains desperately for where I had fucked up. "Why? Was it the B+ I got in freshman writing? Look, I'll take it again!"

He shook his head and glanced back down at the file in his hand—my file. "No you haven't done anything wrong Hunter. But I was looking at your physical record today and saw that you have multiple sclerosis."

"I know, sir, but it's not that bad. I've been managing it with my doctor. He said that we caught it early. I haven't even had any flare-ups since—"

McHenry looked down and held up his hand.

I studied his face desperately. I could feel it slipping away by the minute. The only thing I ever cared about was slipping through my fingers. I tried again. "I'll do double Physical Training. I'll do the night sessions too—"

"Jensen, stop. It's not about how hard you can work. I know you've put in more time than anyone else in the program. This is Air Force policy. The Air Force doesn't accept candidates with your condition."

I shook my head slowly in disbelief. "But I'm fine!" I said, as much to myself as to him. "You've seen me in PT."

"Jensen, look. The Air Force can't risk you having a flare-up while on active duty with lives at stake. The Air Force thinks it's best to avoid the potential for that situation altogether. I'm very sorry, Jensen, but that decision is final."

"The Air Force thinks? What about you? What do you think?" I yelled, feeling betrayed by both McHenry and the organization I had worked so hard towards. I knew I was crossing the line but I didn't care.

McHenry relaxed and looked at me, his eyes softening. "Son, it doesn't matter what I think. I can't change Air Force policy. You're a capable, smart, young man. The military isn't everything, and with your condition, why do you want this anyway? There are a lot of other opportunities for you beyond the military."

A flash of pity flashed across his face and the anger boiling in my chest threatened to spill over. He pitied me. He fucking took away the only thing I ever wanted and he pitied me.

McHenry was talking but I wasn't listening. "I bust my ass, whip everyone in PT, and this is what I get? Kicked to the curb because of some stupid shit disease I have no control over? This is fucking ridiculous!"

His eyes became hard and commanding. "Watch it Jensen. Just because you can no longer be a part of this program doesn't mean you can say whatever the hell you want."

I got up and stared him down. I was shaking with rage and there was a furious pounding in my head. "Fuck you McHenry, and fuck the Air Force."

I left his office bouncing between helplessness and anger as I entered the locker room. I smashed my fist into a locker, rattling the entire row. Other guys looked at me and backed away as I went to my locker; it took every ounce of control to not punch someone. Why did this have to happen to me? What was I going to do now?

I shoved the contents of my locker into a gym bag and slammed the door shut. All that grueling work was down the drain for nothing.

I punched the locker again, leaving a fist-sized dent. McHenry could have fun getting that thing out. My fist aching, I threw my bag over my shoulder and stormed out of the building. After dropping off my stuff back at my apartment, I went straight to the bar. I woke up hungover the next morning and got my first tattoo.

ל ל ל

Two years ago

We were in my apartment having the same argument yet again. Ada and I had been together for around fourteen months; it was now February of my sophomore year. Our relationship wasn't going to make it to the next month if she wouldn't shut up about this.

"Hunter, you can't keep fighting!" she yelled from the couch. "It's just irresponsible! Every time you have a fight I feel like I'm going to get a call that you're in the ER."

I was seated on the floor after another set of pushups, wearing nothing but a pair of mesh gym shorts. "Really? I thought you said it was hot that I was a fighter." I knew that it would piss her off but I said it anyway.

"That was before I knew you had MS!" Ada threw her hands up in the air in frustration."I mean, what if you get hit in the head, or even get knocked out? Don't give me some bullshit about how it won't make it worse. I'm not stupid."

I grinned at her, knowing that I was just pissing her off even more. "I just won't get knocked out. No big deal. Haven't gotten knocked out yet."

"Ugh! You're impossible!"

"I don't need your pity, Ada. I can take care of myself in the cage. Besides, I'm being as safe as I can."

"Being as safe as you can is still killing yourself!" she yelled.

I shrugged. "I don't know, I'm pretty sure I'm still alive."

"You're so selfish," she said bitterly.

"Selfish? It's my fucking body and I can do whatever the hell I want with it. Having MS doesn't change that."

She narrowed her eyes. "I'm not saying you can't do what you want. I'm saying what you want to do is really, really stupid."

I shrugged and got back into position for more pushups.

"This conversation isn't over," she shrieked. "Get up!"

My knees hit the floor and I sat up. "Okay. What else do you have?"

It looked like she was trying to use her eyes to bore a hole into my chest. "You don't respect me. If you won't stop fighting when it's obviously so stupid, I don't think I can be close to you. Every time you fight, I'm worried you're going to get knocked out and die! It drives me crazy."

I locked eyes with her. "Ada, I do respect you. Still, nothing's gonna stop me from making my own decisions. If you don't respect that, then I don't know what to tell you."

She narrowed her eyes in anger. "Oh my god, you're impossible! I can't do this anymore. You've changed, Hunter. I remember when you were driven and had goals. Ever since you got kicked out of ROTC, it's been the same shit with you. Showing people you're in control of your life. Maybe you're showing yourself—I don't know—but all you've shown me is that you're a selfish child."

Fuck her shit, no one was going to tell me what to do. I stared at her for a moment and got back down to doing pushups. She sighed angrily one more time before picking up her bag and walking out the door. We broke up for good the next day.

$$ \text{\textit{ʔ ʔ ʔ}} $$

Yesterday

I lay in my hospital bed, hooked up to more monitors than I thought possible. This was the worst I'd ever felt. I'd had another flare-up. I couldn't ask Lorrie for help so here I was, with Ada. She had driven me to the campus health center a few days before, and since then she had visited every day. I appreciated her help, but I was just waiting for the other foot to drop.

Ada and I had fun when we weren't dealing with my MS. But whenever my MS came up, a bitter argument was soon to follow. If Ada didn't agree with something, she would keep arguing until she got her way. She didn't seem to grasp the words "it's not your business."

Lorrie was different. She didn't know the full story, but she never pried, never tried to tell me what to do. That night, after the fight, I could see it in her eyes: a cool disapproval for the face bashing I just gave the other guy. Even though she didn't know me at the time, I could tell she didn't like it. A girl like her didn't need the fighting, the violence, the feeling of going toe to toe with an angry, out of control monster in a tight confined space, but I did, and she never asked me to stop. I knew I should have told Lorrie about my MS but I couldn't.

Ada broke into my thoughts. "I'll be right back Hunter, going to grab something from the vending machine."

I nodded.

The first time Lorrie ran into me outside the health center, I almost told her. Told her about the disease that was eating through my nerves and would destroy my body eventually. I'd been in the health center getting my monthly treatment. A 10cc dose of corticosteroids, injected directly into my left thigh. Thing was, it always put me in a sour mood. I'd be weak and tired for at least forty-eight hours. Couldn't train, couldn't fight, couldn't do shit. A useless bag of flesh.

Usually, I'd spend those days holed up drinking, watching TV, and fucking girls whose names I barely knew. On the worst days, I'd never let anybody see me. Doctor said no alcohol, but fuck him. Sometimes I'd melt one of the stupid model planes I collected in high school over my stove top until it was a puddle of gray plastic.

I'd clean up the apartment once the side effects wore off. Toss out the beer cans, take out the trash. Get ready to do it all over again in another month.

But that day was different, I ran into Lorrie on my way out of the health center. I told her I'd been getting a couple fight injuries patched up and asked her if she wanted to hang out. Usually I didn't like being around people after my treatment, but Lorrie was different. We ate popcorn and watched some movies. When she fell asleep on my shoulder that night, it almost made me forget about my problems. That was the first night I broke from my post-treatment tradition of getting wasted and feeling sorry for myself. I didn't tell her about the MS though. I didn't want to risk ruining what we had.

Ada came back into the room from grabbing a snack and I snapped back to reality. Ada was the first person I told about my diagnosis. Crazy as it was, that was the tightest bond remaining in our friendship. The only other people who knew were Gary and the hospital staff responsible for my care. Well, them and McHenry.

"How are you feeling?" Ada asked.

"Just tired," I said. I felt a lot better ever since the doctor had come in the previous night and told me I could probably leave midday today.

Her eyes found mine. "Seeing okay?"

Sometimes my vision got blurry during flare-ups but it wasn't bad this time. I nodded. "Yeah, today I'm seeing fine."

"Good."

We sat in tense silence for a moment. The monitors I was hooked up to continued to flash regularly.

"You should tell her," Ada said pointedly, breaking the silence.

I closed my eyes. If there was one thing Ada didn't mind doing, it was having the same argument over and over. I sucked in a deep breath.

"Here," she said, handing me my own phone. Lorrie had texted me a few times, but I hadn't responded. What the hell was I gonna tell her?

"Not now Ada. I'll tell her when I'm ready."

"If you really think she's different from other girls, you should tell her. The fact you won't makes me wonder if you really like her or if there's something else going on."

"What do you mean?" I growled, struggling to keep my voice down. Ada was just trying to goad me.

"Don't take that tone with me Hunter. It's a legitimate question. Are you sure you're not just into her because of her whole 'my-life-is-so-tragic-save-me' act?"

I tried to keep a steady tone, but my chest was getting tight from the way Ada was talking about Lorrie. "Fuck you Ada. You don't know the first thing about her."

Ada glared daggers at me. "Fuck you too. Are you going to tell her or not?"

"I'm crazy about that girl," I said evenly.

She threw her hands up. "Well that's nice, that you're crazy about her! If you're so crazy about her, why not ask her to come to the hospital right now? Do you realize the gossip I'm putting up with because I'm here with you? People think you fucking knocked me up, Hunter. You might not give a shit about what people say with your bad boy rebel act, but I do."

I took several deep breaths and managed to calm myself down. "I'm sorry, Ada. I didn't know people were saying all that stuff. Thanks for coming and checking on me, I appreciate it, but I told you before that you didn't have to come see me every day. Gary's been stopping by to check on me. I'll be fine."

Ada crossed her arms. "If that girl really cares about you, how come she hasn't called you yet?"

It was strange, but I figured it was a good thing since I didn't have to explain being in the hospital. "I don't know. Look, she's got plenty of problems of her own."

Ada continued like I hadn't said anything. "I mean, a few texts, that's it? Come on, you've been gone for almost a week now, what kind of self-absorbed bitch ju—"

"Ada . . . " I clenched my fists, the IV a sharp pain in my forearm. Before I could say something I'd regret, my phone buzzed from the table next to me. Lorrie was calling me.

I froze, watching it vibrate, my insides churning. What would I say if I picked up? *Hi Lorrie, in case you didn't have enough to worry about, let me tell you about my chronic and potentially terminal illness.* Fuck that.

I looked up to see Ada staring at me. "Hunter!" she shrieked. "What the fuck is the matter with you? Why won't you tell her?"

Fucking Ada, everything was always cut and dry for her. Why didn't she understand that it just wasn't that simple.

The moment I first saw Lorrie's face—after fishing her out of that lake—I knew there was something about her. It wasn't the shock on her expression from a near-death experience or even the way her body shivered from the freezing cold. It wasn't anything on the outside. It was that look in her eyes that pierced me to my damn core. I didn't know anything about her, but I instantly recognized that look from seeing it every day in the mirror. She was beautiful. And broken.

Even if she didn't tell me her whole story, she let her walls down for me. I understood her need to protect herself and never pried. I just needed to be there for her. When that asshole at the Tau Beta Pi party said that shit about her parents, he was fucking lucky that Lorrie stopped me. I don't know what I would've done.

No. Lorrie didn't need my sob story and I didn't need her to pity me. She needed me to be strong for her, to wipe away her tears, to hold her shuddering body tightly against mine. Lorrie needed me to take away her pain, not add to it.

I needed her too. Before she came along I was a fucking mess. Maybe she thought I was her savior when I pulled her out of that lake, but I knew the real score. If I hadn't found her, I'd be so lost right now. I would've lost myself in the drinking, brawling, and groupies. Lorrie never let me get away with that bullshit. She saw right through me, but she was never pushy like Ada. Lorrie knew how hard it was to try to make it through each day. She made me feel alive again, like there was still something to look forward to, like I wasn't just waiting for the MS to knock me out.

We were so happy during those days we were holed up in my apartment. It was like a dream that I never wanted to end. Why couldn't we have that for just a little while longer? Why did things have to change?

"If you're not going to tell her then I will." Ada picked up the phone with her hand and my chest tightened. A white hot ball of fury clenched tighter and tighter in my core. If Lorrie found out about my MS, things would never be the same.

"Don't you fucking dare Ada!" I gripped the side of my hospital bed, knowing that once she set her mind to something, it was hard to stop her.

"What's wrong with you Hunter? Someone needs to tell her!" Ada stared at me with accusing eyes.

"No! It'll change everything!" I pounded the mattress pad with a fist, panic coursing through my veins.

"I'm going to tell her, you can't stop me Hunter!" She started fiddling with the buttons on the phone and my panic shifted to horror.

"NO! SHE CAN'T SEE ME LIKE THIS!" I roared, reaching for my phone and violently snatching it from her hands.

Ada backed away as if I'd slapped her, eyes wide and frightened.

I gazed at her harshly, sucking in deep shuddering breaths. "Please Ada. She can't see me like this . . . not like this . . ." I breathed. This was my pain, mine alone to struggle with. I couldn't share it with Lorrie yet. I blinked a few times, my eyes stinging with shame and took a deep breath to calm myself.

Lorrie wasn't ready. No, *I* wasn't ready. I wasn't ready for things to change just yet.

Ada shook her head slowly, her expression shifting from shock to disgust. "Both of you are sick. You deserve each other."

She took a seat in the corner, not saying another word until the doctor came in to discharge me. She put on a fake smile, but I could tell she was still fuming as we walked out of the hospital via the health center entrance on campus. I knew this was far from over.

$$\text{🔨 🔨 🔨}$$

A few hours ago

I wanted to vomit as I looked at Lorrie's shaky handwriting on the note she left me. I had read it again and again, hoping the words would change, but they never did.

Ada was out of control when we ran into Lorrie outside the health center. I wanted to talk to Lorrie, try to fix things to how they were, but Ada was gonna tell her about me and things would never be the same again.

"Give me something, Hunter. Don't leave me with just this." I heard Lorrie desperately call after me. I wanted to talk to Lorrie in private. But I had to stop Ada first. I couldn't let Ada tell Lorrie. Even if she didn't tell Lorrie that day, she would tell Lorrie some other time and it'd ruin everything. So, like an asshole, I ran after Ada, instead of facing Lorrie.

After I convinced Ada to calm down, and she promised me she wouldn't talk to Lorrie, I went straight to Lorrie's room, hoping she'd be able to forgive me. She wasn't there and neither was Daniela. A couple of girls were hanging around in the suite and told me that they hadn't seen Lorrie in a while.

I pulled out my phone and called Lorrie. The phone didn't even ring before going to voicemail. *Fuck, she turned her phone off.* I tried again. Still no luck. Why would she do that? Was she purposely trying to avoid me?

Damnit, I had to find her. I ran around frantically and checked all of her favorite sketching spots, but she wasn't at any of them. After an hour of searching and repeatedly trying her phone, I was almost ready to quit, but then I thought of one last spot to look for her.

Feeling sick, I sprinted across campus. My knees were almost ready to give out when I got to the bridge over Lake Teewee. I saw that the frozen lake was undisturbed and intense relief washed over me.

She was probably out with Daniela somewhere, avoiding me.

I'd fucked it up big time. I should have let Ada go. I should have stayed and talked to Lorrie. She needed me, but I was too afraid to talk to her. Lorrie was right, I should have explained things to her, told her something at least. Now it was too late.

Not knowing what to do and desperate, I went over to the PKD house to talk to Gary. We drank and tried to put together the pieces. Soon we were wasted, no closer to coming up with a way to get my ass out of this mess. I passed out on his couch feeling worse than when I came.

It was only after I woke up hungover that I came back to my apartment and saw Lorrie's note. It was already noon, Lorrie was probably long gone by now. She had come looking for me, she waited for me and she wanted to talk, but instead, I was fucking stupidly drinking away my pain with Gary.

Lorrie needed me but I wasn't there for her. Something had happened and she needed me to be there for her, but I was too fucking selfish and afraid to come clean to her. Now she had gone to deal with her pain herself. I had lost my only chance to explain things, make things right with her. That killed the shit out of me.

As I stood in my kitchen and reread the note she'd left me, a cold sense of dread began to sink in.

Rampage nuzzled against my leg. The little guy didn't know anything was wrong. Or maybe he did. I scooped him up and brought him to my face. His brown eyes looked at me curiously, maybe as confused as I was right now.

I set him down and watched him run off. What the fuck happened that she decided she needed to leave like that?

I exhaled and picked up my phone. Still nothing from her. I had called her a few times but it went straight to voicemail.

How did I keep messing up my life this badly? What was I thinking? I was so fucking selfish. I couldn't see past my own self-pity to think that Lorrie needed me when I was in the hospital during the flare-up. I had fucked up again.

And now it was over.

I punched the kitchen cabinet door to the left of the sink. The door caved in, sending splinters and Cheerios from inside flying everywhere. My fist exploded in pain. Breathing hard, I flexed it to make sure nothing was broken. It hurt, but I was okay.

The kittens had scattered at the loud noise of my outburst, but they were now cautiously approaching the cereal and splinters on the floor. Seeing them brought me back to my senses. If I needed to blow off some steam, I should do it at the gym instead; I didn't want to hurt the kittens.

They were reminders the time Lorrie and I had spent together. Looking at them had always made me happy but now it filled me with grief.

$$\text{🪓 🪓 🪓}$$

One hour ago

I kept my head down and brushed past the rest of the guys at the gym. They saw the look on my face and nobody tried to stop me to chat. I didn't see Gary; he must've been sleeping off the hangover. I headed straight for the heavy bag and began to work it with my bare fists.

Thwack. Thwack. Thwackathwackathwack.

I wasn't just punching the faded leather; I imagined punching my own face in. I deserved it. Lorrie was special and I fucked it up. I couldn't help her and I couldn't save her. I was too weak. Too stupid. Too selfish.

Thwackathwackathwack. Thwack. Thwack. Thwackathwack.
Lorrie, I'm sorry. I'm sorry. I'm so sorry.
Thwack. Thwack. Thwack.
Feeling dizzy, I tripped over my feet. I shot my gloves out and grabbed onto the bag before I could fall. I leaned heavily against the leather bag for a second before pushing it away and getting back up.

Fuck this disease.

I kept hitting the bag until sweat stung my eyes, my arms were sore, and my fists were angry and raw, but I still didn't feel any better when I was done. It didn't matter how hard I punched those bags, I'd never be able to take back the pain that I had caused Lorrie.

I don't know what's going to happen to me if I don't find something solid in my life.

I bent over, breathing heavy, and leaned against the leather punching bag that had just taken all the punishment I could deal out. When I walked over to the water fountain to get some water, the other guys gave me plenty of space.

It was supposed to be me; I was supposed to be that solid thing in her life. I promised her that but I fucked it all up. What the hell was I going to do without her?

As I headed back for another round with the bag, the gym doors swung open and Johnson, the fight coordinator at the Squirrel, came in with a clipboard in hand. I stopped for a second to see why he was there.

"Listen up guys! I know this is real short notice, but I've got a fight lined up in the next hour. So if any of you want a shot at Walter Morris, here's your chance. I had him scheduled for a fight with Dan Evans, but Danny boy's got the flu and canceled this morning."

Walter Morris was one of the top fighters in the area. Six foot four, built like an ox. I'd never fought him before but I knew that I'd have a hard time with him even on my best days.

Johnson looked around the room at the other guys there. No one was volunteering. I didn't blame them. One hour wasn't really a lot of time to prepare to fight Morris. Taking a fight on such short notice against an opponent like that was a deathwish. But maybe I needed that right now.

Johnson was getting desperate. I only half heard him say, "Come on, if you win, I'll double your winnings, you got my word."

I couldn't care less about the winnings but I needed to forget what I had done. I needed to feel that rush of being in the cage, hovering on the edge of violence and oblivion. I wanted the clarity of fighting for survival against a caged animal. I didn't give a shit that this particular animal was going to be Walter Morris.

Lorrie was gone. She wasn't coming back. I was supposed to help her heal, not be a source of her pain, but that's exactly what I ended up being. I was pathetic. I didn't deserve to be happy.

Then I decided.

I locked eyes with Johnson, and just gave him a tilt of my head. That was enough. Johnson knew what I wanted. Understanding flashed between our eyes and he nodded before turning and leaving the gym without another word.

Maybe I could win this fight, maybe I couldn't. Walter was a hell of a lot more prepared than me, but I had one advantage. I'd lost the only person that made me give a damn about myself.

I had nothing to lose.

Chapter Twenty-nine

DAMAGED

Lorrie

It was Hunter.

A sharp pain knifed through my chest. He looked beyond exhausted. His chest heaved and his mouth hung wide open, gasping for breath. There was blood dripping down his face from one of the cuts on his right cheek and the bruise on his left eye was a stormy mix of gray and purple. It seemed to be getting darker and swelling bigger by the second.

A violent shiver ran through my body, and my mouth opened in horror. I'd never seen Hunter like this before. I'd never seen someone so broken.

Finally, the other fighter managed to push Hunter away. The two began circling each other again. Hunter's hands were down by his stomach and his legs wobbled with the effort to remain standing. My heart squeezed in my throat as I watched him struggle.

Something was horribly wrong.

I watched Hunter stumble around the cage. My heart raced, almost ready to explode. There was no way he should be out there. This wasn't the lightning quick Hunter that I first saw in the ring. Maybe he didn't look like he was dying, but it was close.

"Hunter!" I screamed, desperate to do something but unsure what I could even do.

Tension knotting my muscles, I held my breath as Hunter's opponent came forward and took a wild swing. Hunter narrowly ducked the punch and stumbled away without even trying to throw one himself.

Maybe he was just trying to make it to the end of this final round without getting knocked out. If he could just last that long, the fight would be over and he could get some badly needed medical attention. Maybe there was hope after all.

He dodged another punch, but this time tried to throw one himself. It missed, and his opponent countered with a punch to his ribs that landed with a loud thud. Hunter winced and backed away, circling around. I clenched my jaw nervously. Hunter moved in and out, but didn't try to punch the other guy.

The crowd booed at his refusal to engage. Hunter responded by coming forward and trying another wild punch. It missed. His opponent tried to knock him out with a high kick and Hunter just barely got away. This time the crowd cheered. My head swam, dizzy with images of Hunter hurt or worse.

I couldn't let this keep going on. Maybe if Hunter saw me he would stop trying to be a hero and just stay away from his opponent until this last round was over. It was clear Hunter was going to lose the fight. He didn't need to keep trying for a lucky knockout and risk getting hurt himself. People might boo, but at least he wouldn't get injured any worse than he already had. My pulse thundered in my head as I thought of what to do.

"Hunter! Just make it through the round!" I yelled. He gave no sign of hearing me.

I began to swim my way to the front of the crowd, squeezing myself into every opening I could find. There was some grumbling, but I kept pushing forward. I had to get him to see me. He needed to stop fighting.

There was a roar as I got to the front, just feet from the cage. I looked up at the action. Hunter was covering up his face as his opponent hit him with several punches. His opponent was so fast that Hunter could barely defend himself. A shiver of dread crept up my spine, suffocating me and rooting me to the spot. No, this couldn't be happening!

"Hunter, no!" I cried. "It's me, Lorrie! Stop fighting! Please, stop!"

His arms blocked most of the impact, then he hit his opponent with a left jab. The punch stunned his opponent momentarily, giving Hunter enough time to back away.

"You don't have to do this!" I yelled.

Hunter let his hands fall and he looked around with his mostly open right eye. His gaze came to meet mine. Dim recognition flickered across his face as his opponent approached and wound up a right hook.

Hunter tried to dodge at the last second, but the punch landed right on his nose, crushing his face grotesquely with a sickening snap. His body went limp as the blow reverberated through his body. There was a half-second of silence as everyone in the room gasped at once.

My stomach dropped and I felt an intense pain in my chest. "NO!" I screamed, my hands in my hair.

Then the crowd exploded in screams and cheers. I stood stunned, watching Hunter hit the mat stiff as a board. The referee crouched over him and waved his hand over his head. Hunter continued to lay there motionless. His nose was bleeding badly and looked crooked. I couldn't tell, but I was pretty sure it was broken.

I stared at the cage numbly, overwhelmed. My head seemed to float away. This didn't feel real, but I couldn't wake up. The bell was ringing and the other fighter was running around the cage with his arms raised. Hunter didn't move except for the rise and fall of his chest. The referee hovered over him, concern etched on his goateed face.

I tore my eyes away from the scene in the cage, flooded with emotion. Hunter looked badly hurt. Could I have done something different? People were clapping around me, ecstatic at the knockout. They didn't care at all about Hunter's well-being. One figure stood out, stone-faced. He was the only one who looked the way I felt. It was Gary.

He stood by the cage's entrance about ten feet away, looking in. Two medics rushed past him and into the cage with a stretcher. I watched them begin attending to Hunter and was gripped by sadness.

Time passed as I kept my eyes locked on his prone body, trying to grab ahold of reality. He still wouldn't move.

". . . fault," a voice said.

I turned and saw it had come from Gary. He'd apparently walked over to me. His brows were angled sharply downward and his eyes were burning with anger. "What?" I asked.

"This is your fucking fault," he spat.

"My fault?" I said, shocked by his accusation. "Are you nuts? How are you thinking about fault right now? Hunter's hurt!"

He scoffed bitterly. "Trust me, I know. I've been playing this scene over and over in my head since I heard he took the fight. I rushed here to try and stop him but it was too late. I know what a wreck you made of him. For that and a ton of other reasons, there's no way he should've been in there just now. This is your fault!"

I shook my head, confused over why he would think I was the one who made Hunter a wreck. "I sat at his apartment for hours last night waiting to talk to him. It's not my fault he never showed up. What's wrong with Hunter, anyway? He didn't look right in there at all."

Before he could answer, a shout came from above us in the cage. "Make way," a man's voice yelled.

I turned and saw it was one of the medics helping Hunter. They had put him on a stretcher and were trying to get through the crowd to what I guessed would be an ambulance waiting at the front entrance to the bar. People were still packed in tightly, so they put the stretcher down at the top of the steps while one medic went to clear space. The other stayed behind and watched over Hunter.

I peered down at the stretcher and got a clear look at Hunter. My heart sank to the pit of my stomach. His left eye was swollen nearly shut and his right wasn't far behind. Bruises and cuts marred the area around his cheeks and eyes.

The worst was his nose. The medics had wiped away most of the blood and tried to clot it with gauze, but there was still plenty smeared around the lower half of his face. The way it was turned awkwardly to the left made it clear it was broken.

Tears formed in my eyes. Seeing the man I loved so horribly injured crushed my heart. "Hunter, I'm sorry," I said, my vision a blur. "I'm sorry about this whole mess. I just wanted to see you one last time and talk to you. I'm sorry Hunter."

His eyes fluttered open and he looked toward me unfocused. He opened his mouth slightly but no words came out. The small smile that crept onto his lips made me sick with sorrow.

"Dude," Gary said unsteadily next to me, "are you with us? What's your name?"

His eyes slid over toward Gary; they were badly dilated. "Hunter," he slurred.

My heart leaped at the small positive sign. Even if he was slurring his speech, at least he knew who he was.

I looked up at the medic that had stayed with Hunter, desperate for any sliver of hope. "He woke up. That's good, right?"

The man whose nametag said his name was Nick nodded. "Yeah, that's good. If we can get him to the hospital quickly he should be okay. You never know, but waking up is positive."

He should be okay. The thought that Hunter might not be okay— that something might be permanently wrong with him—nearly paralyzed me. Hopefully Nick was right and Hunter would be fine now that he had woken up.

"Lorrie?" Hunter said softly. His eyes darted from my face to the lights at the Bearded Squirrel and back to me lazily. The in and out movement of his breathing had slowed down to a normal rate, which seemed good. It was another sign he would pull through.

The thoughts that had rushed through my mind when I saw him on the mat—that I loved him, that I was leaving him, and that he was badly hurt—finally caught up to me. I began to cry. Sob after sob seized my body so hard I could barely breathe. How had things gone so wrong so fast in our lives?

I wiped my eyes with my sleeve, trying to calm down. "Hunter," I choked out. "It's not your fault I'm leaving. I'm so sorry. I wish I had a choice."

"Lorrie no," he slurred. He opened his eyes as wide as he could, but they had swollen so badly that it wasn't much. It made me feel ill to watch him struggle.

He finally pulled his eyes into focus and stared at me through the purple and black of his bruises. "Lorrie, don't go," he muttered again.

I blinked away fresh tears. "I'm sorry, Hunter. I have to. If I don't take care of myself right now, I'm afraid of what's going to happen to me."

"No, no no no," he trailed off. His eyes drifted unfocused then shut.

My stomach dropped. What was happening to him? I thought once he had woken up he would stay awake. I looked up at Gary, who seemed to be in shock.

"Help!" I yelled. "His eyes closed again."

Nick, who had been watching his partner clear a path to the exit, looked back at us over his shoulder. "Keep talking to him," he said. "We're almost done clearing a path."

"Hunter," I pleaded, clasping his hand. "Please wake up."

I held my breath, every dreadful second dragging on. What if he didn't wake up? Could I leave Studsen if I wasn't sure Hunter would be okay?

His eyes shot open and relief coursed through my veins. He grabbed toward my hand clumsily, making contact with my fingers but not holding on. "I should have told you, Lorrie . . . You wouldn't change. You could still see me."

I shook my head, frantically trying to decipher the meaning of his words. "Hunter, I'm right here with you."

He made another grab at my hand. "I'm sorry," he said, trailing off. "You don't have to go."

His eyes shut once more. Gary, who had been silent, looked up at me, forehead wrinkled with worry. Hunter was breathing hard again with his nostrils flared. Gary's face twisted in panic. "You're stressing him out," he answered. "You need to get out of here before he gets worse."

My face burned with frustration. "Why do you keep blaming me for everything?"

"Because I've watched you turn him into a fucking trainwreck!"

I balled up my fists, barely able to control my rage. My jaw was clenched tight. "What does *that* mean?'

Rather than respond with something nasty, Gary watched as Nick's partner came back.

"We've got a clear path here," the medic said. He and Nick hefted Hunter's stretcher up and began walking it to the ambulance.

"Where are you taking him?" I asked anxiously, walking alongside them. Gary followed close behind.

"Arrowhart College Hospital," Nick replied.

I nodded, my heart racing. "Is he going to be okay?"

"Should be," Nick said as we neared the ambulance. "It will be important that he recover over the next twenty-four hours, but once he's in the hospital he'll be in good hands. I would be very surprised if he had any permanent injuries from this. Nose might be messed up, but nothing worse."

Gary sighed behind me. "God I hope not," he said.

We stopped when we got to the ambulance. Nick and his partner paused in front of the vehicle's back door.

"One of you can ride with us to the hospital," Nick said.

"I will," Gary and I said simultaneously.

Nick grimaced. "I'm sorry, but we can only fit one."

"You're not coming," Gary said to me sternly. He towered over me, his stare rooting me to my spot.

Blood rushed to my face, making it feel extra hot against the cold wind. "Why not?"

"Haven't you done enough damage?" Gary yelled. "Look at him! Look at what you've done!"

Stunned, I opened my mouth to speak. This was all too much.

"Lorrie," Hunter mumbled.

Both our gazes flew down to Hunter. His eyes were open but he wasn't all there. He looked between me and Gary, mumbling incoherently under his breath.

"We need to get out of here," Nick said. He and his partner hefted Hunter up into the ambulance before he turned back to us. "Both of you are welcome to visit him in the hospital during visiting hours. Is one of you riding with us or not?"

"I'm coming," Gary said. Nick looked at me briefly then nodded and climbed into the back of the vehicle. Gary turned to me. "I've known Hunter for a few years now. He has plenty of his own issues, but at least he was working on them. You came along and he got totally obsessed with you. At first it seemed like you made him better, but then he just got worse. A lot worse. He missed training, flipped out at that party, skipped classes, all kinds of stuff. Then you pulled the rug out from under him, and I haven't seen anyone fall that hard. Ever. Listen, Lorrie, I know you didn't mean for all this to happen, but you're no good for each other."

Gary's words hit me hard. I felt like I was the one who had just been punched in the face. I had suspicions that even when Hunter and I were holed up in his apartment, lost in our own little world, that our relationship wasn't entirely healthy, but hearing it from Gary felt like a stake through my heart.

Gary hopped into the back of the ambulance as I stood there stunned and still processing what he'd said to me. He turned back to me with his lips pursed and sighed. "I'll tell him you came to talk to him," he said. "If he wants to talk, he'll come find you. If he doesn't, please stay away. I don't want to do this again."

I nodded limply and he shut the door. The ambulance drove off, sirens fading into the distance, leaving me feeling like an empty husk.

Gary was right. We weren't good for each other.

Chapter Thirty

WRECKED

I sat on the bus back to Indiana and watched the streetlights fly by. They were the only breaks in darkness for miles as we rolled through Illinois farm country. My head pressed up against the glass, I thought about the last few days, trying to hold all my emotions in.

How had it all happened? It was the nightmare I'd been trying to avoid: a messy breakup. Yet again, I'd proven I couldn't trust myself to ride out the twists and turns my life presented. Letting myself get so attached to someone had been a huge mistake. I'd dragged us both down, and now one of us was in the hospital. Sorrow clenched in my chest.

I curled up in my seat and hoped for the hundredth time since the bus left the station that Nick the medic was right and Hunter would be okay. He had seemed pretty confident and I believed him in the heat of the moment, but now I was having second thoughts. I'd never seen someone look so beat up. What was going to happen to him? What had led to a breakdown like that?

A dull ache throbbed in my heart. Whatever Hunter had been dealing with over the past week, he hadn't wanted my help. I looked around the bus at my fellow passengers. Many were sleeping. The man and woman across the aisle from me were nestled together lovingly. The peaceful expression on the woman's face as she lay her head on his chest painfully reminded me of the way I did that with Hunter. She looked like she was claiming that spot for life.

Sighing, I threw myself back in my seat and stared out the window some more, thankful I didn't have someone sitting next to me. I needed space to myself right now. The hurt inside was too much to bear.

If Hunter didn't end up being okay I would never forgive myself. I closed my eyes, letting a tear roll down my cheek. I was never going to see him again. There would be no tearful reunion, no working stuff out. The world wouldn't be that kind to us. Our brief time of happiness together was over.

I began to cry harder, doing my best to stay quiet and not embarrass myself. The tears rolling down my cheeks became warm, salty streams. What was going to happen to Hunter? Did he hate me now? Would he think that I abandoned him? Even when I tried to live a normal life, something always came to drag me back. Dad had been wrong. I wasn't strong enough. I wasn't rolling a giant boulder up a hill every day, I was caught under it.

And I couldn't break free.

Chapter Thirty-one

WAKE

Hunter

My head felt like someone was jabbing a knife into my temple. The second thing I noticed was the unpleasant smell of the hospital and I knew where I was without even opening my eyes. How had I gotten back here? What had happened? I wasn't sure what my last memory was; I couldn't separate my fevered dreams from reality.

I felt pressure on my eyes as I tried to open them. This was a familiar feeling. I'd clearly just had my ass kicked. My entire face felt like shit.

"You there, bud?" a man's voice asked.

It was Gary. He must have come with me to the hospital.

I craned my neck over toward his voice. He was blurry at first, but eventually his face came into focus. "Yeah, I'm here," I croaked, discovering that my throat was bone dry.

He watched me for several seconds, deep concern marring his expression. "Do you remember anything?"

"If you're asking me whether I remember how my face got so fucked up, the answer is no."

He sighed and his jaw worked silently. "Okay. Figured as much, but thought I should ask."

"What happened?"

His eyes narrowed. "What's the last thing you remember?"

My mind was fuzzy, but slowly, it was coming back.

"Lorrie," I rasped quietly.

Gary's expression was a mix of pain and relief. "Yeah."

I took several deep breaths. There it was. We were done. She was on a bus taking her far away from Studsen, to deal with her own pain. I had saved her that cold winter day when I pulled her out of the lake, but I couldn't save her from what she was dealing with now. *Goddammit.*

Clenching my fists, I tried to sit up, but was stopped by the IV hanging from my left arm. I used my right hand to grab the needle so I could yank it out.

Gary grabbed my wrist fiercely. "Whoa, dude, settle down! Where do you think you're going?"

"Get off me," I growled softly.

His grip remained strong. "Stop trying to rip your IV out and I will."

My muscles tensed. I tried to contain my anger, but it was no use. My whole body began to shake. The way Gary was trying to physically restrain me from going after Lorrie seriously pissed me off.

"Lorrie!" I roared. I ripped the IV out of my arm and sat up. A searing pain shot through my arm.

Gary tackled me back onto the bed. He glared, his eyes a pair of thin flames. "Stop!" he yelled. "Hospital security will take a fucking taser to you and strap you to that bed if that's what it takes. Nobody wants that."

I struggled for a second, but it was no use. Weakened as I was, I couldn't fight Gary.

After I'd calmed down, he looked to the door, but nobody had responded to our raised voices. "Now tell me what's on your mind," he said, his voice lowered. "What are you going to do?"

I froze and stared at him. What could I do? Gary was right. I was stuck in a hospital bed while Lorrie was on a bus going somewhere far, far away. Was I going to chase the bus down? In my current state? I could barely move my legs.

Defeated, I slumped back in my bed, my breath coming in thin wheezes. I'd lost this round. Gary watched me for a second, then took his hands off my wrists. My hands dropped heavily to my sides. I wasn't going anywhere.

We sat in silence for a few minutes. My swollen eyes were

focused on nothing in particular. There was nothing to look at. It was a hospital. I was stuck in a sterile room again, waiting until I could go home so I could go do whatever. I'd regret the past few days, mostly. And probably drink too much.

"You good?" Gary asked, breaking the silence. "I'm gonna go hit the bathroom. You're not gonna do anything stupid, right?"

I looked up at him and nodded.

His lips a thin line, he turned to walk out but stopped at the door. "Listen, before she left, she came to the fight. Said she wanted to talk to you. Do you remember any of that? You know what I think of that, but I promised her that I'd tell you."

He watched me for a reaction, but when I didn't give him one, he turned and walked out the door. I wasn't sure how to react. A ringing began in my ears as I rocked back and forth. *Lorrie wanted to talk. She hadn't given up on me.* This wasn't the end of us. This was a blank slate.

I was going after her even if it killed me.

Hunter and Lorrie's story continues in the powerfully emotional sequel,

Rescued

Available Now!